a MURDER Of CROWS

A MURDER OF CROWS

A SIR ROBERT CAREY MYSTERY

P. F. CHISHOLM

Poisoned Pen Press

Poisoned Pen Press
6962 E. First Ave. Ste 103
Scottsdale, AZ 85251
www.poisonedpenpress.com
info@poisonedpenpress.com

Printed in the United States of America

To Barbara Peters and Robert Rosenwald,
who got Carey and Dodd back in the saddle again.

PROLOGUE

A hunchback and a poet met in the glorious gardens belonging to the hunchback's father. The poet was dusty and tired, having ridden up from London to report to his new employer on the sensational events in and around the Fleet Prison the previous Sunday.

The hunchback preferred to sit in the shade, dressed in his customary black damask and white falling band, his lean handsome face tilted slightly sideways to listen more carefully. Beside him, since he liked to make notes, was pen, ink and the very best, most expensive paper, smoothed with pumice so that his pen nib never caught nor spattered. The poet stared at the sheets hungrily, knowing they cost as much as tuppence each and wishing he could afford such a pile. The bench was carved to look as if it had grown from the ground and faced across a labyrinth made of low clipped box-trees, filled in with scented flowers, some of which were making a valiant last flowering in the autumn light. The Queen had often walked in these very gardens and still occasionally did. When the hunchback's father chose to inspect his plantings, he would normally travel around the carefully raked and weeded paths on the back of a small donkey since he was now crippled by gout.

The hunchback generally walked the paths when he was thinking, at a fast pace and with hardly a limp despite the bandy legs of a childhood trampled by rickets.

The poet prided himself on his memory and never wasted precious paper on mere notes. He had been a player and hoped to be one again, used to being presented with a part the night before its first afternoon performance with only one rehearsal in the morning. He could read pages twice and know them by heart. His memory was just as good for what he heard: once he had written out in full a sermon that had lasted three hours for the benefit of his then employer who suspected the preacher of subversive puritanism.

Naturally the hunchback had chosen a bench where the trees behind it would give him shade but the sun would shine direct on the poet's face. He was glad he had done that. The poet's tale was very nearly incredible. Yet there had been reports from Carlisle which were almost as insane but which came from different and unimpeachible sources.

"Are you telling me that Mr. Vice Chamberlain Heneage organised a plot to implicate one of Lord Chamberlain Baron Hunsdon's sons…"

"Edmund Carey," put in the poet quietly.

"Yes, whichever one, in the forging of gold angels by alchemical means?" The poet nodded. "That when he saw the trap closing, Edmund Carey then took cover, as it were, under the nose of the cat and that his brother Sir Robert, whilst disguised as a north country man, later caused a riot there, and ended by breaking Mr. Heneage's nose because Mr. Heneage had taken and beaten a man of his from Carlisle?"

"Yes, your honour," said the poet promptly. "He also…"

The hunchback put up a long pale hand, leaning back as far as he could. "Mr. Heneage was trying to oust my lord Baron Hunsdon from his place as Lord Chamberlain?"

"Yes, your honour."

The hunchback smiled, making his face immediately charming and attractive, never mind the weakness of his body. "Good Lord!" he said. "Who would have thought it?"

The poet considered answering this question, but decided it was rhetorical.

The hunchback sprang to his feet and began pacing. "Sir Robert's antics are not so surprising," he said, more to himself than to the poet, who stood patiently with his hands tucked behind his back. "God knows, he was dangerously bored the last time I saw him at Court and was as badly in debt as he was a couple of years ago when he walked to Newcastle in ten days."

The poet blinked a little at this. The hunchback smiled ruefully. "I lost several hundred pounds on that bet, blast him, and so did a lot of his friends. He made about £3000. It didn't do him any good at all, of course. Once a spendthrift, always a spendthrift."

The poet looked down discreetly.

"That's why I recommended to Her Majesty that she appoint him Deputy Warden of the West March instead of that corrupt fool, Lowther, and also for…good and sufficient reasons."

The poet narrowed his eyes but was far too sensible to ask what they were.

"It's Heneage's behaviour that I find extraordinary," said the hunchback, sitting restlessly back down on the bench and leaning forward now in a confiding way. "What do you think of his proceedings?"

"Ah…" The poet thought very carefully, since he had been working for Heneage at the time. "I felt…unhappy." Unhappy didn't really cover the poet's incandescent rage when he understood just how dangerously he had been set up by the Vice Chamberlain, a man he had trusted. Having played the part of the alchemist, he realised he would have been perfect meat for the hangman if the scheme had worked the way it was supposed to. It still made his innards quake to think about it.

"How about that rival of yours, Marlowe?"

"I wouldn't describe him as a rival," murmured the poet. "I would describe him as a friend and…and teacher."

"Really?"

"For all his faults, Kit Marlowe is a wonderful poet."

The hunchback shrugged. "Nevertheless he's still working for Heneage, as far as anyone can make out."

The poet struggled with his conscience for a moment, and then lost. "I had heard…I believe that he may be trying to use Sir Robert as a means of entering the Earl of Essex's service."

There was a considering silence while the hunchback thought about this. The poet wondered if he had done right telling him.

"Interesting," was all the hunchback said. "So he's unhappy with Heneage too?"

"I imagine so."

"As unhappy as you were when you realised that the delightful Mistress Emilia Bassano was not only Baron Hunsdon's official mistress but was also having an affair with his son?" The hunchback was watching intently for the reaction to this prod.

The poet's ears went pink which was unfortunate because he didn't have much hair to hide it.

"I understand the lady is now in bed with the Earl of Southampton," he said smoothly. "Clearly love blinded me to her unchastity."

"Quite over it?"

The poet bowed. "Of course."

"Good. And what's your opinion of this Carlisle henchman of Carey's?"

The poet paused. "Sergeant Dodd?"

"That's his name. He seems to be…ah…the wild card in the game."

"He appears to be no more than a typical Borderer, very proud of being headman of his little patch of country and holding a tower there…"

"Gilsland in fact controls one of the routes from Scotland into northern England," said the hunchback, who had been reading ancient reports and squinting at maps prepared by his father's agents in 1583.

The poet bowed a little. "…as well as serving in the Carlisle Castle guard under Carey. He looks and behaves like a mere stupid soldier, useful on horseback, and with any weapons but especially with a sword and his fists…"

"But?"

"I think there's more to him than that," said the poet. "Sir Robert certainly thinks so. And I like him."

The hunchback's smile was sunny. "Excellent," he said. "His lawsuit against Mr. Heneage?"

The poet shrugged. "He wants compensation, of course."

"And if he doesn't get it?"

"I think he'll look for another kind of compensation."

With one of his typically sudden movements, the hunchback threw a small full leather purse and the poet just caught it. The hunchback's face was impossible to read for sure but it seemed that somewhere in what he had said, the poet had told him something of value. He bowed again.

The hunchback rose and held out his hand to shake friendliwise. The poet took it and found his fingers were gripped with surprising strength.

"Thank you very much, Mr. Shakespeare," said the hunchback. "It seems we will do well together."

"I hope so, sir," said the poet.

"Keep me informed." The hunchback stood. "I will be back in London by tomorrow." He turned his bent shoulders and walked quickly towards the rows of hazel trees that shielded a raised lawn full of sculptures of minotaurs and fauns and mermaids and other fantastical creatures. The bees browsed on frantically in the late flowers and Shakespeare headed back to the stables and London town.

monday 11th september 1592, morning

"Nothing like an execution, eh Sergeant?" Sir Robert Carey was lounging elegantly against the fence that kept the groundlings in their places, one kid-gloved hand tipped on the pommel of his sword, the other playing with the beginnings of a new Court goatee.

Dodd looked at him gravely for a moment and then turned his attention back to the bloody mess on the Tyburn scaffold. On the other side of the scaffold he noticed a man with a badly pockmarked face who was staring transfixed at the priest. Suddenly, the man turned aside and vomited on the ground. The goings-on didn't upset Dodd's stomach as much—for all the smell of roast meat—since there had been no screaming. They had actually burnt the priest's balls in front of him, a detail Dodd had not expected, though at least they'd done it after cutting them off and before they slit the priest's belly to pull out his guts.

The priest hadn't been screaming because the hangman had given him a good drop off the ladder and had let him hang until his face was purple, eyes set and popping and his tongue cramming his gag in the ludicrous mask of a judicial death. Evidently a kind or well-paid hangman. In fact, the man had been unconscious on the hurdle as he was dragged along the Oxford Road, grey-faced and hollow-eyed. He had seemed only half aware of what was happening when the hangman had put the noose over his neck, though there had been something like a smile around the corners of his exhausted eyes. Impossible to tell with the gag forcing his lips into a grimace, but he had looked confidently up at the sky before stepping off the ladder. The hangman hadn't needed to push him.

Now they were quartering him efficiently with cleavers, working like the butchers at the Shambles. Quartering a man was not so very different from butchering a pig and Dodd had killed and colloped his own pig every November since he'd been a married man and knew something about it.

No sausage-making here, though. Nobody had caught the blood in buckets to make black pudding nor pulled out and washed the bladder to be a bouncy toy for children.

That thought did make his stomach turn so he was glad that Carey was speaking again.

"Eh?" said Dodd.

"I said, he'd been one of Heneage's guests at Chelsea," Carey nodded at the man's wrist which was flopping from the nearly severed arm not far from them. It had a thick swollen bracelet of flesh around it and the fingers were tight-skinned and swollen as well.

Dodd saw that Carey was rubbing his gloved left hand where two of his fingers were still slightly bent. The rings for those fingers were still at the jeweller's to be resized since they no longer fit, and Carey was wearing kid gloves all the time not only because it was fashionable and they were extremely fine embroidered ones, but also to hide his very ugly bare nailbeds while he waited for the fingernails to regrow. All in all he had recovered well from the mysterious damage that had been done to him at the Scottish court. As to body, at least. As to mind and spirit…Only time would tell. He was being irritatingly breezy now.

"Priest was he not?" Dodd squinted slightly as one of the men working on the scaffold held up the peaceful head.

"So perish all traitors to Her Majesty!" shouted the hangman.

"Allegedly," murmured Carey. "Hoorah!" he added at a bellow, and clapped. The crowd cheered and clapped as well, with some wit about the priest's equipment.

"Ay," Dodd had tired of fencing games. "So why did ye bring me here, sir? Ah've seen men hang afore now. Hanged a couple mesen under Lowther's orders while he was Deputy Warden…"

Carey's eyebrows went up and he made a little courtier-like shrug with his shoulders. "Thought you might be interested to see a real hanging, drawing, and quartering, they don't happen so often."

"Ay. Nae ither reason?"

Dodd knew his face was dark with suspicion and ill-humour and didn't care. Why shouldn't he be miserable? He was still stuck in this hellhole of London, still wearing uncomfortable hot tight clothes loaned him by Carey so he could look the part of his natural station in life. He knew what and who he was and he didn't care whether the bloody southerners knew or not so long as they left him alone, so he didn't see the point of the play.

Today, for the first time in his life, he had been to a London barber and had had his hair trimmed, washed, oiled, combed, and his beard trimmed back to a neat pawky thing on the end of his chin. One of the things that was making him bad-tempered was the fact that he had caught himself enjoying it. If he wasn't careful he'd go back to Janet and his tower in Gilsland as soft and wet as any southerner and Janet's geese would eat him alive, never mind Janet herself.

Dodd glanced again at the scaffold where they were sweeping sawdust into clumps and bringing up mops and buckets. The bits of human meat were slung into a cart to be taken to the gates of London for display and the head to London Bridge to join the priest's colleagues.

Carey was already heading off through the crowd and Dodd followed him until he found a little house with red lattices and reasonably clean tables on the Oxford Road near to Tyburn. By some magic known only to him, Carey immediately snared a potboy to take his order and quickly settled down to a quart of double beer and a small cup of brandy. Dodd took mild ale, mindful of what the Portuguese physician had advised about his bruised kidneys.

"Obviously I want you to know what manner of man you're dealing with," Carey said in a random way, blinking into his cup of brandy before swallowing all of it.

"Thank ye, sir," said Dodd in a careful tone of voice. "But Ah ken verra fine what manner o'man he is, seeing he laid about mah tripes wi' a cosh and me wi' ma hands chained and ye had at him yersen, sir, an hour later and he never drew blade nor struck ye back nor sent his man to arrange a time and a place."

Dodd would never forget what had happened on that Sunday, particularly Carey finding him still curled up and half-conscious on the floor of Heneage's thrice-bedamned foreign coach after a thorough beating from Heneage and his henchmen. Those lumps had been intended only as a preliminary to further inter-rogation and one of the henchmen had just come back with thumbscrews to help. Dodd had not personally seen but had heard from several witnesses that Carey had then gone straight for Heneage with his bare fists, being without his sword at the time, until unfortunately restrained by his father. It hadn't been very gentlemanly of Sir Robert, but it had given Dodd some pleasure to see Heneage with a swollen nose, two black eyes, and a doublet and gown ruined by blood a little later.

And Heneage hadn't even called Carey out over it, which just showed what a strilpit wee nyaff he was. Well, lawsuits to be sure would be multiplying like rats, but that was a different matter. Dodd had never heard of a gentleman hitting another gentlemen right in the nose with his fist and not having to at least talk about a duel afterwards. For form's sake. Dodd himself didn't plan to take Heneage's demeaning beating of him as if he was some poor peasant with no surname to back him. He planned revenge.

As well as lawsuits.

Carey coughed. "I want you to remember how powerful and ruthless he is. If you take him on, there's no going back nor crying quarter."

Dodd squinted in puzzlement at Carey. "Ah dinnae understand ye, sir," he said. "Are ye suggesting Ah should beg his honour's pardon for damaging his cosh wi' ma kidneys?"

Carey grinned. "No, Sergeant, it's just he's not some Border reiver like Wee Colin Elliot or Richie Graham of Brackenhill. He's the Queen's Vice Chamberlain, he came this close…" Carey held up his gloved forefinger and thumb an inch apart, "…to outplotting and removing my father, he's wealthy, he's clever and he likes hurting people. He has many of Walsingham's old pursuivants working for him, though none of them like him, and he has taken over Walsingham's old network of spies and informers, although unfortunately not his shrewdness. He's highly dangerous and…well…my father says he'll back you but…"

Dodd breathed hard through his nose: a few months ago he might have been offended enough to call Carey out on it, but now he was prepared to give the Courtier benefit of doubt although it came hard to him. After all, Heneage's nosebleed had been very messy.

"Ay sir," he said. "Ay, Ah ken what he is." For a moment, Dodd considered explaining to Carey some of the things he'd done in the course of his family's bloodfeud with the Elliots, then thought better of it. Wouldn't do to shock the Courtier, now would it? The corners of Dodd's mouth twitched briefly at the thought.

"But?" asked Carey, waving for more beer.

"Ah dinna think Heneage kens what I am."

There was a pause.

"You won't take his offer?"

It had been paltry, offered the previous Wednesday by a defensively written letter carried by a servant. A mere apology and ten pounds. Where was the satisfaction in that? Dodd hadn't bothered to answer it.

"Nay sir. I've talked tae yer dad about it and he says he'll gie me whatever lawyers I want, all the paper in London for ma powder and shot…"

"Yes, father's very irritated at what happened to Edmund," said Carey with his usual breezy understatement.

"Ay sir," said Dodd, "And I'm verra irritated at what happened tae me." Dodd was trying to match Carey with understatement. "Irritated" didn't really describe the dull thunderous rage settled permanently in Dodd's bowels.

Carey nodded, looked away, opened his mouth, shut it, rubbed his fingers again, coughed, took a gulp of his new cup of brandy, coughed again.

"I feel I owe you an apology over that, Sergeant," said the Courtier, finally getting to the point of what had been making him so annoying for the last couple of days. He wasn't looking at Dodd now, he was staring at the sawdust scattered floorboards of the boozing ken.

"Ah dinna recall ye ever striking me," Dodd said slowly.

"You know what I mean. I used you as a decoy which is why you ended up in the Fleet instead of me and why Heneage got his paws on you in the first place."

Dodd nodded. "Ay, Ah ken that. So?"

"So it's my fault you got involved…"

While a penitent Carey was both an amusing and a rare sight, Dodd thought he was talking nonsense. Besides which it was done now and Dodd had a feud with one of the most powerful men in the kingdom. It wasn't a bloodfeud yet but it probably would be by the end. Which reminded him, he needed some information about the size of Heneage's surname. But first he had to clear away Carey's daft scruples.

"So it would ha' bin better if thon teuchter had taken ye instead? Got what he wanted right off, eh?"

Carey frowned. "Well, no…"

"Listen, Sir Robert," said Dodd, leaning forward and setting his tankard down very firmly, "I've done ma time as surety in Jedburgh jail for nae better reason than I wis Janet's husband and the Armstrong headman could spare me for it." And Janet had been very angry with him at the time, of course, a detail he left out. "It wisnae exactly fun but it was fair enough. Same here. Ye used what ye had and what ye had wis me—there's nae offence in that, ye follow? Ah might take offence if ye go on greetin' about what a fearful fellow Heneage is and all, but at the moment Ah'm lettin ye off since ye dinna really ken me either or ma kin."

Carey frowned. "You're not accepting my apology?"

Dodd reached for patience. "Nay sir, I'll accept it. It's just I dinna see a reason for it in the first place."

Carey smiled sunnily at him and stripped off the glove on his right hand. Dodd had to squash his automatic wince at the thought of touching the nasty-looking nailbeds so he could shake hands with good grace.

"Now, sir," he added, "since ye've not had the advantage of partakin' in a feud before, will ye be guided by me?"

Dodd was trying hard to talk like a Courtier, his best ever impersonation of Carey's drawl, and Carey sniggered at the mangled vowels.

"Good God, Ah niver sound like that, do I?" he asked in his Berwick voice, which almost had Dodd smiling back since it sounded so utterly out of place coming from the creature in the elaborately slashed cramoisie velvet doublet and black damask trunk hose.

"Ay, ye do, sir. But nae matter. It's nae yer fault, is it?"

Carey made the harumph noise he had got from his father, thumped his tankard down and stood up.

◇◇◇

Lawyers being the scum they were, most of them tended to clog together in the shambolic clusters of houses and crumbling monastery buildings around the old Templar Church. Nearby were the Inns of Court, new a-building out of the ruins of the Whitefriars abbey. In the long time the Dominicans had been gone, bribed, evicted, or burned at the stake in the Forties, the reign of the much-married Henry VIII, something like what happens to a treetrunk had happened to the old abbey. Small creatures taking up residence, large ones raising broods there, huts and houses like fungus erupting in elaborate ramparts that ate the old walls to build themselves. There was a long area of weedy waste ground stretching down to the river and inevitably filling with the huts, vegetable gardens, chickens, pigs, goats and dirty children of the endless thousands of peasants flooding into London to make their fortune. They were not impressed by the lawyers' writs of eviction. However the writing they didn't know how to read was very clearly on the wall for them in the shape of scaffolding, sawdust, wagons full of blocks of stone, and builders finishing the two magnificent halls for the rich lawyers to take their Commons.

Dodd had almost enjoyed the short walk of a couple of miles along the Oxford Road from Tyburn to the Whitefriars liberties where Carey was more comfortable even though his father had (yet again) paid his creditors. Most of them. The ones he could remember or who had served him with writs at any rate.

He had to admit, it was interesting to see the different styles of working in London and the numberless throngs in the streets and the settled solidity of the overhanging houses. He also had to admit that despite the pathetic lack of decent walls or fortifications, London was impressive. Dodd was still tinkering with his plans for the greatest raid of all time, even though he knew it was hopeless. Where would you sell that much gold and insight? How would you even carry it all back to the Debateable Land?

Very near the round Temple church with its wonderful coloured glass, Carey swung off down an alleyway and up some stairs into a luxurious set of chambers, lined with leatherbound books and with painted cloths of Nimrod the Hunter on the walls. Two haughty-looking clerks surrounded by piles of paper and books looked up briefly as they came in, announced by a spotty page boy with a headcold.

There was a pause. The clerks continued to write away. Carey looked mildly surprised and then leaned on the mantel over the luxury of a small fireplace and hummed a tune. Dodd put his hands behind his back and waited stolidly.

Nothing happened. Surprisingly, Carey cracked first. "Is Mr. Fleetwood available?" he asked coldly, and the haughtiest clerk ignored the magnificence of his embroidered trunk-hose and raised a withering eyebrow.

"Do you have an appointment, Mr...er..." intoned the clerk down his nose. The pageboy had announced them correctly and clearly.

Carey's eyebrow headed for his hairline as well. Dodd leaned back slightly and prepared to watch the fun: would the two pairs of eyebrows fight a little duel, perhaps?

"Robert Carey," he drawled, "*Sir* Robert Carey."

The clerk held his ground. "Do you have an appointment, Sir Robert?"

"I believe my worshipful father, m'lord Baron Hunsdon, mentioned that we might be coming here this afternoon." Carey paused. "To see Fleetwood. Your master." He added as to a child, "About a legal matter."

"Ah yes," sneered the clerk, "The assault at Fleet Prison."

The other clerk glanced up nervously from his copying, then down again. The page boy was hiding on the landing, listening busily.

"And unlawful imprisonment of my man, Sergeant Dodd," said Carey, "and sundry other matters of a legal nature."

The clerk sprang his trap. "Mr. Fleetwood is *not* available."

One Carey eyebrow climbed, the other dropped. Did he know he was doing it, wondered Dodd who was not in the slightest bit surprised at what was happening. It seemed from his face that Carey was surprised. Now the left eyebrow was mounting Carey's forehead again to join his brother in chilly wonder. Did he practise? In front of a mirror?

"How unfortunate," said Carey. "Perhaps tomorrow..."

"Mr. Fleetwood is very busy," said the clerk with magnificent contempt, "for the foreseeable future. A year at least."

"My lord Hunsdon had assured me that Mr. Fleetwood could represent Sergeant Dodd in this matter." Carey was losing ground here.

"My lord was mistaken. Mr. Fleetwood had not first consulted me," sniffed the clerk. "His daybook is full."

"Hm," said Carey, eyebrows now down in a frown.

Dodd stepped forward and leaned his hands not too threateningly on the clerk's desk. "Is Mr. Vice Chamberlain Heneage payin' ye?"

The clerk quivered slightly and then answered with fake indignation, "Of course not, Sergeant, the very idea is outrageous."

Dodd looked around at the other clerk, industriously copying, and nodded. "Ay, so he's threatened ye."

It was satisfying to see the haughty clerk now reading very carefully in Mr. Fleetwood's daybook which seemed to be empty as far as Dodd could see. Nobody said anything.

"Thank ye," said Dodd, remembering a little late some of Carey's lectures about London manners. "Nae doubt it's just as well, Ah wouldna want a man wi' nae blood tae his liver standing up for me in court."

He clattered down the stairs followed by a Carey who was smiling now.

"Well, I never saw that before," he mused. "A lawyer turning down a fat fee. Amazing."

"I have," said Dodd.

Carey wanted to try other lawyers he knew of, Dodd said it wasn't worth the bother. They had an argument about it in the arched old cloister next to the round church.

"See ye," Dodd said, "if it ha' been nobbut a bribe, then maybe, but if Heneage is threatening 'em, he's threatened the lot of them. Threats are cheap."

"I know that, Sergeant," said Carey. "I just want to check."

Sighing Dodd followed Carey on his route through the dens of lawyers and found he was right. No serjeant, utter barrister, attorney, nor even humble solicitor would touch Dodd's case on the end of a polearm. Not that any one of them could have lifted such a weapon.

Frustrated, they sat on a bench facing a small duck pond next to the other shiny new hall, still having its windows installed. Carey had to lean awkwardly with his legs out because of the idiocy of his clothes and their tight fashionable fit.

He pulled out the long clay pipe and started filling it with the mixture of tobacco and expensive Moroccan resin that Dr. Nunez had prescribed for them the previous week. Carey liked it enough to have made enquiries about importing some to Carlisle but it was eyewateringly expensive.

Despite the fact that the practise of drinking herbal smoke was a highly fashionable London vice, Dodd rather liked it too. He took the pipe and drew some of the aromatic white smoke into his lungs and after a moment was blinking peacefully at the tumble of huts going down to the water.

Carey chuckled. "It's a mess, isn't it? Last time I saw him, Sir Robert Cecil was talking about planting gardens down to the river. Of course you'd have to get the riffraff thrown out first."

"What? The lawyers?" Dodd said deadpan, and Carey grinned.

"Good idea, as they won't bloody work for us."

"Ye canna blame them. Heneage will have said to a few of them, tsk tsk, d'ye think the Careys'll take care of yer kine and yer tower while you're lawyering for that Dodd, tsk tsk, and the word will have gone round," Dodd said knowledgeably.

"Metaphorically speaking, but yes. Shortage of Readerships, strange famine of appointments to the serjeantcy, etcetera, etcetera. Quod erat demonstrandum."

"Ay. So. Will we do it ourselves?"

"What, go to court? Certainly not."

"Why not? It canna be so hard if lawyers can do it."

Carey snorted with giggles and Dodd almost giggled as well, feeling pleasantly drunk from the smoke.

"Sergeant, you've run wood. How long does it normally take you to draft one bill? An afternoon? And I'm certainly not studying the law at my age."

"Other young gentlemen study at the Inns of Court," Dodd pointed out. One of the young gentlemen happened to be standing nearby wrapped in his black cloth robe, very like a crow, blinking at the ducks on the pond. For a moment Dodd thought he was familiar, but couldn't place him at all.

Carey took the pipe back from Dodd who had forgotten he was holding it. "Not me. I went to France and wapped a lot of French ladies," said Carey coarsely. "We need a lawyer."

"All Heneage has done is reive our horses," Dodd said.

"Metaphorically speaking," Carey corrected, waggling the end of the pipe at him.

"So then we go after him on foot. We do it ourselves. Ay, so it's slower but…"

Carey shook his head and passed the pipe back to Dodd. "I keep telling you, this is not a Border feud, we do things differently in London. Perhaps Father could twist some arms, raise the fees…Maybe one of the Bacon brothers would take it pro bono if I asked nicely."

Dodd shook his head firmly and opened his mouth to argue but there was a soft cough which interrupted him.

"Excuse me, sirs, but I couldn't help hearing your discourse."

It was the young man in the lawyer's robe. As the man made his bow, Dodd stared at him suspiciously, assuming this must be one of Heneage's spies you heard so much about. The young man was average height, narrow built, with sandy hair under one of the newly fashionable beaver hats. Sharp blue eyes peered out of a face ruined by smallpox, worse even than Barnabus. His attempt at a friendly smile was actually twisted by the scarring. There was a shocking pit right next to his mouth, the size of a farthing.

"Is it true that you are in need of a lawyer?"

"Possibly," said Carey, eyeing the man.

He bowed again to both of them, making Dodd feel uncomfortable. "I am James Enys, at your service, sirs, barrister-at-law."

"And yer daybook is no' full?" asked Dodd cynically.

"Empty, sirs." The man laughed without humour and spread his soft white hands. One of the fingers was dented by a ring newly taken off. "I have just hocked my last ring, sirs, and turned off my clerk."

"Are ye no' rich then?" Dodd asked curiously, "I thought all lawyers was rich."

"Potentially, yes. But generally not when they start, and especially not if Mr. Vice Chancellor Heneage has taken a dislike to them."

This was too pat for either Carey or Dodd's liking. They exchanged glances.

Enys coughed and held up one hand.

"Gentlemen, I know you are trying to launch a civil suit for damages and a criminal charge of assault, battery, and false imprisonment against Mr. Vice, and that Mr. Vice has forestalled you by frightening off all the courageous men of law in this place."

"Ay," said Dodd, putting his elbows on his knees and leaning forwards, despite the damage this made his chokingly high collar do to his adam's apple. "But whit can ye dae to show us ye're no' one o' his kinship come tae trap us in ambush?"

Carey coughed as Enys frowned in puzzlement. "My friend is from Cumberland," he explained, and translated Dodd's challenge.

Enys inclined his head slightly. "Quite right, Sergeant," he said, "you have a point there. Yet the same could be said of any lawyer you hired—if not already a spy, turned into one the minute Heneage found out who he was."

"So?"

Enys shrugged. "Make enquiries, sir. Ask about me. You will find I am a little notorious. I still have chambers in my lord of Essex's court. My...um...my sister keeps house for me there although she does not…um like to keep company. You may find me there any time from ten in the morning."

"Not at Westminster Hall?" Carey asked.

Again the stiff smile. "Frequently, in hopes of a brief. However, Mr. Vice has made it clear that he prefers my room to my company there and the Court officials often oblige him. Please—at least consider my offer."

"Do you know who I am?" Carey was crossing his legs at the ankle, leaning back and tapping his gloved fingers on his teeth. Dodd nipped the pipe from his other hand and smoked the last of the tobacco in the bowl, then tapped it out, his head spinning. Not only did the smoke ease his kidneys, it also seemed to do something to the dull ball of rage in his gut against Heneage.

"I believe you are the son of my lord Baron Hunsdon."

"How did you find out?"

"When I heard you enquiring of one of my brothers-at-law, I asked him and he told me. Also, sir, with respect, you and your family are not entirely unknown to the legal profession."

Carey ignored that. "Well, you'll know then that I'm the youngest and utterly penniless at the moment, so it's my worshipful Father you must convince, not me. He'll be paying you."

Enys bowed. "I should be delighted at the chance to try."

"Hm," said Carey again, "Very well, come to Somerset House tomorrow afternoon."

The young man bowed again and his robe swirled as he walked away, whistling softly to himself. Dodd watched him go. "I dinna trust him."

"Quite right too," said Carey, putting the pipe away again. "Even if he's not Heneage's spy, he's still a bloody lawyer."

When they got back to Somerset House they found that Hunsdon was not there. He had gone upriver to Whitehall Palace in a matter for the Queen and required his son and his son's henchman to join him there immediately.

They got into one of the Hunsdon boats, still munching some hurried bread and cheese. Dodd leaned back and idly watched the flapping standard at the prow. Certainly there were aspects to being a gentleman he could well get used to—such as not being one of the men in blinding yellow and black livery sweating to propel them to Westminster against the tide. Carey sat opposite, upright, tapping his fingers on the gunwale and looking thoughtfully into the distance.

Dodd had nothing against boats and found himself quite enjoying the crowded river, full of vessels crossing in all directions; a red-sailed Thames lugger headed straight for them at one point causing the men on the larboard side to back water in order to avoid it. Derisive shouts echoed over the water from the larger boat. The water was brown but not too bad-smelling, all things considered. Somerset House had its own well and in any case Dodd was sticking firmly to mild ale because it was good for his kidneys. He saw no need to take the suicidal risk of drinking expensive Thames water which was so full of ill humours and mud, although he was quite happy to eat the salmon from it when he wanted a cheap meal. The standard flapped in the breeze on the water.

"What are you smiling at, Sergeant?" asked Carey, who seemed to be worried about something. Dodd realised he had indeed been smiling; he must still be a little drunk from the tobacco.

"Nowt." Dodd hastily averted his eyes from the thing.

"Come on, it's Father's badge, isn't it?"

It had been. Dodd had been wondering, why did the Queen's Lord Chamberlain, one of the richest and most powerful men in the kingdom, choose as his badge the figure of what looked like a rabid duck?

Carey stuck his lower lip out. "It's a Swan Rampant."

"Ay?"

"It's in honour of my Lady Mother, if you're interested."

"Ay?" Dodd was very interested, but tried hard not to let it show. "Is she still alive then, yer...ah...Lady Mother?"

"Oh yes," said Carey, not explaining any more. Dodd wondered where Hunsdon kept her as there was no sign of a wife at Somerset House. Perhaps she was tired: Dodd would have thought she would be after birthing the full Carey brood of eight living children, and possibly more pregnancies depending how many babes she might have lost.

"So…ah…where is she?" asked Dodd in what he hoped was a tactful voice. After all, there was an official mistress at Hunsdon's residence. "Prefers the countryside?"

"You could say that," answered Carey. "She has no interest in the Court and would have to attend the Queen if she lived in London, so…er…she doesn't. She was here in '88 though."

"Wise lady," said Dodd, feeling sorry for her. It could be no easy thing to be married to the likes of lord Baron Hunsdon nor mother to his reckless sons. He pictured the lady in a manor house somewhere, living a dull but respectable life, embroidering linen and doing whatever else ladies did, whilst her husband philandered through the fleshpots of London.

Carey nodded, still looking worried. Just once he cast a glance over his shoulder where the ship-forest of the Pool of London, on the other side of the Bridge, was disappearing round the bend.

"I thought I saw…No," he said to himself, "can't be."

Dodd peered at the bridge himself but the crowded houses gave up no clue and nor did the carrion crows and buzzards squabbling over the new head there. He saw a flight of fourteen crows swoop up and attack the buzzards together, driving them away from the delicacy. He blinked for a moment. Did birds have surnames to back them? Crows all lived together in rookeries, of course, but did they foray out together against other birds like men? It was fascinating. He knew that the proper thing to call such an avian group was a "murder" of crows because of their liking for newborn lambs.

More of Hunsdon's liverymen were waiting for them at the Westminster steps. Carey and Dodd were led briskly not into the palace but to a small stone chapel tucked into the side of Westminster Hall, then down into the cool crypt. From the stairs Dodd smelled death ,and so did Carey for his nostrils flared.

A bloated corpse lay on a trestletable between the various tombs and monuments of the crypt. The body was surrounded by candles to burn out the bad airs. They were not doing a good job. Hunsdon stood before the corpse, hands on his sword belt, his Chamberlain's staff under his arm.

Carey bowed and so did Dodd. "My lord," said Carey, "I was hoping that your business at the palace would be more pleasant."

Hunsdon scowled at his son. "Eh? What are you talking about?"

Carey looked annoyed and uncomfortable. "I was hoping you might have been…ah…mentioning my unpaid fee to Her Majesty and…"

"Oh, for God's sake, Robin," growled Hunsdon, "she'll pay it when she's good and ready and not before. Meanwhile, look at this."

Unwillingly, they looked.

"Besides she's still in Oxford with the court or possibly heading back by now if she takes one of her notions. Odd this."

Hunsdon gestured at the corpse. It was a man wearing a good linen shirt, skin waterlogged and flaking away, eyes and other soft parts already eaten by fish, stomach swollen and pregnant with gas.

"Who is he?" asked Carey, taking a handkerchief out of his sleeve pocket and holding it to his nose.

"Nobody knows his name and he's in my jurisdiction, blast him."

Dodd wanted to ask why but didn't. However Hunsdon swung on him and said, "As Lord Chamberlain to her Majesty I am *de officio* President of the Board of Greencloth with a remit over any murder done within the Virge of the Court, that is, within two miles of Her Majesy's sacred person or her palaces. The blighter washed up against the Queen's own Privy Steps, so he's my responsibility."

With a lurch in his gut, Dodd realised the man had no feet. Carey was approaching the corpse, handkerchief still over his mouth and nose, looking carefully all over it and turning the swollen hands over. Dodd knew Carey had been spending time with Mr. Fenwick the Carlisle undertaker and he seemed to have got a strong stomach from it. The man's left index finger was missing a top joint.

Dodd found that the close air in the crypt with its musty smell of the long dead and the gassy fecal stench reeking from the corpse was on the verge of embarassing him. He didn't have a hanky, so he put his hand over his nose and swallowed hard.

Carey smiled at him. "Look here, Sergeant," he said, "see? It's interesting, isn't it?" Carey was holding up the flaccid swollen fingers. By the guttering light of the candles Dodd could see they were scarred with burns in a couple of places, but also that there was a clerk's callus on the middle finger of his right hand. Yet the palms had the calluses you got from using a spade, not a sword.

He frowned. Yes, it was interesting. What manner of man was it? A gentleman wouldn't have spade calluses on his palms and a commoner wouldn't have a clerk's bump from holding a pen.

"Ay," he said, "He wis wearing a ring too." He pointed gingerly at the mark on the little finger left by a ring.

Carey carefully lifted the other hand. "No other rings, the same marks though."

"And what happened to his feet?" said Hunsdon, watching his son with his head on one side and a look of baffled pride on his face.

Carey moved to that end, past a pair of knobbly knees, and blinked down at the exposed ankle joints. "It looks like they were torn off after the man was dead," he said thoughtfully. "Hmm." He bent closer to look and Dodd peered as well, brought one of the watchlights over.

The bone seemed to have been ground by something hard leaving little grains of red there. Perhaps flakes of rust?

"Hm," said Carey again and went to the head end. "I wonder..."

To Dodd's disgust, he took out his poinard and levered open the man's mouth with it. A trickle of brown came out. Carey placed his gloved hand flat on the man's chest and pressed. More brown water came out of the mouth.

"There's no wound in the body, is there?"

"Stab wound in the back," said Hunsdon, now holding a pomander to his nose, "probably to the kidneys."

"Ah," nodded Carey, taking refuge in his hanky again. Dodd was desperately trying not to cough. "I wonder if…"

At that moment the corpse shifted and farted, as if some horrible wall had been breached. All three of them were at the door in unspoken terror before the air filled with a stench so foul they were coughing and gagging as they ran up the stairs, leaving the watchcandles flickering blue behind them.

"Christ," gasped Hunsdon as they tumbled out into the street with very little dignity, "I hate these cases. Bloody man will have to be embalmed until we can hold an inquest for him." He gestured irritably at three of his men who were standing around holding a large tarpaulin and after an unhappy pause, they went down into the crypt to cover the corpse up again.

By unspoken agreement, all three of them went up the street and into a nearby Westminster boozing ken, a wooden hut but very nicely painted hard by the Court gate, with the traditional red lattices. Its battered patriotic sign bore the Tudor Rose, painted over a carving that looked as if it was of a boar or a pig of some kind. The barman knew Hunsdon immediately and was obsequious, bowing him into a private alcove away from the feverishly gaming young courtiers. Their brandies came from a different barrel under the counter and when Dodd gulped it, he wished he hadn't for it was very much better than the aqua vitae he normally drank when pressed. At least, he thought gloomily, he had held his water and hadn't vomited, though it had been a close thing when the corpse moved…To be sure it was no more than the gas in it and Dodd had seen it happen before, but in a small space and in the light of the candles…As Carey's father had said, Christ!

His heartbeat was settling again. Two more of Hunsdon's men, Turner and Catchpole, stood around nearby. Now Dodd had to suppress another moment of happy smugness. Normally it would be him standing by walls, watching his betters drinking, bored and waiting for an order from Lowther or Scrope, not sitting down and doing the drinking. He had done the same duty for his wife's uncle, the Armstrong headman, Kinmont Willie Armstrong, although on those occasions he hadn't been bored at all because he was waiting for the fight to begin. So this gentlemanning around London was a pleasant change and it worried him that he was getting used to it.

His face settled back into its normal glum scowl and he sipped more carefully at the aqua vitae so he could actually taste the stuff.

"Good isn't it," said Carey, whose face was not quite so pale now. "It's a French aqua vitae, made from cider."

"Ay?" Dodd was interested. "What's normal brandy made of then?"

"Wine usually."

"Is that the same as brandywine?"

"No, that's wine mixed with brandy and usually some spices and sugar. Very good it is too…"

Carey caught the potboy's eye, established that the boozing ken was high-class enough to have brandywine, and a few minutes later Dodd was sipping that as well. Carey hadn't even asked the price—that was what having a rich father did to you, thought Dodd.

"I've already told the Board to convene tomorrow, damn and blast it," said Hunsdon, knocking back his own aqua vitae. "God, I hate council meetings."

"When exactly was he found?"

"Low tide, yesterday," said Hunsdon. "Gave one of the Queen's favourite chamberers a nasty turn."

"So probably carried downriver by the current, not up by the tide."

"Probably."

"Hm." Carey was looking thoughtfully into his wine.

"Any ideas, Robin?"

Carey smiled cynically. "I think you should procure six witnesses to swear that they saw him going to Heneage's house in

Chelsea and the inquest should find him unlawfully killed by person or persons unknown and…"

Hunsdon rolled his eyes. "There's no sign he was one of Heneage's."

Carey shrugged. "And?"

Hunsdon shook his head. "Come on, what could you see from the corpse?"

"Not the face of his killer in his eyes," said Carey. "And I don't know whether he was a commoner or a clerk or a gentleman. But I do know that the stab to his back didn't kill him for he was put in the river still breathing since his lungs were full of water. I suspect that what killed him was the weight of iron chains on his feet pulling him to the bottom from the rust flakes on his ankle bones."

Dodd nodded at this. "Ay, and when his flesh rotted enough, his feet broke off in the currents and the body could fetch up at the steps."

"How long ago was he put in the river?" rumbled Hunsdon.

"Perhaps ten days, two weeks ago? I don't know, it's hard to tell with water."

"Any more of Walsingham's tricks?"

Carey shook his head. "Nothing that would give us his name, my lord, but I expect that's why he had only his shirt on—his doublet would give too much away."

Dodd sat still, transfixed with a sudden thought. If the man was stripped, why *did* they leave his shirt on? Modesty? Not very likely. Och God, he thought, I'll have to go back into that pest pit again.

Fortified by brandy he leaned forward. "Ay, so what's under his shirt?"

Carey frowned and was clearly thinking the same as Dodd. He sighed and stood up. "We'll have to look."

They walked back down the street, took several deep breaths of relatively clean London air, and then went down the stairs and past the guard. The tarpaulin was heavy and the ragged remains of the man's shirt sticky with…something. Carey pulled it back. Dodd and he stared, looking for anything of interest. Nothing, if you ignored the damage done by fishes, except for a small knife scar on the ribs and a recognisable healed swordslash across the chest.

They looked at each other and Dodd's gorge rose. He swallowed hard and held his breath.

Fearful of causing another corpsely fart, they hefted the man onto his left side very carefully. Dodd brought the flickering candle as close to the man's back as he could. And there, at last, they found something interesting—little arrow-shaped scratches scattered at random across the water-swollen skin of his back. There were more grouped near the shoulders, as if the dead man had rolled in a bramble patch. Nothing else—the scars were mostly white and old, although a few seemed more recent.

Neither spoke as they let him down again, saving their breath. They pulled the tarpaulin back and hurried up the stairs.

Dodd was panting from lack of air and both of them were sweating. His head spun. He had to stop and sit on a wall for a moment because of the memories from when he was very little and still in his skirts: the bodies of people he knew, dead from plague, lying unburied around the village, and what had happened to them.

"I hope that was worth it," said Carey. "I wonder what made those scratches. I know I've never seen it before but there's something niggling me about it."

"Ay," croaked Dodd, very ready for more brandywine now, "but he wisnae actually flogged, that's for sure."

Carey nodded, gazing into space intently as if he was trying to read the answer written on the clouds.

They rejoined Hunsdon at the boozing ken who had got in more brandy for them and mild ale for Dodd.

"Just some odd little scratches on his back, and a couple of healed cuts" Carey answered his sire's eyebrows. "They don't help identify him. No tattoos or birthmarks that I could see, although you could cry the fact that his left index finger is missing its top joint."

Hunsdon sighed heavily again and drank. "It's worth looking at the warrants Mr. Heneage has sworn out over the past month just in case the man's one of his, but it's unlikely we'll match them up. We need a proper identification. I'll have the town criers in Westminster and the City cry the news, and bills printed up with his description. All I can do, unfortunately."

"Meanwhile Mr. Recorder Fleetwood's bloody nephew refuses point blank to act for me," said Carey.

"Damn and blast," said his father, sounding no more than wearily irritated, certainly not surprised. "I thought that might happen."

"Is it no' possible to proceed then?" Dodd asked mournfully.

"Of course it is. I'll ask Cecil what he suggests. Or one of the Bacons…"

"Perhaps my lord earl of Essex could help?" Carey put in.

"Possibly. He's back in her Majesty's favour again at least," said Hunsdon and Dodd thought he heard something cautious in his tone.

"The Bacons won't deal with a mere case of assault…"

"They might know someone who will."

"He'll no' come to trial will he, my lord," Dodd said. "Heneage, I mean. He's too important."

"Criminal trial? We can make the attempt though I agree, I doubt it. It's the civil case for damages that I'm interested in." Hunsdon let out a tight little smile.

"And will the Queen no' take his side? Seeing he's her henchman?"

"There's no telling what Her Majesty the Queen my cousin might take it into her head to do."

Dodd knew about this. Hunsdon was indeed cousin to the Queen through his mother Mary Boleyn, the sister of the more famous Anne.

Dodd looked hopeful. "Untouchable, are ye, sir?"

"Good God, no," said Hunsdon with a bluff laugh, "nobody's untouchable. If Heneage could convince the Queen that I've turned traitor, I'd go to the block just like anybody else. Quite right too if the bill was foul and I was guilty."

That was worrying. If somebody like Hunsdon came down, so would anyone associated with him. Hunsdon slapped Dodd on the back.

"Don't look so worried, Sergeant, the Queen's a lot more difficult to fool than Heneage thinks she is."

Dodd nodded.

They sat in the back of the boat while Hunsdon sat in the front. Carey was looking annoyed, possibly because a boat full of musicians was following the Hunsdon boat, playing for all they were worth. Dodd couldn't hear a word of what Carey was muttering.

"Eh sir?" he shouted. Carey tried again but couldn't whisper loud enough. "What are they following us for?" Dodd wanted to know, wishing he'd brought a crossbow, especially for the viol player.

"Father's in charge of the Queen's entertainments at Court," Carey explained. "They're hoping he'll give them a job."

"Och." Dodd shook his head at such folly. "Whit were ye saying…"

"I was saying that I was hoping to start for Carlisle soon."

"Afore ye've seen the Queen?" Dodd was surprised.

"She's at Oxford which is on the way."

"Ah." Dodd felt the corners of his mouth turning down sourly. Typical Carey, no consideration for anyone else.

"I'm surprised you're not delighted, Sergeant."

Dodd scowled at him for his ignorance. "Nay sir, I'm in nae hurry."

"I thought you hated London."

"Ay sir, I do."

"And there's plague about."

"Ay sir." Both of them were quiet for a moment remembering Carey's servant Barnabus and his family. Hunsdon had indicated he would take Barnabus' niece into his household until she could be found a good husband, and young Simon, his nephew, was already lording it over the other boys in the stables where he was a great deal more use than he was as Carey's page.

"So? Why don't you want to go home?"

"I havenae had my satisfaction fra Heneage yet."

Carey barked with laughter. Dodd was annoyed again. He wagged a finger at Carey.

"Say what ye like about Richie Graham of Brackenhill, but he'd know better than to treat a Dodd like that. Wee Colin Elliot might treat me like that if he got the chance, but he wouldnae have the insolence to leave me alive after."

Carey grinned. "Jock of the Peartree did something similar to me a few months ago and I'm not planning vengeance."

"Ay sir, but ye was spying out his tower and forebye it was in the way of battle and retaliation for the lumps ye gave him yersen. That's fair, is that, and ye both know it."

Carey nodded. Dodd leaned back with his hands on his thighs.

"So. I canna leave London until I've given Heneage back what he gave me."

"With interest?"

"Ay. Wi' interest."

"Trouble is, it might take a while and I really want to talk to the Queen and my lord of Essex."

Dodd sighed and looked him in the eye. Carey winced, probably at the horribly sour but valiant viol-scraping in the boat that was now closing on them rapidly.

"Sir," said Dodd, "do ye not ken that the Dodds have a blood-feud wi' the Elliots that goes back tae the Rough Wooing of Henry VIII, over sixty years. If it takes a while, then it takes a while. Or if he dies afore I'm satisfied, then I'll do the same to his son."

"I don't think Heneage has a family."

Dodd shrugged. "If he dies wi'out issue, then I'll take it to his cousins or his nephews." He'd been wondering if Heneage had family to back him as well as the Queen. It was good news that he didn't.

Even so, Carey seemed worried.

Dodd tapped his knee. "Dinna be concerned, sir. It's no' a blood feud, only a feud. It might be composed if he offers enough to me or I can burn his tower or the like."

"Ah," said Carey. "Good. I need you back in Carlisle this autumn."

"As yer father tells it, I can leave the court case with my lawyer once I've made my statements and he'll take it on for me until he needs me again. Once it's well begun I'll come back wi'ye to Carlisle and happy to do it." Dodd thought wistfully of Janet. He would never have guessed how much he missed her visits to him on market days and his visits back to her in Gilsland when he could.

"How much would you take to compose your feud?"

Dodd thought carefully. "Ah dinna ken, sir. Whit would be the London price for twenty kine and ten sheep and five good horses."

At that moment they heard a muttered "God's truth!" from Hunsdon in the prow. He stood and gestured so that the rowers backed water. Then he beckoned the boatful of importunate musicians even closer.

"How much for your viol?" he roared across to them.

The musicians elbowed each other and there was a fierce argument. "He doesn't want to sell, my lord," shouted a harpist with long hair.

Hunsdon fished out a purse of silver and hefted it. "This much?"

There was a scuffle in the boat and one of the flautists brandished the viol in the air while the drummer sat on the viol player. Hunsdon gently threw the purse of silver into the boat and, despite wild protests from the viol player, the instrument was lobbed spinning across the water to be caught by Hunsdon's man Turner. He handed it to Hunsdon, who took the instrument by the neck and smashed it to pieces against the side of the boat. Carey looked mildly pained, then shrugged.

"That's better," shouted Hunsdon, "and don't for God's sake let the man buy another bloody instrument."

The Hunsdon liverymen bent grinning to their oars again and they left the musicians well behind.

Carey and his father were uncharacteristically quiet as the boat sped downriver, helped by the current. As they rounded the bend and came in sight of Somerset House, both men gasped and stood up in the boat, nearly upsetting it.

Another boat was tied up at Somerset steps, a long gig from a ship, also sporting the Swan Rampant that was Hunsdon's badge. Men were standing on the boatlanding who were clearly not Londoners, being barrel-shaped, mainly red-haired and short, and sporting long pigtails down their backs.

Dodd stared with interest at the play of expressions on Carey's face—absolute horror predominating. Strangely Hunsdon was grinning with delight from ear to ear and let out a bellow of laughter.

"Good God, it can't be," groaned Carey.

"It is!" laughed Hunsdon, slapping his son on the back and taking him unawares so he nearly went in the Thames. "I'd recognise that crew of Cornish wreckers and pirates anywhere. Ho, Trevasker!"

The most evil-looking of the men touched his cap to Hunsdon and said something to one of the others.

"Oh Jesus, this is all I need," said Carey, sitting down and putting his head in his hands.

His father stayed standing all the way to the steps and jumped off onto the jetty before the boat was even tied up. The crew of Cornish wreckers and pirates touched their foreheads respectfully to Hunsdon as he hurried past them, through the gate in the wall, and up through the gardens. Carey followed nearly as quickly with a face of thunder while Dodd scrambled after, near to dying of curiosity. He caught up with Carey in the orchard.

"Is it one o' yer creditors?"

"No, much worse. You saw the badge, didn't you? It's much, much worse."

Dodd shook his head, loosened his sword just in case Carey wasn't exaggerating again, and followed up to the house which was blazing with candles in the grey afternoon.

In the magnificent entrance hall stood more short, broad, pigtailed men with hands like hams and a strong smell of the sea on them. Hunsdon hurried through to the parlour where a smallish woman in her sixties with very bright blue eyes was just taking off a large sealskin cloak and handing it to a pink-cheeked girl.

She turned, smiled, and curtseyed to Lord Hunsdon who bowed formally, then opened his arms and bellowed "Annie!" as he scooped her up and swing her round in a delighted hug.

"Put me down, Harry, you old fool!" shouted the woman as she hugged him back with just as much violence, laughing with an infectious gurgle in her throat. "You'll knock my hat off."

Although she otherwise spoke like Hunsdon there was a strong flavour in her voice. It was the sound of the Cornish sailors who plied up and down the Irish Sea in appalling weather, trading tin, hides, wood, and contraband in all directions.

Hunsdon put her down gently and she straightened her smart French hood and smiled lovingly at Carey. "Where's my little man to, then, eh?" she demanded.

Real pain crossed Carey's face. Dodd's mouth dropped open as he finally worked out who he was looking at. Carey stepped past him, swept a very fine Court bow, and bent over the lady's hand with unimpeachable respect.

"My lady mother," murmured Carey in a resigned tone of voice. "What a delightful surprise."

She laughed a gravelly laugh and thumped him in the ribs. "No it ain't, Robin." she said, "Don't try that Court soft soap with me. You're shaking in your fine boots."

Carey smiled wanly.

"Er…"

"You're worried I know what you've been at, boy, and you're right. I do."

"Ah…"

"Meanwhile, who's this henchman of yours?"

Guts cramping, ribs aching, and his face stiff with the effort not to laugh, Dodd stepped forward and made the best bow he could manage.

"Ma'am, may I present Land-Sergeant Henry Dodd of Gilsland, presently serving under me in Carlisle," said Carey in the tones of one going to his execution.

Dodd found himself being looked sharply up and down.

"Hm. So you're the Dodd headman that came out for my son with your kin when he got himself in trouble at Netherby," she said.

"Ay, my lady. Wi' the English Armstrongs o' course."

"And as I heard it, you convinced the Johnston to back you and ran a nice little ambush on the Maxwell to bring the hand-guns back from Dumfries in the summer."

Dodd could only nod. How the hell could she know so much? Carey had his eyes shut and his hands clasped firmly behind his back like a boy reciting a lesson.

Lady Hunsdon swung on her husband. "I take a little trip to Dumfries in summer with Captain Trevasker and the *Judith of Penryn* in Irish whiskey and some vittles for the Scottish court and what do I hear? My youngest son's doings all over the town although the King's gone back to Edinburgh and his mangy pack of lordlings with him."

"Did you sell the cargo?" asked Hunsdon.

"Of course I did, husband, that's why I went. I knew the Court would have eaten and drunk the place bare. Triple prices for the whisky from my Lord Maxwell, no less."

She was advancing on Carey now who backed before her with his shoulders up like a boy expecting to have his ears boxed for scrumping apples. Dodd held his breath in mingled hope and fascination.

"Now one of the things I heard was not at all to my liking," she said, prodding Carey in his well-velveted chest which was as high as she could reach. He flinched. "Not at all. What's this about Lord Spynie and Sir Henry Widdrington, eh?"

Carey smiled placatingly and spread his hands. "I couldn't possibly say, ma'am, are they in bed together?"

"All but." Pouncing like a cat, Lady Hunsdon grabbed her son's left hand and pulled off his embroidered glove. After a moment when it seemed Carey would snatch his hand away and possibly run for it, he stood and let her look, towering over her and yet somehow gangling like the lad he must have been fifteen years before.

In silence Lady Hunsdon reached for his other hand. Carey sighed and pulled the glove off for her. More thunderous silence. Dodd saw tears rising to Lady Hunsdon's eyes and suddenly she pulled Carey to her and hugged him.

"Mother!" protested the muffled voice of Carey. She let go at once and turned to her husband.

"We shall set a price of five thousand crowns on Spynie's head and the same on Widdrington's," she said coldly.

"Er…no, my lady," said Hunsdon, "I think not. Spynie's still the King's Minion, though there are hopes of Robert Kerr, and John needs the Widdrington surname to help him rule the East March."

Their eyes locked and Dodd could see the tussle and then the agreement between them flying clear as a bird. "At least, not yet," amended his lordship.

"Of course, my lord," said Lady Hunsdon with the dangerous meekness Dodd had learned to fear in Janet.

Carey was pulling his gloves back on with fingers that trembled slightly.

"Have you seen Edmund?" Hunsdon asked to break the silence. "Doctor Nunez is very pleased with him."

Lady Hunsdon sat herself down in a carved chair as Hunsdon sat as well. "I talked to him while I was waiting for you, my lord."

At Hunsdon's gesture, Carey and Dodd sat on a bench. Hunsdon's majordomo was bringing in a light supper and spiced wine for them. Carey spoke quietly to him and Dodd saw a small cup of brandy brought and added to his wine. He looked like he needed it and drank gratefully while Dodd helped himself to a mutton pasty.

"Did you plan to put a price on Heneage's head as well, wife?" asked Hunsdon teasingly as he carved a plump breast of duck with a sauce of raspberries and laid it on her plate. Lady Hunsdon sniffed and pulled the dish of sallet herbs towards her.

"Your sister wouldn't like it."

"She wouldn't," agreed Hunsdon.

"He mistreated you too, Sergeant Dodd?" Lady Hunsdon said suddenly to Dodd, who had to swallow quickly.

"Ay, my lady."

"What are you going to do about it?"

"Ay well, milady, if I was at home the bell'd be ringing and the Dodds and Armstrongs would be riding and the man would ha' lost a few flocks of sheep and herds of cattle and some horses if we could find them and likely a tower or two burned."

Lady Hunsdon nodded. "Of course. Powerful long way for your surname to come though, isn't it?"

"Ay, it is. Your good lord has offered to back a court case for me but...ah..."

"The lawyers won't take the brief, ma'am," explained Carey. "None of them will."

Lady Hunsdon nodded at this.

"Except that pocky young man we met the day," put in Dodd. "He said he'd dae it since Heneage disnae like him in any case."

"What's his name?" asked Hunsdon.

"James...Enys?"

"Enys?" said Lady Hunsdon, "That's a Cornish name. Where's he from?"

"No idea. We were worried he might be Heneage's man so we asked him to come here tomorrow so you could look at him, my lord." Lord and Lady Hunsdon both nodded.

"Heneage isn't going to give up just because his last attempt blew up in his face," said Hunsdon, "and Edmund..."

"...has horse-clabber for brains," snapped Lady Hunsdon. "At least you did well there, Robin, from what he said."

Carey inclined his head politely while still studying the floor.

Dodd watched as Lady Hunsdon polished off her wine and nodded at the Steward to replenish it. "So what I'm hearing from you, my lord, is that there's not a thing we can do to pay back Spynie and Widdrington, and Heneage is more than likely going to have another try at pulling you down just as soon as he can think of something twisted enough."

Hunsdon inclined his head in a gesture just like his son's.

"God damn the lot of them," swore Lady Hunsdon, tapping her fragile Venetian wine glass decisively. "Do you need money, Robin?"

Carey coloured. "Ah…well…"

"Of course you do, look at your fancy duds. Cost a couple of farms just for your hose, I shouldn't wonder. Well, I had a lucky voyage coming up the Channel, so here you are…"

She threw a bulging leather purse at Carey who caught it and whistled soundlessly when he looked inside.

"Pieces of eight?"

Lady Hunsdon smiled and wiggled her fingers. "We caught a Flemish trader off the Carrick Roads as we came out of Penryn. And you're not to spend it on clothes," she added, setting off another near-hernia in Dodd's abused diaphragm. "Sergeant, don't you let him go near that devil Bullard and his doublets."

"No, milady," Dodd managed somehow.

"Invest it, Robin," said Lady Hunsdon. "As I've told you before, George Cumberland has the right idea…"

Hunsdon was standing again, leaning over to his wife and proffering his arm.

"My lady wife," he said softly. Lady Hunsdon swallowed the last of her spiced wine, put her hand on her husband's arm, and allowed him to help her up. Then she stood on tiptoe and kissed Lord Hunsdon's ear as they turned towards the door to the stairs.

Carey put his fists on his knees, stood up and hurried after his parents, caught up with his mother at the foot of the stairs and started whispering to her urgently. Dodd followed them. He didn't need to hear Carey's question as he knew exactly what it would be about—the woman Carey was disastrously in love with. She was still married to Sir Henry Widdrington, a jealous husband who had clearly seized the chance to mistreat Carey in Dumfries.

"Mother, how is Elizabeth Widdrington?" asked Carey, "I'm anxious for her. Sir Henry might…"

"I think she's well enough, all things considered," said Lady Hunsdon with a worried frown. "She's very strong. Sybilla's still furious with me for the ill match I made for her daughter."

Carey's inaudible next murmur sounded angry and Lady Hunsdon put up her hand to his shoulder and gripped. "Robin," she said, "I know, I know. You must be patient." Carey's response was a characteristic growl. Lady Hunsdon smiled fondly at him, pulled his chestnut head down to hers and kissed his cheek. This time Carey didn't bridle like a youth but kissed her back and put his arm around her shoulders.

They parted as Hunsdon led his lady up the stairs. Carey avoided Dodd's eye as they made for their respective bedchambers.

"Now you see why my Lady Mother doesn't often come to Court," he said. "She prefers to stay in Cornwall with her sister Sybilla Trevannion and her friends the Killigrews."

"Ay," said Dodd.

"It wasn't my mother's fault that I first met my cousin Elizabeth when I went to Scotland with the message for King James from the Queen about his mother's execution," added Carey. "Which was after she had been married off to Sir Henry."

"Ay," said Dodd, not much interested in the complicated tale of Carey's love-life. If the woman was willing and her husband odious, why did Carey not simply gather a nice raiding party, hit the man's tower by surprise, kill him and take the woman? Dodd would be perfectly happy to be best man at that rough wedding and it would at least end Carey's perpetual mooning over her, alternating with an occasional seduction of some even more dangerous female. "Ah…Does yer mam hold a letter of marque from the Queen?"

Carey's gaze was cold. "Of course she does, she's not a pirate. Father got it for her after she happened to help sink a Flemish pirate off the Lizard." Dodd was proud of himself for not letting a flicker across his countenance.

"Ay?"

"What the Devil do you expect her to do all day, sit at home and embroider?" Carey slammed into his chamber, shouting for the ever absent Simon Barnet to see to his points.

Dodd went to his own chamber and could laugh at last. The wild cherubs over the mantelpiece seemed to laugh back as he carefully worked through all his buttons and laces and folded his suit before climbing into bed in his shirt. As he went to sleep, he thought happily that he now had all the explanation he needed for Carey's wild streak. By God, the Careys were an entertaining bunch. For a while, Dodd felt pierced with loneliness that he didn't have Janet in bed beside him to talk about it. He rather thought Janet and Lady Hunsdon would get on very well.

tuesday 12th september 1592, early morning

Just after daybreak Dodd was enjoying bread and beer in his chamber at his good vantage point at the window where he could watch the doings in the street. What a pleasure it was to be able to look through a window quilted with diamonds like the jack of an Englishman, so the glass kept the wind out but let the light in. Nobody ever bothered with glass in the Borders because it broke too easily, although Dodd thought he had heard that Richie Graham had a couple of windows of the stuff for his wife's chamber which were removeable in the case of a siege. Here in wealthy London, every window glittered like water with it.

The knock on his door was nothing like Carey's hammering. When he opened it he found a square young man with red hair and freckles clad in the Hunsdon livery of black and yellow stripes. The youngster opened his mouth and spoke words that might as well have been French for the sense Dodd could make of them, although he knew the sound from the sailors that came into Dumfries and took copper out of Whitehaven.

"What?" Dodd asked irritably. Why could nobody in the south speak proper English like him? It was worse than Scotch because he could speak that if he had to.

The man tried again, frowning with the effort. "M'loidy wants ee."

"Ma lady Hunsdon? Wants me?"

More brow-wrinkling. "Ay, she do."

Dodd picked up his new hat and washed down the last of his manchet bread. It was a little tasteless for all its fine crumb, he thought to himself, he really preferred normal bread with the nutty taste from the unsieved flour and the ale in it and the little gritty bits from milling. There was something very weak and namby pamby about all this luxury.

He clattered down the stairs after the red-haired lad, trailing his fingers along the wonderful carved balustrade as he went. In the hall were two other wide, pig-tailed Cornish sailors, Will Shakespeare looking neat but a little less doleful than he had the week before, and the fresh-faced, cream-skinned girl in neat dark blue wool.

"What's up, Will?" Dodd asked the ex-player and would-be poet. "Ah thocht ye were well in with the Earl of Southampton?"

Shakespeare shrugged. "These things can take a little time. My lord had to post to Oxford to meet her Majesty. He...er... he took Mistress Emilia with him."

Dodd nodded tactfully. "Ay? And what are we doing now?"

"My lady Hunsdon has a fancy to go into town to do some shopping," Shakespeare explained.

Dodd's brow wrinkled this time. "Why?"

"My lady is a woman and women go shopping," Shakespeare explained patiently, "especially when they are in London in Michaelmas term with the Queen's New Year's present to consider."

"Ay, Ah ken that, but why wi' me?"

"For conversation?" offered Shakespeare with just enough of a twitch in his eyebrows for Dodd to get the message.

The horses were outside in the courtyard, nice-looking animals and one stout gelding with a pillion seat trimmed in velvet.

"Ah, Sergeant Dodd," came the ringing voice tinged with the West Country from the other doorway, "I have a fancy to spend some of my gains in Cheapside and require a man to manage my horse as I shall ride pillion."

Dodd knew perfectly well that there were grooms aplenty in Hunsdon's stables who could have done the job. He sighed. Then he bowed to Lady Hunsdon who was standing on the steps with a wicked grin on her face, wearing a very fine kirtle of dark red velvet with a forepart of brocade. She had a smart matching feathered hat on her head over her white cap. It looked similar to the green one Dodd had bought at outrageous expense for Janet and which was now sitting packed with hay in its wicker box in his chamber.

"Ah, I havenae done the office before, m'lady," he said nervously. "Ah dinna…"

"Good Lord, how does Mrs. Dodd travel then?"

Dodd couldn't help grimacing a little at Janet's likely reaction to the suggestion that she should ride pillion. "On her ain mare, m'lady," he replied, and said nothing about the mare's origins.

Lady Hunsdon nodded, making the feather bounce. "Ah yes, I used to hunt when I was young, though never as well as Her Majesty. There's nothing to it. All you have to do is ride, which I am sure you can do very well, and keep me company."

Shakespeare glanced meaningfully at Dodd and mounted the other gelding which had a less decorated pillion seat behind the saddle. Lady Hunsdon was busy handing out staves to the two Cornishmen so the pretty round-faced girl hoisted her skirts, climbed the mounting block, put a pretty little boot on the pillion saddle's footrest and, while Shakespeare held one of her hands, one of the grooms lifted her up and sat her on the seat. behind him. The girl whispered something in Shakespeare's ear and he smiled over his shoulder at her. Dodd narrowed his eyes. All right. He could do that.

He went up to the gelding and patted his neck, let the long face and inquisitive nose have a delve in his doublet, eased the cheekpiece a little which might chafe. Then he checked the girth, gave the horse a look that warned it not to dare anything, put one hand on the withers and vaulted up to the saddle the way he always did. He shifted the animal over to the block and while he waited for her ladyship, he lengthened the stirrups to his liking.

She came up to the mounting block, puffing a little, and it took the two sturdy Cornishmen to lift her onto the pillion seat, where she settled down, sitting sideways. The gelding sighed and cocked a hoof.

"Would ye no' prefer a litter, m'lady?" asked Dodd.

There was a loud pshaw noise in his ear. "I hate the things," snapped Lady Hunsdon, "Disgusting stinking contraptions. Only thing worse is a bloody coach. Now then, off we go."

Two of Hunsdon's men ahead, one Cornishman on each side of the two horses in the middle, a packpony with empty panniers led by a boy, with a footman to follow as well—a fine raiding party for the pillaging of London's shops. They waited for the gate to be opened for them and clattered out and into the noise and dust of the Strand.

"It's my poor knees," explained Lady Hunsdon, behind him. "And my hip, alas. I much prefer ships. Of course, it's a nuisance to get aboard in the first place..." Dodd was suddenly transfixed by the idea of Lady Hunsdon shinning up a rope ladder. "...but once you're there, that's it. Off you go and you can go anywhere in the world. Wonderful." Presumably she used a gang-plank or they somehow winched her up?

"Ay but..." Dodd was struggling with a truly terrible urge to ask what that noted courtier of the Queen, Lord Baron Hunsdon, thought about his wife gallivanting about the oceans. After all, he could guess what the lady's youngest son thought of it.

"Out with it, Sergeant."

"Ahhh...does me lord no' mind if ye..."

Lady Hunsdon's laugh was a throaty gurgle. "I'm sure he would have played merry hell about it once upon a time. But it was after darling Robin went off to court and Philadelphia's match with Scrope was made and my lord was busy at Court as usual. I was sitting about with nothing whatever to do and a perfectly good steward to run the estates. Once I was tired of embroidering everything that didn't move, I went to visit my sister Sybilla at Caerhays in Cornwall. Ever been to Cornwall, Sergeant?"

They were pushing through the constant jam of people being pestered by stinking sore-ridden beggars at Temple Bar, some of whom had spotted the great lady and her party and were fighting to get through the crowds and do some serious begging.

Dodd could see the prick of his gelding's ears and feel the neck begin to arch at the smell and the noise. He patted the neck again, shook his head to answer Lady Hunsdon. He fixed one of the scabby beggars with his eye and moved the toe of his boot suggestively.

"It's quite beautiful there. But again, very little to do and so I went visiting the Killigrews at Arwenack by the Fal estuary and Kate was fitting out a privateer to be captained by my cousin Henry Morgan, and so naturally, I took a share and went along with her and we caught a pirate out of Antwerp, in the mist just by St Anthony's Point and sank her."

Dodd's mind reeled at the idea of these two stout mothers taking a whim to go privateering. It was truly terrifying.

"Poor Morgan was killed in the melee, so after my lord got me the letter of marque—half in jest, I'm afraid, poor dear—I decided to go into it properly, fitted out my own little ship the *Judith* with Captain Trevasker, and paid for the whole thing and more with our first Spanish merchant full of sugar and timber that we caught in the Channel." She laughed throatily again. "You should have seen the faces of the crew when they saw who had caught them. 'Bruja,' they called me, which is Spanish for witch, and other less flattering names."

"Ay?"

"Of course it's all a terrible gamble, but not if you have good intelligence and watchers along the coast and a good haven for the ships and to land the prizes. And Cornishmen to sail your ship, of course. Penryn is at the neck of one of the finest natural harbours in the world, according to dear Sir Francis Drake. Kate agrees with him—her windows in Arwenack House near Pendennis Fort have stunning views across to St Mawes—and she's used her spoils to buy up most of the land around the bay that the Killigrews don't already own. It's expensive, land-prices in Cornwall are ridiculously high, despite being very poor for anything but pasture or tin-mining."

There was a scuffle as the beggars tried to dodge past their escort. One of the Cornishmen caught a particularly cheeky beggar right in the forehead with his fist. The other shook his cudgel and growled something incomprehensibly Cornish and most of the beggars fell back.

Lady Hunsdon was oblivious to the excitement and didn't seem to need any prompt to carry on talking as Dodd urged the horse on through the crowds.

"Of course, the real reason I go privateering is that it's very entertaining—you never know what might happen or where you might find a fat prize. My lord says that if I were younger and a little more spry, he could see me boarding with the sailors and laying about me with a belaying pin—which is a cruel thing to say since I would naturally use a sword or a pistol."

Dodd winched his jaw shut and managed a neutral, "Ay?"

Lady Hunsdon laughed again. "Which of course I wouldn't either because my hands are too small and my wrists far too weak for a pistol or a sword. And anyway, the last thing the sailors need is another fighter, Sergeant. What they do need is a cool head and an eye for merchandise. That was how we sank the pirate. The sailors were so furious the Flemish had been sinking their fishing boats, they didn't even notice how they were manoevring us into a very dangerous position. Fortunately I did, and we were able to trap them, board them, free some prisoners, and take the ship into Penryn as a prize. We took some very fine jewels as well. I hadn't had such fun since I used to hunt with my lord husband and Her Majesty the Queen."

She leaned against him and put a hand on his belt while she rearranged her skirts with her other hand. "And since then, of course, I've done well enough at the privateering that my lord is quite happy with me. He's planning to begin rebuilding the Blackfriars with my latest spoils, very pleased he doesn't need to go to Sir Horatio Palavicino for a loan after all. Ha!"

Lady Hunsdon subsided into a sudden thoughtful silence. They were ambling up Ludgate hill and into the city, past the the huge Belle Sauvage carter's inn where the players were parading around with drums to announce a terrible and savage and improving tragedy of Dr. Faustus. As they pressed on past St.

Paul's churchyard, Lady Hunsdon called out in a voice clearly more used to a full gale,

"Letty, my bird, I need writing paper, ink, pens ready cut, sealing wax, and a new shaker. Off you go now and don't pay more than a penny a sheet for the paper."

Dodd watched carefully how Shakespeare gave Letty his hand again and braced himself to take her weight as she hopped down and headed towards one of the stationer's stalls in the Churchyard. They waited while she went and spoke earnestly to one of the better-dressed stallmen. He had a brightly-painted and lurid sign over his head of a pen dripping red blood. A pile of the popular though scandalous coneycatching pamphlets decorated his stall as well and a crowd of people were buying them. Despite being busy, he and his wife came over personally with the package to make their bows to Lady Hunsdon. One of the Cornishmen stowed it in the pack pony's basket and Shakespeare and the other man helped Letty back to her seat.

They carried on into Cheapside with the pack pony mouthing his bit and looking sulky. Cheapside was jammed with litters and men on horseback and part-blocked by a cart that was unloading. Lady Hunsdon ignored the bedlam, passed by many fine windows, and stopped at the sign of a Golden Cup beside some barred windows that blazed with assorted gold plate—nothing so common as silver to be seen.

Letty hopped down first and spoke to the scarfaced man in a worn jack standing at the door. Dodd eyed him with automatic interest since he was different from the one who had been there a week or so before. The man's jack was Scottish with its square quilting and some of the details made him think of the East March surnames. The man nodded and turned to shout inside.

Moments later the handsome willowy young man came out with a mounting block for Lady Hunsdon to use, followed by Master Van Emden in his fine brown velvet gown, bowing low to Lady Hunsdon.

Dodd looked over his shoulder at her to see that she had magically transformed into a very haughty court lady. She held out her hand imperiously to him and he took it, braced, and managed not to grunt at the effort of helping her step down to the block where she took the young man's proffered arm to step to the pavement. A page swept the flagstones before her clean of mud and some hazelnut shells from the people idly snacking as they gawped at the goldsmiths' windows. Lady Hunsdon was already in full flow, her voice quite without the Cornish rounding it had when she was relaxed.

"Master Van Emden, I have heard all about your shop from my dear son. You recall that you were kind enough to advise Sir Robert regarding the goldsmith's art a week or two ago and he was very complimentary about the beauty and fineness of your work. I desire you to make the Queen's New Year presents both for myself and for my husband, Lord Chamberlain Baron Hunsdon…"

The play of expressions on Van Emden's grey-bearded face was very funny. It started with understandable wariness at mention of Carey, then continued with delighted surprise to be finished off by a look of quite frightening greed. He settled into an ecstasy of respect as Lady Hunsdon paraded into the shop, followed by one of her Cornishmen, trailing clouds of wealth.

Shakespeare settled back in his saddle, took a small notebook from his sleeve and a small stick of graphite from his penner, and started scribbling. Dodd contented himself with looking about for half an hour, enjoying the sightseeing and idly planning his Great Raid. There were three or four of the goldsmiths' windows which looked worth the trouble of breaking the bars for their contents and they would have to remember to bring a crowbar. Master Van Emden's windows were perhaps the best, but the bars looked too solid to bother with. Dodd had decided that all the insight would need to be taken in a single morning before the City fathers could call out their trained bands to stop Dodd and his gang of men…

A little later when Dodd was starting to think seriously about beer, Lady Hunsdon emerged, followed by Letty holding a velvet bag that clanked, Master Van Emden, his young man and his page, all bowing in unison.

"By the end of the week, I has sketches for your ladyship," the Master was saying, mangling his foreign English in his excitement. "Young Piers shall to Somerset House for your inspection the plans bring."

"Splendid," said Lady Hunsdon with great satisfaction, "I will look forward to it."

The process of setting the ladies back on their pillion saddles was very hard on your back since you had to help lift with your shoulders twisted round. Dodd darkly reckoned Shakespeare had about half as much work to do with Letty as he had with Lady Hunsdon, who was no taller than her maid.

They carried on to an inn next to the Royal Exchange. Looking perky and happy as usual, Letty went in followed by a Cornishman. There was a pause and then she came out, frowning.

"He's not there, my lady," she said.

Lady Hunsdon frowned. "Is he not? Are you sure? Ask the landlord if he's gone out?"

Letty went back in and returned a moment later. "Landlord said he's gone, he's not here any more."

Lady Hunsdon held her hand out to Dodd who swung her down and then, on an impulse, jumped down from the horse himself, gave the reins to one of the henchmen to hold, and followed her into the inn's commonroom to back her up if she needed it.

She didn't really. The landlord was hunched and handwashing with anxiety but he stuck to his guns.

"A thousand pardons, your ladyship, but e's gone. I dunno where, just gone. That's all I know."

"We arranged to meet at this very inn this very day, oh...several weeks ago," rapped out Lady Hunsdon. "Of course he isn't gone."

"He's gone, your ladyship, or rather, I don't know what's happened to him and his bill not paid and he left his riding cloak and some duds here when he went."

Lady Hunsdon's eyes narrowed. "That's ridiculous. Let me see his room."

"I can't your ladyship, beggin' your pardon, but I let it again and I sold his duds to pay his bill wot he hadn't, see."

"When did you last see him?"

"More'n a week ago, ladyship, honest," said the innkeeper. "He saw his lawyer and then he went out to a dice game, he said, and that's the last I seen of him."

"Didn't you look for him?"

The landlord shrugged. "'Course I did, 'e hadn't paid his bill had he, but I couldn't find him."

Dodd's eyes were narrowed too. There was something radically wrong here.

Lady Hunsdon made a harumph noise like both her husband and her son. Behind her, Letty was snivelling into her sleeve. The landlord invited them to a drink on the house and Lady Hunsdon agreed, sharp as a needle. They were shown to a back parlour with some ugly painted cloths hanging on the walls where Lady Hunsdon drank brandywine with a large spoonful of sugar, Letty drank mild, and Dodd had a quart of some of the worst beer he had ever tasted, thin, sour, over-hopped and not very strong. Lady Hunsdon said nothing, gazing beadily at Letty who was trembling and clearly trying not to cry.

Before they left, Lady Hunsdon beckoned the landlord and spoke quietly in his ear. A gold angel passed from the lady to the landlord and his demeanour changed.

"Sergeant Dodd," she said, "would you be so good as to go upstairs with mine host and search the bedroom used by Mr. Tregian?"

"Ay m'lady," said Dodd, not sorry to be leaving his beer unfinished.

He followed the landlord who seemed nervous. The private room was better than the common run, reasonably well-furnished with a half-testered bed, a truckle for the servant, and a couple of straw palliasses for pageboys or henchmen, a chest with a lock and a table and chairs. The jordan was under the bed, not only empty but clean. So the room hadn't been let.

Dodd couldn't slit the mattresses with the landlord watching but he could and did search methodically and carefully, working from one side to the other, like a maiden doing the cleaning. All he found was an old book of martyr stories on a shelf which was a little loose. Dodd jiggled it a couple of times and then looked at the join it made with the wall. It was definitely loose at one end. He peered at it from underneath and saw something folded and wedged up behind the wood of the shelf. With the tip of his dagger he teased it out and found two blank sheets of paper. Presumably they'd been put there to stop the shelf wiggling and he was about to throw them in the fireplace when he caught a faint scent of oranges from the papers. It was an expensive way of fixing a shelf after all.

He folded them carefully and put them in his belt pouch, then went on down the stairs. The ladies were ready to go so Dodd went ahead. Out of habit, he checked under his saddle and his girth, mounted then bent to hand Lady Hunsdon up behind him.

"London Bridge," she ordered.

They carried on, shoving through the crowds, all of whom seemed to be heading for the Bridge, which was hard on the temper.

"Powerful lot of folk here," said Dodd as he pushed on through an argument between three men and a donkey stopped in the middle of the path and all four braying furiously.

"Have you never been on London Bridge, Sergeant?" asked Lady Hunsdon with a naughty sparkle. "Or did you cross several times and simply not notice that the best drapers, haberdashers, and headtiring shops in the world are there?"

"Ay," Dodd admitted, "that'd be it."

They were coming to the gate towers with their fringe of traitors' heads, where you could hear the rush and creak of the newly installed waterwheels, the crowd nearly solid as they passed through the narrow entrance. The gate gave onto the street over the Bridge which was enclosed by the shops and houses built right on it and dim enough to need lanterns at the shop doors. Suddenly there was a gasp behind them as if somebody had been stabbed. Dodd jerked round to see Letty staring up at the row of spikes along the top of the gatehouse. A crow was flapping heavily away from the newest of the heads there, arrived from Tyburn the day before. Letty seemed struck to stone by the sight of the bearded and now eyeless face. Her hands flew to her mouth, she breathed deep, and then she screamed like a pig at the slaughter.

Dodd's gelding took severe offence and, despite the weight of two people on his back, tried to pirouette, then backed frantically into a group of stout women with baskets who all shouted angrily. Letty was still screaming which had thoroughly spooked the mare she was sitting on. Shakespeare was frantically sawing at the reins as the animal lunged sideways, snorting and kicking and starting to crow-hop to get rid of her burden. A gap opened in the frightened crowd and she looked ready to take off for the far hills.

Dodd felt Lady Hunsdon's arms clasp tight around his waist and her hands lock together.

"Help them, Sergeant," came the firm cool voice behind him.

Dodd brought his whip down brutally on his gelding's side, which got the beast's attention. Then Dodd turned him around and drove him after Shakespeare's and Letty's mount, knocking pedestrians and one Cornishman aside. He came alongside the bucking, frantic nag, grabbed the bridle, and leaned over to put his sleeve across the silly creature's eyes. Being a horse, she immediately stood still because she couldn't see and Dodd muttered in her ear, telling her gently how he would have her guts for haggis casing and feed her rump to the nearest pack of hunting dogs he could find. It didn't matter what you said to the animal, so long as your voice was right. At least Letty's screaming had stopped, though a glance over his shoulder showed this was because Shakespeare had a hand firmly on her mouth.

Shakespeare's face was white and there were hot tears boiling down Letty's cheeks, little cries still coming from behind Shakespeare's palm.

"God's truth, mistress, did ye wantae die…?" he snarled.

"Shhh," said Lady Hunsdon behind him in a voice that was an odd mixture of fury and sadness. "She's seen something that upset her. We'll go back to Somerset House now."

"Ay m'lady," said Dodd, and turned both the horses. "Will ye bide quiet now, lass?" he asked Letty who was trembling as much as her mare. She nodded so Shakespeare took his hand away, after which she dropped her face into her hands and started to cry.

Dodd was sweating from all the drama, which was made much worse by the stares and sniggers of the Londoners standing back unhelpfully to watch the show. The Cornishmen were helping Hunsdon's henchmen to pick up and dust down a couple of annoyed lawsuit-threatening Londoners who hadn't moved away fast enough.

Dodd jerked his head at Shakespeare and they closed up the distance between the horses. A Cornishman cudgelled an urchin who had his hand in the heaviest pannier on the packpony as Dodd swatted away a small bunch of child-beggars with their hands up and their sores exposed. Their party formed a tighter group and headed back for the other side of the City as fast as they could.

"M'lady, what the…"

"She's just seen her father's head on a spike at London Bridge," said Lady Hunsdon drily into his ear. "I think that's a reason to be upset, don't you?"

Dodd craned his neck to see. The only recognisable head was the priest's, that he and Carey had seen hacked off the day before. His mouth went dry.

"But m'lady…?"

"Be quiet."

"But…but Ah thought Papist priests couldnae wed…?"

"Precisely. We'll discuss this in private."

A war council of the Hunsdon family convened at dinnertime, with Sir Robert, Lord and Lady Hunsdon, and Sergeant Dodd staring at each other over some marvellous venison and more of the mutton pasties. When the second cover was served and

Dodd could wonder at the jellies and custards that were laid out for no more than a normal meal, the servingmen were sent out of the room. Letty had been put to bed with a strong posset and a girl to watch her, while Dr. Nunez and his barber surgeon had been sent for to bleed her against the shock.

"You are quite certain it is Richard Tregian, my lady?" rumbled Lord Hunsdon, staring at his clasped hands.

"I am, my lord," said his lady soberly. "He had a scar by his mouth from a hunting accident a few years ago and his beard was still red. I knew him at once even on a …at that distance."

"No priest then," said Hunsdon.

Lady Hunsdon snorted. "Hardly. He was a Papist though."

"He was the man you were in London to meet?"

"Yes, my lord. I wanted to find out more before I broke the matter with you, but events are now ahead of me. I discovered from my sister's husband that there have been some very dubious land-deals happening in Cornwall and Richard Tregian was up to his neck in them. He was in desperate need of money to pay his recusancy fines, to be sure, but there was more to it than that. There was Court money involved. The land around the Fal has tripled in price in the last three years, but additonally there have been some very surprising purchases further north in the tin-mining areas near Redruth. I would have gone to Sir Walter Raleigh as President of the Stannary when I had consulted you, my lord, but Sir Walter is in the Tower for venery, I find. I wanted to warn Richard away from whatever deals he was doing and I brought Letty up to town with me in the *Judith* to talk some sense into him."

"Was there any question of treason involved, my lady?"

Lady Hunsdon bowed her head. "Letty says not, but I simply don't know."

Lord Hunsdon sighed heavily. "Sir Robert?" he said formally to his son.

Carey looked at Dodd briefly, then at his mother, before he answered his father quietly. "We watched Richard Tregian die yesterday under the name of Fr. Jackson. He was gagged and had been tortured. The hangman gave him a good drop so he was quite dead by the time they came to draw and quarter him."

Lady Hunsdon nodded. "Thank God for that at least."

"How do you know he was tortured?" asked Lord Hunsdon.

"His wrists were swollen and showed the print of bindings with swelling above and below. I would say the rack or the manacles." Carey's voice was remote.

There was a long moment of silence. "What statute was he sentenced under?" asked Lord Hunsdon.

"Henry VIII's Praemunire."

"Nothing more?"

"Now that I think about it, the announcement was very short."

"He made no sign?"

"He was in no state to do it before he was hanged and moreover he was gagged." More silence. "I wonder whose authority was on the warrant?" Sir Robert added softly.

"It will have been genuine and the authority unexceptionable or Her Majesty would not have signed it."

"Heneage?"

Hunsdon shook his head. "Not necessarily. Sir Robert Cecil or Lord Burghley himself could have been involved, or even my lord the Earl of Essex. Someone of lesser rank could also have originated the warrant, such as the Recorder of London or the Constable of the Tower. Of course, I could do so if I needed to."

"Was yer man not tried?"

After a pause Lord Hunsdon said reluctantly, "Obviously not, Sergeant."

"So what was Richard Tregian actually doing?" asked Sir Robert, leaning his elbows on the table. Nobody had touched any of the elaborate sweet dishes, but Dodd, who had a less delicate stomach, reached for a pippin and started munching it. He liked apples and you didn't get many of them on the Borders because raiders kept cutting or burning orchards down. "Buying land from cash-strapped fellow-Papists and then selling them on to a courtier or two? Or informing on Papists and getting a cut from the lands when they were confiscated?"

Lady Hunsdon shook her head. "I don't see Richard inform-ing—and even if he did, he wouldn't last very long in Cornwall. They don't like blabbermouths there. I would say it was the first. He may even have been an agent, using his principal's money and then taking a cut."

"Well there's nothing treasonous about that," boomed Lord Hunsdon. "Perfectly legitimate thing to do, I use agents myself. Keeps the prices down a bit."

"My lord, I dinna understand," Dodd put in. Lord Hunsdon looked enquiringly at him. "Only, this land was to be sold? To somebody wi' plenty o' money at court?"

"Probably. That's where the money tends to be."

"Ay, so why would they buy it? Cornwall's a powerful long way and…"

"It might be the tin. It's quite a fashion at Court now to start mining works and similar on your land if there's anything there to be mined."

"Is tin worth so much?"

"Not really," put in Lady Hunsdon, "There's more of it in Spain and easier to get at."

Something Dodd had heard in a long drinking session with a miner from Keswick tickled his memory. "There's tin, so is there gold as well?" The Hunsdons were watching him thoughtfully. "Only that would make sense of poor land being worth buying on the quiet until ye could take the gold out."

"If there is it would belong to the Crown anyway," said Hunsdon. "You'd need a license."

"All the more reason for keeping it quiet until ye could take out the gold for yersen."

"Hmm."

"Well the obvious candidate for his principal is Heneage," pointed out Sir Robert, "and that would explain his ending up on a scaffold if Heneage didn't want to pay him."

"I doubt it," said Hunsdon. "Heneage could simply have delayed payment until Richard Tregian got tired of asking or went to jail. There would be no need to kill the man."

"And why did he do it like that," Dodd asked, which was the main question on his mind. "Why be so complicated? Even in London it canna be hard for a man wi' Heneage's power to slit his throat and drop him in the Thames and nae questions asked?"

Nobody said anything.

The steward knocked on the door, came in, and whispered in Lord Hunsdon's ear.

"Oh. Ah. Yes, of course. We will see him in the large parlour. I believe your lawyer has arrived, Sergeant."

"Ay."

"In the meantime," Hunsdon summed up with weary distaste, "we shall keep this matter as quiet as possible until we can discover what really happened. The final decision on any action to be taken will, of course, be mine although I may be forced to take the matter to my sister." There was a warning tone in his voice and yes, he was glaring directly at his wife.

"Of course my lord," she said, "Naturally."

Carey closed his eyes briefly and seemed to be praying while Dodd fought down the urge to snicker. After all, it was hardly a laughing matter. Still the blandly respectful look on Lady Hunsdon's face as she lowered her eyes to her meekly clasped hands was very, very funny to Dodd. Lord Baron Hunsdon seemed quite satisfied and nodded approvingly. "I knew you would understand, my love."

Carey caught Dodd's eye and one eyebrow flicked infinitesimally upwards. However Dodd was ready for it and his mouth drew down and his face settled in its normal scowl.

tuesday 12th september 1592, afternoon

With Hunsdon leading his wife out, they processed to the large parlour where Lord and Lady Hunsdon were seated on two well-carved arm chairs that teetered on the edge of being presumptuous thrones. Hunsdon's bore the lions of England carved into the wood while his lady's was padded with tawny velvet. They had stopped short of a cloth of estate, though.

Following Carey's lead, Dodd sat down on a bench at the side of the room and watched as James Enys came in, wearing a good if out-of-fashion green wool suit and his Utter Barrister's monkish black cloth robe hanging from his shoulders. He took off his velvet cap and bowed low to both the Hunsdons. He was already sweating with nerves. Lady Hunsdon made a noise that sounded a little like "Tchah!" and stared down her nose at the lawyer.

"Mr. Vaughan, good of you to come," said Hunsdon, was politely elbowed by his wife, and coughed. "Enys, yes, of course."

Enys bowed again.

"I understand you are willing to take the brief on behalf of Sergeant Henry Dodd of Gilsland here against his honour Mr. Vice Chamberlain Sir Thomas Heneage?"

"Ah…yes m'lord." Enys's voice was quite light but firm and pleasant to listen to. It carried easily. Dodd noticed he was holding the lapels of his gown with his thumbs under the material in a way which made him look combative but was probably designed to stop his hands shaking.

"Despite Mr. Vice Chamberlain having frightened off all of your legal brethren?"

A faint smile crossed Enys's ugly face. "Ah…yes m'lord."

"Why?" asked Hunsdon bluntly. "Have you no wish for preferment?"

"There is no chance whatsoever that Mr. Vice will ever offer it to me. Whereas you, my lord Chamberlain, have a reputation for dealing justly and I have no doubt but that you will be my good lord, whatever the result of the litigation."

It was prettily put and Lord Hunsdon beamed and expanded slightly. Lady Hunsdon leaned forward.

"We can't help you if you end in Chelsea with that devil Topcliffe questioning you."

Enys shrugged. "I am a good loyal subject of Her Gracious Majesty, I attend Divine service every Sunday, and my brother fought and was wounded in the Netherlands."

"If you go against Mr. Heneage as things are at the moment you may find that these things do not protect you," put in Carey.

Enys shrugged again. "I may die of plague tomorrow if God wills it."

"Hm." Hunsdon leaned an elbow on the arm of his chair and tapped his teeth. Lady Hunsdon had fixed Enys with a gimlet blue stare which would certainly have had Dodd sweating. However, the young man seemed to have calmed somewhat. He took a breath to speak.

"My lord, my lady, may I be quite frank with you?"

Hunsdon nodded while his lady only narrowed her eyes.

"Obviously, you will be wondering if I am in fact Heneage's man."

Hunsdon smiled; his lady remained grim.

"Also, obviously, there is very little I can do to convince you that this is not the case since any test of my truthfulness you could think of, Mr. Heneage could circumvent. Here is my tale. Immediately after I was called to the Bar and whilst I was still in pupillage a year ago, I was approached by a man of business, a solicitor of some fame, and asked if I would take some cases in King's Bench dealing with forfeitures of Papist land and other property dealings. Knowing no more than that Mr. Vice Chamberlain was the principal and that he was high in the counsels of our most worshipful Sovereign Lady, I naturally agreed. I took the cases, drafted the pleadings, and appeared in the initial hearings."

He sighed. "At this point I found that all was not as it seemed and that I could not appear for Mr. Heneage without lying to the court and going utterly against mine honour."

The Hunsdons exchanged glances and then both scowled at Enys. It was quite admirable that he stayed steady and continued with his rhetorical story.

"I withdrew, charging no fee, and Mr. Heneage offered me a higher fee to remain, then a cut of the proceeds plus many further tempting blandishments. I still refused and he said he would destroy me since he would not be denied by anyone, especially not a stripling lawyer. He has gone some way to achieving his threat as I have had practically no cases in the past six months and will soon lose my chamber as well. I have no profession but the law and have no family other than my brother …um and sister…to help me, nor any good lord."

"So?" asked Lady Hunsdon.

"So, my lady," answered Enys, "When I heard two gentlemen discussing their problems regarding Mr. Vice and realised from his speech that one of them must be your son, I thanked Providence that I had stopped by the pool instead of going to sell my cloak, and made haste to offer them my services."

Hanging in the air was the wonder of such a stroke of luck. Lady Hunsdon summed it all up by sniffing eloquently.

Hunsdon smiled on the young man. "Mr. Enys, it could be dangerous to act for Sergeant Dodd. Mr. Heneage has a tendency to attack the smaller fry in a dispute. You could easily wind up in the Tower confessing to Papistry."

Enys smiled back bitterly. "The man is a scandal and a tyrant, m'lord. Yes, I could. But I may do so in any case since he is mine enemy in which case…"

"In which case, Mr. Enys?"

"In which case I might as well take the fight to the enemy first."

Dodd nodded at this piece of good sense. Hunsdon laced his fingers together.

"Mr. Enys, I shall naturally make enquiries about you. What were the cases?"

"Matters relating to the estates of Mr. Robert Boscoba, Mr. John Veryan, and Sir Piran Mawes of Trenever."

"Cornish lands? You're Cornish, aren't you?"

"Yes, your ladyship. My father was from Penryn and came up to London after Glasney College was put down. My sister…" Enys paused. "…My sister was wed to a Cornishman until the smallpox widowed her."

Lady Hunsdon nodded intently. "Do you know a Mr. Richard Tregian who would have come up to London about two or three weeks ago?"

"No, my lady," said Enys, his eyes narrowing, "I have never met him."

"Assuming my enquiries are satisfactory," said Hunsdon, "I shall retain you for the amount of a guinea per week plus refreshers for court appearances."

The lawyer bowed low. "My lord is very generous,"

Lady Hunsdon leaned forward confidingly. "Mr. Enys," she said coaxingly, "what were the cases you withdrew from about?"

Enys's eyelids fluttered. "I cannot tell you more, m'lady, I'm very sorry. Client confidentiality."

"You withdrew from the cases," Hunsdon pointed out.

"I did, m'lord, because they would have gone against my honour." There was a pause whilst Enys nerved himself. "It would also go against my honour to babble about them like a woman at the conduit to anyone who asked." Hunsdon nodded.

"How soon can you draft and lodge the pleadings on Sergeant Dodd's behalf."

"Once I am fee'd and briefed, m'lord, by tomorrow."

"Any ideas on the conduct?"

"Yes, m'lord." The young man took a deep breath and clasped the lapels of his gown tightly. "I would recommend a writ of *pillatus* against Mr. Heneage for the criminal assault and wrongful imprisonment, to be served immediately."

Both Hunsdon and his lady stared at the young man for a second, transfixed, before Hunsdon bellowed with laughter and his lady gurgled. Carey too had a wicked grin on his face. "What's that?" hissed Dodd to him, knowing he was missing something important here.

"He's saying we should get a warrant to arrest Heneage immediately on the criminal charges," whispered Carey, still grinning.

"He'll surely wriggle out..."

"Of course he will, but he'll spend at least a night in prison if we time it right."

Dodd's lips parted in delight. "Och," he said, "I like this lawyer."

"While he's in prison," added Enys, "we should serve writs of subpoena on all potential witnesses and put any that are… frightened…into protective custody."

Hunsdon let out another bark. Dodd understood this. "Mr. Enys," he called across the tiled floor, "one o'them's the Gaoler o'the Fleet."

Enys's pock-marked brow wrinkled. "Then I think he needs to be named on the originating warrant as a confederate and also arrested, or he'll never testify."

Barnabus Cooke's funeral was later that afternoon and a respectable affair, attended naturally by Carey, Dodd, and the young Simon Barnet, though not Barnabus' sister's family which was still locked up in their house with plague. No more of them had died apart from the mother. Hunsdon had paid for Barnabus's coffin and the burial fees and also four pauper mourners, one of whom seemed to be genuinely upset. The Church of St Bride's was convenient and the vicar glad of the shroud money, but had the sense to keep his eulogy of Barnabus short and tactful. Carey had pointedly invited Shakespeare to come as well, but had received an elegantly phrased letter of regret. Apart from a remarkable number of upright men who turned up hoping to be paid mourners too, there were several women in veils and striped petticoats and a round-faced man in a fine wool suit with a snowy falling band whom Dodd felt he had seen somewhere before. Carey seemed to know him and once the small coffin had been lowered into the plot in the crowded graveyard, strode over to greet him.

"Mr. Hughes," he said, "how kind of you to attend."

The man took his hat off and bowed. "Thank you, sir," he said easily, "I try to attend them as gets away."

Carey smiled. "Still smarting?"

Hughes smiled back. "No sir, though I'll allow as I had a rope measured and properly stretched for him. I'm also here to bring the compliments of my brother-in-law and his thanks to your worshipful father for his support of Barnabus Cooke's family."

Carey seemed surprised by this for he paused, and then bowed shallowly. "My father is proud of his good lordship and feels it is the least he could do."

"Nonetheless, sir, there's not many would bother nowadays. My brother-in-law would like you to know that he is obliged to your honours and at your father's service."

With a dignified tip of his hat, Mr. Hughes moved quietly away and through the gate. Carey blinked after him. "Well well," he said, "that's interesting."

Dodd was irritated that again he didn't know what was going on here. "Ay?" he complained.

Carey smiled and led the way to a boozing ken on Fleet Street, filled with a raucous flock of hard-drinking black-robed lawyers and their pamphlet-writing hangers on.

"That, Sergeant," he said as he drank brandywine with satisfaction, "is the London hangman. You saw him performing his office yesterday."

"Jesu," said Dodd, feeling slightly queasy.

"He is also, and this is where it gets interesting, the brother-in-law of the King of London, Mr. Laurence Pickering himself. Who has just as good as offered an alliance to my father for some reason."

"The King of London?"

"Mr. Laurence Pickering, King of the London thieves, chief controller of the London footpads and upright men, main profiter by the labours of the London whores, coming second only to his Grace the Bishop of Winchester who collects their rents."

"Ay," said Dodd with respect. "Is there only the one King of London, then?"

"Oh yes," said Carey drily, "Only the one. Now."

wednesday 13th september 1592, morning.

At dawn the next day, itching in tight wool and with a new highcrowned beaver hat on his head, Dodd went with Carey to take a boat at Temple steps with Enys for Westminster Hall. Enys was carrying a sheaf of papers in a blue brocade bag and looked tired with bags under his eyes. He pulled his black robe around him and held his hat tight to his head. It was hard to tell the expression on his face, so thick were the scars from the smallpox, but he looked tense.

"Sir Robert, is your father providing bailiffs to back up the court staff?" he asked Carey.

Carey was busy smiling and taking his hat off to a boatload of attractive women heading downstream for London Bridge.

"Hm? Oh yes, the steward's arranging for it and they'll meet us at Westminster once you have the warrant."

"Ay, but we'll niver arrest him, will we?" Dodd said, thinking of Richie Graham of Brackenhill's likely reaction to any such attempt, never mind Jock o'the Peartree's. Jock would still be roaring with laughter at the joke as he slit your throat.

The Hunsdon boat was butting up against the boat landing. Carey and Dodd hopped in, while Enys seemed very nervous of the water and nearly fell as he stepped across. He sat himself down and gripped the seat hard with his hands, swallowing.

"I rather think we will, Sergeant," said Enys, "although I'm sure not for long. And as there is no doubt at all that as soon as he's bailed he'll be trying to intimidate the witnesses, I have drafted a writ against him for maintenance to keep in reserve."

Carey blinked as if puzzled for a moment and then shouted with laughter. "That old Statute against henchmen?"

"Old and from Her Majesty's grandfather's time, but still on the books. It's not the oldest statute I shall be citing."

"What is?" asked Dodd fascinated, although he had no idea that henchmen were illegal.

"Edward III 1368," said Enys. Dodd used his fingers to work it out.

"It's two hundred and twenty-four years old," he said. "What good is that?"

"It's a highly important principle," said Enys, looking annoyed. "You might say it is the foundation of our English liberty. It says that no man may be put to the question or tortured privily without trial or warrant. In effect, habeas corpus."

Once again Dodd struggled with foreign language. He supposed they meant something about dead bodies.

"I don't recall Mr. Secretary Walsingham paying that much attention to the statute when he was questioning some Papist," Carey pointed out.

Enys looked at him distantly. "Sir Robert, it is a fact that a man who murders another for his money may pay no attention to the statutes against murder. It is in the nature of sinful men that they break the law. It is a very different thing to hold that there is no such law to be broken, which Heneage does by his actions."

"And if the law be changed in parliament?" asked Carey.

"If it be changed, then we must abide by the new law," said Enys. "But this law has not been changed nor repealed. It was excluded from matters of treason and the Henry VIII statute of Praemunire made many religious matters into treason. Therefore Mr. Secretary Walsingham could and did rightly ignore the statute since he was seeking out Papist traitors against Her Majesty and the Commonweal of England."

Carey nodded while Dodd stared in fascination to hear such a young man speak in such long and complicated sentences, using such pompous words. Now the lawyer lifted one finger in a lecturing manner. "However, this is not a matter of treason at all. Sergeant Dodd was neither guilty of nor accused of any crime whatsoever when Mr. Vice falsely imprisoned and assaulted him. There was a fortiori no trial and no warrant. I have seldom heard of such a clear case."

"Ay," said Dodd, catching up with most of the last part of the speech, "that's right." His head was buzzing with the legal talk.

"Perhaps Mr. Vice will simply claim that he was looking for me and laid hold of my henchman to track me down," said Carey.

"I'm sure he will," said Enys. "However the fact remains that you were not accused of treason either, Sir Robert. Even your brother was accused only of coining, which may indeed come under the treason laws as petty treason…"

Dodd stretched his eyes at that. Was coining treason? Did Richie Graham with his busy unofficial mint know about it? Did he care?

"...but it is not a direct attack upon her Majesty nor upon the Commonweal of England. And in point of fact, if what you have told me is correct, I believe that Mr. Heneage may be vulnerable to a charge of coining and uttering false coin himself, with your brother and the apothecary Mr. Cheke as witnesses against him."

Carey whistled through his teeth. "I thought we couldn't prove that?"

Enys shrugged. "Heneage will bring oath-swearers to disagree but it will depend on the judge. It's arguable. At this stage it doesn't have to be provable."

They came to Westminster steps and jumped out—Enys seemed clumsy again and hesitant as he stepped onto the boat landing at just the wrong time. He might have wound up in the Thames without a quick shove from Dodd.

"Thank you, sir," he muttered, looking embarassed. "I am still weakened by my sickness."

"Ay, but your face is healed?" said Dodd, immediately worried because he had never had smallpox in his life.

"Oh it is, I am no longer sick of it. But the pocks attacked my eyes as well and my sight and balance are not what they were," said the man, rubbing his hand on his face and jaw. Dodd could see the pits on the backs of his hands going up his wrist. Jesu, that was an ugly disease as well, worse than plague in some ways. Of course you were far more likely to die of the plague, but that was relatively quick and if your buboes burst you'd probably get better with no more than a couple of scars on your neck and groin and never be afraid of getting it again. You weren't going to be hideous for the rest of your life. As for pocks on your eyes... Jesus God. At least there wasn't much smallpox on the Borders, though Dodd had had a terrible fright when he was nine when his hands had got blistered from a cow with a blistered udder.

Both his parents were alive then; it hadn't been anything, and the blisters on both him and the cow got better soon enough.

They walked up through the muddy crowded alleys to the great old Hall of Westminster, hard by the Cathedral. The place was teeming with a flock in black robes, some wearing silk with soft flat square hats on their heads and followed by large numbers of young men carrying bags and papers.

"Lord above," murmured Carey, "It gets worse every year. Michaelmas term hasn't even started yet and look at them."

Enys took a deep breath at the doorway into Westminster Hall, gripped his sword hilt lefthanded, and forged ahead into the crowd of lawyers around a desk who were shouting at the listing officers.

He came threading out again, his hat sideways. Just in time he grabbed it and clamped it back on his head.

"Sirs, we shall go before Mr. Justice Whitehead in an hour to swear out the pleadings and have the warrant granted."

Dodd nodded as if this were all quite normal but he thought that it surely couldn't be so simple. Normally it took months for a bill to be heard in Carlisle and years if it was a Border matter. Hunsdon had handed Carey a purseful of silver that morning to be sure the matter was well up the list which he had passed to Enys. Perhaps that had worked.

They ventured into Westminster Hall which was split into a dozen smaller sections by wooden partitions while the old fashioned ceiling full of angels and stone icicles echoed with the noise. You couldn't see the floor at all because it was covered in straw and dung from the streets. Dodd rubbed with his boot and saw some pretty tiles under the muck.

It was indescribably noisy. Not all the partitions had judges sitting behind a wooden bench, but in the ones that did, red-faced men in black gowns were shouting at each other and waving papers. Bailiffs and court servants shouted at each other for the next cases to come to whichever court. There was a hurrying to and fro and an arguing and shouting between lawyers, between litigants, between lawyers and litigants. At every pillar it seemed, there was a huddle of mainly black-robed men engaged in some kind of argument at the top of their voices. It was exactly like a rookery.

Dodd was already starting to get a headache. Although lacking the clang of metal and the snort of horses, the row was as loud as a battlefield, or even louder.

Enys seemed to have spotted his judge and was beckoning them over to stand next to him by the partition.

"I wanted to see what kind of mood his honour is in."

Dodd peered around the high wooden boards. The judge, sitting with his coif on his head and a pen in his fist, pince nez perched on his nose, was scowling at a shivering young lawyer in a rather new stuff gown.

This judge seemed a little different from the others: an astonishingly luxuriant but carefully barbered grey beard decorated his face and his grey eyes glittered with wintry distaste.

"Mr. Burnett," he was saying witheringly, "have you in fact read your brief?"

The young lawyer facing him trembled like a leaf and gulped. Judge Whitehead threw his pen down.

"This matter, Mr. Burnett, clearly comes under the purview of the Court of Requests, not King's Bench. Why you have seen fit to plead it in front of me is a mystery. Well?"

The young lawyer seemed to be choking on his words while behind him his clients looked at each other anxiously.

"God's truth," said the judge wearily, "Get out of my court and go and redraft your pleadings, paying due attention to the cases of Bray v. Kirk and the matter of the Abbot of Litchfield v. Habakkuk. Adjourned."

The young lawyer scurried off, trembling. An older lawyer warily approached the bench, trailing his own clients. "Yes, Mr. Irvine, what is it now?" said the judge in a voice as devoid of welcome as a winter maypole.

Dodd glanced at Enys to see how this was affecting him. To his surprise he saw Enys was smiling quietly and his brown eyes sparkling.

"Disnae sound verra happy the day," said Dodd, tilting his head at the judge who could be heard berating the unfortunate Mr. Irvine from the other side of the partition, his weary voice cutting through the hubbub like a knife.

"Shh," warned Enys, with his pocked finger on his pitted lips, "Mr. Justice Whitehead has very good hearing."

"Ay."

"Mind you, he may not be able to understand you for all that."

Dodd sniffed, offended. It was southerners who spoke funny, not him. Meanwhile Enys was listening to the judge's comments with his head tilted as if listening to music. At one piece which seemed to be entirely in foreign, he chuckled quietly.

"Whit language are they speakin'?" Dodd wanted to know.

"Norman French," said Enys. "Generally most cases are heard partly in English nowadays, but a great deal of the precedent is in Latin or French."

"Jesu. And what's sae funny?"

"His honour just made a rather learned pun."

"Ay?"

Enys chuckled again in the aggravating way of someone enjoying a private joke. Carey had found a pillar he could lean languidly against and had crossed his arms while he surveyed the passing throngs through half-shut eyes.

"D'ye think he'll be on my side?"

"Sergeant, his honour will find what is correct in law, you can be sure of that."

"Ay, but will he be on ma side?"

"My father was wondering if a gift…?" said Carey delicately.

Enys shook his head. "Asolutely not, sir…It would guarantee the opposite decision."

Carey looked surprised and worried. "Yes, but if we can't buy him…"

"If we *could* buy him, then so could Mr. Vice—it would become not a court case but an auction," said Enys. "I had rather deal with someone that gives justice without fear or favour."

Carey's eyebrows went up further. "I hadn't thought that any judges did that."

"Remarkably, sir, there are a few. In fact, I am in some hopes that Mr. Vice might make the mistake that we will not."

Dodd was listening to the learned judge asking Mr. Irvine if he had ever heard of the relevant law and precedents to this case, and if he had, why had he quoted the wrong ones? Enys had an appreciative grin on his face.

"He sounds a terror," said Dodd.

The bailiff gave mournful tongue with their names five minutes later as Irvine and his clients fled with their case adjourned until the lawyer could learn to read.

With a spring in his step and an expression on his face that looked remarkably like Carey's before he launched into some insane battle or gamble, Enys led the way into the little booth and bowed to the judge. Watching Carey out of the corner of his eye and seeing him uncover and bow, Dodd scrambled to do likewise, dropped his new beaver hat on the disgusting floor, and had to grovel to pick it up again before somebody stood on it.

"Mr. Enys," growled the judge, "I had heard you had thought better of the law and gone back to Cornwall?"

"No, my lord," said Enys surprised. "Who told you that?"

"Evidently a fool," snorted the judge. "Well?"

Enys handed over the sheaf of pleadings and the warrant written in a fine clear secretary hand. The judge paused as he saw who was named as the Respondent and shot a piercing grey stare over his spectacles at Enys who stared straight back, not a muscle moving in his face. Not that you could have told if it had, thanks to the scarring, thought Dodd. That lawyer would be a nightmare opponent at primero.

The judge turned to the warrant. Very briefly, something like the ghost of a smile hovered near his mouth.

"You have started proceedings in the Old Bailey?"

"Yes, your honour. Not wishing to waste any time, I briefed a solicitor to file the necessary criminal indictment about an hour ago. We are here because although the crimes were committed in the City, Mr. Vice Chamberlain Heneage is in fact resident at Chelsea which is for our purposes in the borough of Westminster."

Another small smile. The judge turned to Dodd. "Mr. Dodd…"

Dodd coughed hard with nervousness, but he was not going to go down in the record as anything other than what he was and what he was came to more than a mere mister.

"*Sergeant* Dodd, my lord," said Dodd. "Beggin' your pardon."

"You're not a lawyer, surely?" said the judge, his brow wrinkling.

Crushing his immediate impulse to challenge the man to a duel over the insult, Dodd coughed again.

"Nay sir, Ah'm Land-Sergeant o'Gilsland, in Cumberland. On the Borders, sir."

The judge's lips moved as he worked this out. "Really? My apologies. How do you come to be in London, then, Sergeant?"

"Ah come with Sir Robert Carey, my lord."

The judge transferred his attention to Carey who stepped forward and swept him another Courtier's bow.

"*Carey?* Is my lord Baron Hunsdon involved in this matter, Sir Robert?"

"Yes, your honour," explained Carey with a face so open and innocent, Dodd felt the judge was bound to get suspicious. "My most worshipful father is outraged that Mr. Vice Chamberlain Heneage should have falsely imprisoned and assaulted Sergeant Dodd who serves under me in the Carlisle Castle Guard where I am Deputy Warden under my Lord Warden of the West March. My father is very kindly helping Sergeant Dodd seek redress for his injuries and the insult."

Even Carey shifted slightly under the impact of the judge's skewering glare and silence. "Is this a matter of Court faction, Sir Robert?" he asked at last.

"No your honour, of course not. It is a matter of seeking justice for an abhorrent and illegal assault and…"

"Yes, yes, Sir Robert, thank you," sniffed Judge Whitehead. "Mr. Enys, I suppose you had better open these pleadings."

This Enys did with verve and in detail, not seeming to need to shout to be heard quite clearly in the court, quoting various laws in parliament against which Heneage had offended and various legal precedents establishing the same. More than half of what he said was in Norman French but Carey, who spoke French, whispered a translation for Dodd. Enys came to the end and Dodd was surprised to find he had understood most of what had been said that wasn't actually in foreign.

"Sergeant Dodd," said Judge Whitehead, "are those the facts as Mr. Enys has related them? You were arrested in error instead of Sir Robert on a warrant of debt and not believed as to your true identity. You were shortly after removed from the Fleet by Mr. Heneage who was fully aware that you were not in fact Sir Robert Carey since he complained of it. You were then falsely imprisoned by him in his coach and interrogated by him therein, during which time he himself as well as his servants and agents laid violent hands upon you?"

"Ay, my lord." Dodd felt himself flushing with anger, enraged again at being beaten like a boy or a peasant of no account and not able to fight back.

"Mr. Heneage produced no warrant and did not accuse you of any crime?"

"No, my lord."

"What religion are you, Sergeant?"

Dodd blinked a little at this although Carey had prepared him for it. "My lord …eh…I am a good English Protestant and attend church whenever my duties at Carlisle permit it." Dodd had practised saying this. It wasn't strictly true—like most English Borderers, Dodd worshipped where and how he was told to and concentrated on avoiding the attention of a God who was so terrifyingly unpredictable. It was only powerful Scottish lords like the Maxwell who could afford to go in for actual religions such as being a Catholic.

"No dealings with Papist priests?"

"No, my lord," Dodd said, then ventured, "I might have arrested one once, a couple of years back. For horse-theft." He had never been quite sure whether the man had been a priest or a spy or indeed, both. Lowther had been doing a favour for Sir John Forster.

Carey coughed, Enys blinked, and the judge looked down at the papers for a moment.

"I see, thank you, Sergeant." The judge was rereading the papers in front of him. He snorted.

More silence. Dodd stole a glance at Enys to see if he was going to say anything, but he wasn't. He was watching the judge carefully.

"On the face of the case and on the facts here presented to me, Mr. Enys, we have here a quite shocking incident. Ergo…" The words degenerated to foreign again.

Enys's face split in a delighted grin.

"You may take two of the Court bailiffs when you go to execute the warrant, Mr. Enys."

Enys bowed low. "Your lordship is most kind, thank you."

The judge scribbled a note on the warrant and passed the pleadings to his clerk who was looking alarmed. "I shall look forward to seeing you again, Mr. Enys," said the judge in a chilly tone of voice. "You have been admirably succinct."

A flush went up Enys's neck as he bowed again, muttered more thanks and then led the way out of the court. As he threaded at speed through the shouting crowds, Carey called,

"And now?"

"Time to arrest him."

wednesday 13th september 1592, late morning

The Court bailiffs were two stolid looking men who took the warrant and went down to the Westminster steps where two of Hunsdon's boats were waiting. The second was low in the water with the weight of some large and ugly Borderers. Among them Dodd recognised jacks from the Chisholms and the Fenwicks which reminded him that Hunsdon was also the East March Warden. The Berwick tones were now pleasantly familiar to him, mingled with the rounded sounds of the incomprehensible Cornish who made up the other half of the party in the first boat.

Dodd, Carey, Enys, and the bailiffs got in the first boat and they headed upriver, past leafier banks, straining against the flow, to the oak spinneys of Chelsea where Heneage maintained his secluded house on the river frontage.

Dodd's heart started beating harder as they came near. He looked about him to spy out the approaches to what he couldn't help thinking of as Heneage's Tower. There was a boatlanding and a clear path heading up through market gardens and orchards. Not bad cover, no walls to speak of, no sign of watchers on the approaches. He jumped onto the boatlanding with the rest of the men, loosening his sword, then felt Carey touch his elbow and draw him aside.

Some of the men went round the back of the house while the bailiffs strode up to the main door, surrounded by the largest of Hunsdon's men.

"You and I stay out of this," said Carey to Dodd.

"Ay sir. I wantae see his face when…"

"You'll see it but from a distance. I don't want any risk of a counter-suit if you whack him on the nose. And you're definitely not allowed to kill him."

"I know that," said Dodd with dignity. "This isnae a blood-feud yet. But…"

"No. It's bad enough that I lost temper and hit him myself after I found you. I don't want to give him any more ammunition."

"Och sir," moaned Dodd rebelliously. It was typical of Carey that he let some bunch of Berwickmen have all the fun.

The bailiff was speaking to Heneage's steward whose expression was one of astonishment and horror. Not only, explained the bailiff, was there a warrant for Mr. Heneage's arrest, there was also a warrant to search the house for him if he didn't come out, which warrant they were minded to execute immediately.

The steward was objecting that Mr. Vice Chamberlain was not there, had gone out, had never been there and…The bailiffs shouldered past him, followed by Mr. Enys, who was wearing an oddly fixed and intent expression.

There was a sound of shouting and feet thundering on stairs. Carey's face clouded. "Hang on," he said, "that's not right."

He headed for the door and brushed past the still protesting steward, followed by Dodd who was pleased to be in at the kill.

The house was expensively oak panelled and diamond-paned, there was an extremely fine cupboard with its carved doors shut, and the steps going down to the cellar truly reeked.

The bailiffs had fanned out and were checking all the doors. Enys had hurried down the stairs and into the arched cellar where there were a few barrels of wine and a central pillar. Barred windows level with the courtyard paving let in some light. Bolted to the pillar about eight foot off the ground was a pair of iron manacles. Somebody had dug a pit in the earth underneath them which was soiled with turds. The manacles were darkened and rusty with blood.

Carey paused, took a deep breath and then went forward to where Enys was opening both of the smaller doors that gave onto two further cellars that were tiny, damp, and had not been cleaned since last there were prisoners there. However they were otherwise empty and Enys turned away, the shadows making his face hard to read, though Dodd could have sworn he saw a glint of something on the man's face.

"Who were you looking for?" Carey said quietly, his hand on Enys's narrow shoulder.

"No one…" Enys looked down. "My brother. I heard…I was afraid…Heneage might have taken him."

"So you used me and my father…"

"No sir," said Enys, looking straight at him. "It's clear that Heneage was warned to be away from here by someone, probably the clerk of the court. But we had to make the attempt to begin the case."

Carey nodded. "And? Is Cecil involved in this? Raleigh?"

Enys shook his head. "Not to my knowledge, sir, only I had to try. My brother has been missing for over two weeks. We should leave immediately so we can…"

Carey took his hand away from his sword. "Oh not so fast," he drawled. "I think we should check more carefully for Mr. Vice. Now we're here."

Starting at the top of the house, moving from one room to the other while the Cornishmen stood around the steward and the couple of valets busied themselves with the horses in the stables, Carey searched the place methodically. In one room that had a writing desk and a number of books in it, he found a pile of papers newly ciphered which he swept into a convenient post bag. In a chest he found another stack of rolled parchment, one of which he opened. He whistled.

"Mother would be interested by these," he said. "It seems our Mr. Vice has been busy buying lands in Cornwall—look."

Dodd looked, squinted, and sighed because the damned thing was not only in a cramped secretary hand but was clearly in some form of foreign.

"You can see it's a deed—see the word 'Dedo' which means I give, and that says 'Comitatis Cornwallensis'—which means Cornwall. We'll just borrow this one, I think." Carey dropped it in the bag.

There was a book on the desk, much thumbed, which Carey looked at and which turned out to be Foxe's Book of Martyrs.

Dodd had been attending to the cupboard with the carved doors. Eventually the lock broke and he opened it. There was a nice haul of silver.

"Jesu, Sergeant, put that back," Carey said behind him, "we're not here for the man's insight."

Dodd was puzzled. "Are we no'? I thocht that was what we were about. Can I no' nip out that fine gelding in the stables then, the one wi' the white sock?"

Carey grinned. "We're not raiding the man, we're searching his house for evidence of wrongdoing and I'm certainly not losing my reputation for the sake of a second-rate collection of silver plate and one nag with the spavins. The man has no taste at all." Dodd scowled. Who cared what the silver plate looked like since it was going to be melted down? And the gelding certainly did not have the spavins and was in fact a very nice piece of horseflesh, as Dodd knew, and probably Carey did as well.

At the foot of the stairs Enys was anxiously waiting for them. "I had no intention of taking Mr. Vice Chamberlain's papers…" he began.

"Of course not," said Carey breezily. "We came to arrest Heneage but in the course of our search for him we came upon some papers which might possibly relate to treason and which my Lord Chamberlain, as his superior, would naturally wish to know about. We'll give them back as soon as we can find Heneage himself."

He led the way out of the door and along the path to the boat-landing. To the steward he gave a shilling to pay for the damage to the cupboard and to convey his compliments to Mr. Vice Chamberlain—he was sure they would meet soon.

It seemed a very long row back to Somerset House steps, even though Dodd wasn't rowing and the current was helping the men sweating at the oars in the warm afternoon sun. Enys remained silent, staring into space, and Dodd had nothing much to say either. Carey watched Enys for a while before remarking, seemingly at venture, "Have you truly seen nothing of your brother for more than two weeks?"

Enys turned his gargoyle's face to Carey's. "Nothing. And he would be back by now. He…he was concerned in something dangerous connected with Heneage, something to do with land, but that's all I know."

Carey handed over the deed he had taken. "Is it real?"

Enys squinted his eyes, read the deed, and nodded. "Yes, quite in order, a few hides of farmland near Helston. In Cornwall they call them 'wheals.'"

"Are these anything to do with the cases you withdrew from?"

Enys shook his head. "Not this piece of land, no. Were there other deeds there?"

"Plenty of them."

Enys smiled bitterly. "It's a popular game. Arrest a man for non-payment of recusancy fines, offer to release him in exchange for some land sold at a very low price, and then release or don't release him, depending how much land you think his family have left. There is nothing, alas, illegal about it."

"But you find it dishonourable?"

Enys shrugged.

"Are you a Papist?" Carey demanded, voice harsh with suspicion.

"No sir," Enys said with a sigh, "but my family were church-Papists and I find it hard to cheat their friends and neighbours."

"Are they still Papists?"

"No sir, all of them are buried in good Protestant graves. My brother is my only living relative apart from my sister."

"Was?"

Enys lifted his hands, palms up. "What else can I think?"

Dodd nudged Carey's foot with his boot. "D'ye think...?"

Carey sighed. "We can but try."

The men were very happy to stop off at Westminster steps and have ale and bread and cheese bought for them for their labours. Carey, Dodd, and Enys hurried to the crypt of the little chapel by the court.

The undertakers had been and the smell was less appalling since the entrails had been taken out and the cavity packed with salt and saltpetre. Now the corpse was wrapped in a cerecloth. Carey lit the candles with a spill from the watchlight.

Enys swallowed hard, took a deep breath. He had his hands clasped together at his waist as he went forward and Dodd peeled the waxed cloth from the dead man's face. He looked intently for a few moments and then let his breath puff out in a sigh of relief.

"This is not my brother, sir," said Enys. "Poor soul." His gaze travelled down the body and he made a jerky movement with his right hand, then looked down.

Dodd grunted and put the waxed cloth back as carefully as he could. There was a sound behind him and he saw a small, fragile, very pregnant girl coming down the steps being carefully helped by a large man wearing a buff coat. With them was one of Hunsdon's liverymen.

"Yerss," said the large man to the liveryman, "it's Briscoe, Timothy Briscoe. And this is my wife, Ellie."

Carey stepped back from the corpse and so did Dodd. Enys was already in the shadows.

"Only she 'eard about a corpse being found wiv a bit of 'is finger missing," Briscoe continued, "and she was scared it was 'er big bruvver who she 'asn't seen for years and so I brung 'er so she wouldn't worry 'erself and upset the baby."

Dodd thought that if anything was likely to bring the baby on, it was the sight and smell of a corpse that had been in water for a while. The girl was shaking like a leaf and gripping tight to Briscoe's arm. He looked a dangerous bruiser but his square face was full of concern and the girl crept close to the corpse and peered at the man's left hand. There was a gasp and a gulp.

"Ellie, my love," Briscoe rumbled. "You mustn't…

"I've got to know," trembled Ellie. Carey stepped forward and lifted the cerecloth from the man's face. He was watching the girl carefully. She stood on tiptoe and stared, gulped again and again, and the tears started flowing down her face.

She turned her face to her husband's shoulder quite quietly. "I'm not sure," she whispered, "'is face is different, but it might be Harry. It could be."

Carey was good with distressed women, Dodd thought. He beckoned Briscoe and his wife up the steps and into the sunlight, gestured for them to sit down on a bench. He sat next to her and offered Mrs. Briscoe a sip from his silver flask of aqua vitae which she took gratefully.

"Mrs. Briscoe," he said gently to her, "if you haven't seen your brother Harry…What was his surname?"

"Dowling," Briscoe said and his wife sniffled, fumbled out a hankerchief and blew her nose. "Harold Dowling was his name."

"If you haven't seen him for so long, why did you think it might be him?"

She gulped again with her hand resting on her proud belly. Thank God it didn't look as if the babe had been brought on by shock yet. "I thought I saw 'im in the street a few weeks ago, only he wouldn't talk to me. I was so sure it was him and I was so pleased but he wouldn't stop and he wouldn't speak."

"Where did you see him?"

"Seething Lane, near Sir Francis Walsingham's old house."

"How was he dressed?"

"He looked like a gentleman which is what he always wanted to be, you see. He went off to Germany after he had a big fight wiv my dad and went for a miner, but we never heard nuffing more from him and my dad said he'd probably died in a mine and good riddance." She sniffled. "He was always in trouble, Harry, so maybe he was soldiering as well. It's a good thing my mam never saw what he come to after she spent all that money to put him to school."

Carey nodded. "But you're not sure it's him?"

She shook her head. "It might be because of the finger, that's why I came. When I heard the crier say that about the body. He lost the tip of it when he was a boy and he caught it in a gate and the barber cut it off cos it went bad."

She stopped, frowned and blinked at him. "Who are you, sir?"

"I'm Sir Robert Carey. My father asked me to try and find out why this man ended in the Thames with a knife wound in him."

She gasped again. "I don't know about that. He was a lovely bruvver," she said, "'e took to me to Bartalmew's Fair when I was little and every year after and he was such fun, always laughing and full of ideas for making money. He was certain he'd end as a gentleman."

"I believe the inquest will be tomorrow…" said Carey, looking for confirmation at Hunsdon's man who nodded, "in front of the Board of Greencloth. Afterwards you'll be able to claim the body to bury."

The girl nodded again and blew her nose again. "Thank you, sir."

"May we help you to your home. I have a boat waiting for me." Carey was watching the girl with concern.

Briscoe coughed. "Thank you kindly, sir, but we don't live far from here and my wife prefers to walk, don't you, Ellie?" The girl nodded as she heaved herself off the bench. "I've been walking a lot today, haven't I, Tim?" she said with a watery smile. "It's easier than sitting, to be honest, sir. And I don't know if I could get in a boat at the moment, I'm so clumsy."

"I see," said Carey and smiled at her. "Well, God's blessing on your time, mistress, I hope all goes well for you." Ellie Briscoe went pink and dropped him a clumsy curtsey as she waddled off with her husband's arm around her into the molten light that the sun was pouring into the Thames like a beekeeper measuring honey. Enys headed with his shoulders bowed towards the boatlanding.

"Will you not take a quart of ale, sir?" said Carey.

"If we do not presently round up the witnesses to Mr. Heneage's assault on Sergeant Dodd, be very sure we will never find them," said Enys in an oddly strangled voice. "Since he himself has given us the slip, I'm sure the lesser fry can and will."

"Ay but surely they'll be feared for their kin," said Dodd who deeply doubted there was any point in finding the witnesses at all. Unpaid ones, anyway. "They'll no' testify, naebody would." He'd thought that their only chance of persuading anyone to do it was being able to say "and Mr. Heneage is locked up now, what do you say to that?" while persuasively bouncing heads off walls. He'd assumed that was what they were about.

"You have a point," said Carey regretfully as he followed the lawyer, gestured to the oarsmen and bailiffs who were sitting in the sun by the red lattices of the alehouse, and headed to the boat again.

Enys had a list of witnesses that Dodd had drawn up. Most of them were in Heneage's pay. And Dodd had been looking forward to wetting his whistle which was starting to go dry, which was his own fault.

Scowling he got back in the damned boat again and sat there watching as Enys fumbled and wobbled his way to the seat. Carey stepped across and sat down at the prow, trailing his finger in the water and looking thoughtful.

"It's a pity Mrs. Grenville's a woman so she can't testify," he said. "All the rest are Heneage's men, apart from Mr. Cheke."

Enys frowned. "Nobody else?"

"The Gaoler and the gaol servants."

"Hmm. Sergeant, you were marked in the register as Sir Robert."

"Ay, but I writ me own name in the book, clear as ye like," said Dodd proudly, "not me mark but me name and office as well." It was almost worth the missed football games and beatings from the Reverend Gilpin to be able to say that to the hoity toity London lawyer.

Surprisingly, Enys didn't seem impressed by Dodd's clerkly ability but he did look pleased.

"So under whose name were you removed from the gaol? Yours or Sir Robert's?"

Dodd thought he'd been through this with Enys the night before. "Well, it couldnae have been Sir Robert's name because Heneage knew fine Ah wisae him for he was angry about it."

"Did he say anything?"

"Ay, he did."

"In front of the Keeper and the gaol servants?"

"Ay, he was furious. So he kenned verrah well who I wis and called me *Mr.* Dodd forbye. Like ye said to the judge."

"I believe we should pay a visit to the Fleet and arrest the Keeper," Enys said to Carey. "It's possible he has not been warned by Heneage and putting him in gaol might help to flush out the Vice Chamberlain."

"He'll get bail," Carey said.

"I expect so," said Enys placidly, "but the point will have been made. And with luck we will be able to establish something very damaging to Mr. Vice in the process."

Dodd leaned forward. "Ay, but surely Heneage will get away wi' it in the end," he said, realising as he spoke that that was why he had been in a dump since they left Heneage's house in Chelsea. Jesu, the man had his own personal dungeons and torture chamber. He was going up against someone more dangerous than the Grahams, that was sure. He couldn't bring himself to admit it but it had been the blood on the manacles bolted high on the pillar in the cellar that had sent him queasy. Him. A Dodd from Upper Tynedale. At the age of sixteen he had taken a fine and bloody revenge for his father's murder by the Elliots and…

No, he wouldn't take the insult from anybody…but was law the right way to go about it? For all Carey's father's fine talk about paper weapons and lawyers as men at arms and champions.

"On the criminal charge, yes, he'll likely compose with a fine which you should accept. On the civil…" Enys shrugged. "If we are before Mr. Justice Whitehead and any of the witnesses agree with you…Again it will be in the nature of a fine."

Dodd grunted. It all came down to money for these folk, didn't it. Well, was money what he really wanted? And since Heneage was still at large, would they find he had called out his affinity and descended on Somerset House while they were away. Och God, was that where he was?

He was about to mention the possibility to Sir Robert when Enys interrupted.

"It is certainly worth subpoena'ing the henchmen to testify that Heneage laid hands on you himself. Was he the only one?"

Dodd blinked at him. "Nay, they all had in wi' a boot or a fist, tho…" Dodd paused and brightened. "Ay, but they might not mind admitting that Heneage laid into me wi' a cosh if I said that he was the only one. Ay, I'll say that."

Enys coughed and looked at the bottom of the boat. "If we are in front of Mr. Justice Whitehead, may I urge you to tell the truth at all times. His honour is most perspicacious."

Dodd didn't care how much he sweated, he wanted to know how to get the judge on his side and keep him there. If telling the truth was what it took, then so be it. He sighed. "Ay, so it were all of them with Heneage in the lead."

"How are you now, Sergeant?"

Dodd shrugged. "Ah've had worse, I think." He couldn't recall exactly when, mind, certainly since he'd learned to fight, but he had woken up hungover and aching as badly on more than one occasion.

"Did you see a surgeon?"

"Ay, better than that, my lord had his ain physician tend to me."

"Would he testify as to your injuries?"

"He might," said Carey, "for a fee."

"He give me this stuff for medicine, which is very fine indeed," said Dodd taking out the clay pipe and the henbane of Peru again. Once he'd got it lit he took a good lungful of smoke which was tasting better and no longer made his head whirl so badly. He liked the odd sensation of mild drunkenness without the rage that booze normally uncovered in him, and it definitely helped with aches and pains. He offered the pipe to Carey first, who shook his head, and then to Enys.

"I've never drunk tobacco," said Enys.

"Ay? I thought all the students at the Inns of Court were terrible for it."

"Oh they are," said Enys ruefully, "drinking, gambling, fighting. It never appealed to me, drinking smoke. What are chimneys for?"

Nonetheless Enys took the pipe and cautiously sucked some smoke. Then he burst into a mighty coughing and wheezing, handing the pipe back to Dodd just before he would have dropped it.

"Ay, it takes you that way first," Dodd agreed, smiling wisely as the medicine took hold. "I thought my head would fall off with the phlegm. It's better now. You wouldnae think it wis medicine at all since it disnae make you purge."

Still coughing, Enys nodded and mopped his eyes. That henbane of Peru surely did blast the phlegm out of you, though Dodd was hazy as to how that might help your kidneys.

They went first to Mr. Cheke's apothecary shop, but did not even knock on the door. The windows were shuttered and on the door was the painted red cross and the printed warrant saying that the house was under quarantine.

Dodd felt sick. Poor man. Of all the physicians and apothecaries in the city, he had at least tried to fight the plague… Which was probably why he had caught it himself, despite all his terrifying precautions.

Ignoring the danger of infection, Carey shouted up to the shuttered windows. "Mr. Cheke!" he roared, "Mr. Cheke! Can you hear me? Do you need food or water?"

There was no answer, no sound, no movement. Carey stood for a moment with his head bowed and then turned wordlessly, heading away from the stricken shop.

In a methodical manner, they went round making sure the bailiffs delivered subpoenas to all the names on Dodd's list after dumping the bag of Heneage's papers at the Somerset House gate. One more witness was dead of plague. The Gaoler of the Fleet was quite upset to see them again, even more upset to be served with court papers, and positively horrified when Enys impounded the register as vital evidence. Slightly to Dodd's surprise, there still witten in it as clear as day was the Gaoler's wobbly painful letters which read "Sr Rbt Carey Knt" and next to it "Sgt Henry Dod" in Dodd's own hand. Dodd thought he'd written it quite tidily, if large.

wednesday 13th september 1592, late afternoon

Inevitably they ended up in the Mermaid again where Marlowe was playing primero with Poley and Munday and some obvious barnards as if nothing at all had happened. Marlowe stood up as they came in and bowed elaborately. "Ave, vos moriture saluto," he said.

Carey returned the courtesy with a lordly nod, sat himself down on a bench, stretched out his legs and crossed them at the ankles. Then he smiled and said, "If that means what I think it does, we're not going to die yet."

"Of course you are, gentlemen," said Marlowe, waving at the potboy, "but it will have been worth it. You've tried to put the honourable Mr. Vice Chamberlain into gaol. Wonderful idea. What would you like to drink?"

The two barnards looked in horror from Carey to Marlowe and back again, gathered what was left of their money, and practically ran out the door. Munday tutted quietly.

"Aqua vitae from the barrel under the counter and sherry sack," said Carey promptly. "Did Heneage pay you your wages at last then, Kit?"

Marlowe smiled and kissed his fingers at Carey.

"I'll have a quart of double, if ye're buying," said Dodd suspiciously. "This here is Mr. Enys, he's our lawyer."

"Better and better," said Marlowe becoming more dramatic by the minute. "Mr. Enys if you were the man who had the balls to draft the pleadings, please do join us."

Enys coloured slightly and smiled. "Mild for me, thank you," he said, sitting himself down nervously on a stool with his robe wrapped around him.

"Many tongu'd Rumour is rampaging up and down Whitefriars and the Temple," declaimed Marlowe, who had clearly been drinking all day, flinging out an arm as if to introduce her. "Is it true Mr. Vice tried to escape and was stopped by Sergeant Dodd here leaping on board the coach, wrestling the driver to the ground, running across the backs of the horses, and halting the coach just before it should tragically fall into a ravine with Heneage in it, at which Mr. Vice ran into the woods and escaped."

"No," said Carey dampeningly, "he wasn't there."

Marlowe struck his forehead with the heel of his palm. "Such a pity, another wonderful story sadly exploded by prosaic reality."

"Somebody must have warned him what was afoot."

"Ah yes, the clerk of the court. As always, a useful purchase. What will you do tomorrow?"

"I have other matters to pursue," said Carey, "but I expect I shall go to court again. What's the book?"

Marlowe produced a small notebook from his sleeve. "Here we are. Five to one on that the Sergeant composes the criminal assault with Heneage and makes a deal for the civil damages. Ditto that it's taken out of Whitehead's court on account of his notorious honesty. Ten to one on and no takers that you're both in the Tower for treason by the end of the month." Carey smiled faintly. "Are you in?" asked Marlowe, reaching for his pen.

"Probably," said Carey, "I'll have to think about it. I'll put in a noble on myself to stay out of the Tower."

Dodd gulped. Six shillings and eightpence wasn't much of a bet in Carey's scheme of things. Plus he hadn't said "myself and Dodd."

"Your father's backing this, isn't he?" asked Poley suddenly as he added some coins to the primero pot and took another card.

Carey had his eyes shut and had not been dealt into the game. "Obviously."

"Why? I mean why is he backing it?"

"Oh, high spirits and a love of justice, I expect."

Poley had a pale oblong face with eyes that seemed not to blink very much. Dodd considered that he would certainly not buy a horse from the man. "Surely he's taking revenge for what happened to your brother?"

"Of course not," said Carey, still smiling with his eyes shut.

"Must be," said Poley, relentlessly. "He wouldn't want to leave it lie."

"Whatever you wish, Mr. Poley," said Carey, which made Dodd blink at his unaccustomed soft-spokenness.

"They've never got on, have they, the Lord Chamberlain and Vice Chamberlain?" Poley continued to poke, "And your father wouldn't like..."

"Mr. Poley, I can't imagine why you think I'm going to discuss my father's plans with the likes of you," said Carey. "If I wanted to tell it all to Heneage I'd write a letter and get Marlowe to deliver it which would probably be quicker." Marlowe had been over by the barman, talking quietly to him.

Poley coloured slightly. "I don't..."

"Oh tut tut," said Marlowe silkily, coming back, picking up and laying down his new cards, "Chorus. Mine I think. If you want my lord Baron Hunsdon to employ you when Heneage goes you'll have to do better than that, my dear..."

Poley gave Marlowe an ugly look. "I..."

"Crows white, noonday night, hills flying, pigs roosting in the trees," murmured Carey seemingly apropos of nothing.

"Eh?" Poley paused in a blindingly deft shuffle of the cards.

"He means," Marlowe told him patronisingly, "that these things will happen before Hunsdon employs you. Very poetic I'm sure, Sir Robert, since you've nipped it straight out of a Border ballad."

"I don't know why I'm being insulted," sniffed Poley as Marlowe took the cards from him to shuffle again.

"Tell me about the body in the Thames," said Carey.

"Which one?"

Carey's eyebrows went up. "A gentleman or seeming like one, dark hair, sallow complexion, marks of burns and stains on his hands, top joint of his left forefinger missing."

It was the merest flicker, but Poley looked uncertainly at Marlowe and then quickly back at his cards. Meanwhile Marlowe had paused infinitesimally as he dealt Carey in. Dodd shook his head and stayed out of it. So did Enys who was sitting quietly on his stool, sipping his small beer and watching everything. From the corner of his eye Dodd saw the potboy trot through the common-room and out the door into the street where he speeded to a run.

"No idea," said Marlowe glibly, "Where was he found?"

"Washed up against the Queen's Privy Steps."

Marlowe raised his eyebrows, very Carey-like. "So?"

"In the jurisdiction of the Board of Greencloth. My father wants me to investigate. He also wants me to look into rumours of crooked land dealings in Cornwall."

Marlowe shrugged. "It's all the rage at court, I believe. Bald Will was talking about how the Earl of Southampton is buying himself a sheaf of godforsaken Cornish hills."

Carey nodded, picked up his cards, glanced at them, put them down, leaned forwards and put his chin on his clasped hands. "And?"

Marlowe shrugged again. "I don't know. I'm certainly not about to buy some dubious marshy fields somewhere I am never likely to go. No matter what they might have under them. And even if I had the money."

Carey murmured something to Enys who had been blinking at Marlowe as if tranced like a chicken. Enys started, coloured, and fished in his satchel of papers and brought out a stiff piece of paper, written and sealed. Carey took it and handed it to Marlowe who took it absent-mindedly while adding his bet to the pot, glanced at it, and then scowled.

"Damn it, Sir Robert."

"You've been served, Christopher Marlowe. I'm calling you as a witness to Heneage's dealings with my brother and the incident with Sergeant Dodd here."

Dodd's spirits lifted slightly. That had been nicely done. Marlowe's face was a picture and no mistake.

Marlowe screwed up the paper furiously. "You tricked me!"

Carey shrugged. "I can't appear in open court against Heneage."

"Yes you can," said Carey. "Until it's time to testify you can stay at Somerset House and we'll organise you a boat to take to to Westminster."

"I can't appear," said Marlowe through his teeth. "I was not a witness. I wasn't there. I was in Southwark."

"Were you now?" said Carey easily, not seeming ruffled by this abject lie. Poley's eyes darted from Marlowe to Carey and back. "Any corroboration, any witnesses to that?"

"Oh yes. Mr. Poley here for one."

Poley didn't look happy at this. "That's right," he said, "I was with Mr. Marlowe on...ah...the day in question and he was in Southwark."

"Was he?" Carey's eyes were half-hooded. "You sure about that, Kit?"

"Yes," Marlowe was giving Carey back stare for stare.

"Despite all the witnesses I have to you sitting in the Mermaid waiting for me on the day in question?" Carey was smiling. "Come on, I know Heneage is powerful and wealthy but so is my father and he likes poets for some reason. He'll protect you."

Marlowe finished his brandywine, checked his cards again, and folded. "Does your father employ Richard Topcliffe?" Now where had Dodd heard that name before?

"No. Who's that?" From the look in Carey's eyes, Dodd suspected he did know but wasn't admitting it.

"You've never met him?"

Carey shrugged. "No."

"Consider yourself lucky," said Marlowe. "Topcliffe is...well he's ingenious and he's very good at his job which he likes very much."

"Really?"

"He's a freelance inquisitor. He often works for Heneage. He has the breaking of most of the Papist priests we...the pursuivants catch. He's at the Tower working on one called Robert Southwell at the moment. That's why you haven't seen him and why he wasn't at Chelsea."

"And?"

"And? I don't want him after me. Because he's completely insane and kills for fun and Heneage protects him, gives him completely free rein."

Dodd nodded, struck by a memory. "Ay, Shakespeare was saying there was someone he was more affeared of than me... Which was a surprise to me, ye follow."

Marlowe blinked at Dodd as if he'd forgotten his existence and then nodded. "That will be Topcliffe."

"Come on, Marlowe," said Carey comfortably, "this isn't like you. Where's the student of the lofty spheres…"

"The student of the lofty spheres prefers to keep his own fleshly spheres away from Topcliffe who likes playing games with men's stones. I mean it, Carey, I'm not testifying against Heneage."

"I heard Topcliffe buys the bawdy-house boys that get poxed and nobody ever sees them again," put in Poley.

"How does he get away with it?"

"The Queen protects him because she's been told he's useful. He's mad, of course. Bedlam mad. He'll tell anyone who listens the dreams he has of the Queen where he…Well, you'd expect her to hang him if she'd heard what he says, so I assume she hasn't. And he has other friends at court, powerful friends. And although he's old now, he's a very good pursuivant." Marlowe lifted his hands palms up. "I'm not doing it."

"Isn't anyone going to play primero?" said Poley. Enys shook his head and pushed the cards he'd been dealt back towards Marlowe, who picked them up with his eyebrows raised. "Mr. Enys, I'm surprised, I thought all Gray's Inn men were shocking gamblers."

Enys smiled faintly. "Not me, sir. Or rather I am a shocking gambler as I generally lose. I lost so much last Christmas that I have sworn to my sister that I will have no more to do with play."

Marlowe nodded but said nothing more. "Sir Robert?"

"Oh eighty-five points," said Carey languidly, dropping a sixpenny stake into the pot. Dodd shook his head as well, filled a pipe, and lit it. Once again the aromatic herb and incense mixture made him feel as if some tight knot in his stomach was being slowly unwound. He passed the pipe to Enys who took some and hardly coughed at all this time. As the pipe went round, Dodd considered that there were London vices he would be sorry to leave behind him and he'd have to buy in a good stock of the doctor's medicine before he went north.

Although Dodd hadn't drunk very much by the end of the long evening he was feeling peaceful and light in the head as he left the Mermaid and all three of them headed up past the Blackfriars monastery wall. They were heading for Ludgate and

Fleet Street to pass onto the Strand and Hunsdon's palace of a place. Only a madman tried to cut through the Whitefriars liberties at night after curfew and they were no longer using the little tenement Hunsdon had given them earlier in the month. He and Carey had felt that if they were taking on Vice Chamberlain Heneage in the courts they were better off somewhere with walls and a large number of serving men. Dodd was thoroughly enjoying the luxury of Somerset House, now he had got over his shock at having an entire chamber to himself. He was even starting to get used to the ridiculous hot tight clothes Carey insisted he wear.

There was a movement of something too large to be a cat in a shadowed alley. The hair on Dodd's neck stood up straight. Automatically he loosened his sword and took a quick glance behind him under cover of a coughing fit. A large shape moved into shadow in the corner of his eye. Heart thundering and his head still swimming with the tobacco, Dodd paused and then turned left into the nearest alleyway, feeling for his codpiece laces. He needed a piss anyway.

"Och, Sir Robert," he called, "Will ye look at this?" and pretended to be squinting into the alley.

Carey had been trying to persuade Enys to sing "A Shepherd to His Love" in harmony with him, to Enys's giggly but steadfast insistence he had no voice. Now Carey swung back and Enys trailed after them, still sniggering.

Dodd shook his head violently, trying to clear it. "'S' a place here looks a lot like Tarras Moss," he slurred. "Would ye credit it?"

Carey sauntered over, whistling happily. For a moment Dodd thought he hadn't got the reference until he saw Carey's hand go stealthily to the poinard dagger hanging at the small of his back.

Dodd looked down, annoyed. Sheer tension meant he could not actually piss.

"Och damn it," he moaned, wishing he hadn't had the beer. Carey was leaning one arm against the wall, singing softly and pretending to fumble at his own lacings.

"How many?" he muttered very quietly.

"Ah've seen two," Dodd muttered back, quickly tying again, "so I'd bet on five or more."

"Me too. Break for the Temple, not Somerset House."

"Ay sir," said Dodd. "Will we charge 'em now?"

"Not exactly," said Carey with a smile, "Let's see if we can avoid a trial for murder, shall we?"

He drew sword and dagger and crossed them. Dodd drew his sword and faced the other way. Enys was leaning against a wall, still giggling.

Carey stepped out a little so that a public-spirited torch in a sconce on one of the linen shops, showed him up in the blackness.

"Gentlemen, I know you're there. Shall we talk?"

There was a pause and then a heavyset man moved from the shadows of an alley and another came out of the bulk of Temple Bar itself where he must have been pretending to be a carved saint. Dodd strained his eyes to penetrate the other shadows and thought he caught a glimpse of metal as someone drew a dagger. Three visible, so a possible six in total.

Seeing Enys still leaning against the wall giggling from the tobacco fumes, he kicked the man on the ankle. "Ow," said Enys aggrievedly, "Why...?"

"Will ye draw, ye fool?" Dodd hissed furiously.

"Wha'?" Enys tried to stand upright and blinked about himself. Yes, definitely a fourth man visible next to the huge permanent dungheap a little way from Temple Bar. Probably that was where the ambush had been planned for. Dodd squinted hard looking for the fifth and sixth whilst Enys hiccupped and fumbled at his sword hilt. No help there then, damn it, typical soft southerner.

"Talk?" said the large man in a jack who seemed to be the leader. "Wo' abaht?" His voice was as full of glottal stops as Barnabus' had been, very hard to understand.

"Oh nothing much," said Carey, doing a couple of showy juggling tricks with his dagger and sword, swapping them over and then back again. "Just talk. What a pleasant night it's been. How you gentlemen must be tired of waiting for us. Who's paying you. That sort of thing."

"Nuffink to talk about."

Dodd saw what Carey was doing. He was deliberately drawing attention to himself, aiming to draw the attackers out so they'd show themselves. Presumably it would then be up to Dodd to kill them...Except what was that the Courtier had said about avoiding a trial for murder in London?

There was a scrape behind Dodd, he spun, saw a large moon-face looming near him with a veney stick raised over his head, and slashed sideways with his sword. He heard a yelp and smelled blood as the man reeled backwards, clutching a spurting arm. Dodd heard a cry behind him and saw Enys clumsily trying to block with his sword against a man battering down on him with a club.

Another club? No blades? Ay, the Courtier's right, Dodd thought in a sudden slow moment of icy clarity, this is to get us all arrested for murder.

Furious at the man who had hired roaring boys and set them deliberately against fighters who could kill them, Dodd ran up behind the man who was so intent on Enys, his prey, that he had no defence against Dodd's powerful boot in the arse which sent him sprawling.

Enys had dropped his sword and had his hands over his face as he crouched in a corner, moaning. Jesus, thought Dodd as he went past the ninny, what a pathetic sight. What's wrong with him?

Dodd grabbed the club-wielder who was just trying to climb to his feet, picked him up bodily and crashed him backwards over a stone conduit filled with slimy horse-slobbered water. Dodd shoved the man's head deep into the water and held him there while he clawed at Dodd's arm. Meantime Dodd looked around cannily for more attackers. Something complicated was going on down Fleet Street, involving Carey and the big man-at-arms, but the other two men, if they existed, were still waiting their moment, or possibly had run.

Dodd let the man with the club crow in some air, and then had him blowing bubbles again.

"Wh…what are you doing?" came a slurred voice behind him. Dodd glanced over his shoulder and saw the soft southerner staggering over, trailing his sword in his left hand and twisting his right as if it pained him. Perhaps he'd sprained it somehow. He was panting and wild-eyed.

"Ah'm drowning this pig's turd," Dodd explained casually, letting the man up for a second so he could hear.

Enys watched the renewed bubbles and then jumped at a further clang and ting down Fleet Street followed by Carey's customary bellow of "T'il y est haut!"

"What about Sir Robert? Won't you help him?" trembled the soft lawyer.

Dodd leaned an ear expertly in the direction of the clanging.

"Neither o' them are trying to kill each other," he said. "And yon Courtier nearly held Andy Nixon to a draw for three minutes in the summer, he'll be well enough while I make sure of this loon. Will ye fetch his dagger?"

The loon's hands were flailing more feebly now, so Dodd let the man up to breathe while Enys gingerly fished the dagger from its sheath. What was it doing still there, Dodd wanted to know.

"Now then," Dodd said to the man, who was coughing and spluttering fit to bust his lungs, "who was it set ye on tae *me* wi' nobbut a stick and a knife, eh?"

"Heeh…heh…"

Dodd said it again patiently, only more southern. He hoped.

"Hur…ha…he said you was only a farmer, and not a gentleman."

"Ay," said Dodd, "I am certainly no' a gentleman and I am a farmer, did he tell ye where I farm?"

The man shook his head, spattering slime everywhere. Dodd told him.

"I have boys that scare crows for me that are better fighters than ye, ye soft southern git, so who was it that tried to get ye killed? Eh?"

The man gasped for breath then said the name. Dodd sighed and dunked him again until the flailing had stopped, then hefted him out and laid him on his side on the filthy cobbles to puke and cough his way back to consciousness. On a thought, he picked up a nice piece of brick from a nearby pile of rubble. He realised with irritation that his sleeves were wet to the elbow and hoped they wouldn't shrink too much.

Then he sauntered over to where Carey was seemingly playing a veney with the large man who had been first to show himself. The man was now backing up carefully, probably trying for one of the many alleys off Fleet Street that led into the liberties without actually turning his back on Carey. The Courtier was quite breathless by now but clearly enjoying himself, fencing like a sword instructor and never trying to come to close quarters with the lethal twenty inch long poinard in his left hand.

"If ye can leave off playin' yer veney wi' yon catamite," called Dodd as southern as he could, "we might catch Marlowe afore he runs for it."

Carey missed a beat and nearly lost the tip of his nose before coming back to the attack with more purpose. "Oh for God's sake," he groaned in disgust.

"Ay," said Dodd, narrowed his eyes and threw the brick hard at the man-at-arms' chest. It caught him in the rib cage, giving Carey the chance to beat past the man's blade and smash him in the face left-handed with the pommel of his poinard. The man went down like a sack of flour.

Carey pounced on him at once, bashed him a couple more times with the dagger hilt, then straightened and caught his breath for a moment. He started dragging the large man over to his mate who was still heaving and coughing by the conduit. Dodd glanced at Enys who was staring at the swordsman as the blood came gouting out of his nose and down his face from the nasty cut on his forehead caused by one of the jewels in Carey's poinard hilt. So that's what they were for, eh? That made sense of why anyone would want a pretty dagger hilt.

Dodd sheathed his sword which was still clean and gave the puffing Carey a hand to carry the man to his mate and lay him down in a suggestive position behind Dodd's victim. Carey grinned and pulled off both men's belts, then tied them tightly together with the swordsman's wrists in front of Dodd's man and that man's hands belted behind him as far around the bulk of the swordsman as his arms would go. The swordsman started to struggle and mutter so Carey bashed him a couple more times, while Dodd tied their feet in a tangle.

It was a cosy sight and would give the Fleet Street wives a good laugh when they came to fetch water at the conduit in the morning.

"Ay," said Dodd, deeply satisfied at justice done. He unbuttoned his sleeve cuffs because they felt tight.

Enys still seemed upset for some reason and was saying nothing. Dodd took his sword from his unresisting left hand and put it back in his scabbard, then examined the man's wrist which was unusually thin and seemed mildly sprained.

"Caught a blow awkwardly, did ye?" he asked with not much sympathy. Enys nodded. It was hard to tell colour in the flickering light from the Gatehouse Inn torch and the one on the linen shop, but it looked as if Enys had gone beetroot-cheeked and so he should.

"Sergeant, I apologise, I'm…well…I'm no good as a swordsman. I only wear one because the Inn regulations say I have to."

"Ay." Dodd nodded with dignity at this apology, "When yer wrist is well, would ye like me to teach ye a few moves?"

Enys blinked rapidly. "Ah…yes…if you don't mind."

"Ah dinna care one way or the other, I just dinnae want the trouble of finding a new lawyer to take my case. Why did ye no' kick him in the cods, he was open for it?

Enys smiled shakily. "I didn't think of it."

Dodd sucked his teeth. "Ye've never fought before?"

"My brother."

Dodd nodded sourly. "Ay but he wasnae trying to kill ye. Generally."

"Come on, gentlemen!" called Carey from up the street where he was heading briskly towards the Blackfriars again. "He's an arrogant bugger is Marlowe, there's a chance he might still be there."

Dodd speeded to a sprint to catch up with Carey, followed slowly by Enys who seemed to run in a lumbering fashion that boded ill for his sword-fighting. He seemed remarkably tired by the short sprint of a few hundred yards as well. He walked behind them, hunched, breathing hard, and pressing at his ribcage.

"You should consider going to your home, Mr. Enys?" Carey said to him, "This might get nasty."

Enys shook his head. "I'm afraid I shall be…no use to you gentlemen…at all," he panted, "but I would prefer to stay with you, if I may."

Carey raised his brows at Dodd for his opinion and Dodd shrugged.

"If it a' goes wrong, we wilnae protect ye," he warned Enys. Looking at Carey he thought it was quite likely to go wrong. Carey's lips were compressed in a thin line and the light of battle gleamed in his eye.

"D'ye think he'll be there?" Dodd asked.

"Oh yes. He'll want to know what happened. His calculation will be either…"

"We got a beating and think better of it, or we kill someone and wind up in gaol wi' yer friend Hughes measuring a rope for us," said Dodd.

"Or, in my case, sharpening an axe, of course," pointed out Carey the aristocrat. "I am more sick than I can say of Marlowe's stupid plotting…bloody idiot. What does he think he's playing at?"

"Trying hard to get back in Heneage's good opinion."

"A week ago he convinced me that he wanted to switch to my lord of Essex's affinity."

"Ay, but that was a week ago. He's changed his mind, nae doubt."

"Though I did have his head buried in a pile of the Queen's old bumrolls at the time so he may not have been telling me the whole truth."

Dodd hid a smile at the picture this presented. "Did ye now?" he said still glum, "Why did ye not slit his throat then and save us all trouble?"

"Didn't want to get her Majesty's linen all dirty," said Carey very prim. "Also, despite his faults, Marlowe's a remarkably fine poet and it would be a pity…"

Dodd shook his head at such an irrelevance.

wednesday 13th september 1592, night

Carey paused as he turned towards the Mermaid Inn, checking round the corner. "God, I wish Barnabus was here," he said, "this is the perfect job for him."

Dodd said nothing, never having much liked Carey's thieving manservant. Before they came to the Mermaid, Carey ducked into an alley that wound its way between the old walls of the monastery and the new shacks of incomers, to the sturdy wall at the back of the inn's yard. An unmistakeable reek of malt came from it. Carey looked thoughtful then climbed up on a shed roof and thence to a wall. Dodd boosted Enys onto the shed, then climbed up himself. Carey was peering down into the courtyard which was empty apart from a couple of goats tethered near a wall.

"Stay here," he whispered, and climbed quietly down from the wall, using a hen house as a step.

There were sounds of activity in the common room and the noise of somebody playing a lute much less expertly than he thought he could.

"Mr. Enys," breathed Dodd in his ear, "can ye understand me?" Enys nodded. "If it a' goes wrong I want ye to leg it for Somerset House fast as ye can. Dinna fight, dinna stop to wait for us, get to Somerset House and roust out my lord Hunsdon's kin. D'ye follow?"

Enys took a breath, possibly to argue, then nodded firmly. "How will I know?" he whispered. Dodd thought.

"Ye'll know if ye hear fighting or me yowling like a cat as a signal."

In Tynedale they gave a yell but Dodd didn't want to give too much away. Meanwhile Carey had crossed the yard without waking the chickens or the goats and got to the horn-paned window of the scullery. He knocked on it. Out came the sleepy-eyed potboy with wet hands red raw from lye. After quiet conversation and the transfer of a coin in the normal direction—away from Carey—the boy ducked back inside and a few minutes later, the innkeeper came out. He was carrying an empty barrel. Another quiet conversation and another transfer of coin.

Meanwhile Dodd had been thinking and none of what he thought pleased him at all. Even he was wishing for Barnabus now who would have been the ideal man for what he needed done.

The innkeeper went back inside, Carey crossed the yard again and used the henhouse to climb back up onto the wall. This time the hens inside clucked anxiously.

"The innkeeper tells me Marlowe is on his own and I've bribed him to get Marlowe out into the yard and…"

"Nay sir," said Dodd, coming to a decision. "I dinna think so."

"I beg your pardon, Sergeant?" Carey's voice was cold. He always hated being contradicted. No help for it, Dodd was not about to stand by and watch Carey run headfirst into an ambush again.

"Sir, did ye never run a raid on someone wi' but a few men and have the rest lying out in a valley to ambush them when they rode in on the hot trod?" It was so obvious, it was painful.

"This isn't the Borders, Sergeant," sniffed Carey, "and I've seen that…"

"Sir, ye've seen nothing, ye've been told." With decision, Dodd moved to the end of the wall and climbed quietly down into the alley again, helping Enys down as he went. "It's a' too bloody convenient," he muttered to himself.

"Where are you going Sergeant?" hissed Carey from the wall.

"I'm gonnae see for meself," Dodd told him, trotting quietly down the alley and then into another one on a sudden thought. Aggravatingly the alley suddenly twisted on itself and ended up at some riversteps, so Dodd moved along the bank to another alley and then jogged along it back to the main road.

There he saw exactly what he had suspected: a large group of large men in jacks carrying loaded crossbows. They were filing down the alley he had just accidentally avoided coming out of.

"Och," thought Dodd with fury, "Will I niver get to ma bed?"

He opened his mouth and let out what he thought was quite a good caterwaul, heard running feet stumbling down Fleet Street for the Strand. Two urchins who had been asleep on a dungheap for its warmth were sitting up and staring at him. Dodd nodded at them and beckoned them over, gave each of them sixpence which was all he could bear to part with, and told them what they were to do.

There was no sign of alarm from the men at arms who had paused at Dodd's imitation cat. Moving quietly and deftly through the shadows, Dodd came round by a different direction to the front of the Mermaid where the sign hung over a coach waiting outside, with the horses half asleep, their hooves tipped. Dodd recognised the damned thing, and crept up to it on the other side with his heart thundering.

The coach itself was empty. Dodd peered round and saw one man standing by the door to the tavern, who was probably the coachman, looking in with interest.

Suddenly there was a shouting and yelling followed by the loud twang of a discharged crossbow. Then a grumble of voices.

Dodd sighed. Instead of waiting for Dodd to come back with his report, the daft Courtier had got himself captured and he hoped that he hadn't got in the way of that crossbow bolt.

"Thish ish an outrage!" came Carey's voice at its loudest and most affected. "How dare you, shir, unhand me!"

Dodd nearly smiled, it was all so theatrical. Had he done it on purpose, perhaps? Peeping around the coach he could see Carey through the diamond paned windows, lit up by candles and menaced by several crossbows, dusting mud off his hat.

Dodd skulked back behind the coach and very quietly, using the point of his dagger and a fingernail which broke, pulled out two of the axle pins in the coach wheels. He then went back down the alleys, past the two urchins who were bent over a tinderbox, and climbed onto the wall of the courtyard again. The goats were up, giving occasional excited bleats, the chickens were complaining to each other but not daring to come out of their hutch, which in any case was bolted against alleycats. With infinite care, Dodd climbed down from the wall and crossed the yard. In front of him was the usual shamble of kitchen sheds and storesheds and the entrance of the cellar. A gabble of talk came from the commonroom.

Holding his breath, Dodd tried the back door to the kitchen which was latched on the inside. Very carefully he put his dagger through the hole and jiggled. For a wonder the bar was not pegged and came up. He went into the scullery where the pots and pans were piled up and into the kitchen where the boy was fast asleep by the fire, wrapped in his cloak with the spit dog huddled in his arms.

A loud growling came from the spit dog. In any case, Dodd needed to talk to the boy. He went over, gripped the dog's nose with one hand and clamped the other one over the boy's mouth. The boy woke and squeaked with fright.

"Can ye understand me?" Dodd said patiently, and told the boy what he had come to say. The boy shivered and stared at him, so Dodd hoped he had got the message, tapped the dog on the nose, and padded on to the serving passage, closing the door behind him as he went. He heard a scramble of feet and excited yipping.

There was a second door to the commonroom and Dodd put his ear to it.

"I have no idea what you're talking about," came Carey's pained tones, "Jusht...on my way home from an evening'sh card-play with my friendsh and I am shurrounded...shurrounded, sir!...by Smithfield bullyboys who threaten me with croshbows and make me come in here, no idea why, sure it's illegal. Eh?"

There was a quiet ugly murmer which Dodd could not make out. He was sure it didn't come from Marlowe, being too deep and not nearly cocky enough. It contained rather a dull certainty. The owner of the coach, then? But Heneage's voice was lighter than that.

"Yesh, I wash, marrer of fact, wiv him, your friend and mine, Mr. Kit Marlowe, playwright. Got lorsht."

More muttering. "Mr. Topcliffe," said Carey's voice with magnificent boozy arrogance, "my friendsh have all gone home and I would like to ash well. What…ish the problem?"

More murmering. Carey laughed theatrically. "Don't be ridiculoush," he said, "I can't turn Papist. I'm the Queen'sh bloody nephew. And her coush…cousin. If I so much as think about it, which I wouldn't because it'sh evil and treashon as well, I'd already be in the Tower with my head chopped off. So to shpeak."

Dodd risked a peek round the door. Carey had sat himself down on one of the settles by the fading fire with his right leg propped on his left knee and a mannered right hand placed just so on it. Standing nearby with a strange expression of mixed fear and amusement on his face was Marlowe. In front of Carey at an angle from the door, arms folded, dark gown with hanging sleeves trailing off his shoulders and men behind him, was an old man with a sword. At odds with the lines on his face was his hair and beard which was a sooty black colour. Dodd didn't know him.

Marlowe was staring straight at Dodd and must have seen him. Infinitesimally he moved his head to right and left at Dodd, then lifted his brows and his gaze went over Dodd's shoulder. He turned back to the black-bearded man.

Dodd's stomach froze twice. First when he knew Marlowe had seen him, once again when he realised what Marlowe was urgently trying to tell him.

A click of the safety hook coming off a crossbow trigger. Dodd sighed softly, let the door shut, and turned with his hands up.

One of the henchmen was standing there grinning gap-toothed, a beer mug in one hand and a crossbow in the other. That was the nuisance of crossbows. Unlike firearms you couldn't hear them because there was no match to hiss.

"Ha ha!" said the henchman, "Got yer." He took a pull of beer from his mug and waved the crossbow slightly. "Wotchoo doin 'ere, yor sposed to be watchin ve coach."

Dodd paused for a moment, completely mystified then said as near to London-talk as he could get, "Ah wis 'opin to find booze."

It didn't work. The man's eyes narrowed so Dodd gave up on subtlety and kicked him as hard as he could in balls, hoping he wasn't aiming the crossbow straight. The man's eyes crossed, he slowly started to crumple up. Dodd's hand closed on the crossbow and took it off him to find the thing wasn't properly loaded and the bolt had stuck fast. There were too many men backing the black-bearded man in the common room, so Dodd changed his plan.

He ran back through the kitchen where the kitchen boy was methodically helping himself to meat hanging up in a larder while the spit dog yipped excitedly. He grabbed the boy by the ear. "Ah tellt ye to run, now run!" he growled and propelled the boy out the door in front of him, followed by the spit dog, still yelping.

The boy ran across the courtyard, slammed open the gate, and disappeared into the alley. The tied-up goats set up a loud bleating and the chickens clucked. Dodd sprinted round the side of the lean-to, found a water barrel, and climbed up it onto the slippery wooden-shingled roof.

He watched with interest, counting under his breath, as a stream of broad men in jacks came rushing into the yard, across it and through the gate, followed by the black bearded man who was pointing with his sword and shouting furiously as he hobbled after.

Wishing again, pointlessly, for Barnabus who would have been very useful with his throwing daggers, Dodd stayed as flat as he could and listened for the sounds to die down. Then he climbed up a little to a balcony, hearing the whispering and giggling of the urchins down in the yard.

It was a struggle to get over the rail thanks to the stupid stuffed hose he was wearing. He tried the door to the best bedroom but it was locked. He used his dagger to attack the hinges of the window shutters where the wood was old and a moment later after some stealthy cracking, managed to lever the shutter back and off, leaving a space large enough for him to climb through and into the empty bedroom. He hoped. He held the useless crossbow out and waited for the shout and scrape of steel but there was no sound of breathing in the room.

The corridor was also empty. Dodd clattered down the stairs with his sword in his right and the crossbow in his left, and came upon a fascinating picture.

Two men must have been left to guard Carey but they were both in crumpled heaps on the floor. Marlowe and Carey were standing over them. Carey looked up as Dodd came down the stairs, slightly breathless no doubt because of the tightness of his doublet.

Carey beamed at Dodd. "Excellent, Sergeant, I told Kit you wouldn't be long."

Dodd crushed the impulse to grin back like some court ninny. They were very far from being safe and in fact he could smell smoke already. He went over and checked the men on the floor and was happy to find a pouch of quarrels on one of them, which he took. He then carefully discharged the crossbow in his hands which popped the bent bolt out onto the floor, put his toe in the stirrup, rebent the bow and hooked it so he could slot in a new bolt. Much happier, he shook his head at Carey and Marlowe's move for the kitchen and instead went straight for the main entrance to the inn where the coachman was sitting on the coach driving seat, looking worried.

Dodd pointed the crossbow at him and he froze and sat back down again.

"Ay," said Dodd. "Ye didna see nothing."

The coachman nodded wildly. Carey and Marlowe looked at each other.

"Shall we steal the coach?" asked Marlowe, giggling slightly.

Dodd sighed. This was a serious business, not a boy's escapade. "Ah wouldnae advise it," he said coldly.

Carey looked over his shoulder. "Somerset House," he said.

They bunched together and headed up to Ludgate and then left into Fleet Street over the Fleet Bridge that stank to high heaven. Dodd's eyes were itching with tiredness.

Behind them were heavy running feet and shouts. After one glance to see the black-bearded man's henchmen coming after them in a close-packed crowd and several crossbows being raised, all three of them picked up their heels and sprinted along the Fleet, running like hell for Somerset House or one of the little alleys leading into the Whitefriars if necessary. After about half a minute of serious running, Dodd was starting to feel breathless and tightchested. A crossbow twanged and he ducked instinctively, was outraged to see Marlowe drawing ahead of him as they pounded up the cobbles and wondered, in some cranny of his skull which was not in a panic, what had happened to his wind?

There was the rumble of coach wheels on the cobbles behind him, changing to scraping as they came onto the rutted muddy disgrace of the Strand. He risked a glance over his shoulder to see the black coach hammering after them, the horses nearly at the gallop, then the sound of clattering as it turned to avoid the margins of the dungheap. There was a crack and an ear-jangling crunch and crash as the wheels on one side of the coach tilted inwards and fell off. The coach toppled over sideways in a heap as the coachman leaped desperately for safety and landed on a soft pile of rotten marrows. Now that was a highly satisfying sound. Dodd had taken a great dislike to that coach and he risked another glance to see it in its splintered ruin, half on the dungheap with the coachman climbing groggily out from the muck. The horses had come to a stop with their traces trailing and were eating a London wife's herbal windowsill.

Then he heard another cry and squinted ahead and his heart sank: up ahead was another large body of men jogging towards them, torches held high. Dodd immediately swerved left to the awning of the Cock Tavern and eyed the red-painted shutters with a view to climbing them for a good vantage on the roof. Marlowe too dodged behind a stone conduit. Carey however picked up speed and kept running forward.

"Mr. Bellamy!" he yelled. "Don't shoot…"

There was a shout and the group of men stopped, Carey was among them, and Dodd heard his voice carolling, "How very good to see you."

"Likewise sir," said Bellamy, and Dodd recognised the voice of Hunsdon's deputy steward.

Men in Berwick jacks and black and yellow livery were fanning out into the street to block it. They raised an interesting variety of weapons. The black-bearded man's henchmen came to a halt and the two parties stared at each other across a gap of a hundred yards.

Dodd decided he fancied some height, so despite his lack of breath, he swung himself up on the lattices and hoisted himself to the join with another shingled roof, prayed devoutly that it wouldn't collapse nor slip, and eased himself to a squatting position at the corner. Trying to control his ridiculous puffing, he aimed his crossbow carefully for the black-bearded man. Am I ill, Dodd wondered anxiously, och God, I must be. His heart was pounding, his breath so short that his hands wobbled on the stock of the bow, and he couldn't get a clean shot. Ah Jesu, maybe it was plague?

Marlowe had broken from the shelter of his conduit for the Hunsdon liverymen, and he and Carey were now invisible in the mass of them. There was a thud of hooves on the mud behind the Hunsdon party and two horses skidded to a halt. The foremost was being ridden by a broad grey-haired man in clothes that glinted with gold brocade.

The black-bearded pursuivant was staring in rage and horror, himself panting and leaning on his sword. His mob of bully-boys were close-packed and yet he had a gap around him Dodd noted, which would be helpful for a killing shot if only his own breathing would quiet.

Lord Hunsdon sent his horse through his men who parted for him and up alongside the black-bearded man. He had his white staff of office as the Queen's Chamberlain under his arm.

"What the devil do you think you're playing at, Mr. Topcliffe? What is the meaning of this outrage?" rumbled Carey's father.

Topcliffe's face drained of blood, making his face and beard more like a balladsheet woodcut than ever. He had forgotten to dye his eyebrows which were grey. The mouth moved but no words came out. Dodd squinted in the darkness and saw that the rider of the second horse was his puny lawyer, riding a little better than he ran at least.

"I am…arresting…some notable Papist priests," panted Topcliffe's voice in a blustering tone.

"You were attempting to arrest *me*, Mr. Topcliffe, with no warrant," called Carey's voice reproachfully.

"If you had nothing to hide, why did you run?" said Topcliffe insinuatingly. "My lord, it's a wise father that knows all his son may…"

"I had a fancy to keep my balls," called Carey, "I've got more use for 'em than Papist priests do. Or you."

"My lord, the Queen's grace must be protected from the Jesuitical plots…"

"Good God almighty," said Hunsdon in disgust. "Mr. Topcliffe, shut up. You may not be aware of it but my youngest son is possibly the least likely candidate for the Roman Catholic priesthood since the death of my revered and worshipful natural father, King Henry the Eighth of that name. And my half-sister, Her Majesty the Queen, knows it and has a considerable liking to him."

There was a silence in which Dodd could actually hear Topcliffe swallowing stickily.

"A…a…mistake, my lord," stammered Topcliffe, "A case of… mistaken identity. We are seeking one Father Gerard who is… well-known…to go about dressed as a gentleman."

"Is he?" said Hunsdon, heavily. "My lord Burghley told me the man was in Worcestershire."

"Quite so," said Topcliffe, "We had the word of an informant…clearly wrong."

"Clearly."

"I shall reprimand him. Many…many apologies, my lord, Sir Robert," gabbled Topcliffe, "I…I shall continue the search."

"Excellent."

Out of sight there was a loud clanging of a bell and the shout of fire at the Mermaid. Dodd winced. He had forgotten about that. Ah well, it would teach the innkeeper better manners than to help set up ambushes for his regulars.

Topcliffe turned and walked with some dignity towards Ludgate Hill, past the wreckage of Heneage's expensive coach. His men gathered round him but the coachman seemed to have run.

Carey was at his father's stirrup, talking fast, Marlowe not far behind. Dodd saw the flash of Hunsdon's teeth as he sat back in the saddle and grinned.

"Sergeant Dodd?" called Lord Hunsdon, looking around him. The City Watch shambled into view at last, with their lanterns, rattle, and bells, cautiously peering around to make sure that the trouble was truly over. One of them went over to the coach and picked up a broken bit of door, tutting.

"Ay," said Dodd, raising an arm, "up here, my lord."

Hunsdon contemplated him for a second, taking in the crossbow in his right hand.

"There you are, of course," he said. "By God, I do like having a Dodd on my side again."

He nodded at Carey who came over with a self-satisfied look on his face to help Dodd down from his narrow perch.

The Watch wandered away again with a couple of shillings each to help them forget all about the exciting events they had just missed and Hunsdon's small war party went back in the direction of Somerset House. The local urchins, whores, and beggars were already gathered around the coach looting it for firewood, saleable bits of metal, cushions, and leather. By the morning it would probably be completely gone. Dodd allowed himself a satisfied smile. One to me, he thought.

"Your mother was furious when Mr. Enys brought the news," Hunsdon said conversationally as Carey walked at his stirrup.

"Oh Jesu."

Hunsdon was thoughtful. "Very sharp-tempered she is at the moment, my lady wife," he rumbled. "Took a lot to stop her coming out with me along with her entire crew of Cornish cut-throats."

"Thank you, sir," said Carey with feeling.

"Don't thank me, lad, I can't have your mother loose in London in the temper she's in. Richard Tregian is still…unaccounted for."

Dodd heard the intake of breath from the lawyer whose horse was right behind him and gave the man a sharp look. Enys caught this and smiled a sickly smile.

Somerset House was ablaze with torches, intense activity on the boat-landing at the end of the gardens. Lady Hunsdon was standing in the doorway to the marbled hall, fists on her hips and two Cornishmen on either side of her with torches. She looked terrifying.

Carey stepped up to her swiftly and bowed. "Madam," he began, but his mother stood on her tiptoes and boxed his ears violently.

"That's for falling into a trap as clear as the nose on your face," shouted Lady Hunsdon while Carey scuttled crabwise away from the backswing. "What were you using for brains, boy?"

"Mother!" he roared, ducking another blow. Lord Hunsdon had dismounted and was very busy thanking and dismissing his men, half of whom were trying not to grin.

Lady Hunsdon swung on Marlowe who was watching the scene between mother and son with a supercilious expression. "As for you, you goddamn sodomite, how dare you come into my lord's house after what you…"

Carey had edged closer to his enraged mother, caught her elbow, and was whispering urgently into her ear. Lady Hunsdon listened and her jaw set.

"Is that a fact?" she sniffed, "Well, I'll leave it for now if my son says you helped him, but you watch out, boy." This was snarled at Marlowe. "If you try one of your games, I'll have you. I don't like you nor I don't trust you."

Marlowe bowed in his superior way. "Likewise, madame, I'm sure."

Lady Hunsdon paused and like a witch shape-shifting was suddenly the haughty Court lady again. "Oh, very smart, aren't we, young Mr. Marlowe, who spied for Walsingham all those years for money and a crumb of silence about his boy punks and now thinks Heneage and Topcliffe are his friends. Pah!"

She turned her back on him with the finality of an offended lioness and hooked her arm through Hunsdon's.

"Mr. Bellamy, see to Mr. Marlowe and Mr. Enys, they will be our guests…" said Hunsdon.

Enys was pale again and came anxiously up to Hunsdon. "Sir, my lord, I…I must get back to my chambers in case…"

"Nobody is leaving Somerset House until the morning," said Hunsdon flatly. "As for your chambers, Mr. Enys, I think you can assume that they will be ransacked tonight and there is nothing whatever you could do about it even if you were there. Best not to be there."

Enys looked horrified. "But…"

"Mr. Enys," said Lady Hunsdon, "You are, I fear, in a war with Heneage and his men. If you weren't prepared for it, you shouldn't have got into it."

Enys said nothing as the Hunsdons processed stately fashion up the stairs, lit on their way by servants carrying candles.

Enys had gone meekly to his bedchamber and Carey and Dodd were sitting up in the Lesser Parlour over a flagon of brandywine and a pile of papers, the contents of the bag Carey had raided out of Heneage's house earlier. Carey had set up as clerk with clean paper and an ink bottle and pens, plus a large candelabra of expensive wax candles.

"Walsingham had me taught something of this art by Thomas Phelippes when I was in Scotland with him all those years ago," said Carey picking up a piece of paper covered in code and putting it neatly to one side. "Of course, at the time I had no idea why…" He laughed softly for a while as if recalling a very great joke. Another piece of paper, this time mostly in ordinary writing, went to a different pile. A third piece, all over with numbers except for a sequence of letters at the top, and a third pile begun.

Dodd watched the piles grow with Carey setting a few letters aside, wondering what was nagging him, why he was sure he had forgotten something.

"Now then," said Carey, picking up the first of the letters in clear and taking a gulp of brandywine. He held it up against the light of the candles, shook his head and then put it back in the bag. Several more letters followed.

"What are ye looking for, sir?" Dodd asked at last, thinking about another pipe but then deciding against it. He didn't like the way his chest had felt tight when he ran and it couldn't be blamed on his doublet because he had undone the buttons in what Carey called the melancholik style. He poured himself brandywine instead.

"Oh…I'm not sure. Something to do with Cornwall. Something about Richard Tregian or Harry Dowling or whoever the poor soul in the Thames may be."

"Ay sir, but they're both dead. What's the point?"

"Good question." Carey had taken off his kid gloves the better to handle the papers, and he now put up an elegant but nailless finger. "Imprimis, Richard Tregian was judicially killed in the place of another man—the Jesuit called Fr. Jackson. It's certainly an alias. So where is Fr. Jackson? Did he escape? Did he turn his coat and then get released? In which case why go through all the palaver of having Tregian hanged, drawn, and quartered in his place. Normally when a Jesuit turns, the Cecils trumpet it abroad so why hide this one so lethally? And why Tregian? He's a respectable gentleman, even if he is Cornish. If you were going to murder the man, you would be better advised to slit his throat in an alley and blame it on a footpad, as you pointed out before. It's not as though there's a shortage of them in London."

"Ay sir, though I've not been troubled recently."

Carey grinned. "No, Dodd, good news like you gets out quickly."

"Ay," said Dodd, wondering if this was a compliment.

"Secundus, we have a corpse from the Thames that might be Mrs. Briscoe's brother or not, yet nobody else has claimed yet despite my father having had the announcement cried at Westminster and in the City and offering a reward for information."

Dodd nodded.

"There's something odd about the corpse though I can't place it." Carey frowned and stared into the fire in the fireplace for a moment. "Very irritating."

"Ay," said Dodd.

"Tertius, and possibly not connected at all with any of this, we have Enys who mysteriously turns up and offers to be our lawyer just when we need one. He has a Cornish name. His brother, he says, has disappeared and must have gone at roughly the same time as the corpse wound up in the Thames, but he says the dead man isn't his brother."

Dodd thought back to that. "Ay sir, but he didnae say he didn't know the man."

Carey nodded. "No, he didn't, did he? Hm." He paused and put up a fourth finger, this one still with its nail. "And item, we have mysterious land-deals happening in Cornwall, a Godforsaken place good for nothing but tin-mining, wrecking, and piracy. My mother likes it there, but I do not see the likes of the Earl of Southampton going and farming sheep or mining tin for that matter. It's too far from London. Riding post and hoping not to be waylaid on Bodmin Moor, you'd feel pleased if it only took you three days to get there. If they had post houses in Cornwall, which they haven't. A ship is a better option, frankly. More comfortable, the Cornish probably won't rob you or wreck you if you're sailing in an English ship, and it only takes a week."

He paused, thoughtfully and put up the thumb. "And item, of course, we have my esteemed lady mother's interest in the whole matter which I frankly find very worrying. As does my father. The connection to our family of Richard Tregian is close enough to be dangerous under the wrong circumstances. Also the connection to my Lady Widdrington's family—her father is the Trevannion who holds Caerhays Castle."

Dodd nodded politely. It always got back to Lady Widdrington somehow.

Carey blinked at his spread fingers, then closed them into a fist. "Topcliffe running about the city with an armed band of men. My father here instead of going back to Oxford where the Queen still is—though she ought to be coming back to London in October despite the plague. She'll probably stay in one of the outer palaces like Nonesuch or Greenwich, well away from the city."

"Why did the judge ask about court faction?" Dodd asked from idle curiosity. It had been like the question a sensible juror would ask on the Borders—is there a feud here? And then take tactfully sick if there was.

"Good question. Why did he? What's he heard about, or been told."

He looked down at the pile of papers. "We'll have to give these back at some stage and I don't have time to copy them all out."

For some reason that was the thing that tripped Dodd's memory. He fumbled in his belt pouch and brought out the folded pieces of paper he had found wedged behind the bookshelf in Tregian's chamber at the inn. He explained where it had come from as Carey passed the paper under his nose, smiled, and held it near the candle. Soon the brown numbers appeared written in orange juice and Carey had Dodd calling them out while he copied them out carefully. All were numbers except for a letter at the bottom which Dodd read out as a letter A, upside down.

As Carey dipped his pen and wrote them down, he paused. "Hang on," he said, and pulled one of the other papers towards him. Two of them were also covered with groups of numbers and the same letter at the top. An A, upside down.

Immediately he dipped his pen and started copying them out as well, ending with three sheets of paper entirely covered with groups of numbers.

"D'ye know what they say, sir?" Dodd asked, fascinated.

"No, not yet. But I know how they've been coded," said Carey with satisfaction, wiping off his pen and sharpening the nib.

"Ay?" said Dodd, very unwilling to admit how little he knew about codes and ciphers.

"Well, you see, these are just number substitution codes—where you write out the alphabet and then replace each letter with a number. There's two ways of doing it. Either you do it in a pattern—say call A a 1, B 2 and so on, or you do it at hazard where A is 23 and B is 4 or whatever. Follow me?"

"Ay," said Dodd cautiously. It seemed a lot of work to be sure nobody could read what you wrote—why write it down at all then?

"Of course the random one is better than the one in a pattern because believe me, someone skilled in the art like Mr. Phelippes or Mr. Anriques can find a pattern like that in a matter of minutes and then they can read all the correspondance you think is so secret—that's what happened with the Queen of Scots."

"Ay," said Dodd, who felt he was now on more familiar ground. Hadn't he gone into town with his father and all his brothers and sisters to have a good gawk at her while she was being kept at Carlisle? Carey had told him before how Walsingham had trapped her, twenty years later.

"Now if you do it randomly, of course, you have to make sure everyone you write to has the key. That's dangerous as well—you could lose it or your enemies could capture it. A good codebreaker can break that one as well if you've written enough or been careless."

Dodd looked at the uncommunicative numbers. Surely Carey couldn't do something like that?

"I know some of the common patterns used so when I have the time I can try a few out on it. And we can try and find a code book. Do you think you could go back and search Tregian's room again?"

"Nay sir, I dinna think so. It's likely got a new man in it."

"Hm. It might be worth going and charming mine host for it. Failing a code book I'm just going to have to try and break the bloody thing." Carey puffed a sigh out. "God, I wish I'd paid more attention to my lessons with Mr. Phelippes instead of chasing Scottish ladies."

Dodd grunted. That was no surprise.

Dodd looked again at the numbers and at the letters at the start. "A," he said. "Is that the codebook?"

"Could be. And of course the really interesting point is what is a ciphered letter in invisible ink which comes from either Topcliffe or Heneage—or perhaps is intended for them—doing in Richard Tregian's chamber? Especially if he's going to end up being executed by them."

Carey blinked at the copies and yawned cavernously. "We'll have a try at possibilities tomorrow," he said, "I'm going to bed."

thursday 14th september 1592, dawn.

Dodd was woken by a hammering on the door. He woke up fully to find himself at the door in his shirt with his sword drawn and raised to strike whoever it was had just ruined a very fine dream about Janet. Carey's voice rang out.

"Come on, Sergeant Dodd, get your arse out of bed, the sun's nearly up…"

From the sound of it Carey too was in a temper and as usual full of energy and enterprise at a time when more decent folk were still asleep. The London sky had barely started to pale. Dodd lowered his sword regretfully, unbolted the door, put the sword on the bed and started assembling the daft confection of cloth he had to wear in this Godforsaken hell hole. He refused to let a man help him with it which was why it always took him so long, especially with it happening in the morning and all. He looked longingly at his nice comfy homespun suit Janet had woven for him and that he had been so proud of when he first came to London. At least he had to admit that he was the target of a lot fewer London coney-catchers when he wasn't wearing it.

There was another bang of fist on panelling. Shrugging the braces over his shoulders and bending to pull his boots on, he called, "It's no' locked," and Carey burst through the door looking furious.

"That bloody lawyer's bolted," he snarled at Dodd, who just sighed.

"Ay, o'course."

"Why of course?"

"Anybody could see he wis hiding something."

"Course he was, he's a lawyer, but why'd he bolt?" Dodd said nothing and Carey started to pace up and down after finding that the wine flagon was empty. "Steward says he went to his bed-chamber last night and this morning there's no sign of him at all."

Dodd was struggling into his doublet. "Nae doot of it, he's out of London and heading for his ain country," he said wistfully because it was what he would have done.

"May I remind you, Sergeant, that we have to appear in Court this morning in order to swear out a bill against Heneage in his absence. For that we need a lawyer and Enys' the only one we've got."

Dodd sighed again, fumbling with his multiple buttons. Carey came over impatiently and twitched it into place on Dodd's shoulders, then briskly started rebuttoning. He was, inevitably, immaculate in black velvet and brocade, though his breath was as bad as a dog's.

"So let's get over to the Temple and see if we can find the blasted man before he leaves."

"He'd go back there first would he?" Dodd said, wondering if even a lawyer could be so stupid.

"Course he would, you could see how upset he was about it being ransacked. Probably got a little treasure trove of fees and bribes there."

"Ay sir, but I wouldnae…"

"He's an idiot. That's where he'll be," said Carey looking distinctly furtive as he stepped into the corridor. "Come on, hurry up before my lady mother wakes and insists on coming too."

Despite not having had any breakfast or small beer to wake him up, Dodd's mouth turned down with the effort of not laughing at Carey's tone of voice when speaking of his mother. Dodd rather liked the old lady, but he could see how she was a terrible trial to her sons.

The steward had orders that Carey was not to stir without a bodyguard—no doubt by order of Lady Hunsdon, and equally doubtless to keep him from leaping into trouble as well as protecting him in case trouble should come to find him.

After considerable argument they went out with two Berwickmen in buff coats and Shakespeare. According to him Marlowe wasn't up yet which was perfectly normal. Or had he shinned out of the window too, Dodd wondered.

"His window overlooks the courtyard and his door is locked," Shakespeare said primly in answer to Carey's suspicious look. "I have seen to it that he has paper, pens and ink, food, booze, and tobacco any time he cares to call for them. He'll be no trouble, trust me. He will know that Topcliffe will wait until he shows his nose and then arrest him for thwarting the ambush in the Mermaid at Sir Robert's urging."

Which Marlowe himself had set up by sending the potboy to Topcliffe and paying the roaring boys earlier to make their feint attack on Fleet Street. What a fool the poet was, Dodd thought. Heneage must have ordered him to do it as soon as the clerk of the court warned him to avoid Carey's arrest. Mind, it must have been fun to watch him, he would have been enraged. Perhaps that was why Marlowe had gone along with it.

They found Enys' chambers by asking around. It was at the very top of a tottering building facing a dilapidated courtyard that had apparently just been bought by the Earl of Essex. They left Shakespeare and the Berwickmen in the courtyard and went up. At the top of the rickety stairs was a door that had plainly been broken into and then set back carefully in place later. Carey started by knocking politely. After a long wait there was a sound from inside. Carey hammered on the wall next to it.

"Mr. Enys," he bellowed. "Enys, God damn your eyes, open up!"

"One moment," came the cry. They waited. Dodd went to the small window on the landing and peered out at the Berwickmen who were standing around looking bored. Shakespeare was sitting on a mounting block scribbling in his notebook. At last there was the sound of furniture being scraped back and a broken panel was pulled away. A woman peered through the gap. In the dim light they could see there was something wrong with her face as well as her eyes being swollen with tears.

"Is Mr. Enys within, mistress?" asked Carey, moderating his tone a little.

The woman sniffled and shook her head. "He was away from home last night and he came back in a hurry very early this morning and then was away again, he said, to see that Mr. Heneage's bill was fouled in his absence as quickly as possible."

Carey looked taken aback. "Oh. Westminster?"

"So he said."

"Well, Mrs. Enys…"

"No sir, Mr. Enys is my brother. My name is Mrs. Morgan."

Carey paused. "Ah? Really? My mother's family name is Morgan…I wonder if there's a connection."

"I don't know, sir. My husband's cousin Henry Morgan was a well-known…er…sea trader."

"Can we come in?"

For answer the woman started removing a piece of door. Dodd and Carey helped her and entered Enys' chambers.

There were two rooms visible. In the light from the small window they could see that the smallpox had made as bad a mess of her face as it had of her brother's. She was quite a tall woman, a little stooped, in a plain grey wool kirtle and doublet bodice, with her hair covered by a linen cap that was crooked. Carey bowed to her and she curtseyed.

"I'm sorry not to be able to offer you anything, sir, but… you can see…"

She waved a hand helplessly. Carey took a deep breath.

"Mrs. Morgan, I am Sir Robert Carey, and this is Sergeant Henry Dodd, your brother's client."

"Yes, my brother has told me about you."

"Can you tell us what happened, mistress?"

Mrs. Morgan bit her lip and shut her eyes tight. "They came and battered the door in and they said if I stood facing the wall and did not scream they wouldn't hurt me."

"They kept their promise?"

She shrugged. "Yes sir."

It was easy to recognise the handiwork of pursuivants. Every chest had been upended, every book opened and dropped on the floor, the great bed and the truckle in the bedroom with the curtains ripped and the mattress slashed so that wadding bled out of it.

Carey sighed. "Did they get all the papers?"

"I expect so, sir," said Mrs. Morgan. "They took every piece of paper they could find, even things that were nothing to do with your case."

"Who were they?"

"They had their cloaks muffled over their faces and their hats pulled down. I didn't know them. My brother said he needed to consult some books at his Inn and then he felt he could apply for a judgement immediately. Is there anything else I may help you with, sir, as I have a great deal to do?"

It was a clear, though polite, invitation to leave. Carey looked at the woman seriously, not seeming put off as Dodd was by the pock scars disfiguring her face.

"I now understand why Enys was reluctant to stay at my father's house last night. He should have mentioned you."

The woman said nothing and curtseyed.

"Would you feel safer in Somerset House under my father's shelter and protection, mistress?"

Mrs. Morgan curtseyed again.

"I would prefer to stay here. There's…a lot to do." She coloured under Carey's gaze and stepped away from the light.

"Are you sure?"

"Yes sir. Thank you for your offer."

Carey shook his head. "As you wish, mistress. If you change your mind simply come to my father's house on the Strand and tell the porter that I sent you."

She nodded and looked at the ground until they left.

They went in silence down to the Temple steps and waited an unconscionable time for a boat. Just as one finally rowed languidly towards the boat landing where Carey was pacing up and down impatiently checking the sun and the tide every minute, there was a clatter of boots behind them and Enys appeared, running down the steps towards them, holding his sword awkwardly up and away from his legs.

"Ah, Mr. Enys," said Carey, "there was I thinking you might have left town?"

Enys was puffing and wheezing alarmingly. He shook his head, unable to speak.

They all got in the boat with the Berwickers and Shakespeare looking as if they were prepared for a boring day. Soon the boatman and his son were rowing upstream to Westminster. Once Enys had got his breath back, Carey looked at him consideringly.

"Why didn't you mention Mrs. Morgan to us last night?" he asked.

"Um…" Enys looked panicky.

"Mr. Enys," said Carey pompously, "what my mother said is true. We are in a war with Heneage and Topcliffe, but luckily my father has the capacity to protect his counsellors and servants and friends at the moment. He would have sent men to guard your chambers or bring your sister to safety if you had said something…"

Enys coloured red. "I know, sir. I am afraid I was in a panic. I…my sister is very shy and prefers not to be seen in public, or at all."

"She has Lady Sidney's malady."

"I beg your pardon?"

"My Lady Sidney—Sir Philip's sister, you know—caught the smallpox whilst nursing the Queen when she had it and took it very much worse than Her Majesty. She was a very beautiful lady before but now considers herself hideous and never comes to Court. She meets with poets and writers at her house which she refuses to leave. And yet, we would all delight to see her at Court for never was a kinder nor wittier lady. Even the Queen, who dislikes any kind of ugliness, has often said how she misses her."

Enys was an even darker red.

"I…"

"No one can convince Lady Sidney that nobody is laughing at her and that if anyone should dare to laugh an hundred swords would be drawn in her defence, including mine. I have told her so myself but she only smiles sadly and shakes her head," said Carey, tilting into the romantic flourishing speech of the court. "And so we are deprived of the company of the finest jewel that could adorn any court, saving the Queen's blessed Majesty, a woman of intellect and discretion and wit, all because she fancies a few scars make her hideous."

Enys seemed unable to speak. He coughed a couple of times and mopped his face with his hankerchief. Shakespeare was staring at him with interest but he seemed not to notice.

"I'm afraid, sir, my sister is not of so high blood as my lady Sidney," he said at last, his voice husky. "And all…er…all she ever wanted was to marry her sweetheart and bear his children."

Carey nodded. Enys stared out over the river.

"Three years ago I heard that my best friend that had married my sister had taken the smallpox," he was almost whispering as if he had difficulty getting breath to speak even slowly. "He…I posted down to Cornwall when I heard and found him dead and buried and his two children sickening. After they died my sister took sick and so I nursed her for I would not bring any other into that house of ill fortune to do it. Then when she recovered, I took sick of it as well and so turn and turnabout she nursed me. We lived, barely, hence we have such similar scars, but my sister says…No one cares how ugly a man be, so he be rich enough and kindly, but for a woman to lose her complexion and her looks is an end to all marrying. And so, since her jointure was small and her husband's land reverted to his brother on the death of his issue, we shut up the house in Cornwall and came to London together to try if the law would make our fortunes."

Carey nodded. "Her Majesty says that Lady Sidney's scars are as much honours of battle as any gallant's sword cuts. And so I think yours and your sister's must be too."

Enys inclined his head at the compliment, then turned aside to stare over the water again. "My apologies, sir, but I hate to remember that year."

Carey and Dodd left him to it. The tale was common enough, Dodd thought, but hit each person it happened to as rawly as if no one else had ever caught smallpox. He might catch it himself and die with his face turned to a great clot of blood as the blisters burst—though they said that when the blisters came out you were on the mend so long as none of the blisters turned sick. That was why they tied your hands to the bedposts so you wouldn't scratch.

Dodd shuddered and trailed his fingers in the waters. Fish rose to him from the depths and he wished vaguely for a fishing rod.

Westminster steps was again clotted with lawyers in their black robes, Enys dug his own robe out of a drawstring bag of fashionable blue brocade and slung it round his shoulders. At once the transformation happened; he seemed to relax and settle as if he had put on a jack and helmet and was waiting for the fight to begin.

"Did they get all the papers?" Carey asked him.

Enys smiled for the first time, even if lopsidedly. "No sir, not all." He scrambled to get out of the boat and nearly fell in the Thames again when his sword got between his legs. Dodd rolled his eyes regretfully. God preserve him from ever having to take Enys into a real fight.

In the din and confusion of Westminster Hall they found no trace of Heneage appearing to answer their plea.

"Calling Mr. Enys in the matter of Sergeant Dodd versus Mr. Vice Chamberlain Heneage et aliter," shouted one of the court staff.

Once again they lined up in front of Mr. Justice Whitehead who scowled at them from under his coif.

"Mr. Enys?"

"Yes, my lord."

"I regret to inform you," said the judge in English, leafing through the papers before him with the expression of one skinning decayed rats, "that Mr. Heneage's case has been transferred under the Queen's Prerogative to the court of one of my brother justices and has been adjourned sine die. He has seen fit to rescind all warrants of pillatus on Mr. Heneage and all and any co-defendants. "

Enys sighed.

"What?!" shouted Carey. "God damn it!"

Dodd's hand went to his swordhilt and his face set into what his men would have recognised as his killing face.

"Mr. Enys" snapped the judge, "be so good as to inform your clients that if I hear any more blasphemous disrespect from them, I shall have them committed for contempt of court."

Both Carey and Dodd subsided. It seemed that the only one who was unsurprised was Enys who was looking exceedingly cynical.

"Which honourable judge was it?"

"Mr. Justice Howell," said the judge with a sour expression.

Enys nodded. "Thank you, my lord,"

"By the way," said the judge, "for completeness, I have had copies made of the papers filed this morning under the Queen's prerogative by a Mr. Evesham. I believe he is the clerk to Sir Robert Cecil." He leaned over and gave a sheaf of papers to Enys who took them with an expression of cautious surprise. Carey's lips were formed into a soundless whistle.

"My lord," he said. "Sir Robert Cecil, Privy Councillor?"

"Yes," said the judge, glaring at Carey over his spectacles. Carey swept a magnificent bow.

"Then my apologies to you, my lord," he said, "for having unintentionally misled you yesterday. It seems that this *is* a matter of Court faction, a complication of which I was unaware."

The judge nodded and rubbed the margin of his beard with his thumb. "Quite so, Sir Robert."

"Thank you very much, my lord," said Carey, and led all three of them from the Hall. Behind them they heard Judge Whitehead's weary voice. "You again, Mr. Irvine. I hope you have the correct pleadings this time…"

Once again they needed a drink with even Enys accepting a small cup of aqua vitae. He was reading the papers he had been given very carefully, eyes narrowed, his lips moving as he reread some of the words.

Carey was cutting into a large steak and kidney pudding which was the ordinary for that day. "Well?" he said.

"The case has been adjourned sine die, which means indefinitely, for reasons good and sufficient to the Queen's Prerogative. That means both the civil and the criminal case. We can apply for a new court date but this will set the proceedings back by weeks…"

"Does the Queen no' like my case, then?" asked Dodd, wondering if he should leave the country immediately. Then he thought of something. "Ay, but how does she know about it? Is she no' still at Oxford?"

Carey looked thoughtful. "Yes, we only tried to arrest Heneage yesterday. I suppose he could have sent a message the forty odd miles to Oxford and back in the time, but the man would have had to ride post and ride through the night as well."

"Eighty miles. Ay," said Dodd, "ye could dae it if ye could see the Queen immediately…"

"No, the Queen will not have heard anything about it. These papers are from Sir Robert Cecil acting for Lord Burghley who, as Lord Chancellor and Lord Privy Seal, may wield the Queen's Prerogative during pleasure."

Carey nodded. "Hm. Interesting. I wonder…Hm. Must ask my father."

"Can I no' sue Heneage then?"

"You can continue with the litigation by requiring reasons for the adjournment and you can make representations to the Privy Council asking for the case to be heard in a different court," said

Enys, narrowing his eyes. "Obviously it would be ridiculous to take it in front of Mr. Justice Howell who is notoriously corrupt."

"So I get nae satisfaction?" said Dodd mournfully.

"Well, you might…" began Enys.

"I think I should go and talk to Her Majesty about this," said Carey, through a mouthful of kidney.

Dodd grunted and pushed away the rest of his pudding. He hadn't expected much justice, but he had allowed himself to hope he would get some down here in the foreign south. Ah well, serve him right for being a silly wee bairn about it. His face lengthened as he considered the matter.

Carey washed down the last of his meal with the reasonable beer and leaned back with his fingers drumming on the front of his doublet. "I wonder what the surnames are up to at the moment?" he said to Dodd.

Dodd shrugged. Early autumn, the horses and cattle fat, bad weather not set in yet, but the nights not long enough. The planning would be feverish.

"It's October and November they'll start at the reiving," he said, "when they've killed their pigs and calves. We've time yet."

"Wouldn't want to miss the fun," agreed Carey, who probably meant it, the idiot. "Well then, I think I'll find out about that corpse which annoyed my father. The inquest might not have happened yet—shall we go to the Board of Greencloth?"

The Board of Greencloth was held in a meeting room at the business end of the Palace of Whitehall, a short walk from Westminster Hall. Carey spoke gravely to the yeoman of the guard at the entrance and they were all three admitted to a wood-panelled room whose dusty glass windows let in very little light. The corpse itself was not present for which Dodd heartily thanked God, but there were several women there. One of them was Mrs. Briscoe, as round and pregnant as a bomb. Mr. Briscoe stood behind her looking nervous as if ready to catch her when she fell. Another was a grave looking lady in a dark cramoisie woollen kirtle with a doublet-bodice and small falling band. She had grey hair peeking under a white linen cap and black beaver hat, and a very firm jaw. Behind her stood a pale-faced young woman in dove grey furnished with a modest white ruff.

The men who served on the board filed into the room, led by Hunsdon who already looked bored and was carrying his white staff of office. The others were pouchy-faced and dully-dressed, men of business who ran the complex administration of the palace. A couple of them were distinctly green about the gills which might have been because they had gone to the crypt to view the body in question. Or it might have been the green baize cloth that covered the trestle table boards in front of them, a cloth which made some sense of the name of the Board. All of those waiting bowed to the members of the Board who sat down. One drank some of the wine in a flagon before him and took a little colour from it.

"We are here," intoned Hunsdon, "to enquire as to the probable identity and cause of death of the corpse found by Mistress Wentworth, Queen's Chamberer, at the Queen's Privy Steps. Have we all viewed it?"

Everyone nodded, one swallowed again. "I have had the body cried three times in the cities of Westminster and London. Has anyone any…"

The grey-haired woman stepped forward and curtseyed to Hunsdon. "My lord, I am here to claim the body which I have identified as Mr. John Jackson who went missing in London some three weeks ago."

Hunsdon's bushy eyebrows climbed his forehead. "Indeed, mistress. And you are?"

Carey was staring at the woman with his lips parted in a half-smile and his eyes narrowed. "Hm," he said, in a tone of great interest.

"His cousin, sir, Mrs. Sophia Merry, gentlewoman."

"Ah."

Mrs. Briscoe had a puzzled expression on her face, mixed with some relief. Hunsdon looked shrewdly at her. "And you, mistress? Have you anything to say?"

"Oh, ah." Mrs. Briscoe seemed confused at being addressed so courteously. "Um…I thought it was my bruvver, but I wasn't sure."

"You are willing to yield the body to Mrs. Merry?"

"Oh yes, my lord, if she's sure. I'm not, see. His face...Might not have been him." She looked down and frowned.

Mr. Briscoe put his arm across her shoulders and whispered in her ear. "My lord, may I sit down?" she asked in a whisper.

"Of course, mistress," said Hunsdon, no more eager to have her go into labour there and then than any man would be. One of the court attendants brought up a stool for her to sit on.

The rest of the inquest went quickly. No mention was made of the man's missing feet, all the attention was on the dagger-wound in the back and the missing joint of his finger. The Board of Greencloth found that Mr. John Jackson had been unlawfully killed or murdered by person or persons unknown and released the corpse into the keeping of his cousin Mrs. Sophia Merry.

They all bowed, the Board filed out of the room, and moments later they were in the little alley behind Scotland Yard where were the kilns that fired the staggering quantities of earthenware the palace kitchens used.

"Why did Poley say, which corpse?" Dodd asked, the thought having just struck him. "Do a lot of deid men wind up in the Thames?"

"Of course, it's very convenient if you don't care about the dead person coming back to haunt you—no questions and no shroud money. Dead children too, dead babies. He could have been joking."

"Or he could have known of more than one that he'd heard tell of or had to dae with."

"He could. I think I should ask the watermen." He stopped and frowned. "Except I can't because I haven't got Barnabus, damn it. They wouldn't talk to me and if they did they'd lie."

"Whit about the hangman?"

Carey smiled. "Hughes? Hm. I don't know if the watermen would talk to him, but I wonder if..."

He immediately changed direction and headed northwards. Dodd sighed and followed, whilst Enys looked bewildered.

"Verrah impulsive gentleman, is Sir Robert," said Dodd to the lawyer. "If ye'd like to tag along, I doot he'll notice now he's got a notion in his heid."

Enys nodded, rammed his robe and the papers back into his brocade bag, slung it over his shoulder, and hurried after them.

Mr. Hughes lived near his normal workplace at Tyburn, in a pretty cottage surrounded by the shanties of the poor. He had his doublet off and his sleeves up and was working in his garden, carefully bedding out winter cabbage.

Carey stood by the garden wall watching with interest. After a while Hughes looked up and took his statute cap off.

"Well sir," he said.

"Mr. Hughes, what would you say if I told you that the man you executed on Monday was the wrong one?"

"I'd say, they're all innocent if you listen to…"

"No, I meant, genuinely was the wrong man."

Hughes put his cap back on again slowly, narrowing his eyes.

"I'd be very surprised, sir." Something about his eyes said he wouldn't.

"You never get substitutions?

"Never, sir, though I suppose it could happen."

"What about the priest? Fr. Jackson?"

"What of him?" Now the eyes were wary although the mouth was innocent.

"It wasn't a priest, in fact it was a friend of my mother's called Richard Tregian."

Hughes came to the gate of the garden and opened it. "Come inside, sir," he said, with a bow. "Try some of my fruit wines."

The main room of the cottage was clean and swept though bare. They sat at the small wooden table that had a bench beside it and one stool and Hughes bustled into the storeroom to bring out a pottery flagon with a powerful smell of raspberries. He poured them a measure into horn cups, then sat down on his stool and braced his hands on his knees.

"Mr. Topcliffe brought him on the day. I had not seen him before to weigh him and calculate the drop, but Mr. Topcliffe said it was no matter, he was to be dead before he was drawn and gave me a purse for it as well."

"Did he speak?"

"No sir, he was in…er…no condition to speak, he had been given the manacles and then he had been waked for a while and could hardly hold his head up nor see straight."

"Waked?" asked Carey.

Hughes studied the floor. "He had been stopped from sleeping for many days, sir. It sends a man mad and kills him quicker than starving. Topcliffe prefers…other methods, but waking is a speciality of Mr. Vice Chamberlain."

Carey had a look of disgust on his face. "And what was the purpose of this waking?"

"Dunno sir, usually it's to make him talk so they'll let him sleep, but sometimes all they get is nonsense and vapours of the brain from the poisonous humours, sir."

There was a penetrating silence.

"And it don't show, sir," Hughes added, still staring at the floor, "So the mob don't get too sympathetic." More silence. Dodd realised that Carey was using it as a weapon. "See, if it's a Papist priest, I wouldn't mind sir, not since they sent the Armada—I heard tell they tried again this summer too, sir, only God saved us again. But this…I was worried, see, sir, cos he didn't look like a priest."

Carey blinked. "How could you tell?"

Hughes looked up with enthusiasm for the first time. "Oh it's remarkable what you can tell from a man's body and his clothes, if you know what to look for. See, your papish priest is always doing some sort of penance, see, and it shows. Like most of them have knobbly knees, see, from kneeling at their prayers."

Carey shook his head. "Could mean he's a courtier, I've got knobbly knees myself from kneeling in the Queen's presence and I'm no priest."

"True, sir. But it all goes together, you see. Or if he's been wearing a hair shirt, even if it's been taken from him, he's usually got a rash in the shape of a shirt on his body and often a lot of lice cos they don't take them off at all, sir. Or if he's been using the discipline—that's a little scourge with wires on it—you've got the marks of that—sort of criss-crossing scratches as if he's been rolling in a bramble bush, more on the shoulders 'cos they're easier to reach…"

Carey's head had gone up, as had Dodd's. They exchanged satisfied glances. Enys was staring at Hughes in some kind of mute horror.

"So you could see none of that on Richard Tregian?" asked Carey.

"No sir, nor he didn't say nothing except gibberish, but still Mr. Topcliffe would have him gagged—in case he made some kind of Papist sermon which Topcliffe couldn't allow, so he said."

"What kind of gibberish, Mr. Hughes?" asked Enys.

"Ahh…Funny words like Trenever and Lanner and Kergilliak, couldn't make head nor tale of them. Bedlam he was, far as I could tell. Slept like a baby while he was being dragged on a hurdle to Tyburn which is something you don't often see and gave the mob a bit of a turn, too."

Carey nodded.

"Course it's not my place to ask the likes of Richard Topcliffe the wheres and whyfores but I…I was troubled, sir."

"Why?"

"'Cos I asked to see the warrant and it was for Fr. Jackson right enough but it didn't look right."

"Why not?"

"The ink, sir. The warrant was nicely done in Secretary hand, but the places where Fr. Jackson's name went and the date, the ink was darker there, like they'd put it in later. They're not supposed to do that. Each death warrant is for each person, it's not respectful otherwise. You can't just have a general warrant with spaces to fill in to hang anyone you fancy…"

"No, indeed. Is there anything else you can tell us about Richard Topcliffe?"

"I don't like him, sir. Bring him to me when I'm working with a proper warrant for him and I won't charge you a penny for the rope nor nothing for my services."

"Do you often have cases like this?" Hughes paused, took breath to speak, paused again with reluctance.

"Not often, no sir," he admitted. "Mr. Secretary Walsingham did it a couple of times, but this year…"

Carey was scratching the patch on his chin where his goatee beard was regrowing. "More?" he asked.

Hughes seemed to remember something and stopped suddenly, gulped. "Couldn't say, sir," he mumbled.

Dodd sipped his raspberry wine and was stunned. He had never tasted anything so delicious in his life. He drank a little more and then finished the cup. Perhaps Janet was right in her planting of fruit bushes. He wondered if the blackberry wine Janet made for her gossips to drink and which he had always disdained as fit only for weak women was anything like this wonderful stuff. He had to concentrate to pay attention to what was going on.

Carey leaned across to Hughes. "Mr. Hughes," he said, "thank you, you've been very helpful. Would you mention to your brother in law that I appreciated his compliment and so did my father?"

Hughes nodded and stopped looking so frightened. "I'll mention it. He…er…he was wondering if you would be interested in a primero game at Three Cranes in the Vintry on Thursday evenings—he had heard you were quite a player."

Carey coughed modestly. "Oh, I wouldn't say that, Mr. Hughes, Her Majesty and Sir Walter Raleigh regularly beat me hollow."

Hughes' gaze was steady. "Perhaps you should try your luck at the Three Cranes, sir."

Carey smiled. "Perhaps I shall. Thank you, Mr. Hughes."

Now nothing would do but that they must walk south to Westminster to the crypt by the palace to take another look at the mysterious corpse with no feet, to see as Carey said if his knees were knobbly or not. When they arrived they found the crypt empty and no sign of a corpse, embalmed or stinking. Carey was annoyed.

"She collected the body already?" he demanded. "That's smart work."

"Gentleman's cousin, since the Board of Greencloth concluded killing by person or persons unknown. She collected him wiv a litter, sir, for immediate private burial," said the church-warden in charge of the crypt. "I have her name in the book here, sir." He was pointedly not opening the pages and finally Carey got the point in question and handed over a penny. The name and address at the sign of the Crowing Cock were neatly written there, and the woman had made her mark as well.

They took a boat to the Bridge and walked to the street by London Wall where there was no house with the sign of the Crowing Cock and nor had any of the neighbours ever heard of a Mrs. Sophia Merry.

Sitting on a bench at yet another alehouse, drinking beer, Carey was scowling with thought. Enys had said nothing what-ever the whole time but finally Carey noticed him again.

"Mr. Enys," he said irritably, "have you no cases to attend to?"

"No sir," said Enys humbly, "I told you. Mr. Heneage has seen to it my practice is almost extinct."

"Why are you tagging along?"

"I might be of some assistance…"

Dodd snorted. "It's allus better to let the women clear up after a raid on their own, otherwise they start sharpening their tongues on you for letting it happen."

Enys coloured up. "I had no intention of…"

"Did I say it was ye? I was speaking in general."

Enys steepled his fingers. "I will of course be on my way, as you are quite right, my sister has much to do. But I have been wondering about this matter."

Carey lifted his brows forbiddingly. "Oh yes?"

"The gentleman from the river was…not unknown to me. I told you, I think, that my family were church Papists. We went to church when we had to but in our hearts…in my parents hearts we still considered ourselves Catholics."

"What do you consider yourself now?"

"A good obedient subject of the Queen who worships where I am told," said Enys without a tremor. "I have no interest in the ambitions of any Bishop of Rome nor Spanish king to take this land under the colour of a crusade, except to do whatever I can to stop it."

Carey nodded approvingly. "And the man from the river?"

"I don't recall his name. I saw him a few years ago when he first came to Cornwall as a stranger and he was a man of many accomplishments. He was an alchemist and metal assayer and a mining engineer. He could devise wind pumps to take the water out of the tin workings that went deep. He was strong for the Catholic faith and I am not surprised if he was indeed a priest although I am surprised he should end in London for he said he hated the place." Carey waited but Enys spread his hands. "That's all I know, sir."

"The words that Tregian was babbling are place-names in Cornwall aren't they?"

"Yes, they are. None of them are in the tin-mining areas though as far as I know."

"Could there be gold there?"

Enys shrugged. "I…doubt it. They say gold breeds out of tin in some places so perhaps there is. I know there is gold in some places in Cornwall though never very much, not as much as in Wales or Ireland."

"Would this metal assayer be able to tell if there was gold?"

"Oh yes, sir, he could, and he knew how to take the gold out of the ore as well."

"Ah hah!" Carey looked pleased with himself.

"In the meantime, sirs, please excuse me. Sergeant Dodd has touched my conscience, I should not leave all to my sister who has no gossips in London to help her."

He rose, finished his beer, bowed to both of them, and walked away. Carey grinned at Dodd.

"Christ, I thought he'd never go. Now then, let's take a look at St Paul's."

Expecting Carey to spend the rest of the afternoon parading up and down Paul's Walk with other overdressed, overbred, underworked Court ninnies, Dodd was surprised and suspicious when Carey went to the Churchwarden's office instead and asked to see a register of churches in London both old and new. He studied it carefully for so long that Dodd got bored and began peering at the Cathedral treasure chest and wondering if it was full and if it was, would it be hard to get the lid off? It certainly looked securely locked and the iron strapping looked strong as well. Which argued that there was some good plate inside. It didn't move when he accidentally toed it with his boot.

They did go into the cathedral, but Carey went to the serving-man's pillar where the men who wanted work stood about near their notices pinned on the stone arch. He went straight up to the largest of them and asked him a question, only to receive a firm shake of the head. He asked all of them, all seemed to say no, and Carey rejoined Dodd looking irritated.

"Blast it," he said, "word's gone round obviously. None of them want to work for me."

Dodd thought it showed there was some sense amongst the servingmen of London.

"Or at least, none of them want to work for me in Carlisle," Carey amended, proving that Londoners were idiots.

Carey was now hurrying out of the main door and heading north across the city. Dodd hurried after him and noted that despite the rebuff of the servingmen, Carey was wearing an expression as smug as a bridegroom. On general principles, he loosened his sword.

They came to a very small lane not far from London Wall. It was one of the poorer places and was full of houses that seemed to have been patched together from pieces of something larger, some of them still clinging to the foundations made of large granite blocks.

People were passing up and down the street, and occasionally one of them would turn seemingly on impulse and head down an alleyway. Carey watched for a while and then headed for the alleyway himself. On the corner a crowing cockerel was chalked on the wall.

Dodd followed him full of forboding. The alleyway seemed to end, but in one corner were steps leading down and a boy sitting there. Carey smiled at him, spoke for a moment, and then beckoned Dodd to go down the steps with him.

It was a small crypt with an arched ceiling and thick plain pillars. At one end was a table laid with linens and six black candles about the coffin and a large number of people were standing about, talking quietly. In an alcove was a worn chipped figure of a man fighting what looked like a bull—perhaps some Papistical saint? Carey looked about him and took his hat off, so Dodd did the same.

"I don't like the looks of this," Carey said quietly to him. "I was expecting something quieter."

Dodd didn't like it either. He hated being in a place that only had one exit and he certainly was not planning to listen to a Papist mass which would be in solid foreign from start to finish and even more boring than a proper church service. Besides being treason outright. He saw that there was a door in the side of the opposite wall which was some comfort but...

There were some young men near the front with worryingly holy expressions, praying hard for something. Dodd didn't like the looks of that either. He threaded through the crowd, some of whom were praying rosaries of all dangerous treasonable things, and squinted at the door. Was it clear? He tested it gently but it didn't move.

Shaking his head, he went back up the steps and hurried round the corner to where he calculated the door should come out. It too was down some steps, but when he went to look at it, he realised it had been nailed shut and the nailheads were still shiny.

Dodd spine froze. Carey was in a stopped earth and so were all the other people. He looked about the street. He couldn't actually see Heneage's men but he knew they were there. If they had nailed this exit, probably they wouldn't be very interested in it, although there would be someone checking it soon to make sure. Somebody must have been following the grey-haired woman when she collected the body.

He leaned against the wall by the entrance and felt for his pipe, started filling the bowl with fingers that shook slightly. How Carey had found himself a secret Papist requiem mass he wasn't quite sure, but he was certain that it would be raided once it had properly got going and Carey would be the biggest prize.

Of course there was one possible option for Dodd. He could simply walk away, head for the Great North Road, and keep going until he got to his own tower where, by God, he would stay.

He puffed angrily. He wouldn't do it. Couldn't do it. Any more than he could have given Heneage the name he had wanted so badly the week before. Damn it, there was something wrong with his brains, that was sure.

He leaned against the door and looked about him at suspiciously little activity for a London alley and there were no plague-marked houses hereabouts to provide an excuse. Any minute now Heneage or Topcliffe and their human terriers would arrive and go into the stopped earth and...

Dodd smiled toothily, tapped out his pipe which was a pity because he hadn't finished it, spat in the bowl to cool it, and put it away in his belt pouch. He looked about casually again; nothing, not even someone visible at a window across the street. Ay well, no help for it then.

He hammered with his fist on the nailed-shut door in the slow, fear-inspiring way he had seen Lowther use on farmers who hadn't paid up their blackmail money.

"Open up," he roared, imitating a London voice as well as he could. "Open in the name of the Queen."

He banged again, roared again, and waited. There was absolute silence inside. As he sauntered around to the front alley again, he saw a couple of men in travelling cloaks, then a group of women talking merrily, then the young men who had been praying, then a mother with children. Everybody was walking as calmly and normally as if they had not just been about to commit treason.

"What the hell are you doing still here, Dodd," hissed a voice at his elbow. Dodd turned and saw Carey emerging from amongst the women with a pale and anxious-faced Letty Tregian clinging to his arm. Her brown hair was trailing from under her hat and she seemed to be on the point of collapse. "Heneage and his…"

"Ay well," said Dodd. "That were me."

Carey's eyes turned to points of ice. "If that was your idea of a joke…"

"Nay sir, I saw the escape door had been nailed shut and I thocht I'd get ahead of them a bit."

Carey frowned for a moment before his face split in a broad grin. He cupped his hand over Letty's confiding paw, slowed and backed under an awning so he could turn to look over his shoulder. A large contingent of buff-coated men were heading for the steps down to the crypt, at the back of them Topcliffe with his matt black hair and jerky gestures. Dodd allowed a brief smile at the heart-warming sight before hurrying on in Carey's wake.

"They certainly know what to do in a crisis, these Papists," said Carey as they sat down again in yet another boozing ken where Carey had already called for brandy to restore some colour to Letty's cheeks. "Never seen anything like it. You banging on the door and shouting the way you did, everybody stops what they're doing—the priest had just arrived and was setting out his Papist trash on the altar. Next thing, everything on the altar is cleared away, the priest has disappeared, the candles are gone, the altar has turned into a mere table, and the people are nearly gone as well. Nothing but the coffin and a bad smell. Only Letty here was upset and some women were helping her and when I told them I was a son of her mistress, they insisted on bringing us both out amongst them. A most delightful escape."

He laughed with the kind of boyish delight that particularly annoyed Dodd. "Best of all I got to see Topcliffe and his men going in to roust out an empty earth. Wonderful."

He turned to Letty and smiled at her. "And I managed to fish you out of a muddy puddle that would have been a difficulty even for my redoubtable lady mother. So, my dear, what were you doing in there?"

Letty started trembling again, cupped her hands around her mouth, and as the tears spilled out of her brown eyes, Carey whipped out a large white hankerchief from his padded sleeve's pocket and handed it over to her. She buried her face in it, sobbing.

Carey leaned back, crossed his ankles, lifted one finger to the potboy and ordered more booze by no more than a nod, then sighed tolerantly. Dodd, who was not at all accustomed to maidens who wept so openly and freely, being bred amongst much less delicate women, was staring at Letty with pure horror.

"It's all right, Sergeant, no point hurrying her," said Carey. "Doctor Nunez explained it to me once. Something about a maiden's womb being not so securely fixed as a woman's and apt to rise and wander up to her head, causing hysterics, fits of tears and fainting, and so on. They really can't help it. Best you can do is wait for the storm to pass."

For some reason this kindly explanation caused Letty to sob even harder. Dodd considered chancing the theory on a Carlisle damsel one day when she was in a mood and decided that he simply didn't have the bollocks—and even if he did, he wouldn't keep them. He was reaching for his pipe again when he stopped and scowled. He had better get used to doing without the London vice as he was certainly not planning to stay there, nor ever come there again.

"Now then, Letty," said Carey to the girl as she blew her nose. "How did you know the Mass was happening?"

"I got a message to say they were saying a mass for my f..f… father's soul and where it was and if I liked I could come if I brought the message to show. So I did. I didn't know it was a requiem. Who was it in the coffin? I thought he was…he was…"

"Show me the message."

She handed over a scrap of paper which was neatly written in the Secretary script used by half the clerks in London. It gave clear instructions to reach the place.

"Who brought you this?"

"Just Will, you know, Bald Will who everyone says is a poet. He said it had been left with the gatekeeper."

"And it was addressed to you?"

"Yes, to Lettice Tregian, which is what everyone calls me in Cornwall though your mother calls me Letitia which I think is French."

"Latin."

"Oh. And I just thought it was nice of them to invite me so I went."

"But you're alone. What would my mother…"

"She said I could. I asked if I could go to church and she said I could."

"You didn't tell her what kind of church? Or why?"

Letty shook her head. Her eyes filled up with tears again. "Oh what will she say to me?"

"She'll say you have horse-clabber for brains, probably," said Carey, "because you clearly do. Don't you know how dangerous it is to go to a Papist mass? Never mind the danger to your soul, it's the danger to you of getting into Topcliffe's hands and what my mother would have to do to get you out again."

Dodd felt this was a bit rich coming from the man who blithely stuck his head in any noose that happened to be handy, but said nothing.

"But we g…g…go in Cornwall and nothing happens," sniffled the girl.

"This isn't Cornwall," said Carey, scratching his patch of beard. "Listen, Letty, you must promise me faithfully not to do it again."

She nodded vigorously. "I was so frightened."

"Rightly so. God's teeth, *I* was frightened when Dodd roared out like that."

"I saw you half-draw your long thin dagger," said Letty.

Carey nodded seriously. "That's what I do when I'm frightened. It's lucky I was there at all and I certainly didn't expect to see you there."

"I had to go," explained Letty, finally making a start on her pork pie with her very pretty little pearl-handled eating knife. "That's why I came up to London with my Lady Hunsdon, you see. I had to bring Fr. Jackson's survey with me. My father had a copy and he was going to meet Fr. Jackson and talk about it with him and then talk to…to the lawyers and other people for he said there was some great land piracy afoot in Cornwall and he wouldn't have it because of what it was doing to the common folk and the tinners."

"And what was this land piracy?" asked Carey with a tone of indulgent disbelief. "I'm sure there was nothing wrong going on."

"That's what I said, but he said something about gold and how the Cornish wouldn't be able to live on their own lands and half of them weren't even recusants, just foolish. And then off he went, only he sent a message to my Lady Hunsdon saying he was going and she was in such a taking about it when she came back from visiting Mrs. O'Malley in Ireland and sailing the whisky up to Dumfries that we went straight to the *Judith* and sailed out of Penryn and up the coast. That's where we caught the Spaniard, you know."

"So my mother said," Carey answered drily. "So Mr. Tregian was part of whatever this was."

"And it wasn't treason, I know it wasn't. It was just boring old buying and selling of land."

"Yes," said Carey, staring into space. "And what's in this survey?"

"I don't know," said Letty, rolling big tragic eyes at them, "I haven't got it. That's what I went to tell them. I don't know where it went. I had it when we went to meet my father and then when I…when I…" She clutched the hankerchief and gulped hard. Dodd had to admit that seeing her father's head on London Bridge must have been a shock to her just as seeing his father dead with an Elliot lance through his chest had been a shock to him. "When I saw my father was dead I…well, I don't know what happened to it."

Dodd had the satisfaction of seeing Carey momentarily lost for words. His mouth opened and then he shut it again.

"You lost it?"

"I think so. I can't find it anywhere. It was in my purse, you see, and something funny happened to my purse because the cord was cut and it was proper safe under my kirtle you know and I didn't notice nothing and then when I got home I realised it was gone."

Dodd and Carey exchanged looks. "Your purse was cut and this survey was in it, yes?"

Letty nodded brightly. "Yes. I even said to my lady, oh I don't know where my purse is to, lucky I didn't have any money in it, and we both laughed, sort of in the middle of crying about my father, you see."

Carey sighed again. "What was in the survey?"

Letty shook her brown curls at him. "Oh sir, you are funny. I can't read. My dad wouldn't have my brains roiled up with it, he said it was bad enough he'd had to learn and him not even a priest."

Dodd nodded at this wisdom. You couldn't argue with that, reading was nothing to do with women.

"That's a pity," said Carey, very strangely, "because if you could read there are all sorts of good books I could recommend you to read to help you get away from your Papish superstition…"

Letty's brow wrinkled. "I heard the heretics *are* always abusing their brains with reading, even the Queen herself, poor soul, but luckily I don't need to for Fr. Jackson tells me everything I need to know."

Carey shook his head. "Was…er…is he in London too?"

"Oh yes, my father came up to town to talk to him. Fr. Jackson went a month or two ago. He was very cross about it, said he hated London and was only going because he had to prevent a crime and a scandal and if he didn't come back I was always to be a good girl and do what my father told me and pray to Our Lady and obey my husband." Letty beamed at them. "Which I will," she added in tones of great piety, sounding just like a very self-righteous little girl.

Neither Carey nor Dodd had the courage to tell Letty what they thought might have happened to Fr. Jackson in case of reopening the floodgates. Dodd was frowning and blinking at the sunlight trying to remember what had happened when they made Lady Hunsdon's abortive shopping expedition and when exactly Letty's purse might have been cut. Just after she saw her father's head and screamed and the horses bolted? Perhaps? Did the cutpurse know what he had or had he perhaps dumped the survey somewhere?

"Ah," said Carey gravely, "excellent. Though of course you should pray to God, not Our Lady."

Letty shook her curls again with great good humour. "Oh no, I'm only a silly maid so He wouldn't be interested. Our Lady is much kinder."

Carey blinked and then seemed to give up his attempt at theology. "And what can you tell me about Fr. Jackson?"

That opened another kind of floodgate entirely. Fr. Jackson was, apparently, the most perfect specimen of manhood alive on this sorry world of sinners. He was not only handsome and well-built, he was very very clever and could tell gold-bearing rock from the other kind with his strange waters and his touchstone, and he knew how to build things as well which he had learned in Germany. And then he became a priest for he heard God calling him, which was something that happened to men who were going to be priests, and all he wanted was to be a good priest to the people in Cornwall.

Carey sighed again which Letty didn't notice. Fr. Jackson came to Cornwall as a priest from the Jesuit seminary in Rheims, but he wasn't evil or a traitor. He travelled around helping people and advising them how to pay their recusancy fines and which bits of land to sell because of course nobody wants to sell land and usually the land he sold for them was poor or fit only for pasture and…

"Fr. Jackson would sell land for people?"

"Not exactly," said Letty, "It was only because he was clever and knew some people in London. My father did as well, I think. So when somebody had a terrible lot of fines to pay—because they changed the magistrates a year ago and now they're much more strict—he would write to his friends and sometimes someone would buy the land in exchange for the fines so there wouldn't be any more fines or bailiffs or court cases but the person in London owned the land, you see?"

"Hm. Yes, I do. What else did Fr. Jackson do?"

"He said Mass of course, like priests do, you know and he would hear your confession…" Letty went very pink at that and Dodd wondered why. "…and he was very kind though I once had to say a whole rosary a day for a week which was a bit much…. And he would catechise and baptise and marry and all that. He was very busy."

Carey nodded. Letty smiled. "I know he's a priest and every-thing and I know a priest is dedicated to God and can never marry like the heretic priests do…Sorry, the Church of England priests do, so…well…I…but I was thinking I might go beyond the seas to be a nun which would be…um…almost as good."

Carey raised his brows. "Oh, I wouldn't advise that," he said. "Did you know nuns have to cut all their hair off and never talk to anybody again except other nuns?"

Letty stared. "Cut all their hair off?"

"Yes. Very short. I used to see nuns when I was in France and they had everything except their faces covered up but a…a friend of mine told me they have to keep their hair very short or even shave it all off."

There was a silence. "Oh. But I'm sure they're quite beautiful."

"I didn't see a beautiful nun all the time I was there. They all looked cross and disagreeable," said Carey blandly.

Another silence. "Well," said Letty.

"I'm sure my mother will help you find a good husband when you're old enough," said Carey kindly, "if you ask her."

Letty brightened at that, then her face fell again. "I suppose…" she said sadly…"I was hoping to see Fr. Jackson again. They did say the priest might hear confessions after Mass and I was going to tell him what happened to my father—in private when I made my confession, you know—and ask his advice. But the priest wasn't him at all and then Sergeant Dodd shouted and…Do you think we'll see Fr. Jackson?"

"Oh I doubt it," said Carey easily. "I don't think he's even in London any more. Not if he has any sense."

The blue glare warned Dodd but Dodd was in no hurry to cause another waterfall. In fact he was spending a good half of his attention on not taking another pipe of tobacco. What was wrong with him now? It wasn't as if he was hungry, he had had a pork pie with a few winter sallet roots and some pickled onions and bread and was quite full. Yet, there it was. He wanted a pipe.

He growled and pulled it out, cleaned the bowl, filled it and lit it and sighed with satisfaction. He would have to try and buy some before they left, that was all there was to it. He wondered if it was possible to grow the herb in Gilsland and if he would be able to persuade Janet to do it if he could get the seeds.

"What now?" he asked as Carey stared into the distance while Letty engulfed her pie. "Are we going to take Letty back to Somerset House?"

"Letty, didn't my mother send someone with you?" Carey asked after a moment.

Letty went pink. "Yes, she did, it was Will but I…er…I lost him."

Carey's eyebrows went up.

Letty's shoulders hunched and dropped. "I didn't want him following me around with his calf eyes trying to be witty and everything and besides…er…I wanted to go to my father's Mass by myself and he would have told my lady and…umm…" Her face squinched in the middle. "Oh, Sir Robert, do you think your lady mother will beat me?"

Carey spread his hands. "Ahhh...possibly, she's never hesi-tated to box my ears any time she thought I needed it. But she soon forgets all about it. So where did you dump poor old Shakespeare?"

"I left him in Paul's Churchyard and just speeded up when he started reading something off a stall because once he does that he has no idea what's going on around him and he once had his purse taken out of his cod-piece without even noticing."

"Perfect," said Carey, smiling at the picture this made. He piled money on the table in an amount Dodd was beginning to get used to. "Come on, if we get back there quickly enough he may not notice you ever left."

Letty immediately brightened and she swallowed the rest of her meal in two large gulps, brushed crumbs off her chin and small ruff.

"That's a wonderful idea, sir..."

"I'll still have to tell my mother, mind you, but at least you won't be embarassed in front of Bald Will."

They hurried through the crowds with Carey offering Letty his arm so she wouldn't fall off her pattens on the muddiest parts—though London was less muddy than Dodd expected, considering the horses clattering through and the pigs, goats, and chickens wandering around the place. However, crowds of urchins fought each other to shovel up the dungpiles on street corners and several little stalls offered it for sale to those who had gardens. The king's share was picked up early in the morning by the nightsoil men and taken out to Essex. Dodd had learned to sleep through their shouts, their clattering and banging every morning. In London everything had a price. Water was more expensive than beer, for instance, if you had it from one of the men with barrels on their backs, and it tasted far worse.

Paul's Walk was thronged as usual and the churchyard filled with people reading books in a hurry next to the various stationers' stalls. Shakespeare was deep in discussion with the printer who had served Lady Hunsdon when they found him and blinked at Letty in bemusement. He had clearly forgotten all about her.

Carey dusted off his hands as she departed, chatting happily about watching the young courtiers in St Paul's and how there was one in tawny velvet and lime green satin who seemed to be having a contest with another one in cramoisie and tangerine as to who could cause the worst headache. Carey had pointed them out as they passed through the huge old cathedral.

"Now where?" moaned Dodd, as Carey immediately headed purposefully for Ludgate.

"I want to know precisely what lands in Cornwall were sold and who bought 'em. Particularly who bought them. I'm beginning to wonder if it matters which lands."

"Eh?" said Dodd.

Carey shook his head. "Lands in exchange for recusancy fines. That's quite an old system for getting rich. Anthony Munday's been at it as hard as he can for years. But what was it about them that brought those two up to London and then both of them wind up dead—one as a substitute for the other as well."

"What system? I dinna ken nowt about land buying and selling."

Carey had the grace to look a little ashamed. "Well…if a Catholic landowner continues to be foolish and obstinate and go to Mass, he gets fined for it. After a while, if he doesn't pay the fines, he could be arrested on a warrant for debt. Now if someone…er…with influence could buy the warrant, he could then exchange it…ahem…for the deeds to some of the man's land and it would…er…be perfectly legal."

From the way Carey was avoiding Dodd's eye, he assumed Carey had either dabbled in this system or his father had. More likely his father; Dodd didn't see Carey having the sense or the ready funds.

"Ay," he said, "it's like when the Grahams first came south to the Border Country."

"Is it?"

"Ay, in King Henry's time. The brothers—that'd be Richie of Brackenhill's grandad, Richie and his great-uncles, Jock and Hutchin Graham. They decided they liked the look o' the place

A Murder of Crows 145

and they had some men with them. So they took the land for theirselves and kicked the Storeys off it and naebody did nothing about it for the King of Scotland had just hanged Johnny Johnstone."

"It's not like that at all."

"Ay, it is, but wi' warrants not torches and fists and swords," said Dodd firmly.

"You're not seriously suggesting that Papists should be allowed to simply…be Papists."

Dodd shrugged. "I dinna care one way or the other," he said, "so they dinna bring in the King o' Spain—now that's not right. Nor try to harm the Queen. That's terrible treason, and who wants to end up like the Scots, forever killing their kings?"

"Quite."

"Still, when ye take a man's land wi'oot paying him fairly for it, I dinna see the difference whether ye come in wi' your kith and kin and boot him off to lie in a ditch and greet, or do it all nice and tidy wi' bits o' paper."

Unusually, Carey said nothing.

They came to the Temple and climbed up the stairs to the top of the rickety building where James Enys had his chambers.

Carey knocked on the new door. "Hello? Anyone there?" he called.

There was a pause and Mrs. Morgan's face looked out. Just for a moment in the semi-darkness at the top of the staircase, Dodd thought it was Enys himself, so close was the resemblance, but the polite matron's white linen cap and small ruff disabused him.

Her brother was not there and had gone out. No, she did not know where. No, she didn't know why. She had spent all day clearing the mess left by the pursuivants and had had to buy a new door which she could ill-afford, even if her brother was about to be paid by Lord Hunsdon.

"It's your other brother's papers I came for?" said Carey. "The one who disappeared?"

There was a long pause. Then, "Yes?"

"The lands he was selling in Cornwall. Does Mr. Enys still have any papers connected to that?"

"I don't know, sir, you must ask him when he returns."

She shut the door on them. Carey stood there a while with his head cocked as if listening and Dodd thought he could hear a stealthy sniffle.

Finally Carey banged his hand on the wall with frustration and led the way back down the stairs and into the courtyard where two lawyers in their black robes stood conferring together. Carey went straight up to them with a shallow bow. "Your pardon, sirs, do you know a man called James Enys?"

One looked at the other and smiled. "Oh yes," he said, "a fine lawyer when he pleases, but I think Mr. Heneage doesn't like him."

"Do you know where he is now?"

The other shrugged. "In his chambers…There he is coming out of the door."

Carey spun on his heel to see Enys coming towards them looking tired and anxious.

"Can I help you sirs?" he asked, nodding to his brother lawyers who tactfully moved away, one of them suppressing a laugh.

"I need to see the documents about the land sales in Cornwall, Mr. Enys," said Carey, his eyes narrowed. "I think they were not taken by the pursuivants though I'm sure that's what they were after. I think you have them somewhere safe."

Enys swallowed convulsively and seemed to be thinking. "Very well, Sir Robert," he said. "I have them in a safe place and I can fetch them for you, but you cannot go into it. Can you not ask me what you want to know about them?"

Carey hooked his thumbs in his swordbelt. "I want to know who bought them, Mr. Enys."

Enys paused. "Ah," he said. "Worshipful gentlemen at the Queen's Court…"

"No sir, I want the names."

"Of the sellers?"

"No, of the buyers. Was my father among them?"

Enys looked at the ground. "Er...no."

"The sales were secret, yes? But at high prices?"

"Yes."

"Who bought them?"

"I...I cannot say, sir."

"Cannot? Will not?"

"Dare not, sir. They were mainly proxies for a very...noble gentleman who would be...offended if his name were linked with the matter."

"Hm. Burghley?"

"I really cannot say, sir."

Carey showed his teeth in a grimace of frustration. "If you should change your mind, Mr. Enys," he said evenly, "please let me know."

They both turned to go but Enys called after them, "Sergeant Dodd."

Dodd turned. "Ay?"

"Would you like me to continue the civil suit?"

Carey's father was paying for it after all and it would likely annoy Heneage even if nothing came of it. "Ay," said Dodd, "see what ye can get."

Enys nodded. "You may be surprised, Sergeant."

"I will be if aught comes of it," said Dodd, and continued with Carey out onto Fleet Street.

Naturally the Cock Tavern was beckoning and they were soon sitting in one of the booths inside, drinking ale. Dodd crushed the impulse to reach for his pipe.

"Well for what it's worth, here's what I think," said Carey. "Last year the magistrates changed in Cornwall and the recusants started getting squeezed. A couple of them had to sell some land and whoever bought the land went to look at it. He found some interesting looking rocks and had an assayer who happened to be in the area—Fr. Jackson—check it for gold."

"D'ye think they found it?"

Carey paused significantly. "I think they did. Perhaps quite a lot. Everyone knows that gold comes from base metals which are forced to change and change again until the true principal metal emerges. There's tin in Cornwall, and where there's tin there's lead usually, and sometimes silver. It would be strange if there weren't gold, in fact."

Dodd nodded. "Ay."

"Of course they didn't want to let out that there was gold, because then it would belong to the Crown, and in any case the price of the land would go up. So they kept it quiet and started buying more and more land, probably using Richard Tregian as their agent. They want to start getting the gold out of the ground—probably covered by tin mining so they get the Papist priest Jackson to come up to London to talk to him and for some reason he turns difficult, he threatens to spread the word or perhaps just demands more money for his silence. They don't need him any more as there are plenty of mining engineers in Cornwall, so they kill him and dump him in the Thames. Who does it is difficult to say, but I would suspect Mr. Enys's mysterious brother who has so conveniently disappeared. Or, more likely, there is no brother and Mr. Enys did it himself." Carey leaned back looking triumphant. "Which is why he keeps following us around and also won't tell us who was buying the land."

Dodd didn't think Enys would be able to kill anyone, but knew there was no point arguing with Carey in the grip of a pretty idea. "And Richard Tregian?"

"Heneage or Topcliffe are after Fr. Jackson and instead of catching him, they catch his friend Tregian. They need to produce a priest and so they use him."

"Ay well then," said Dodd, thinking this was distinctly thin and far-fetched, puffing on the pipe he had just lit, "all we need to do is grab Enys and get him to tell us he did it. Ah dinna think he would take much thumping."

Carey gazed wearily on him. "Dodd, that's simply not the way I do things."

Dodd shrugged. It was the way most people did things and it generally seemed to work for Lowther.

"And it doesn't work," Carey insisted, "if you're beating someone up for information, either he'll spit in your eye and say nothing as you did to Heneage, or he'll tell you whatever he thinks you want to hear, whether it's true or not. It's a complete waste of time."

Dodd shrugged again. "Worth trying on Enys though."

"Well, do you want him to work for you as your lawyer?"

Dodd sighed through his teeth. On the whole he did, so grabbing him and beating him was not the way to go. On the other hand...

"Why can we not go home now, sir? The criminal case is lost and the civil will take far longer than I wantae stay in this place."

Carey scowled. "My parents want me to find out what happened to Richard Tregian, particularly my mother. Until I've done that, we're stuck here, so you might as well help me."

"Ay, but why do they care? Somebody stabs a priest in the back and dumps him in the Thames. Ye might think Heneage would be pleased about it. Heneage then hangs, draws, and quarters Richard Tregian in his place. It's all done wi' and the men'll not be back again. What's the point of your parents sending ye hither and yon in London to find out about it?"

Carey started to answer and then stopped. He leaned back with his eyes half-hooded and a lazy smile on his face. "As ever, Sergeant, you ask the right question. Why indeed? Hmm."

"D'ye think your...eh...lady mother might have bought some of the lands in Cornwall? She said the prices were high."

"She might have. She has to do something with what she gets from her privateering."

"And she came up to London to talk wi' Tregian as well, she said so when we went to find him at his inn and he wasnae there, on account of being on a pike on London Bridge instead," said Dodd thoughtfully. "She was no' best pleased when Letty said he wasnae there and she had me go and search his bedchamber."

"That was where you found the paper with the cipher on it?"

"Ay, tucked in behind a shelf."

"Did you show it to her?"

Dodd opened his mouth to speak, then paused. "Ah, no, it slipped me mind, what with the heid on a pike and Letty screaming, ye ken."

Carey was looking thoughtful. "Well, we've read the invisible ink now and it shows, but we haven't cracked the cipher so we've no way of telling who it was addressed to. I wonder if…"

"Ay," said Dodd who was well ahead of him. "We should try giving it to her. Only I might get in trouble for not giving it to her before."

"She won't be very pleased, but at least she won't box your ears and call you clabber-brained," said Carey with some edge.

Dodd hid a smile. Carey stood and went out the back to the jakes. He came back with a small purse of gold that he must have been keeping in his codpiece, gave it quietly to Dodd.

"I've taken half out of it and I want you to look after it for me and not give me any of it, understand?" said Carey very seriously. "If we're going to play in the King of London's game, I want still to be solvent afterwards."

"We're gonnae go there, are we?"

Carey blinked at him. "Of course. I've been before but we were very clearly invited tonight and I'm going. Only…" He spread his hands and shrugged.

"Will they be cheating?"

"Oddly enough, they won't. Laurence Pickering, the King of London, guarantees his game against all pricksters, card-sharps, and highmen and lowmen, and kicks out anyone who breaks that rule. Which makes it more difficult for me because if I'm playing against crooked players, I can usually guarantee to win whereas if I'm merely playing against good players, I can't be so certain."

thursday 14th september 1592, evening

According to Carey, Pickering's game moved around a lot so you could only find it if you were invited. When the sun started to go down they walked into the city and along the busy wharves until they came to Three Cranes in the Vintry. There the men inside the great treadmills that worked the three enormous cranes were just finishing and jumping down to drink their beer and be paid for a day's work. The last of the barrels of Rhenish and Gascon wine were being hurried on handcarts into warehouses to be locked up, watched by the Tunnage and Poundage men who put the Queen's seal on the locks.

Other brightly dressed young men were standing around in casual ways, so Carey and Dodd took their ease on a bench by the water and Dodd kept his hands away from his tobacco pouch. They saw the lad in cramoisie and tangerine, large ruff, haughty nose, highly coloured, acned and with a target all but pinned to his back.

Once the Tunnage and Poundage men had gone off in their boat, things changed. At the back of one of the securely sealed warehouses, a part of the wall slid aside and two imposing men in buff coats came to stand stolidly by the opening. Dodd recognised one of them but Carey held Dodd back from going in at once.

"Let's see who's there," he said, and watched the other well-dressed courtiers and merchants who went in by the entrance after a muttered conversation with one of the men in buff coats.

At last Carey stood and followed them, trailed by Dodd. At the door he nodded at one of the men. "How's your wife, Mr. Briscoe?"

Briscoe smiled and nodded back. "Near her time, Sir Robert," he said. "It's a worry. She says she'll stop wearing herself out about her brother now she knows it was a man called Jackson and it wasn't him. Which is a relief, you know."

Carey smiled. "By the way, did you happen to hear about the veney I played the other night with some Smithfield brawlers working for Topcliffe?"

Briscoe's broad face broke into a grin. "Nearly split my sides, sir. And what came after. I heard it was that mad poet Marlowe wot hired 'em and he'd better be careful if he goes near Smiffield again, cos none of 'em are 'appy about it."

Carey laughed. "Well if you should happen to hear anything else about it, I'd be grateful if you'd pass it on."

"I will, sir."

"Anything else going on?"

Briscoe's brow creased. "Well, Mr. Pickering's very worried by the plague in the city, though none of the City Aldermen is bovvered. It's in the Bridewell now, you know?"

Carey grimaced. "Thanks for the warning."

"And I heard tell one of the bearwardens was sick of it yesterday and died and one of his bears run wild for sorrow."

"Not Harry Hunks?"

"No sir, he's retired now. Gone back to the Kent herds to sire more bears. That was Big John and they 'ad to shoot him in the end."

Carey shook his head as he handed over the price of entry in gold. "The city fathers think all they have to do is shut the theatres and the plague will disappear, even though it never does."

Dodd was thinking of what that poor apothecary had said a couple of weeks before—that the plague always started in St Paul's, not the playhouses. He resolved not to go near the place again, never mind the rats in the crypt gnawing on only God knew what remains from two hundred years before.

Briscoe tipped his hat and they climbed the wooden stairs to an upper room lit with ranks of candles and glass windows, with fair rush mats on the floors and painted cloths on the walls. It all seemed very wealthy and respectable until you looked more carefully at the cloths which were covered with pictures of shockingly naked people wearing leafy hats and playing cards and dice and drinking. Some of them seemed to be doing...what they shouldn't have been. Dodd's eyes stretched as he took in the details. Somewhere at the back of his mind he wondered if he and Janet..? He gulped and turned away, hoping his face hadn't gone guiltily red.

Carey had put on the Courtier again and was also wearing a suspiciously knowing look. Dodd was beginning to suspect that the real article was the Berwick man who showed up occasionally when Carey was under pressure, but Carey as Courtier never failed to irritate him with his breeziness and arrogance. As the Courtier sauntered into a group of glaringly-dressed young men and greeted them affably, Dodd found a padded bench to park his padded hose on and felt for his pipe.

A small bullet-headed man with a smiling face sat down next to him and offered him a light so Dodd passed him the pipe.

"You're the northerner, ain't you," said the small man, puffing away appreciatively, "what's come sarf wiv Sir Robert?"

"Ay," said Dodd, taking the pipe back.

"I've 'ad the word out to leave you be and not try to tip you any more lays."

Dodd nodded politely at this because he had no idea what the small man was talking about.

"Fing is," said the man, "I can't be seen talking to Sir Robert in public and he knows it, 'cos that cove over there is one of Cecil's boys..."

Dodd followed the man's glance and saw the pale oblong face of Poley.

"So when you see 'im go in the back, I want you to go wiv 'im. Understand?"

Dodd bridled slightly at being told what to do but simply nodded. "Ay," he said.

The small man smiled, held out his hand. "'Course, I can see you don't know me. I'm Laurence Pickering."

Dodd shook. "Ah...Henry Dodd, sir. Sergeant of Gilsland." He blinked. Was this the King of London in dark brocades and furs, his balding head bare? Brother-in-law to the London hangman and master of the thieves of the City? He looked like a very prosperous merchant. Which in a way he was, just as Richie Graham of Brackenhill was very much the lord of his manor, never mind where his family came from nor how they got there.

Pickering winked at him, jumped up, and headed into the throng of players in the corner. The way everyone parted for him told Dodd a lot more than the man's compact size and modest manner.

Carey was deep in a game of primero, with the boy in cramoisie and tangerine clearly set out before him like a peacock ready for carving. He drank and smiled and laughed and shouted eighty-five points as he always did and casually tossed an angel—a genuine gold angel this time—into the pot.

Dodd, shuddering at the idea of a week's wages being where you started in this game, stood up and wandered over to the dice players. They were playing with very fine ivory dice with gold pips—perhaps to make them more difficult to palm and swap which had been one of Barnabus' specialities—the women cheering as one of them threw two sixes and scooped the pot. It was all shillings and crowns there and as Dodd generally played dice for fractions of a penny, he didn't fancy that game either.

He hid a yawn. He could have spent the time gazing at the naked women all over the painted cloths, but didn't want to risk being tempted by one of the girls with her tits peeping over the lace edging of her stays. Although there were musicians in the corner, they were playing quiet complicated music on lutes with no drums at all which was boring to listen to. He had thought that rich folks in London somehow had more fun but as far as he could make out, they did the same things as poor folks only their boredom was more expensive and complicated and took a lot longer. In fact it was worse because with horse-racing you had the excitement of reiving the nags first.

He could see there were special arrangements to make sure none of the games were crooked. For a start the floormats were clean and white and obviously changed often, while the light from the banks of candles made the room quite bright if very warm. There were no handy shadows where you could hide things or drop inconvenient cards. Young men in tight jerkins with tight sleeves moved about, picking up packs of cards and dice between games and inspecting them. One player had his cards taken and then he was grabbed by three of the burly men standing near the door. Two of them upended him while the other searched him and pulled out several high-ranking cards. He was removed, squawking, down the stairs and some of the gamers peered out the window to wait for the splash as he was thrown in the Thames. There were cheers and catcalls and Pickering leaned out of a window.

"Don't come back. If you do, I'll give you to my brother-in-law."

Much obsequious clapping from the young men in jerkins and the women in very low-cut bodices. That was when Dodd spotted him. He frowned. What was Enys doing here—he didn't gamble? Or he said he didn't. As casually as he could, Dodd got up and sauntered over to the table where he had seen the heavily pock-marked lawyer.

They were playing primero, the play tense and close and the pot large. Dodd couldn't quite make out Enys's face because he was sitting well back in a corner so he waited until the man had lost and got up to get a drink.

"Mr. Enys," said Dodd as breezy as he could, "fancy meeting you here…"

The man seemed to jump, but then bowed shallowly. "I'm sorry, sir," he said, "I fear you mistake me, my name is Vent, not Enys." Dodd blinked at him, puzzled. Certainly the voice was different, but the face…The face was definitely familiar though not really Enys's.

"Ay?" said Dodd, "ye're nocht ma lawyer?"

"Er…no," said the man, Vent, "though I have heard I have a double practising law in the Temple at the moment." He coughed or perhaps hid a laugh. "Possibly I should sue him for defamation of character."

"Good Lord, Ah'm sorry, sir, I was sure it was ye."

"No matter," said Vent, "Perhaps you would give your lawyer my compliments, and tell him I would be delighted to meet him over a hand of cards."

"I will," Dodd answered, now feeling awkward. After all, he never liked it when people thought he was the legal type of Serjeant as opposed to a Land-Sergeant. They bowed to each other and Dodd turned back to watch Carey at his game. Several others were watching the game, including Pickering and three of his bully-boys.

Carey nodded and laid his cards down. "Prime," he said. The boy in cramoisie and tangerine stared fixedly and then laid his own cards facedown without another word. Carey smiled sweetly at the lad and pulled the pot towards him. As he pocketed his haul, two of Pickering's men came and stood behind him, one murmured in his ear. Carey looked surprised and then stood up, headed for the door at the back of the room.

After a moment of concern, Dodd quietly followed them and into a small parlour with a bright fireplace where Laurence Pickering was standing blinking at the flames.

"Well, Sir Robert?"

Carey smiled. "Well, Mr. Pickering?"

"How's 'e doing it? Young Mr. Newton?"

"He's not cheating in any way I can see," said Carey thoughtfully, "although he's not as good a player as he thinks he is."

"So why does he win?"

"I'm not sure," said Carey spreading his hands. "He might simply be lucky."

"Or 'e's got a magic ring."

Carey's eyebrows went up. "Hm. I've heard of them and a number of astrologers and magicians and whatnot have tried to sell them to me but I've never heard of one that actually worked. It's like alchemy. It's always going to work, or it would have worked if you hadn't scratched your nose at that particular moment, or tomorrow when the stars are conjunct with Jupiter it will work, but today, right now, when you want them to, in my experience, they never work."

Pickering had his head on one side, exactly like a blackbird eyeing up a worm. He looked sceptical. Carey smiled his sunny, lazy smile. "Besides, if you had a ring like that which actually did work, would you sell it?"

Pickering hesitated and then burst into laughter, slapping his knee. He poured Carey brandywine and offered some to Dodd who shook his head. He wanted to keep a clear head for whatever was going on here. That was why he hadn't had another pipe since the first one he had shared with Pickering.

"So that's a relief," said Pickering. "None of my boys could understand it. We actually let him win a night wiv Desiree de Paris so we could check his clothes properly, but nothing. 'E's just lucky and one day 'is luck will run out."

"I expect so," said Carey easily. "Comes to us all, I'm afraid."

"'Course the only ovver one I've known win so often wivvout cheating, is you, Sir Robert."

Carey bowed a little. "Since my love-life is a catastrophe, this is only to be expected."

Pickering smiled shortly. "All right, then, you've done what I asked. Now. How can I help you, Sir Robert? Or your worshipful father, of course?"

"Both really. Firstly information about Heneage."

"Hmf." Pickering was rubbing his lower lip. "What do you want to know?"

"Anything you feel may be of interest, Mr. Pickering."

"He's short of money,"

Carey's eyes went up. "You'd think with all his loot from catching Catholics and so on that he'd be rich."

"Well, he's short enough that he's wanting me to pay him rental for him leaving me and my people alone."

"Oh really?"

Dodd was surprised. Heneage claiming blackmail money from someone like Pickering? Was the man mad?

Pickering's lips thinned. "Yes, really."

"You had an arrangement with Mr. Secretary Walsingham…"

"Yes I did, Sir Robert. He left me in peace. I made sure that there was reasonable peace in London and if he needed to know anything, he knew it, no questions asked."

"And Heneage…?"

"Wants paying."

Carey tutted quietly.

"And sends Topcliffe to collect." Pickering spat deliberately into the fire.

"Dear oh dear. He certainly seems in a hurry at the moment, Mr. Pickering. Are you aware of the problems my father and brother had with him a week or two ago."

"I'd 'eard somefing," said Pickering cautiously. "You was in a good stand-off in the Fleet's Beggar's Ward, I 'eard all about that."

"Mm. And you'll be aware that Sergeant Dodd here has been trying to bring Heneage to court over his maltreatment."

Pickering snorted quietly at this, an opinion Dodd shared.

"Now there's something afoot over Cornish land," Carey said. "I asked your brother-in-law about the hanging, drawing, and quartering of a purported priest named Fr. Jackson." Pickering's small bright eyes narrowed and sharpened at that. "The man whose head ended up on London Bridge was in fact a Mr. Richard Tregian, a respected Cornish gentleman and a... an acquaintance of my mother's."

Pickering nodded.

"He had been involved in the selling of Cornish lands that had gold in them, working with a surveyor and assayer, who was the priest Fr. Jackson under whose name Tregian ended being executed—if that was actually the man's name. In fact my mother came up to town herself to talk to him—although I don't yet know why. His daughter is in my mother's service and came with her—bringing a copy of a survey of the areas in question."

Carey paused to take a drink of brandywine. "She had it in her purse under her kirtle—she's a Cornish girl and nobody there would steal it from her so she had no idea...Anyway, she comes up to town with my mother in the *Judith of Penryn*, she cannot find her father where he is supposed to be lodging, she goes with my mother shopping on London Bridge, and there she sees her father's head on a spike."

Now it was Pickering's turn to tut.

"Understandably she screamed the place down, spooked her horse and gave Sergeant Dodd here some trouble to control the nag. In the flurry she thinks her purse with the survey in it was stolen, or at any rate, she didn't have it any more when she got home and the cord had been cut."

Pickering nodded. "If it was any of my people wot nipped that bung, I'll have the survey back in your hands by tomorrow, Sir Robert," he said in measured tones. "There's no chance she might of sold the survey and then..."

Carey smiled and shook his head.

"Who would she sell it to? She knows no one in London, she's only a country maid. Besides she has been with my mother the whole time she's spent in London."

"Hm."

"And one other matter. A corpse fetched up against the Queen's Privy Stair a few days ago, but in a state that showed it had been in the water considerably longer. The man had been stabbed but died of drowning—perhaps because he was wearing leg-irons at the time he fell in the Thames. It fell into my father's jurisdiction, and at the inquest today a woman turned up calling herself Mrs. Sophia Merry, claimed the body as Mr. Jackson, and then almost held an illegal Requiem Mass for him this same afternoon. I want to know if any of the watermen saw him going into the water? He had the top joint missing from his left index finger."

Pickering nodded again. "They might know. I'll ask around, Sir Robert. Now. If…ah…if any of these Cornish lands was to be offered to me, just for argument's sake, what would you advise?"

"Mr. Pickering," said Carey with a shrewd look, "I would advise you not to touch it with a boathook."

"Not even as an investment? In case…ahem…there was gold?"

"And what if there were? It's Crown prerogative in any case. You would have to dig it up, refine it, and then share anything you made with the Queen's Majesty. Or do it in secret and risk having the whole thing confiscated. And the land is in Cornwall, for the Lord's sake, Mr. Pickering. What do you know about Cornwall? You wouldn't even be able to understand what they said to you, nor they you. It's at five day's ride from London and there are no posthouses beyond Plymouth."

"I could take ship…"

"Mr. Pickering, if you have bought any of these lands, I advise you to sell as soon as you can and buy any land at all you can lay hands on around the Blackfriars."

"Oh yes?" Pickering's beady little eyes were wide open. "I fort your father owned the lot."

"Not all of it. And he's not selling. Nor can I tell you what his plans are with my elder brother, however…At least if it's in London you can go and look at the place." Carey smiled confidingly. "Please don't tell my father I mentioned it, though."

Pickering nodded, eyes shrewd. "Well, that's interesting. Thank you, Sir Robert. Can I offer you gennlemen any…ah… further entertainment?"

Carey hesitated and then regretfully shook his head. "I think I should return to Somerset House, Mr. Pickering, especially as my lady mother is in town and has…er…sources of her own."

Dodd had to hide a smile at this one, as did Pickering from the slight clamping of his teeth. Both Carey and he stood to leave.

"I'll send a couple of my boys wiv you, Sir Robert," said Pickering with a wink. "We don't want no more veneys in Fleet Street, now do we?"

"Indeed not," said Carey primly. "Thank you."

In fact, they took a boat, which turned up the minute Mr. Briscoe roared "Oars!" from the wharf, and got out at Somerset House steps, a highly convenient way of travelling. On the way, Carey seemed thoughtful.

"How is it that ye're sae friendly wi' the King o' the London thieves?" Dodd asked for pure nosiness. "Ah wouldnae have thought…"

"Oh, it's a long story, Sergeant. Long time ago too. When I was first at Court, before I went to Scotland, I…ah…somewhat over-reached myself at a London primero game…"

"Ay?"

Carey's expression was rueful. "Yes. Lost my shirt, actually. Literally."

Dodd's mouth turned down. "Ay?"

"Well, I wasn't going to let that bother me so I was heading for my lodgings as I…ah…was…"

"Wi'out yer shirt?"

"Nothing but my underbreeches, I'm afraid. It gave a couple of punks a terrible turn, I think. Anyway, Mr. Pickering caught up with me and gave me back my cloak which was kind of him.

He said he liked the way I'd carried it off and as he had suspicions about the cards, he would take it as a compliment if I would allow him to buy me some temporary duds at a pawnshop he knew on a loan so as not to…er…frighten anybody."

Dodd was enchanted at this picture. "Ay."

"Of course, he wasn't the King then, he was working for the man who was. We got talking over a few quarts of beer and I told him if he wanted to draw in the courtiers with money, he should set up a game which was absolutely clean, no cheating at all, guarantee it and charge for entrance. And make sure it was somewhere comfortable."

Carey took his hat off to a lady wearing a velvet mask as she went past in another boat. She turned away haughtily.

"And whit was it about that boy in the terrible get up?" Dodd asked.

"Occasionally, if Mr. Pickering has a player in who wins too much but he can't work out how, he asks me to check up on him," Carey said casually.

"And was he cheating?"

Carey gave Dodd a warning look. "No, or I would have said so," he said, "He was simply counting cards and playing by the odds. It isn't cheating but it does give you an advantage. There's an Italian book explains how to do it and I expect he's read it. That's what I've been teaching you to do, by the way."

Dodd remembered about the Italian book and its notions about numbers. "Why did ye no' tell Pickering about that?"

Carey looked amused. "What, and have him work out how I do it myself? I don't think so."

Back at Somerset House Dodd was hoping for his bed. But no, it seemed, despite both of them being weary and the hour a ridiculously late eleven o'clock, Carey had to speak to his parents if they were still up.

They were companionably playing cards together in the little parlour in the corner of the courtyard, with wax candles on the table and a little dish of wafers to dip in their spiced evening wine.

Carey bowed to his parents and his mother immediately stood up and hugged him, and then to Dodd's horror, gave Dodd a hug as well.

"Letty told me how you helped her when she was such a fool," said Lady Hunsdon. "What with Sergeant Dodd spotting the trap and giving warning and you helping her leave so quickly…She said you were both wonderful. Lord alone knows what trouble there would have been if she had been taken by that evil bastard Topcliffe. She isn't really a Papist, she's just a silly maid that's been wrongly taught, but in Topcliffe's hands…"

Hunsdon smiled fondly at his wife. One of the footmen standing by the wall came forward and brought up another small table while more wafers and wine arrived so that Dodd could do something at least about his aching belly. The pork pie he had had in the afternoon was long gone and Carey, being Carey, hadn't stopped since then.

"Well Robin?" said his father as Carey leaned back in his chair, crossed his legs at the ankle, and took a long draught of wine.

"The Devil of it is," he said, seemingly at random while his mother frowned at him for swearing, "there's a pattern here and I know there is, but I can't seem to see it."

He told the whole tale of their very busy day from start to finish, with no embellishments at all.

"How did you know where the memorial service was to?" asked Lady Hunsdon. "Letty said she couldn't imagine."

"Oh that." Carey smiled faintly. "The Papists themselves told me. It was in the book at the crypt—the woman who claimed the priest's body gave a false address and called herself Mrs. Sophia Merry."

"Never heard of her."

"Of course not, my lord, it's a false name as well. But it told where the service would be—at the site of the old church of St Mary Wisdom."

Hunsdon gave a shout of laughter. "Ha! I didn't realise you'd actually managed to learn some Greek as a boy, between reiving cows and playing football."

Carey smiled ruefully. "I didn't, my lord, I'm afraid. But while I was in Paris I…er…knew a lady whose name was Sophia who told me often that her name meant wisdom and very proud of it she was too although she was as feather-brained as a duck."

Lord Hunsdon seemed to find this very funny whereas Lady Hunsdon only smiled briefly.

He finished with his account of Pickering's game, then wet his whistle and waited for his parents' reactions. They were a time coming. Lady Hunsdon in particular seemed very interested in her cards.

After a moment, Carey said gently, "I find it alarming, my lady, that Pickering seems to have bought some of these Cornish lands on the grounds that there's gold in them."

Lady Hunsdon said nothing. She was dipping a wafer in the wine.

"I advised him to sell immediately," Carey added, "on the grounds that even if there was gold, he would get no good of it since it was so far away and well out of his manor."

There was more thundering silence.

"My lady mother?" said Carey, even more softly. Lady Hunsdon refused to meet his eyes. He sighed. "Well then, my lord, I don't know what more I can do. Perhaps it would be best if I went north again…"

"Not yet," said Lady Hunsdon sharply.

"No," said Lord Hunsdon at exactly the same time. The two of them looked at each other while Carey watched the pair of them with hooded eyes and a cynical expression.

Dodd had woken up to the fact that there was something complicated going on between Carey and his parents and indeed between Lord and Lady Hunsdon, but he wasn't sure what it might be. His own parents had been very much less complicated and furthermore were both long dead. Inside the silence there seemed to be some kind of three-way battle going on.

In the end Carey broke it by uncrossing his legs and planting his boots firmly on the black and white tiles of the floor.

He stood up and then went formally on one knee to his parents.

"My lord father, my lady mother," he said quietly, "I am urgently needed in Carlisle before the autumn reiving starts. I will not investigate this matter any further until I have a true accounting of the background to it from both of you." His eyes were on his mother as he spoke. Then he stood, bowed gracefully to both, backed three steps as if from royalty, turned and left the parlour.

"I told you Robin would…" Hunsdon began but his wife slammed her cards down, stood and marched out of the parlour, her cheeks flaming as if she had painted them. Hunsdon followed her, leaving Dodd sitting at a cardtable all alone except for the servingman standing by the door, seemingly dozing where he stood.

Dodd finished the spiced wine, which was very good, crushed immediately the impulse to steal the silver cups and the candelabra, and headed for his own bed. To his disgust he found Carey sitting by the small fire in the luxurious fireplace, busy mulling the wine which was normally left for him in a flagon on a table by the wall. Dodd's eyelids felt as if they were lined with lead and sand.

"Och," he moaned.

"God damn it," snarled Carey in general, ramming the poker back among the coals as if stabbing someone. "She still thinks I'm a boy that can't see the nose on his face because his head's too full of football, she thinks I still can't add it up. What the hell does she think she's playing at?"

Bewildered, Dodd sat on the edge of his bed since Carey had his chair.

"Ay?"

"As for my father…Why the devil doesn't he keep her under control? Privateering at her age. Dodgy land-deals with God knows what bloody Papists. He should bloody well assert his authority and make her behave!"

Dodd was open-mouthed at this notion as he rather thought Hunsdon would be. He decided not to say anything since Carey was evidently spoiling for a fight with someone, and if he didn't dare fight his parents combined, might well pick on Dodd. Who hadn't the energy for it.

Carey drank some wine and then seemed to remember his manners, poured another gobletfull and handed it to Dodd, who had really drunk enough but didn't feel like arguing either. Would he never get to his bed?

"Don't you understand, Sergeant?" Carey said more quietly. "My mother doesn't like the Court and doesn't really know how it works. You know my father is the Queen's half-brother through Mary Boleyn, Anne Boleyn's older sister? Who was King Henry's official mistress before Anne."

Dodd had heard something about it, but discounted it as the usual overblown nonsense. His eyes stretched but he nodded once.

"Now if King Henry had married Mary instead of Anne, my father would have been king and I would have been a Prince of the Blood Royal." He shuddered briefly. "And my ghastly elder brother would have been the heir to the throne, Heaven help us. But the bastardy means that can't ever happen, thank God, which means my father is her Majesty's closest kin and also her most trusted man at court. As Lord Chamberlain he runs the entire *domus providenciae* of the Court. The…ah…I suppose you'd translate it 'the House of Supplies' which is to say, the servants, supplies, kitchens, laundries, and what-have-you. Courtiers are generally part of the *domus magnficenciae*, the House of Magnificence, and very much worse treated. My father also guards her Majesty against assassinations. Everyone thinks of him as no more than a knight of the carpet, a courtier and patron, never mind what he did during the Northern Earls rebellion. And never mind that he's kept the Queen safe all this time. Heneage wants to destroy him and take his job—he thinks he could have enormous influence with the Queen which my father, on the whole, rarely uses."

Dodd nodded again, still not sure where this was going.

"That means that if my mother has been indulging in some half-baked scheme involving Cornish lands and Papist priests and Heneage gets wind of it and goes to the Queen, my father could be in the Tower on a charge of treason by the end of the year."

"Ay," said Dodd, wondering if it was too late to steal a horse from Hunsdon's stable and head north as fast as he could.

"That's the thing about the Court. Nothing is steady, nothing is certain. People plot and lie and scheme for power. My father has never been very interested in political power which is one reason why the Queen trusts him. He's also seen to it that she stays alive, with God's help. But if Heneage can convince her he's turning Papist or has been dealing with them in some way, no matter how ridiculous the charge would be, the Queen would turn on my father. And her anger can be as terrible as my grandfather's."

"Ay."

"And as lethal."

"Ay."

"Then there's the fact that the Cecils have intervened on Heneage's behalf. Generally speaking they're at loggerheads because Sir Robert Cecil wants to run Walsingham's legacy instead of Heneage. So why would he organize the adjournment of our case for Heneage? Either it's some kind of trick to lull him along or Heneage blackmailed him. Or Cecil's after something else entirely and this is just byplay…" Carey's voice trailed off leaving Dodd feeling he was a very small pawn on a very large chessboard full of extremely dangerous, heavily armed chessmen. Carey had a wary, calculating look on his face. After a moment he began again.

"My father wants me to find out what's going on, in case my mother hasn't told him everything. Meanwhile my mother wants me to find out how Richard Tregian was swapped for a priest and what happened to the priest—although I think we know—and how. And in all of it I must ask questions, but if I don't know what they're up to, how can I be sure to ask the right questions and still protect them?"

"Ay."

"So that's it. I'm not doing any more. I think I'll go hawking tomorrow."

Carey smiled tightly and finally, thanks be to God, headed for the door. He paused.

"We'll probably be on the road north in a day or two," he said.

It was while Dodd was fighting his way out of his suit that he found it. A piece of paper which had been slipped into the little pocket in his sleeve. When he opened it, he found a short and imperious note.

"Please be so good as to meet me in the main courtyard at dawn."

The thing was signed with Lady Hunsdon's initials. Dodd groaned aloud. Dawn? It was past midnight now. He'd get hardly any sleep at all.

Feeling hard-used, he shucked the rest of his stupid clothes, dumped them on the chest, and climbed into bed, closing the curtains around him against the foul ague-producing airs of the Thames.

friday 15th september 1592, dawn

Dawn found the courtyard full of horses. It seemed that when Carey went hawking near London, he couldn't possibly do it the way he did near Carlisle, which was to ride out with only Dodd or another man of the castle guard and a tercel falcon on his fist, a couple of dogs at the heels of his horse. That was fun.

This kind of hawking involved the dog-boy and the Master of the Kennels plus two or three dogs including the lugubrious lymer that had hurt his paw but was much better now, half a dozen mounted servingmen, the Baron's Falconer, and at least five birds with their hoods on and a couple of boys to climb trees for the falcons in case they didn't come back. Dodd saw Marlowe for the first time in days: he was looking out of a second-storey window smoking a long clay pipe while everyone mounted up and lengthened stirrup leathers and argued. They were seemingly headed for Farringdon Fields.

Carey raised his hand in salute to Dodd as the whole cavalcade clenched and gathered itself around him and waited for the main gate to be opened to let them pass.

"Off we go now," said a firm voice at Dodd's elbow, and he looked down to see Lady Hunsdon in a respectable but ordinary tawny woollen kirtle, holding a walking stick and wearing a very determined expression.

"Ah…" Dodd began.

"We'll take a boat and you can explain it all to me," she said. Dodd looked about for her normal gang of Cornish wreckers and found only the wide and freckled Captain Trevasker standing behind her, looking highly amused.

"Ay m'lady," said Dodd, since there was evidently no help for it.

They walked down through the gardens with their polite boxtree knot designs and orchard at the end, hedged with raspberry and gooseberry bushes and a row of hazels. Lady Hunsdon didn't lean much on her walking stick since she had her hand laced into the crook of Dodd's elbow, not quite a jailer. They got to the boatlanding, where Dodd found that Captain Trevasker had already hopped into the smaller of the two Hunsdon boats, and handed Lady Hunsdon down to the cushioned seat at the end. The rowers were waiting there in their headache-producing black and yellow stripes. Once Lady Hunsdon was settled and had nodded to the chief of them, they set off.

In the middle of the river, Lady Hunsdon leaned over and tapped him on the knee.

"Now then, Sergeant Dodd," she said, and her eyes had a roguish twinkle in them which went some way to explaining why the bastard son of Henry VIII had married a West Country maiden with only a small dowry. "Let's find out what that scallywag son of mine has been up to. Tell me everything you've been doing."

Dodd coughed, thought hard and then decided that the unvarnished truth was easier to remember than any improvement of the story. He started at the beginning, went through the middle, and ended with Pickering. He left out his discussion with Carey the night before.

"Hmm," said Lady Hunsdon. "Well then, let's go and see that young lawyer, shall we?"

It was only a little way along the Thames bank to Temple steps where Trevasker hopped out first and handed the Lady up while Dodd helped make fast and jumped out onto the small boatlanding.

A group of lawyers in their sinister black robes were clattering down the steps and tried to get into the Hunsdon boat. Trevasker moved in front of them and growled that it was a private craft. One of them had the grace to bow in apology for the mistake to Lady Hunsdon while the others started bellowing "Oars!" None of the Thames boatmen seemed in a hurry to take them anywhere, probably because they were students at one of the Inns and law students were notoriously almost as bad as apprentices for not paying tips and being sick in the back of the boat on the way home.

Lady Hunsdon climbed the steps and then headed in the direction of the Temple. Dodd led the way to the ramshackle buildings where Enys had his chambers. Lady Hunsdon looked narrow-eyed at the steep uneven stairs and sat herself down on a nearby pile of flagstones.

"Ask Mr. Enys if he will come down to meet an old lady," she said. "I doubt my poor old knees will take me to the top of that lot. Off you go Sergeant. Captain Trevasker shall bear me company."

Dodd headed up the stairs. Halfway there he heard shouting and speeded up, taking them two at a time until he came out on to the landing where the pieces of Enys's door were stacked in a corner, the new raw wood of its replacement wide open and two men standing facing each other in the still half-wrecked sitting room. There was a curtain across the gap to the second room.

One was Enys pale-faced and furious, the other was Shakespeare, hat off, bald head gleaming in the light from the small window, and a certain smug look on his face. They had obviously stopped their quarrel when they heard Dodd's boots on the stairs.

Shakespeare peered out of the window and smiled. "I see my lady has come to see you as well," he murmured. "I shall leave you to consider matters."

With a bow to Dodd he left and trotted down to the court-yard, humming some ditty to himself. Dodd glared after him. If they had been on the Borders, he would have been certain the man was putting the bite on for protection...Mr. Ritchie Graham of Brackenhill is willing to protect your barn from burning while it has such a wonderful quantity of hay in it, but will need his expenses paying...That kind of thing. It was the expression on the face. That smugness. Dodd scowled. Having once felt sorry for Shakespeare for being a poet, he no longer did. The man was nothing but trouble.

"Sergeant," said Enys, sounding tense again, "Can I help you?"

"That poet," said Dodd, "what did he want?"

Enys paused, frowned, took breath, then let it out again and smiled cynically. "Nothing good, you may be sure. However, it is confidential."

"Ay," said Dodd, being rather tired of the word and the general atmosphere in London of people not telling other people things they needed to be told. "Milady Hunsdon wants tae know if ye'll be kind enough to come down to her..."

"Of course," said Enys, putting on his hat.

Down in the shade of an old almond tree perhaps planted by one of the Knights Templar, Lady Hunsdon looked Enys sharply up and down. "What did that poet want?"

Enys bowed. "Unfortunately," he said, "I am not at liberty..."

"He's not one of your clients, is he?"

"Not exactly. However..."

"Well then, what's he up to. I know he spies for somebody, probably Heneage."

Enys blinked and tried unsuccessfully to hide his surprise. Then there was another cynical smile pulling his face. "I cannot say I'm surprised, ma'am, but the matter is still confidential."

"Indeed?" said Lady Hunsdon, very chilly. "When you change your mind you may speak to me about it. Now then. Mr. Vice Chamberlain Heneage. How far have you got with your case for Sergeant Dodd?"

Enys gave her the situation pretty much as Dodd had described it, only in legal-talk. Dodd might have been offended a month or two earlier, but he knew that this was simply the way Carey proceeded and no doubt he had learned it from someone.

"Attend upon me at Somerset House tomorrow," milady ordered. "I shall have the steward make you a payment and I may have a little more work for you. My son tells me he was impressed by your abilities in court."

Enys coloured at that, bowed to her.

"We shall see how you are at drafting. Do you have a clerk?"

"No milady, but I myself can write a fair Secretary or Italic, as needed."

Lady Hunsdon nodded and wiggled her fingers at him. "Off you go then, Mr. Enys. Oh by the way, are you any kin to the Enys twins from the farm near Penryn?"

Enys paused, breathed carefully. "Cousins, my lady," he said. "There are only two of them but three in my family."

"Hm. Interesting. I didn't know that old Bryn Enys had a brother?"

"Perhaps second cousins?"

"Hm."

Enys bowed and turned back to his chamber. "Sergeant, may I ask you something." Dodd went with him up the stairs again. "I was wondering if you meant what you said about teaching me to fight?"

Dodd rubbed his chin. "Ay, I did. I dinna want tae be put to the trouble o' finding another lawyer. And it's a pity for a man to wear a sword and not know how to use it."

Enys nodded and swallowed hard.

"Is it a duel," Dodd asked nosily, unable to help himself. "Wi' Shakespeare?"

"Er…no, only…Ah. I think you're right. I mean about not knowing how to use my sword properly."

"Ay. Where's yer sword?" Enys picked it up out of the corner and handed it to Dodd. "And is yer wrist better?"

"A little sore still but…"

"Ay. Draw yer sword then."

"But…um…surely we cannot practise in such a small space…"

"No, we're no' practising. I wantae see something."

Enys obediently drew his sword from the scabbard with some effort and stood there holding it like the lump of iron it was.

"Ay, I thocht so," said Dodd, holding Enys's wrist and lifting his arm up to squint along the blade. "It's too big for ye and too heavy. When would ye like a lesson? I cannae do it now for I'm attending on her ladyship."

"Perhaps this afternoon? Should I buy a new sword?"

"Not wi'out me there or they'll cheat ye again wi' too much weapon for ye." Of course, in London you could simply go to an armourer's and buy a sword instead of having to get it made for you by a blacksmith. He kept forgetting how easy life was here.

Dodd tipped his hat to Enys and trotted down the stairs again to Lady Hunsdon who smiled at him.

"What did he want?" she asked as they set off again.

"Swordschooling fra me."

"A very good idea. I'm sure you would be an excellent teacher, sergeant, if unorthodox."

"Ay," He might as well agree with the hinny, even though he didn't know for sure what unorthodox meant.

"Try and find out what Shakespeare was about for me, will you?" added Lady Hunsdon. "I'm sure it's important."

"Ay milady."

"Now then. About the documents that Robin has been keeping from me."

Dodd said nothing. There was that roguish twinkle again. She tapped his knee as well. He suddenly realised where Carey got some of his more annoying habits. "Come along, Sergeant, the pair of you managed to raid Heneage's house a few days ago and my son could no more keep his hands off any interesting bits of paper he found there than turn down the chance of bedding some willing, married, and halfway attractive Frenchwoman. Also you searched Richard Tregian's room for me but didn't tell me what you found there—quite understandable in the circumstances but no longer acceptable." She smiled at him, dimples in her rosy cheeks.

Dodd leaned back on the seat and sighed, wishing for his pipe. "They're in his room," he said, deciding to save time. "I dinna think he had decoded them yet, but…"

"He might not tell you if he had." She nodded.

The boat was heading back to Somerset House steps where they climbed out—Lady Hunsdon was lifted bodily up to the boatlanding by Captain Trevasker without noticeable strain, something that impressed Dodd.

He went with her back to the house and followed her up the stairs and along the main corridor into the chambers that Carey had been given, along with Hunsdon's second valet to help with the perenniel labour of his clothes. Dodd felt awkward, snooping about in another man's property, but Lady Hunsdon marched in and looked about her.

"At least he has grown out of dropping his clothes in heaps on the floor," she said, "now he's learned the cost of them."

Dodd considered that it was hardly thrift that had cured Carey of dropping his clothes, much more likely it was vanity and the training that serving the Queen at court had given him.

She went over to the desk Carey had been using and looked at the pile of papers there. Her eyebrows went up. "Well well, are these the ones?"

Dodd recognised the copy of the paper he had found in Tregian's rooms and the paper itself, still smelling faintly of oranges. Lady Hunsdon was frowning down at it.

"Ay," said Dodd, wondering why Carey hadn't hidden them. Presumably he hadn't bothered to lock his door because he knew his mother would have the key but…He stole a look at Lady Hunsdon.

"Hm." She went to the fireplace, picked up the poker, and stirred the ashes. There was a mixture of charred wood, the remains of one of the withered oranges that cost outrageous prices in the street until the new crop arrived from Spain nearer Christmas. Also there was a lot of feathery bits of burnt paper. She bent and picked up a charred fragment and peered at it closely.

"Sergeant, my eyes are not what they were. Can you make this out?"

Dodd came over and looked at the burnt paper—there were letters on it in Carey's handwriting but that was all he could see.

"Ah canna read it, but it's Sir Robert's hand right enough."

"I thought so." Lady Hunsdon glared at the fragment, then went to the chest in the corner where Carey kept some of his books and started sorting through them.

Dodd checked the desk and found a pile of books, including two bibles, poetry, a romance, and a prayerbook. He also found a cancelled pawn ticket which he quietly picked up and put in his beltpouch.

Lady Hunsdon sighed, closed the chest, and sat on it.

"I think Robin has managed to decode the two letters," she said. "But I don't understand why he burnt his translations yet kept the coded copies. Damn it. I shall have to ask him when he comes back from hawking this evening, although no doubt he will be very full of himself. Walsingham trained him well when he was in Scotland."

Dodd was thinking about going out into the courtyard and filling his pipe since he hadn't had one today yet when he realised Lady Hunsdon was looking at him beadily again.

"I wonder what that big-headed sodomite has been up to all this time," she said. "Shakespeare says he's quite happy, writing a play and drinking our cellars dry. Would you go and see him, Sergeant?"

At least with Marlowe he could get a pipe of tobacco. Dodd stood up in something of an unseemly hurry and Lady Hunsdon followed him out of the room, bending to lock it with one of the keys she was wearing on her belt. When in her husband's house, it seemed, she was the lady of the house and no other. Emilia

Bassano seemed to have moved permanently to the household of the Earl of Southampton which was tactful of her. Although it left unsettled a number of problems, including the question of who was the father of her unborn babe.

Dodd bowed to milady and then went to the back of the huge house, where the second floor guest chambers overlooked the courtyard. Sitting by the door to one of the lesser rooms was one of Hunsdon's servingmen who gave Dodd a cautious look and forebore to stand up.

"I've come tae speak tae Marlowe," Dodd explained.

The servingman waved at the door. "He's got it locked from the inside," he said. "My lord says he can go out any time he likes but I have to go with him. So far he hasn't."

Dodd went to the door and knocked on it.

"Go away," came a slurred voice.

He knocked again. Not loudly, he just kept knocking. There was an explosion of swearing and the sound of a chair being pushed back, then a bolt being shot. Marlowe's unshaven face looked round the door, eyes frighteningly bloodshot and a reek of tobacco and booze blending into a fog around him.

"Oh, it's you," he said ungraciously. "What do you want?"

"I want tae speak to ye, Mr. Marlowe," said Dodd as politely as he could. "Can we share a pipe o' tobacco?"

"No we can't because I've bloody run out and that boy hasn't come back yet."

"Ah could go and buy ye some?"

Marlowe grunted.

"Or ye could come wi' me and…"

"Look," said Marlowe through his stained teeth, "I'm busy, understand? I'm writing a play that will never be performed and it's the best play I've ever written. I don't care what you want to talk to me about and I don't care what Sir Robert wants but if you'll fetch me a pouch of Nunez's New Spanish mix, I'll be grateful."

Dodd shook his head regretfully at the insanity of writers, along with the servingman, and trotted off down the stairs. The gateman opened for him with a smile and he headed for Fleet

Street where the tobacconist was in his shiny new shop with printed papers and ballads of the wildmen of New Spain. That was where you went if you wanted gold or silver, over the sea to the New World, everyone knew that. Not marshy Cornwall.

On impulse, once he had the tobacco he went into the pawnbroker's at the end of Fleet Bridge where an old skinny man in a skullcap and long foreign-looking robe sat reading a book back to front.

"Ah," said Dodd, not sure how to start, "are ye the master here?"

The foreigner unfolded himself and came to the counter where he smiled. "Senhor Gomes," he said with a bow and a strong sound of foreign in his voice. "At your service, senhor."

"Ay," said Dodd, pulling out the cancelled ticket. "D'ye ken…Ah, do you recall if Sir Robert Carey redeemed anything here today?"

Senhor Gomes took the ticket. He smiled at once. "Ah, milord Robert, of course, senhor. He said you might enquire. He has repaid his loan on his court suit, the doublet with lilies and pearls upon velvet, and a cloak he had pawned before."

"When did he do this?"

"Yesterday, very late. He woke me up to do it, he said it was very urgent."

"Ay?" Dodd was puzzled. Why would Carey need his court clothes urgently to go hawking. In any case, he had left for Finsbury Fields wearing his hunting gear, the forest green and nut-brown doublet and hose that was now a little ill-fitting, or so he complained proudly. "Did he pawn anything else?"

"No, Senhor. Forgive me, but can you tell me your wife's full name?"

"What?"

"Your wife? Her full name?"

Dodd's eyes narrowed and his neck prickled. Once again he caught the scent of deception and intrigue where nobody can be trusted simply by their face. And why on earth would Carey want his Court clothes. "Janet Armstrong," he said with a gulp.

Senhor Gomes reached under the counter and brought out a letter addressed to Sergeant Dodd and sealed with Carey's carved emerald ring—the Swan Rampant again. Dodd broke the seal, opened the letter and read a short note: "Sergeant, I have decided to go to Court to discuss recent events with my liege Her Majesty the Queen. Please reassure my parents if necessary. Use my funds as you see fit to solve the problem. I will look forward to seeing you in Oxford or at Court if the Queen decides to move." The letter was signed with Carey's full signature.

Pure rage practically lifted Dodd from the ground. He could feel his neck going purple and his teeth grinding. The bastard. The ill-begotten limp-cocked, selfish popinjay of a...

Senhor Gomes was backing away from the counter and quietly reaching down for a veney stick behind him. Dodd folded the paper, his fingers clumsy with the urge to throttle the man for betraying him and leaving him in the complicated, confusing pit of iniquity that was London. Unfortunately, Carey was not immediately available so he stuffed the letter in his belt-pouch. Then he stood for a full minute, fists quivering, breathing hard through his teeth until he had calmed down enough to talk and act like a normal man.

"Ay," he said. "Is that all?"

"Yes, senhor."

Dodd walked out of the shop and stared up at the awning unseeingly. God damn it. God damn it to hell. On a thought he turned back. "Er...Thank you, Senhor Gomes," he said. The old foreigner was again reading his book back to front and raised his hand slightly in acknowledgement. Poor old man, not knowing which way round you read a book. Even Dodd knew that.

He hurried up the street, keeping a weather-eye out for attacks as always, and came to Somerset House without a single person claiming him as their cousin. It must have been true what Pickering had said, that he had ordered his people not to try anything with Dodd.

Marlowe opened his door a crack and reached for the pouch, but Dodd held it out of reach and scowled at him meaningfully.

Marlowe scowled back, his hand dropping to where his sword would have been if he had been wearing it. Dodd dropped his hand to where his own sword actually was and showed his teeth in as pleasant a smile as he could muster. In the temper he was in, he was half-hoping that Marlowe would try something on with him so he could have the satisfaction of beating somebody up.

Marlowe cursed and opened the door so Dodd could come in. He almost fell over a tangled heap of shirts by the door and then had to wade through screwed up papers, bits of pen, drifts of hazelnut shells and mounds of apple cores, and several books lying on the rush mats face down. The bed looked as if a pack of bears had played there and the desk was piled high with paper and more pens. The place reeked of aqua vitae, beer, wine, and pipe smoke, and someone who has been cooped up indoors for too long. At least there were no old turds in the fireplace, although the jordan under the bed badly needed emptying.

Marlowe was standing by the flickering fire with his arms folded across his embroidered waistcoat. He had his doublet off, presumably lost somewhere in the junk on the floor—no, for a wonder it was hanging on a peg—and his shirtsleeves rolled up and stained with ink. There were bags under his red eyes big enough to hide a pig in and his voice was hoarse with smoking.

"Well?" he demanded. "What's so important that you're bothering me with it?"

"Have ye been in here all this time?" asked Dodd, tucking the tobacco into his sleeve again.

From the contempt on Marlowe's face it was obvious he thought this was a very stupid question. "Yes, of course I have. Where else would I be? I'm writing a play."

"What's it about?"

"Edward II, a King of England who loved boys and was not ashamed to show it," snapped Marlowe.

"Like the Scottish king?"

Something in Marlowe's face softened slightly. "Perhaps."

"Ay," said Dodd. "And what happened to him?"

"First his favourite and minion Piers Gaveston was murdered by his lords as happened in Scotland with the Duke of Albany. Then the King was murdered at the orders of the Earl of Mortimer. It is said, by a red-hot poker up the arse."

"Ay," said Dodd after a moment's assessment to see if the poet was joking. It seemed he wasn't. "Verra…poetic."

Marlowe frowned. "It depends on your definition of poetic. Do you mean appropriate?"

Dodd coughed. He did, but wasn't going to admit it.

"That was done so there would be no mark on the body, you know." Marlowe explained in a distant tone of voice. "Since he was a king they wanted it to seem that he died of natural causes. However, his screams gave them away."

He spoke in a disinterested way as if what he was describing was not quite enough to turn your stomach. He then took a sip from a cup of aqua vitae and Dodd realised that he was actually drunk. Not staggering drunk, nor fighting drunk, just thoroughly pickled. It surprised Dodd that anyone could write anything at all in that condition, but then Robert Greene had been able to scribble away when he was just minutes from death.

Marlowe sat down again at his desk, picked up his pen, and dipped it.

"Go away," he said. "I'm busy. Leave the tobacco on the mantelpiece."

God, the man was rude. Dodd considered simply hitting him and seeing what happened. No, he had to talk first. "I bought it because I wanted tae ask ye about a matter of spying as there's naebody else I can think of."

"Why not ask Will?"

"Ah dinna think he'd tell me. If he knows."

Marlowe grunted, dipped, and wrote. It was amazing how fast he did it as well, all the letters flowing out of the tip of his pen as if he didn't need to think about it at all and the pen not even catching a little, it was so well cut, just sliding smoothly across the paper. Incredible. Dodd enjoyed watching a craftsman at his trade. He noticed that Marlowe didn't hold the pen the way he did, in a clenched fist that soon became dank with sweat, but lightly, as if it were a woodcarver's awl.

"There's code I need to work out. Ah need tae find out how to break a code? How do you work it out?"

Marlowe grunted again.

"Well?"

"Well what? Are you still there?" He was counting something under his breath. "Why don't you go away?"

Dodd reached for patience. "Ah wis askin ye…"

"About codes. Why should I care? I only worked for Heneage because he has been known to pay well for it and I don't want to go on working for him which is why I'm here, as well as the fact that this is the first time I've had the peace and quiet to write my play since I drank the money the Burbages paid me for it…"

Dodd sighed. Why did Marlowe always have to be difficult? The man was as spiky and arrogant as if he had his own tower and a large family.

"Is this your play?" Dodd asked idly, putting a finger on the pile of paper in front of Marlowe.

"Yes it is and you can leave it alone…"

Dodd picked up the pile of papers and wandered over to the fire with it. He crumpled up the first page and fed it into the flames, which made Marlowe jump from his stool with a yelp of horror.

"What the hell…?"

"Ah wanted yer attention, Mr. Marlowe," said Dodd, judiciously feeding the next page into the flames. "Have I got it?"

"You can't burn my play…I…"

"Ah can," said Dodd, puzzled at this irrationality, "And Ah am." Another curled into red and yellow and fell to ash.

"I'll kill you."

"Nay, I dinna think so," said Dodd, smiling with genuine enjoyment at the humour of this idea. "Besides, there's nae need. All I wantae know is how ye work out a code."

"What code?" Marlowe was staring at the pile of papers in Dodd's hand, particularly the fourth page which he already had near the fire. He knew enough not to dump the whole lot onto the flames at once because that would put them out. In any case, this method worked better.

"A code made of numbers. Ah ken that Carey worked it out and I wantae know what he found but I've nae experience of spying." Dodd shook his head. "It's verra annoying."

Marlowe was actually trembling, although whether it was with fear or anger only time would tell. "And how the hell do you think I would know? Is it one of Heneage's codes?"

"Ah dinna ken, one paper wis in his office when we searched it, the other was…ah…in another place." Dodd stopped himself just in time. He didn't think Marlowe ought to learn anything he didn't already know about Richard Tregian and the mysterious Father Jackson.

"And do you know what kind of code it is?"

"Sir Robert said it might be one that used a pattern to change letters to numbers or that changed them at hazard and he'd need a codebook. There's been nae codebook found so he must have worked it out but I dinna ken what pattern it could have been and I havenae the time to puzzle ma heid over it." Dodd grunted with sour humour. "Nor the talent forebye. Ah'm no' a clerk, me."

Marlowe's eyes were narrowed. "There are other kinds of code. I doubt Carey could puzzle out either kind of numerical cypher by himself either. If he managed to work it out that means it must be tolerably obvious and simple because the man isn't nearly as clever as he thinks he is."

"Nor are ye, Mr. Marlowe," said Dodd pointedly, moving the pile of paper in his hands.

Marlowe paused and then added grudgingly, "There's a simpler kind of code which is where you use a very common well-known book as the key and refer to particular words by page number, line, and word number in a sentence. Then all you need to do is tell your correspondents which book it is and they can do the rest. The system has the benefit that you can use different codings for common words like "and" and "but" which makes it harder to crack. You also don't have a written key lying around which always looks suspicious. In some ways it's very secure, but simple to work out if you can guess the book being used."

Dodd thought about this. That made sense. "How d'ye find out what book it was?"

"Usually there's a symbol or name in another code which sets it out."

"Could that be an upside down A?"

Marlowe shrugged. "Could be, yes. You have to use that, then get the correct book, decode some of what's written, and see if it makes any sense at all. Generally you use a book that has been commonly printed but isn't obvious. For instance, nobody uses the Bible because it's too obvious. Why don't you ask Carey when he comes home from his hawking?"

Dodd wasn't about to answer that question. "Ah wantae surprise him."

"I'm sure you will. Now can I have my play back?"

Dodd showed his teeth. He would probably never get a better opportunity to find out what Marlowe had been up to. "Not sae fast, Mr. Marlowe." It was interesting to watch him: he folded his arms, his eyes half-closed and he leaned back slightly.

"If this is to be an inquisition, Sergeant, would you object if I got myself a cup of aqua vitae to wet my whistle?"

A rare smile lit Dodd's face. "Well now," he said, "On the one hand I *would* object, for a cup of aqua vitae's a fine thing to throw in a man's face when ye're about tae try and stab him and I'll thank ye to take yer hand fra yer eating knife, Mr. Marlowe."

Marlowe scowled and uncrossed his arms.

"There again," Dodd continued thoughtfully, "On the ither hand, Ah wouldnae object for I'm in a bad enough temper that Ah'd be fair grateful to ye if ye gave me the excuse to give ye the beatin' of yer life."

Marlowe looked sour. "What is it you want to know, Sergeant?"

"Ah wantae know what the hell ye've been up tae these past few weeks, Mr. Marlowe," said Dodd, "I know Sir Robert thinks he's got it worked out but fer me, it's a' a mystery."

Marlowe said nothing. To encourage him, Dodd put another sheet, taken at random from the middle of the pile, into the fire. The poet winced.

"I'll tell you what I can," he said sulkily, "If I know myself."

"All I wantae know whit were ye thinkin' of, setting a pack of roaring boys on us the ither night? Eh? And then bringin' in Topcliffe tae ambush us all? Ah take that as unfriendly, Mr. Marlowe, I surely do."

Marlowe was squinting slightly and Dodd realised he was talking too northern again. But before Dodd could try and repeat it more southern, Marlowe began to speak.

"Heneage was furious when you raided his house. He got the word from the clerk of the lists when he went to see how another case of his was progressing and instead of going to his house in Chelsea, he called upon me instead. He blamed me for…for arresting you instead of Sir Robert and for destroying his fine plan against my lord Hunsdon. He reckoned the whole mess was my fault and threatened me with a treason trial and Topcliffe, everything."

"Speakin' of which, why *did* ye arrange for me to be arrested?"

Marlowe shrugged. "It's not important, I made a mistake. I thought Carey and you would have changed clothes when I sent the men in to take you."

"Did ye tell Heneage this?"

"I did. He didn't believe me. He said I was working with Carey and accused me of betraying him."

"Ay?"

"He offered me the chance to redeem myself if both of you ended up either in the Fleet or dead. I warned him that if he killed Sir Robert, Lord Hunsdon would cease to be a Knight of the Carpet and become again what he was when he defeated Dacre in the Rebellion of the Northern Earls. And that his lady would be even more dangerous. We had an argument about it. At last he said I had to work with Topcliffe, who was with him, as it happened."

"Ay?"

"So Topcliffe and I laid a plan. I hired some roaring boys in Smithfield that I had used before, to lie in wait for you in Fleet Street that night in case you didn't come to the Mermaid. I told them you were not to be killed and if they were asked who had paid them, to make a show of resisting and then give my name. I thought that might bring Sir Robert into the Mermaid where Topcliffe could take him."

Dodd grunted. So he hadn't needed to get his sleeves wet half-drowning the man, he could have just asked him. That was annoying.

"Meanwhile Topcliffe went to gather his men and waited with them at another boozing ken near the Mermaid. I sent for him as soon as you arrived but he wasn't there—he had been called to the Tower on another matter. You had left by the time he came back and he was threatening me with the rack though it was all his fault. So when the boy told me there was a gentleman in the back yard asking questions, I near as damn it praised the Lord for it. Topcliffe sent for all his men and we took Carey easily enough, playing drunk, but you weren't with him and that worried us. We were right. Once Topcliffe had gone chasing after you into the night, Carey said something to me which...well, which made me reconsider. I wanted sanctuary, that was all. So...I helped him by knocking out one of the guards Topcliffe left behind and Carey dealt with the other one. Then you turned up and you know the rest."

Dodd nodded. Most of this fitted quite well. He would have to think it through very carefully before he trusted it, but just for the moment he would accept it.

Marlowe had crossed his arms again. "So, Sergeant? Are you satisfied?"

"Mebbe," Dodd allowed. "It isnae an obvious lie."

Marlowe gritted his teeth, obviously working hard to be civil. "Will you give me my play back now?"

Dodd put his head on one side, assessing Marlowe's temper. He remembered that the man had actually been arraigned for murder once, but got away with it on grounds of self-defence and probably Walsingham's pull and good lordship on behalf of his pursuivant.

"Nay sir, Ah've too much respect for ye. I'll take it wi' me, and leave it by the door when I'm done."

"But…"

Another page edged closer to the flames and Marlowe withdrew again, took his hand off his dagger hilt. Dodd tilted his head at the part of the room on the other side of the bed. "Ah want ye to stand ower behind the bed where I can see ye."

Marlowe went there with ill-grace.

"Ay, now lie on the floor wi' yer legs in the air against the wall where I can see them."

"What?"

"Ye heard me, Mr. Marlowe." Dodd screwed up some pages at random from the pile and put them in the flames where they flared and the iron salts in the ink thickly covering the paper turned the flames red. As always there was a feeling of relief to see something burn when he was angry. Marlowe made a choking sound in his throat. He lay down slowly, and put his legs up against the wall. Dodd thought of pinning him down with the clothes chest but then decided it was too much trouble.

He put the wad of paper under his arm, grabbed a handful of tobacco out of the packet he had brought and tucked it in his own pouch, then went very quietly to the door, opened it and slid into the passage. There he left Marlowe's precious play about boy-lovers, as he'd promised, although the play had made a good hostage and he didn't think he'd ever get any co-operation again from Marlowe. And it wasn't as if anybody would ever actually want to watch the thing in a playhouse. Not even London could be that full of buggers.

Dodd walked back to Carey's chambers—Carey had a bedroom and a parlour as well, which was twice the size of the little hut where Dodd had come to manhood after the Elliots burnt them out. Ridiculous—what would anyone want with all that echoing space? He tried to go in, but then stopped. Damn it. Lady Hunsdon had locked the door.

A low groan came from his lips. But Carey had clearly wanted him to solve the conundrum of the man who wasn't a priest being executed, and the man who was, dying in the Thames. Therefore…Dodd felt along the top of the doorframe and along the edge of the panelling by the tiled floor. There was a chest with a silver candlestick on it which caught Dodd's eye, so he went and picked it up and found a key tucked up in the base. He snorted, took the key, put the candlestick down, opened Carey's chamber door, went in and locked the door behind him.

He sat down and stared at the papers with the upside down As at the top, looked at the books. None of them began with the letter A, nor were they about anyone whose name began with A, nor were they by men whose names began with A. Yet Carey had worked the thing out and as Marlowe had said, he wasn't that clever, bloody sprig of a courtier that he was. Nor did he have magical powers, God damn him, unless you counted overweening self-confidence and the luck of the devil.

Dodd wandered around the room again, looked in the chest, and nodded. Carey had taken his dags with him, somehow, and his sword. He must have sent someone to meet him in Finsbury Fields with a remount and packpony.

A thought occurred to Dodd. He carefully locked up behind him, went back to his own chamber, found the wickerwork box stuffed with hay in which was Janet Armstrong's highly valuable new green velvet hat, and picked it up. Another thought occurred as he saw his old homespun doublet and hose hanging on a hook at the back of the door. Time to do something about them, so he took out some of the hay and stuffed the clothes and his old hemp shirt and a few other things into the box. Then he wandered down to the kitchens off the back courtyard where he had a quiet word with the undercook and appropriated a bag of sacking that had contained pot-herbs. This he shook out carefully and wrapped around the package with string, wrote a label addressing it to Mr. Alexander Dodd, the Guardroom, Carlisle Castle in his best handwriting. He thought a moment

and added a note to say that he, Sergeant Dodd, would pay back
the man that paid the carriage on it.

Then with a bellyful of good brown bread, cheese, and
pickled cabbage, and a quart of remarkably good ale that he
had cadged as well, Dodd went out the gate of Somerset House
and carried the whole surprisingly heavy thing all the way to
the Belle Sauvage Inn on Ludgate. It took him half an hour to
find a carter who was heading for York and knew another one
that made the round as far north as Carlisle, carrying supplies
for the Castle. He payed an eyewatering amount for a deposit
to the carter, plus more for the man who would take it on from
York, and hoped that his brother Sandy would be kind enough
to stump up the money if it got to Carlisle. He could imagine
the stir when the thing arrived, especially if his men were nosy
enough to open it, and was quite cheered up by the thought of
their mystification.

He walked back a little quicker and went down an alleyway
into the dens of lawyers that clustered around the Inns of Court,
found Enys's chamber, and knocked on the door.

Enys put his head out immediately. "One minute," he said.
Dodd heard his voice murmuring and then another higher
pitched voice—it seemed he was urging his sister to greet
Sergeant Dodd but she adamantly refused.

Then Enys was on the landing, hat on his head and his too-
heavy sword at his side.

"Where will we get a new sword?" Enys asked as he locked
the door.

"We'll go to an armourer's I saw near Cheapside," said Dodd.
"Sir Robert said they made good weapons there."

In fact Carey had been trying to persuade Dodd to buy a
gimcrack unchancy foreign-style rapier with a curly handguard
and a velvet scabbard to replace his friendly, balanced, and
extremely sharp broadsword that had been made for him by
the Dodd surname's own blacksmith and fitted his body like a
glove. Dodd had sniffed at all Carey's reasons why rapiers were
the coming thing and then smashed the entire argument to bits

by enquiring why, if rapiers were so wonderful, Carey was now bearing a broadsword himself.

"You know my rapier broke last summer when I hit that Elliot who was wearing a jack…" Carey had said incautiously.

"Ay," said Dodd, feeling his point had been made for him. Carey grinned and started campaigning for Dodd to buy a twenty-inch duelling poinard instead until Dodd had lost his temper and asked if Carey was working on commission for the armourer.

Enys nodded and trotted down the stairs and out into the sunlight. The year was tilting into winter right enough, with the orchards full of fruit and nuts and the hedges and gardens full of birds stealing the fruit, and angry wasps.

They walked up Ludgate, past St Paul's, and Dodd found the armourer's shop he wanted. It was not at all showy and didn't have parts of tournament armour and wonderfully elaborate foreign pig-stickers hanging outside in advertisement of the weaponsmith's abilities. On the other hand, his barred windows were of glass and the swords hanging there seemed nicely balanced.

They went in, Enys hesitating on the threshold and looking around in wonder.

"Ay," said Dodd, "it's odd not to have yer sword made for ye, but…" He shrugged.

The armourer remembered Dodd as having come with Carey since he was wearing the same unnaturally smart woollen doublet. Soon there were several swords laid out on the counter with the armourer excitedly pointing out the beauty of the prettier sword. Dodd picked up one of the others, with a plain hilt, a grip of sharkskin and curled quillions. He felt the weight, drew it, sighted along the blade, flexed the blade, sniffed it, balanced it on his finger, then handed it to Enys who nearly dropped it.

Enys swung it a few times experimentally while Dodd and the armourer retreated behind a display post with breastplates mounted on it. Enys smiled.

"That's much better, much easier."

"Ay," sniffed Dodd, "I thocht so, Mr. Enys. The one ye've got is a couple of pounds heavier."

He turned to the armourer and asked if he would do a part-exchange while Enys eagerly fumbled his sword belt off and handed it over for inspection. The armourer frowned when he saw it, looked hard at Enys, then shook his head.

"You're right, sir," he said, "this is the wrong sword for you. May I ask where you got it?"

"It's mine. My brother gave it to me."

"Ah. I see, sir. And I expect your brother is a couple of inches taller and wider-shouldered? Well, I can certainly make a part-exchange. Shall we allow an angel for the old sword and thus I will require fifteen shillings."

Dodd thought that was very reasonable for a ready-made sword and so Enys handed over the greater part of what Hunsdon had paid him for his court work to date, buckled on the new weapon, and went to admire his fractured reflection in the window glass.

"Sir, I should tell you that I've seen this sword before," said the armourer quietly to Dodd. "Seeing as you're Sir Robert's man."

"Ay?" said Dodd.

"I sold it to a man who called himself James Enys but who was not that man."

Dodd found his eyebrows lifting. "Ay?" he said, rubbing his lower lip.

"Taller, broader-shouldered, something similar in the face and just as badly marked with smallpox."

"Hm."

"Also, he was wearing the exact same suit. But it wasn't him, sir, I'd stake my life on it."

Dodd quietly handed over sixpence, ignoring the small voice at the back of his head that protested at this outrage. "Thank ye, Mr. Armourer," he said, quite lordly-fashion, "That's verra interesting."

He went out into the sunny street where Enys was waiting for him and gave the lawyer a considering stare.

"Now where shall we practise?" asked Enys. "Will you teach me to disarm people?"

"Ah'm no' gonnae teach ye nothing special," said Dodd with a shudder. "Just the basics."

On a thought he went back into the shop and came back out with two veney sticks the armourer had sold for a shilling—he liked them because they had hilts and grips like swords but were still sticks. They made adequate clubs, but were best for sword practise with someone who was unchancy and ignorant.

As they made their way to Smithfield, Dodd was thinking hard. There had always been something not quite right about Enys and it seemed Shakespeare had found it out. Perhaps Enys had killed his brother and taken his place and then pretended to look for him afterwards? Perhaps Enys's brother was still in the Thames as the priest had been?

Or perhaps he was playing cards at Pickering's? The man Dodd had thought was Enys—what was his name, Vent?—fitted the armourer's description exactly. And what about the sister? Where was she? He'd heard her voice but…Why had Enys locked the door of his chambers when his sister was within? Was she his prisoner?

Eyes narrowing, Dodd led the way to a corner of the Smithfield market that was not already occupied by large men loudly practising their sword skills, generally sword-and-buckler work which was the most popular fighting-style. Some of them watched him cautiously out of the corners of their eyes. In another corner were better-dressed men doing what looked like an elaborate dance composed of circles and triangles and waving long thin rapiers. Foreigners, no doubt, doing mad foreign things.

Dodd gave Enys one of the veney sticks and decided to see if the man was faking his cack-handedness. He took him through the en garde position for a sword with no shield or buckler, with his right leg and right arm forward as defence, and showed him the various positions. They went through a slow and careful veney using the main attacks and defences that Dodd's father had first taught him when he was eight. Dodd's face drew down longer and sour at that thought.

Once Enys had corrected his feeble grip and got out of the habit of putting his left hand on the hilt for the cross-stroke, as if he were wielding an old-fashioned bastard sword, Dodd bowed to him, saluted, and attacked.

Enys struggled to do what he'd been shown but that was not in fact the problem. He defended slightly better now, but even when Dodd spread his hands, lowered his veney stick and stood there completely unguarded, Enys still did not attack. Dodd scowled at him ferociously.

"Och?" he said, "whit's wrong wi' ye, ye puir wee catamite of a mannikin? Want yer mother? She's no'here, she's down the road lookin' for trade."

Enys stopped and blinked at him with his veney stick trailing in the mud. Dodd, who had never seen anything so ridiculous in his life, lifted his own veney stick and hit Enys hard across the chest with it. Enys yelped, staggered back clutching the place, and nearly dropped his stick.

"It's ay hopeless," said Dodd disgustedly. "If ye willnae attack me when I'm open nor when I strike ye…"

For a moment he thought there were tears in Enys's eyes, but then at last the man made a kind of low moaning growl and came into the attack properly. Dodd actually had to parry a couple of times and even dodge sideways away from a very good strike to his head. There was a flurry when Enys came charging in close trying for a knee in Dodd's groin and Dodd trapped his arm, shifted his weight, and dropped the man on his back on the hard-trampled ground in a Cumbrian wrestling throw he hadn't used for ten years because everyone in Carlisle knew it too well. Enys was still struggling, mouth clamped, face white, so Dodd twisted his arm until he yelped again.

"Will ye bide still so I dinna have to hurt ye?" shouted Dodd in his ear, and Enys gradually stopped. He was heaving for breath and even Dodd was a little breathless, which annoyed him. "Now then. That was a lot better. Ye had some nice blows in there and ye came at me wi' yer knee when ye couldnae touch me wi' yer weapon, that's a good thing to see. Ah like a man that isnae hampered by foolish notions."

"What?" Enys was still gasping.

"Ye'll need tae watch yer temper," added Dodd, helping the man up and dusting him down. "Ye cannae lose it just because ye got thumped on the chest."

"You deliberately made me lose my temper?"

"Ay. Ah cannae teach nothing to a man that willnae attack and if ye've the bollocks to attack when Ah touch ye up, then there's something to work wi'? Ye follow?"

Dodd was aware that Enys's eyes were squinting slightly as he tried to follow this and so Dodd said it again, less Cumbrian. He was getting better at that, he thought. Enys laughed shortly.

"So should I get angry or not?" he asked, still rubbing the bruise on his chest. "Lose my temper or not?"

Dodd shrugged and took the en garde position again. "It depends. If ye cannae kill wi'out losing yer temper, then lose it. But if ye can get angry and stay cold enough to think—that's the best for a fighting man. Not that ye're a fighting man, ye're a lawyer, but still…There's nae harm in being able to kill if ye need to."

Enys nodded, and guarded himself. Dodd attacked again. He was still as careful as he could be and pulled most of his blows, but Enys was at least taking a shot at him every so often, even if he generally missed or was stopped. He lost his stick half a dozen times before he learnt not to get into a lock against the hilt since he wasn't strong enough for it. And on one glorious occasion, he caught Dodd on the hip with a nice combination of feint and thrust. Dodd put his hand up at the hit and grinned.

"Ay," he said, "that's it. Well done."

Dodd decided to stop when he saw that Enys was alarmingly red in the face and puffing for breath again, even though they had only been practising for an hour or two. Dodd had taken his doublet off and was in his shirtsleeves, but Enys seemed too shy to do it.

He seemed relieved when Dodd lifted his stick in salute. "Ah'm for a quart of ale," he said. "Will ye bear me company, Mr. Enys?"

"God, yes."

Over two quarts of ale at the Cock Inn, hard by the Smithfield stock market so rank with the smell of livestock, and a very fine fish pie and pickles, Dodd lifted his tankard to Enys with an approving nod.

"Ye're a lot better than ye were," he said, "though I'd not fight any duels yet."

Enys smiled and flushed. "I never thought I could be able to fight."

"But did ye no' fight any battles wi' yer friends when ye were breeched and got yer ain dagger?" Dodd asked with curiosity. He remembered with clarity the great day when he had been given his first pair of breeches made for him by his mother and his dad strapped his very own dagger round his waist. He must have been about six or seven and very relieved to get away from baby's petticoats and being bullied into playing house all the time with his sisters' friends. After that he spent most of his time play-fighting with his brothers, cousins, and friends when he wasn't having to go to the Reverend for schooling. Within months he had lost a front tooth in a fistfight over football and got a birching from Reverend Gilpin and several thick ears from other outraged adults for damaging things by carving them with his dagger. He still liked to whittle when he could.

Enys looked down modestly. "I was a sickly child," he said. "I don't think I did."

The ale tasted wonderful when you were so dry, Dodd finished his quart in one and called for more. He shook his head. "Well, if ye keep on wi' it and hire yerself a good swordmaster, there's nae reason ye couldna fight yer corner if need be."

"It's interesting," said Enys after he'd found a bone in a large lump of herring from the pie. "The manner of thinking for a fight that you explained to me is very similar to that needed for a courtroom—being angry without losing your temper, so you can think. Only in the case of a courtroom, of course, the weapons are words."

"Ay?" Dodd thought Carey had said something similar about legal battles. "Surely ye need to be verra patient as well."

"That too," Enys agreed, "and also well-organised and thorough. But there is very little to equal the joy of disputing with a fellow lawyer and beating him to win the point. I used to greatly enjoy mooting at Gray's Inn."

"Ah." The second quart was going down a treat and all Dodd's worries about what would happen that evening started to fade away. Not his fury with Carey, though. That still nested in his gut. He could find out what mooting was later. "A man I met the day said I should give ye his compliments—he had very much the look of ye and I thocht he was ye at first, but his voice is deeper, and he's taller and broader as well." Enys had stopped chewing and was staring at Dodd. "Could it be yer brother that ye thought Heneage had taken?"

Enys swallowed the piece of pie whole and nodded vigorously. "Yes sir, it could indeed. May I ask where you met him?"

"He denied his name was Enys, said it was Vent, James Vent."

Enys smiled at that. "Even so. Where was he?"

"He were at Pickering's game, playing cards and losing."

Enys banged his tankard down. "Almost certainly it was my brother," he said. "I never met a man who was worse at cards nor more addicted to playing."

Dodd nodded. "Would ye like to meet him? Ah ken where Pickering's game is at the moment and Vent said he'd welcome a meeting wi' the man that wis insulting him by impersonating him to be a lawyer."

To Dodd's surprise Enys laughed. "That's my brother. Yes, I would. Thank God he's not dead. I had given him up and thought he was surely at the bottom of the Thames like poor Jackson whose corpse you showed me."

"Ay."

"How much had he lost and was he playing for notes of debt?"

"Nay, Pickering willnae allow it, he was playing for good coin and a lot of it."

"Oh," Enys frowned. "How unusual for my brother."

He looked thoughtful and pushed away the remains of his pie so Dodd polished it off and washed it down with the rest of his ale. He checked the sky for the time.

"It's too early for Pickering's game to start. I wantae go back to Somerset House now to…ah…do something. I can meet ye at sunset by Temple steps and we'll take a boat?"

Enys put down the money for his part of the bill and Dodd put down his. They went companionably enough out of the alehouse and headed across London. Enys went down one of the little alleys off Fleet Street to his chambers whilst Dodd ambled along Fleet Street to the Strand, thinking hard about the damnable book code that Carey must have broken the night before. It was the only thing that explained his actions today. And Dodd didn't have much time to solve the thing either. He had to be out of Somerset House before the trouble started.

What had Marlowe said? A commonly printed book but not predictable, therefore not the Bible. Obviously to make a code from it, you had to have it to hand…Now what was the book that Richard Tregian had had on the shelf where Dodd found the paper? Something quite common, as Dodd recalled, but a little surprising. What the hell had it been? He couldn't quite remember it.

Not realising he was scowling so fiercely that people were taking a wide path around him as he walked down through the crowds on Fleet Street, Dodd stopped and stared unseeingly at an inn sign for the Fox & Hounds, a few doors up from the Cock Tavern where he and Carey usually went out of habit. He'd looked at the book, recognised it, and dismissed it as uninteresting. Damn it to hell. It had been…

The inn sign was particularly badly painted, mainly out of over-ambition on the part of the sign painter, with the fox running as it were towards the sign and the hounds in the distance behind him, so it looked as if his head made the shape of a capital letter A upside down…

The backs of Dodd's legs actually went cold as he realised what the answer was. He blinked up at the inn sign which may have inspired the original code and almost certainly had inspired Carey to guess what it was. He cursed under his breath. Next thing he had loped along Fleet Street, past Temple Bar, knocking the beggars flying, along the Strand, and in at the gate of Somerset House which was quiet that afternoon. He went up the stairs two at a time to Carey's chambers and sat himself down sweating and puffing slightly at Carey's desk where he pulled Foxe's Book of Martyrs towards himself and set to the first coded letter.

It took him a long time and at the end of the hard labour he realised he actually had one and a half letters: one was from Fr. Jackson to somebody he addressed as "your honour" explaining that the trap was ready to be sprung as most of the lands were now held by the one called Icarus. The other was from Richard Tregian and also addressed to somebody he called "your honour" explaining that he had found out why certain lands were being sold for inflated prices as full of gold ore and good sites for gold mines. He was horrified and alarmed at it and was about to… The letter was unfinished.

Dodd leaned back and stretched his aching ink-splattered fingers. He stared into space for five minutes and then gathered up his translations and the original letters, folded them all and put them in his belt-pouch along with Carey's infuriating message. Hearing the cacophony of hounds and horses returning to the courtyard by the main gate, he stood up quickly and ran down the passageway to his own chamber where he collected his cloak and his new beaver hat that Carey had bought him a week before as a celebration of Carey's deliverance from his creditors.

He clattered down the back stairs and into the kitchen where he quietly grabbed half a loaf of bread and a large lump of cheese, then put them back because he had nowhere to stowe them since he wasn't on a horse and wasn't wearing a loose comfy doublet..

In the rear courtyard that led to the kitchen garden, the cobbles were covered in hunting dogs, very happy to be home and already gathering around their dog boy, tails wagging, tongues hanging, waiting to be fed.

"Sergeant Dodd, have you heard…" sang out the dog boy excitedly, but Dodd just waved a hand at him, slipped through the gate into the main garden, and headed down for the orchard and the boatlanding.

All the way there he was quietly praying there would be a boat waiting for him. There wasn't, of course. Still, Temple steps wasn't very far away, so Dodd climbed from the boat landing to the narrow strip of land between the orchard wall and the Strand itself, then eased himself along until he came to a fence which he climbed over, followed along until he came to the other fence, climbed over that, and continued through a narrow alley that led to a secret set of steps hidden by a curve in the river. That wasn't the one so he struggled along the top of a sea wall and then to another alley that passed through a shanty town full of hungry looking children in nothing but their shirts and dogs scuffing hopefully through the mud.

Finally he was at Temple steps, his ears itching in anticipation of the hue and cry that would be made for him once Lord and Lady Hunsdon realised who was missing. Enys was standing there, wrapped in cloak and hat, his expression a strange combination of hope and fear.

"Ay," said Dodd, not explaining why he was arriving by climbing out of a tiny handkerchief of herb garden, guarded by a ginger tomcat.

Enys raised his arm and yelled "Oars!" A Thames boat arrived quickly, the boatman looking very hopeful—ah yes, of course, the taste of students at the Inns for the fleshpots and dissipations of the South bank.

"Three Cranes in the Vintry," Dodd ordered, practically vaulting aboard. As usual Enys dithered over stepping in and nearly fell in the Thames again before he sat down.

"Are you sure, sir?" said the boatman. "I heard there's a good game at Paris Garden tonight…"

"Ye heard what Ah said," snarled Dodd. The boatman shrugged and started rowing the hard way.

They came up against the wharf which was quiet and Dodd paid the man and jumped out. Jesu he was getting as high-handed with his cash as Carey was—mind, it wasn't his cash, it was Carey's. That gave him a warm cosy feeling in the place where the rage was still packed tight.

As before there were a few well-dressed exquisites and one or two prosperous merchants hanging around not doing very much, including the boy in the tangerine paned hose and cramoisie doublet, a walking headache everywhere he went.

Mr. Briscoe was on the door as before, looking haggard with bags under his eyes. He touched his hat sadly to Dodd before stepping forward to stop Enys.

"Do I know you, sir?" he asked very politely.

"Ah, Sir Robert asked me tae bring him to meet Mr. Pickering." Dodd tried. Briscoe hesitated "It's Mr. Enys, my lord Baron Hunsdon's lawyer. He wis at the inquest, ye recall?"

Briscoe allowed them past and they climbed the steps to the gambling chamber with its banks of candles and white mats. Enys seemed quite open-mouthed at the women standing about there, with their strangely cut stays that cupped their white breasts but left them bare so the nipples were visible peeking over the lacy edge of their shifts like naughty eyes, prinking and pinking in the draught from the door.

Dodd dragged his eyes away and swallowed hard. It seemed his kidneys were recovering. Then he stopped one of the comely boys running past with trays of booze, and asked if Mr. Vent was there.

"No sir," said the boy. "Shall I tell Mr. Pickering you're here? He has some information for you."

"Ay."

Dodd took two cups from the tray as the boy turned to go and gave one to Enys who was bright red again. Dodd knew how he felt. All those round plump tits just begging to be cupped and fondled and licked…

He took a large gulp of brandywine and tried to look at something less entrancing. But the walls were hung with the cloths painted with completely naked people doing lewd things with swans and bulls and such. It was impossible to concentrate, which no doubt was half the intention.

"Mr. Pickering will see you gents now," said the boy at his elbow, so he tapped Enys on the shoulder and followed the boy into the back room where Pickering sat by the fire with a large plump man in a dark brocade doublet and snowy white starched falling band.

Pickering smiled as they came in and Dodd made his bow to include both of them, reckoning that a bit of respect to a headman on his own ground never did any harm and might do some good. Enys sensibly bowed too, rather more gracefully.

"Welcome back, Sergeant Dodd," said Pickering. "Sir Horatio was 'oping to meet Sir Robert. Is 'e here?"

"Ah. No," said Dodd, hoping he wouldn't have to explain further.

"Is 'e on 'is way?"

"Ah. No," said Dodd.

Pickering frowned and so did Sir Horatio. "I'm sorry to hear that. I hope I haven't offended him in…"

"Nay sir, nothing like that. He…ah…he found he had urgent business at court."

The plump man stood up and turned out to be as tall as Carey. He held out a hand to Dodd who shook it.

"Sergeant," he said in a smooth, deep, slightly foreign sound-ing voice, "I was hoping to discuss the question of the Cornish lands with your Captain, Sir Robert. I am Sir Horatio Palavicino, Her most gracious Majesty's advisor on matters financial and fiduciary."

Dodd wasn't quite sure what that meant.

"'e's the Queen's banker, Sergeant," said Pickering, spotting Dodd's confusion. "He sorts out the Queen's money."

Dodd's mouth went dry. "Ah," he said. Oh God, had the Queen bought some of the worthless Cornish lands? Was it too late to steal a horse and head north?

Yes it was. Much too late.

"Sit down, Sergeant, and you, Mr. Enys."

They sat on stools noticeably lower than the chairs seating Pickering and Sir Horatio. Sir Horatio smiled genially.

"I assume that Sir Robert has gone to Court to apprise the Queen of what he knows?" Dodd was relieved to be asked something he could answer with confidence.

"Ay sir," he said, "he couldnae do it safely by letter so he went tae speak to the Queen hisself."

Sir Horatio smiled and nodded. "As ever," he said, "Sir Robert is precipitate but correct."

From flushing an unbecoming shade of red as a result of the ladies outside, Enys had now gone an equally ugly pale yellow.

"Sirs," he said, leaning forward, "excuse my interruption, but is it true that the Queen does not know of this…ah…this land fraud?"

Sir Horatio sighed. "As far as I know, she does not."

"Ay she does now," said Dodd with confidence, "Sir Robert will have left this morning when he gave the huntsmen and falconers the slip and it's ainly forty miles. He'll be at court for sure by now."

"It may take him some time to gain audience with Her Majesty," said Sir Horatio. "But yes, correctly put. She *did* not know, Mr. Enys."

"Ah hope she hasnae bought none?" Dodd asked, voicing his main worry.

Sir Horatio laughed kindly. "Why would she need to," he asked, "since if there were gold there, she would own it in any case through Crown prerogative?"

Dodd nodded. "Ay," he said. "That's a relief."

Sir Horatio seemed highly amused by this. "Indeed it is."

"But…sir…" Enys was frowning with puzzlement, "I drafted many of the bills of sales and the deeds of transfer and I told Mr. Vice Chancellor Heneage that I thought the thing was not what it seemed. I told him that I knew many of the places had been assayed for tin many times and found to be barren of all metals including gold. It was why he dismissed me as his lawyer and then took steps to destroy my practice because he would not have what he called the falsity told abroad. But I assumed he had told Her Majesty at least."

There was a silence at this. Mr. Pickering seemed the least surprised at it, and in fact had a cynical smile. Sir Horatio turned and stared at Enys with an expression of mixed anger and calculation while Dodd groaned softly under his breath.

"When did you tell him this, Mr. Enys?"

"Months ago. He was very angry. I think because he had bought some."

"Hm. He was not the only one," said Sir Horatio. "Mr. Enys, I understand that you were in contact with the assayer, a Mr. Jackson."

Enys lifted his head. "No sir," he said, "that was not me, that was my brother whom I came here to find. And it was Father Jackson SJ."

"Society of Jesus."

Enys nodded.

"The man that was hanged, drawn, and quartered by Mr. Hughes?" said Pickering with a puzzled frown.

"Nay sir, that wasnae him. It was one Richard Tregian." Dodd corrected him. "Mr. Topcliffe substituted him for the Cornish gentleman."

Palavicino was leaning forward, his face full of bewilderment. "Substituted him?"

"Ay sir, and Fr. Jackson seemingly ended up in the Thames wi' a knife in his back but we dinna ken how or why."

Enys drew a deep breath. "Sir, my brother has been calling himself James Vent. Do you know where he is? Sergeant Dodd said he thought he had seen him here?"

"Vent?" Pickering's glittering little eyes had gone hard. "He was here but he ran out of money. Said he was going to the Netherlands again to make his fortune and headed for a ship he knew of in the Pool of London."

"Do you know which ship, sir?"

"The *Judith of Penryn*,"

The name didn't seem to mean much to Enys but Dodd recognised it. Och God, he had to get back to Somerset House after all.

"Thank you, sir," Enys was saying. "Will you excuse me, gentlemen. I must try and track down my brother and speak to him urgently. Sir Horatio was looking very thoughtful while Pickering was scowling."

Enys was already bowing to Pickering in thanks and heading for the door, no doubt to find a boat to chase his brother. For a moment Dodd wondered about telling him who owned the ship, then decided he would find out soon enough. As the lawyer clattered down the stair, Dodd had a thought about the now decoded letters. He had been wondering about it but now he made a decision. If Palavicino was the Queen's banker, perhaps he was the best way for Dodd to get the information safely out of his keeping and into the Queen's. It clearly all hinged on whoever Icarus might be a codename for and he had no idea, although he suspected Carey did. Icarus had been in normal letters, not numbers, so he supposed it was doubly important. He pulled out the coded letters and his laborious translations and handed them to Palavicino.

"That one," he said, tapping it, "I found hidden in Richard Tregian's chamber. The ither one…" He coughed, not sure how this would be received. "…ah, the ither one we found when we had a warrant to arrest Mr. Heneage for assault in my case and we were searching his house for him."

It seemed both Pickering and Palavicino knew about that because they both smiled.

"As usual, ingenious and appropriate," said Palavicino, not making a lot of sense as far as Dodd was concerned. "And what have we here?"

"The translation's there," said Dodd, quite proud of what he had done in only an afternoon. Sir Horatio looked hard at the writing and his lips moved as he read it. Then he looked up and nodded.

"Sergeant, thank you," he said. "I shall see the Queen receives this at once."

"Ay," said Dodd, thinking it might be about time to be going. Pickering stopped him. "Just a word before we go, Sergeant, about Sir Robert's enquiry," said Pickering quietly. "I've asked around and I will lay my life on it that not one of my people 'as lifted that survey out of the Cornish maid's purse."

"Eh?" said Dodd, then remembered. "Ay?" He was surprised. "Are ye sure?"

"Certain. I'd've 'ad it in my 'ands by yesterday night if any nip-purse or foist or any of their friends 'ad it, believe me."

Dodd nodded. That left only one place the survey could have gone to and now, he thought about it, made perfect sense.

"As for what the watermen think about whoever did in the Papist priest…It's only a rumour but they say 'e was escaping from Topcliffe's place in south bank marshes when it happened. I haven't found the man who rowed the boat for them so I can't say for sure. Unfortunately, he disappeared a couple of days ago."

"Thank ye, Mr. Pickering," said Dodd, thinking he knew what had happened to the poor boatman. "If ye hear any…"

There was a thunderous banging on the doors downstairs. Pickering jumped to his feet and stood there with his fists clenching and unclenching.

"What the 'ell…?" he said.

"Open in the name of the Queen!" came the roar from below. Dodd moved to the window and peered out. The area around the warehouse was full of large men in buff coats, another boat pulling up with more men in it. Out of it stepped Mr. Vice Chancellor Heneage with a very prim and satisfied expression on his plump prissy face. Dodd had forgotten how much he disliked the man. At least he was still sporting green and purple around his eyes and his nose was swollen.

Poor Enys had obviously walked straight into an ambush as he left to find his brother. He was being held with his arms twisted behind him by two men who looked pleased with themselves. Enys looked as if he might be sick and was still struggling.

"Och," said Dodd, cursing himself for a fool. He looked at Sir Horatio who was still frowning at the letters.

"Get him out o' here, Mr. Pickering," he said to the King of London who seemed too shocked to react. "Have ye no' a bolthole?"

Pickering blinked, shook himself and moved. "'Course I do. Come along, Sir Horatio."

He went to the corner of the small room and rolled back one of the mats. Dodd lifted the trapdoor, revealing stairs leading down. To his surprise, Pickering did not go down the steps but motioned to Sir Horatio.

"At the bottom is a door into a basement, it's a bit wet but don't worry. Open the door and go along the passage and you'll be in the warehouse over by the third crane, see?"

Palavicino looked out the window and nodded. "Now Sir Horatio," gravelled Pickering, making the two words sound like "sratio", "'ere's the key to the door of the warehouse. The seals is fake and you can put them back. Bring me the key when you can."

Palavicino nodded, took a candle from the mantlepiece, shook hands with Pickering, and then went down the stairs, moving remarkably quietly for so large a man.

There was more thundering and a banging downstairs and Heneage ordering the door to be opened in the name of the Queen. Pickering, short sturdy and bullet headed, looked at the door, pursed his lips, sucked his teeth, and squared his shoulders. From a mere wealthy merchant he had become something much more dangerous.

"I'm going to welcome in our visitors. I think you should slip away as well as I'm quite sure 'e's got a warrant for you."

Dodd quietly loosened his sword despite what Pickering had said, then followed the man through the gambling room where the players and the half-clad women were staring through the windows. "Mary," said Pickering to one of them, "put 'em away, luv," and the women started pulling their shifts up and relacing their stays so as to look a little bit more respectable. "Start moving out, girls," he added as he went past, quite quietly. The girls started ushering all the wealthy players to the back room where the trapdoor and secret tunnel were.

Dodd went down the polished stairs. Briscoe and the other henchman were standing on the inside of the barred and locked door as it shuddered to the blows of a battering room.

"Yerss," said Pickering, "plenty of time, gentlemen, these doors was put in by the Tunnage and Poundage. The girls are still busy upstairs. Meantime…What would you do if some jumped up court clerk did this to you in your own country, Sergeant Dodd?"

Dodd was amazed Pickering needed to ask. "If it were the Queen herself as did it, then I'd do nowt," he said, heavily, "but if it were aye one o' her men, then I'd have the Border alight in two hours, Mr. Pickering, the bells would a' be ringin' and the men would a' be riding. But Ah'm nobbut the Land-Sergeant of Gilsland and Ah could ainly call on the Dodds and the Armstrongs there and mebbe the Bells and the Storeys, four hundred men at best. If it were Richie Graham of Brackenhill that had his tower burned, by God, Mr. Pickering, there'd be fifteen hundred men i'the saddle by daybreak and Carlisle in flames the day after."

The King of London smiled briefly. "Hm," he said, "it ain't quite like that here in London, mind, but I agree wiv you, I will not be treated like this and I won't 'ave my men treated like this either. So, Sergeant, wot do you reckon?"

"Me? There's a man I'd like to talk to first and then…I wantae talk to the owner o' the *Judith of Penryn* and find this man Vent. And then, Mr. Pickering, Ah'm at yer disposal."

Pickering looked consideringly at his men. " Mr. Briscoe," he said quietly as the battering ram hammered home again, "would you do me the kindness to come and speak with me…"

To Dodd's surprise the man called Briscoe suddenly looked hunted and made for the stairs. His mate caught hold of him firmly by the neck and held him there.

Pickering went up to him. "Easy way or hard way?" he said softly through his teeth.

Briscoe licked his lips and started to cry. "Only, 'e took my Ellie, my missus, what's gonna have a baby, he took 'er down to his house and he said to me, 'e'd have 'er belly cut open to get the baby out and then 'e'd make me watch while 'e…"

"Heneage?"

Briscoe shook his head "Topcliffe."

"And?"

"And so I told 'im where the game would be and that we was waiting for Sir Robert to come back and…I told 'im."

"Topcliffe still got yer mort?"

Briscoe nodded, then hid his face in his hands. "I signalled when I saw the Sergeant," he whispered, his voice muffled.

Pickering shook his head. "Tim," he said in a low voice, "Why didn't yer come and tell me?"

"'e said 'e'd know if I did and 'e'd kill 'er right away."

Bang went the battering ram again. You had to admire the way the doors were standing up to it, thought Dodd. Surely Heneage would try gunpowder next?

Pickering nodded once. "I'm 'urt Tim," he said thoughtfully, "I'm 'urt you didn't find a way to tell me what was going on,"

"I know, Mr. Pickering, I'm ever so sorry, I couldn't fink 'ow to do it."

"Well, the damage is done now. What do you fink I should do about you?"

Briscoe studied the ground, and sniffled. He muttered something Dodd couldn't make out.

Pickering smiled. "'Course I'm going to kill you, Tim, but what should happen first?" He put his hand up on Briscoe's burly shoulder. "'Ave a fink about it, tell me later. Meanwhile, see Sergeant Dodd here?" Briscoe nodded. "'e needs a man at 'is back if 'e's to get away and do somfink about yer mort and yer kinchin. Will yer do that? Wivvout tipping 'im no lays?"

Briscoe nodded convulsively and looked up at Dodd who was now halfway up the stairs.

"Come on," Dodd grunted, and Briscoe followed him up to the room where the girls were just staggering down the steps carrying large bags of money, but still leaving some scattered about the tables. Dodd approved of that—the money would slow the searchers down considerably. The girl called Mary stood waiting by the trapdoor and a couple of the younger ones were bunched around her, looking angry and frightened.

"You're slow," she snapped. "I've got to lock it. Hurry up, we ain't got all night."

She looked somehow familiar but Dodd couldn't think where he might have seen her before. He went down the steps, followed by Briscoe, a long way down, to a passage that was dripping and evil-smelling but quite wide and well-flagged. It looked to have been built a long time ago. The trapdoor shut and locked behind them and there was a scraping sound of furniture going over it.

"Wait," said Briscoe, and paused by a grating. Dodd stood next to him and peered through the bars.

They were at foot-level. Like giants the men with the battering ram ran past them, hit the door...And went straight through, landing with shouts and crashing on the other side of it. Stepping over their legs, delicately, came Laurence Pickering, the King of London.

"Good evening, your honour," he said to the Vice Chamberlain of the Queen's Court with a perky bow. "How may I serve Her Majesty?"

Heneage brandished a paper at Pickering. "I have here a warrant to search for ill-doers and malefactors engaged in unGodly gambling and whoring within the bounds of the City of London and I have here one warrant for the arrest of one James Enys for assisting in the escape of a prisoner of Her Majesty and a further warrant for the arrest of Henry Dodd for high treason."

The pursuivants were already in the building, thundering and crashing around, Palavicino and the girls carrying the coin were somewhere ahead of them but Dodd couldn't tear himself away. From the odd angle, he could just make out Enys who was now standing very still between the two bullyboys who had hold of him, his face as white as his falling band. From the way he was part-hunched over, Dodd assumed somebody had kneed him or punched him in the gut.

Soon the men in buff coats started bringing out the girls who had been left behind and there was a gull-like clamour of furious argument, insult, and insinuation from them.

Heneage gave a smile of triumph. "You are James Enys, member of Gray's Inn, Utter Barrister?" said Heneage to Enys who hesitated for a moment and then nodded convulsively. Heneage struck him across the face as he had once struck Dodd: an experiment, to see what reaction he would get.

"Answer me properly," he said.

"Yes, I am now," said Enys softly, his eyelids fluttering. "God help me."

Heneage slapped him again. "You say, Yes I am, *your honour*," he corrected with a spiteful smile. Enys looked him gravely in the face and managed a lopsided smile in return.

"Your honour is of course, most wise and just," he said in his court-voice. "I am most grateful for your honour's elucidation in this matter."

Heneage's lips thinned and he raised his hand again. However for no good reason, he seemed to think better of it.

Dodd found his hand gripped so hard on his swordhilt, it hurt. He forced himself to relax and take his hand away. No point drawing a sword in a little tunnel, there was no room to wield it. He thought he had most of the whole mess worked out now, but not all of it, and he stared at Heneage as if the simple pressure of his gaze could damage the bastard.

"Your honour," came Enys's low voice. "Who was it saw me…"

"The boatman you hired. Did you think I wouldn't find him?"

Enys nodded, looking at the ground. The print of Heneage's hand was bright red against the pockmarks.

At last Heneage turned away from Enys to shout at the pursuivants who were crashing and ripping through Pickering's gambling room to bring any money to him. The girls were being loaded into one of the boats, still arguing and cursing and complaining that the Bridewell was becoming a pesthouse.

"Well, Mr. Heneage, ain't you going to arrest me too?" asked Pickering conversationally.

A muscle twitched in Heneage's cheek. "Later," he said. Pickering chuckled quietly.

"Queen's Warrant still in force then?" he said. Heneage said nothing.

That was interesting but Dodd heard another loud banging and crashing above. They had better get on. He hurried along the passage and then paused at a side turning.

"Whit is this place?"

"Smuggler's passage," said Briscoe, "to get the wine in and out of the bonded warehouse."

"Ay then, there'll be a door ontae the river to get to the Pool."

Dodd scratched with his dagger on the corner and then went down it. The passage tilted downwards and came to a grill that seemed to be locked. There had to be a mechanism or a lever or…

Briscoe had leaned down and pulled and the grill came up. They ducked under it and he let it go down again. A wooden door that was part rotten from the damp was a little further on. When they peered around the door, they found watersteps washed by the river.

As always the Thames was busy in the twilight. Dodd put his fingers between his teeth and whistled sharply. A boatman paused, changed direction, and came up to the steps. "Where to, masters?"

"Pool o' London, the *Judith of Penryn*."

"No chance, mate, I'm not shooting the bridge now. I'll take you to the bridge and you can walk."

Dodd shrugged and stepped into the boat, followed by Briscoe, who sat down in the back.. no, the stern…his face working.

"Never seen no one take a boat at them steps before," said the boatman. "What are they from?"

"Ah, a private house. Of a merchant," lied Dodd, even though Pickering would probably never use the place again and the Tunnage and Poundage men would have lost a useful source of income.

"Hm. Shows you never can tell. I thought I knew every set of watersteps on the river. I was telling my lord of Southampton just the other night that…"

Dodd was thinking as hard as he could. If Heneage truly did have a warrant against him for treason, then the only possible sensible place to hide was the *Judith*. And he hoped that the man who called himself Vent would be there as well. But now he had the time to think, he realised that there was someone else he urgently needed to talk to first. He tapped the boatman on the shoulder as he prosed on and on about the Earl of Essex who seemed to be a very fine fellow and said, "Ah've changed ma mind, I wantae go to the Blackfriars."

The boatman tutted and rolled his eyes. "Well that's double, with the tide as it is. Are you sure?"

"Ay," said Dodd. He was too. He glanced at Briscoe in the back…stern of the boat but the man was too hangdog and miserable to say anything about the change of plan. He had better not try any signalling. Still Dodd was annoyed with himself about that: he had noticed the man was hollow-eyed but he had done nothing about it.

On impulse he leaned over and touched the man's shoulder. "Mr. Briscoe," he said, "Ah need tae find a man by the name o' Will Shakespeare and Ah cannae spare much time for it. He could be at Somerset House, he could be at the Earl o' Southampton's place, or he could be…"

He didn't want to risk Somerset House just yet, if ever, and the Earl of Southampton had gone to the court according to Carey. That left two places.

Ordering the boatman to wait, Dodd ran up the steps and down an alley. The Mermaid Inn was half-empty, the landlord looking as if he was staring ruin in the face now Marlowe was drinking somewhere else. A greasy damp smell of fire came from the half-burned kitchen at the back. Only Anthony Munday sat alone by the bar, scribbling into a notebook and looking very dapper in a pale grey woollen doublet and hose.

"Nobody's here," said Munday dolefully. "Have you seen Marlowe? He owes me ten shillings."

"Ay?" said Dodd, "I dinna ken where he is the day. Have ye seen Shakespeare?"

"No," said Munday viciously. "With a bit of luck he's got plague and died of it."

"Ay," said Dodd, having almost forgotten about the plague that was running round the city still.

One place left to try, but Dodd decided to swing through the Temple and quietly check on one of his ideas for solving the mess in front of him. He found Essex's court and climbed the stairs to Enys's chamber where he had locked the door as he left. Dodd hammered on the door.

"Mrs. Morgan," he roared, "are ye there?" Silence. No sound of fire, no sound of breathing, nothing.

Dodd pulled out his dagger, levered the hinges of the new door with it, and then used one of the bits of the old door to prise into the crack and break the door open. He'd pay for it after, if it came to that, but above all he needed information. The room was dim in the dusk now, so he used the tongs to pick a coal out of the fireplace and lit a tallow dip with it. The smoke was choking,but it gave just enough light.

The place was completely empty. Dodd went through into the second room where there was a bed and a trundle under it, which bore no signs of having been slept in for some time. Somebody had put back the remains of the mattress and there was the clear print of one body in it. The jordan was emptied, most of the mess of the pursuivants search had been swept away. In no place was there any sign of Mrs. Morgan, Enys' unfortunately pock-marked sister.

"Ay," said Dodd, putting the tallow dip in its sconce on the mantleshelf. He was fully satisfied he had it right. There were not three siblings, there were two. And if one brother was now calling himself Vent and hiding out on the *Judith of Penryn* in the Pool of London then that left…

"What are you doing here?" It was Shakespeare's voice, nasal flattened vowels and doleful tone again.

Dodd drew his dagger, strode across the floor, grabbed Shakespeare by the front of his doublet and slammed him against the cracked wood panelling with the dagger threatening to split his nose. Shakespeare looked down at it cross-eyed.

"Ah'm lookin' for Mrs. Morgan or Mr. Enys, depending," Dodd growled., "Ah'm also searching for the land-survey that Lady Hunsdon's maidservant brought up from London and which ye stole, ye bastard."

Shakespeare's eyelids fluttered. "I...I..."

"Who'd ye give it tae?" Dodd bounced Shakespeare against the wall, "Eh? Mr. Heneage?" Bounce. "Mr. Topcliffe?" Harder bounce.

Shakespeare was breathless with fright and what he said came out as a hiss. Dodd nearly slit his nose for him before he realised what Shakespeare was trying to tell him.

"The Cecils?"

"Sir Robert Cecil, my lord Burghley's second son, the hunchback."

Dodd stopped banging the man against the wall and stared into his bland face. "That who ye serve and spy on the Hunsdons for?"

Shakespeare flushed and nodded. "I cut young Letty's purse while you were busy calming the horse," he explained. "And then I took the survey to Cecil myself because...well, I thought it might interest him even though it said there was no gold. And he said that he needed to keep it secret before the matter could be revealed."

"Was he surprised or shocked at it?"

Shakespeare's very large brow wrinkled slightly. "No, he wasn't. In fact he seemed amused to hear that my lady Hunsdon had come up to London specially to put a stop to the dealings in lands she knew to be worthless."

"Whit did he say?"

Shakespeare shrugged. "Only that the horse had bolted and there was nothing she could do."

Dodd let go of the man's doublet front and smoothed it out for him. "Ah'm glad I saw ye," he said. "Why did ye come here?"

"I…ah…was hoping to have an answer from Mr…er…Enys,"

"And whit answer was that? How much ye wanted payin' to keep quiet about what ye knew?"

"No," said Shakespeare warily, "I wasn't going to ask her for money, only for assistance, advice."

Dodd paused, speechless. Her? He had assumed that Mrs. Morgan was Mr. Enys in disguise, not…

"*Her?*"

"You must have realised what I did: she had no adam's apple, her feet were small, and her doublet had been taken in at the shoulders whilst her hose had been let out."

"Ye saw that, did ye?" Dodd was starting to recover a little.

"Of course. In the theatre we go to a lot of trouble to turn boys into passable girls and women . Once I had noticed one hint, it was easy to put the others together. I think she may have been passing as a man for a while though, she does it very well."

"Ay, though she canna fight." A thought struck Dodd. "That's whit she wanted me tae teach her swordplay for, she was gonnae have a try at killing ye, Mr. Shakespeare."

"Why would she want to do that?"

"Mebbe she didnae like givin' ye the *assistance* ye wanted." Dodd's sneer made it clear what kind he thought that probably was. To his surprise and disbelief Shakespeare shook his head vigorously.

"No, not at all. I wanted her advice."

"Ay?"

"Really and truly! I thought it was marvellous what she had done, quite extraordinary. Here she is, a woman alone in London, whose brother has disappeared mysteriously, and she puts on his clothes and sword, appears in court before a judge, and sets about finding out what happened to him. A mere weak woman to do all that and even show enough learning at the law not to be discovered."

Dodd hadn't thought of that part of it though he had to admit it was clever of her. He was only thoroughly annoyed with himself for not seeing through the game quicker. There had been plenty of clues, after all. Had Carey worked it out, he wondered. Shakespeare was pacing up and down now.

"I wanted her to advise me on the law and describe her feelings as she went from woman to man and I was hoping to write her story as a play and put it upon the stage at the Blackfriars when the hall is ready for plays. *Justicia or The Woman at Law*. How could I possibly miss such a chance?"

Perhaps he had been unfair to the poet. "Ay well, ye'd best be quick for Mr. Heneage has arrested her...him...Enys the lawyer for helping the escape of a prisoner of state. Ah didnae ken fully until I saw that and then I did."

"Arrested?" Shakespeare had gone pale.

"Ay. Heneage raided Pickering's game this evening. Ah came here to be sure I was right about Enys and then I'm gaunae roust out Carey's kin and fetch her and Mrs. Briscoe away from Heneage."

Shakespeare's jaw dropped. "You can't do that."

"Can I no'?" asked Dodd, full of interest. "Watch me." At the very least they could ransom her before Topcliffe got started on him...her—had they discovered Enys's sex yet, he wondered. He looked at Shakespeare who seemed genuinely concerned and upset and something inside him said it could do no harm to bring Cecil's man along. So he took Shakespeare's elbow and hustled him out of the chambers and down the stairs, down through the Temple to the river where he found Mr. Briscoe still there with the mutinous looking boatman who was lighting his stern lamp.

"Thank ye," he said, in a lordly fashion, giving the boatman some more of Carey's money. "Ah'll double that if ye'll take us tae the Pool of London right now."

The boatman looked at the pile of silver in his palm and then at Dodd. "All three of you?" he asked and Dodd said "Ay." Briscoe was looking at the planks, Shakespeare licked his lips. but neither of them disagreed. "Sure? In the dark, with the tide on the ebb?"

"Ay," said Dodd.

The boatman laughed a little, leaned over, and put his hand in the inky waters. "Well the flow's not too vicious for the bridge, but it'll be fast."

"Good," said Dodd, wondering why he didn't get on with it.

"I've never done it at night," said the boatman with a grin, tossing the coin and catching it on the back of his hand. The Queen's head shone bright silver from the sixpence in the light from the rising moon. "Well, we'll see if the old girl likes us or not, eh?" With a little dip of his head, he tossed the coin again and deliberately let it fall into the river. Next minute he had shoved off from the Blackfriar's steps and rowed the boat round to point down stream at the bridge.

"You'd best hold on tight," shouted the boatman. "Hold onto yer 'ats, gentlemen."

It certainly was fast. The boatman rowed out into mid-stream, well away from likely eddies and whirlpools around the sandspits near the bank. You couldn't tell easily in the darkness, but the faint ruby lights to their left seemed to be speeding past.

The tide being on the ebb with the flow of the river doubled the speed. The boatman was rowing hard to keep the prow aimed straight. His only guide was the torches hanging on the sides of London Bridge which were not easy to see. As they bounced and slid nearer and nearer the noise of the water against the starlings and the grind and clank of the waterwheels still working at the ends were enough to take your head off.

Suddenly, at a horrible speed they were approaching the dark arches with their single lanterns hung over the two central ones. The wet bricks swooped towards them like mouths of sea monsters intent on eating them. Next second they were under the echoing arch with the dripping brickwork and the great beams going across to brace them, the roar of the waters battering their ears and brains far worse than thunder, nearly as bad as cannon. For a second, Dodd saw eyes peering at them from the narrow ledges and realised there were creatures so poor that they tried to sleep in that awful place. The second after that they had shot across the churning white water and out into the relative peace of the Pool of London with its waterborne forest of ships, each showing its sternlight and mainmast light.

The boatman backed water and caught his breath. "Done it!" he crowed. "Nobody of my lodge ever did that, ha! Old Noah'll be proud!"

He reached over and shook Dodd's hand, laughing with delight at himself. Dodd gave him a golden angel since it wasn't actually his money and the man had done well by them. He didn't plan to shoot the Bridge on the ebb ever again, night or day, but it had been...exciting.

They were coming close to the *Judith of Penryn*, a long slender ship with three masts crowded on the deck. There were cannon ports along the side and movement on deck. Dodd saw more lanterns being lit.

He blinked across the dark waters and had to shut his eyes and refocus carefully: a small rotund figure in the stern was aiming a pistol at him, he could clearly see the match burning.

"Mr. Briscoe, Mr. Shakespeare," he said quietly, raising his hands. "Lie down."

They stared at him, followed his gaze, saw the pistol in Lady Hunsdon's steady hands, and ducked immediately. Briscoe drew his dagger and convinced the boatman to keep rowing. Carefully, slowly, Dodd stood up and balanced. There wasn't a lot of chance she could hit him at that range, but you never knew.

"My lady Hunsdon, can Ah talk wi' yer ladyship?"

"If you have any information on my son who went missing whilst hawking in Finsbury Fields, Sergeant, yes."

"He's gaun tae Court. Naebody's taken him, he went off by hissel. I didnae ken until this afternoon."

"How do you know for sure, Sergeant?" That gun was still pointing at him, steady as a rock except for a gentle movement to allow for the rocking of the ship.

"He used yer money to get his Court duds out o' pawn, my lady," said Dodd, coming up with the only piece of evidence that would have convinced Janet. "And he left me a letter wi' Senhor Gomes." There was a thoughtful pause.

"Explain why I should believe a word of this considering I think that you are the most likely man to have betrayed him."

"It's the truth!" shouted Dodd, outraged to have his word doubted. The match glowed brighter as she blew on it and settled the dag on her forearm to aim better. "Ah, if ye let me on yer boat wi'out my weapons, my lady, ye can kill me wi' a dagger if ye're not convinced. Which will save ye the recoil on the pistol."

The pistol was still steady. After a very long time, she simply nodded. The boatman rowed carefully up to the tall wooden side of the ship. Dodd unbelted his sword, looked at the ropeladder, and climbed it as fast as he could so he wouldn't have time to think about it. At the top as he climbed puffing over the rail, Captain Trevasker steadied him, a long carved stick in his left fist, and then walked him up some steps to the rearcastle where Lady Hunsdon was waiting. She looked magnificent and was wearing a steel gorget as the Queen had been rumoured to do when the Armada came. Captain Trevasker drew his long knife.

Dodd ignored this and pulled the crumpled sheet of Carey's letter to him out of his pouch, gave it to Lady Hunsdon. Some of the lines of fury on Lady Hunsdon's face relaxed as she read in the light of her lantern. "Well, Sergeant?" she said and so he told her what had been going on. After a little more time, she pinched out the dag's match with her gloved fingers and laid it down. As the tale went on she began to get angry again.

"Is the man completely without commonsense?" she asked haughtily at the news of Heneage's raid on Laurence Pickering, "What a wittol, eh Captain?"

Dodd added the facts on James Enys' true nature, expecting surprise, and found that Lady Hunsdon simply shook her head.

"Of course I knew that, Sergeant, I knew they were twins and there was no spare brother. I also could see for myself that Enys had no adam's apple and walked like a woman when she wasn't concentrating. I didn't see any need to talk about it."

Bitterly Dodd wondered if he was the only one to be taken in.

"Well Heneage has got her and he's got Mr. Briscoe's wife forbye to use for anither hostage."

There was a moment's silence. Lady Hunsdon had her chin on her chest in thought.

"And Laurence Pickering's got some plans, but he didnae tell me what they were," added Dodd. "He said he'd find out where they were keeping her."

"Who else is in the boat with you?" Lady Hunsdon asked.

"Tim Briscoe, Pickering's man and…er…Bald Will," said Dodd.

"Any idea who he's working for now?"

"Ay milady, he told me he stole the survey Letty had and giv it tae Sir Robert Cecil."

Her very bright eyes glittered slightly at this, but all she said was "At least that's an improvement. Why did you come to the *Judith*?"

"Ah had a mind tae speak wi' this Vent, who I think is the real James Enys. He disappeared in the last two or three weeks which makes me wonder what he's been at. Heneage arrested Enys for helping the escape of a state prisoner."

"If he hasn't jumped off, he's on board now. The bo'sun's a cousin of his."

Dodd nodded at the sense this made. Naturally if you were on the run in a foreign city like London, you'd take refuge on a ship from your own county so you could get back there eventually. Also they might be less likely to betray you. He'd do the same. In fact it might be worth finding out if there were any Newcastle coasters in the Pool since it was a long way by sea to Carlisle.

There was a clattering. First Shakespeare's head appeared and he climbed over the rail to be followed by Briscoe, who had evidently been pushing him.

Dodd realised he had scuffed his knuckles and made a hole in his hose which thoroughly annoyed him. Still, what could you expect from fancy, expensive, but delicate duds? How the devil did the elderly and stout Lady Hunsdon get aboard?

Briscoe and Shakespeare were looking around themselves nervously at the short, mostly red-headed men bustling about in the lantern light with ropes and barrels.

A man was brought up from below through a hatch, dressed in workman's clothes, but with soft hands and a pocky face that might have been good-looking once. It was definitely Vent the card-player. Dodd squinted at him in the flickering light and there was indeed a resemblance to Enys the lawyer. He was a little taller and broader in the shoulder, but the hair-colour was the same and the general cast of the features very similar. His voice was deeper and rougher though.

Lady Hunsdon sat herself down on a cushioned seachest with Trevasker beside her, and rested her hands on the top of a silver and ebony cane and her chin on her hands. Bright beady eyes raked Enys like gunfire.

"Well, James Enys, I want a full accounting of yourself."

The man bowed nervously. "My lady, I asked for refuge on your ship being a Cornishman because I am a little entangled in gambling debts and I…"

"Pfui. You are on the run and your sister has taken your place as a man of law. Heneage arrested her in place of you not an hour ago for assisting the escape of a state prisoner. Well?"

The man paused carefully. "I don't understand…" He sounded as if his breath was short with shock.

"Och, my lady, this canna be the man," said Dodd sourly. "I heard fra his sister while I thought her to be a man that she had sae loving a brother he came and nursed her while she was sick of the smallpox and her husband and children had died, and then caught it himself."

"Who are you?" said the man.

"Sergeant Dodd, Sir Robert Carey's man. I saw the woman calling herself James Enys taken by Heneage. He slapped her about a bit, mind, but what he and Topcliffe will do to her when they find she's a woman, I darenae think." He paused. "And they'll find it oot as soon as they strip her for the rack."

The man swallowed convulsively.

There was a pause broken by shouts and an occasional long creak as the ship swayed at her mooring.

"My lady, I…perhaps I should speak in private…"

"You can speak here, now. This is all tangled up with the coney-catching practice about Cornish lands, isn't it?"

Enys nodded.

"And the killing of Fr. Jackson," added Dodd, since he thought he might as well. "It was ye killed him, was it no'?"

Suddenly Enys sat down on a coil of rope and put his face in his hands. "I couldn't think what else to do…"

"Shh," said Lady Hunsdon kindly. "Nobody minds you killing a Papist priest. We haven't much time. Oh, while I remember…Mr. Shakespeare!" The bellow could have cut through a full gale. After a moment, Shakespeare appeared at the top of the companionway to the rear castle, looking frightened.

"Go and find your master Sir Robert Cecil immediately and tell him I want to speak to him here on the *Judith*."

Shakespeare's mouth opened. "But milady…"

"Don't argue. Go and fetch him immediately."

"But what if he won't come."

Lady Hunsdon's eyes narrowed. "He'll come." Shakespeare bowed.

A man came running up to Trevasker and whispered in his ear. Dodd noticed the ship moving and creaking more and seeming to move at its anchorage. Lady Hunsdon nodded. "Good, the tide will turn in an hour," she said to Trevasker. "Will you have the men get ready for a cutting-out expedition?"

The imperturbable Trevasker's jaw dropped slightly and he stared. "Where'd that be to, milady?"

"Oh, somewhere around here." She turned her head, looked straight at Dodd and winked. Dodd almost snorted with amusement.

Then she rapped with the cane on the deck. "Come along, come along, James," she said. "Just spill it all out, you'll feel so much better. When did your sister—Portia isn't it? I remember that. Her mother named her after a little fishing village in Cornwall for some reason. When did Portia start playing at being a man?" No answer. "Do you want me to ask Dodd to encourage you a little? Just to salve your pride with a black eye, or something?"

Not for the first time, Dodd's ribs were hurting with the effort of not laughing James's face reappeared from behind his hands and scowled at Lady Hunsdon.

"Ah'll dae it and glad to," said Dodd, wishing he had leather gloves on to protect his scabbed knuckles. "It might be safer for him if ye have a man holding him though."

"That's not necessary," growled the real James Enys.

"Och," said Dodd, quite relieved, but did his best to look disappointed.

"It started after we both came up to London from Cornwall, after it seemed everybody we had in the world had died of smallpox. I went back to Gray's Inn to continue my legal studies which I had broken to try my fortune in the Netherlands. I had no enthusiasm for it any more, after...after the smallpox. Portia came with me to keep house for me and because she had nowhere else and we always agreed very well so it seemed the best idea. I found that...I was falling behind and so she would help with my studies and write briefs for my moots. The first time she wore my clothes and pretended to be me was a day when I had a terrible megrim and fever..."

"I expect you were hungover, weren't you? Distempered of drink?" came Lady Hunsdon's scalpel-like voice.

James looked at the deck. "Yes, my lady, I was. She went and mooted for me and did immensely well, carrying her point and utterly destroying my opponent that I had been afraid of. She came back in the best spirits I had seen her in since the death of her children and husband and the next time I had to moot, she went on my behalf again as I never liked doing it."

"Ehm...milady, what's a moot?"

"As it were a practice court case for the law students at the Inns of Court, like a veney with words," said Lady Hunsdon. "Often on very foolish subjects."

"Whiteacre and Greenacre arguing over a square yard of land upon which is an easement and a flying freehold, generally," said James incomprehensibly. "Utterly tedious. But Portia enjoyed it and was much better at talking Norman French, so I…well, it seemed kinder to…"

"You were very relieved at not having to do the work yourself and let her do it."

"Yes. She studied and began taking some clerk work to support us and even began being approached for some court paperwork. When it came time for me to be called to the Bar…She was in the hall, not I, and it was she that was properly called. It seemed only just."

Lady Hunsdon nodded. "Had she no wish to marry again?"

"My sister is convinced that no man will look twice at her since her complexion is now so hideous."

Lady Hunsdon nodded sympathetically.

"And she has no inheritance for all her husband's land went to his brother with the death of his issue and very little jointure, nor no dowry from me neither. A man would have to take her in her smock or not at all."

Lady Hunsdon nodded again.

"In the meantime, as she says, she must eat and as it seems she has an ability and an understanding for the law—which to be sure, I have not—then she will carry on being a man to do it for as long as she can."

Enys sighed, spread his hands on his knees. "I have been a very ill brother to her. I did find some clerkwork for Heneage but that went wrong too. For him I drafted many of the deeds for the Cornish lands that were supposed to have gold. They were all being sold by a Mr. Jackson—a man I only knew as a correspondent in Cornwall. I didn't realise he was a Papist priest. I even found him new buyers. It became quite the fashion at Court and many of the lands have been conveyed at higher prices—so much that I began to wonder at it. I was sure most of the lands I was dealing with bore no gold. To be sure there was gold in Cornwall—there are a couple of places near Camborne where there were gold mines in the olden days, but they are all worked out now."

"Then suddenly Jackson came up to London and…I had never met him face to face and he was being elusive. So I spoke to a lady who had lent him a chamber in her house. It turned out he was a Jesuit."

"You are not a Catholic, Mr. Enys, are you?"

Enys coloured and stared hard at the deck. "Not really, my lady, not a proper Catholic. My parents were and tried their best with me but…I attend church service when I should and…" He shrugged. "It seems very unimportant to me what exact flavour of religion we should follow, when it's most likely that we are simply howling into the void and mistaking the echoes for divinity."

There was silence at this shocking statement and Trevasker crossed himself and fingered an amulet. Dodd felt for his own; just because it was probably true didn't mean you should go shouting about it like Marlowe and offending…Something.

"It was the children," said Lady Hunsdon gently although she had frowned at first. "Seeing the children die of so evil a pestilence as smallpox?"

Enys nodded, gulped again, and continued in a rush. "Suddenly, somehow, everything went wrong and Heneage arrested Jackson."

"How did you find out?"

"I…heard about it. Then I was in terror it would be me next for being with him—after all, once they put him to the question mine would be a name he would give. I was hiding at the Belle Sauvage under another name. Then I recognised Richard Tregian when he came to town—God, I was pleased to see him. I asked his advice and he warned me off the Cornish goldmines himself. He said he had been sent up to London by you to warn the authorities and that you would bring his daughter with a true survey of the lands in question to prove they had no gold-bearing ore in them."

"So who was it ordered you to help Fr. Jackson escape from Heneage?"

"From Topcliffe in fact, Jackson was being held at one of his private properties upriver in Chelsea so Heneage could deny knowing about…what was happening."

Lady Hunsdon leaned forwards and spoke very clearly. "Who ordered you to break him out?"

Enys licked his lips. "Sir Robert Cecil."

Lady Hunsdon sat back with a triumphant smile on her face. "I thought so," she said smugly, "No wonder Robin bolted for the Court."

"I had gone to him to ask for an audience for Richard Tregian and when I explained why, he just smiled. Then he asked me if I would do a dangerous job for him for fifty pounds and I said yes. I was desperate for money to go abroad in any case, it seemed to me that the Netherlands was the only hope I had of ever being able to find my sister a husband.

"Cecil gave me a map to show where he thought Fr. Jackson would be kept and a password and key for the dungeon. I went there at a time when Heneage was overpressed with business to do with another matter, and I managed to fetch Fr. Jackson out of Topcliffe's hands before he had been badly hurt.

"I had him in the boat with me, in his shirt, crowing with triumph, boasting of how he had destroyed the Queen's best men through their own greed. And I had trusted him and recommended him and found buyers for his lands and..."

"And had bought some yourself, I'm sure."

"Yes, my lady, I had. And he told me that none of it was true, it was all a lay to coney-catch the great men at Court, there was no gold or hardly any, but that he had turned many worthless Cornish wheals into money and freedom for Catholic families."

"And so?"

"I had taken his manacles off, but not the chains on his feet. I stabbed him in the back and heaved him into the Thames."

"Where?"

"Upstream of Whitehall. Near Chelsea. And then I realised that if Cecil had ordered me to break him out then they must have known what he was doing and so...and so..."

"It was all a great deal more complicated than you thought. What did you do then?"

"I lay low. I tried to win some money to take me to the Netherlands but I couldn't and Heneage was looking for me. Pickering was willing to help.

"And then?"

"Heneage arrested Richard Tregian."

Silence.

"Why didn't you rescue him?"

"I was sure it was a trap to catch me. And...I didn't dare. I got drunk."

Lady Hunsdon nodded. "You were probably right," she said. "It doubtless was a trap to take someone they knew to be your friend. Why did Cecil not help?"

"I tried to see him and talk to him, but I couldn't get an audience."

"I see."

"And then came the news that Fr. Jackson would be executed at Tyburn and I wondered how it could possibly be. So I went to observe—and found they had substituted Mr. Tregian. I think you were there too, were you not, Sergeant? With Sir Robert?"

Dodd didn't answer.

"And then?"

"I...er...lay low again. I couldn't understand why they would do that—the poor man was only trying to stop people being fooled by Jackson's con-trick. I was even more afraid and didn't dare go back to my sister or my chambers. I tried to get a message to her, but it failed. I was beginning to think I might be safe when Sergeant Dodd saw me at Pickering's game and knew me."

Dodd nodded. Enys had carried it off well.

One of the ship's boys came and doffed his cap to Lady Hunsdon. "We'm all ready, my lady," he said. "Where's the battle to, then?"

She smiled at him and beckoned both Dodd and Enys closer. "Gentlemen, I have a mind to break your sister Portia Morgan out of Topcliffe's clutches and also poor Mr. Briscoe's wife. I am very certain of the illegality of his whole proceeding from start to finish. Mr. Enys, do you recall where you released Fr. Jackson?"

Enys nodded. "Do you still have the key and the password?"

"The password is likely to be different."

Lady Hunsdon grinned roguishly. "I don't think you'll be needing the password, really, except for the purposes of confusion. You will accompany Sergeant Dodd and Mr. Janner Trevasker and give them whatever aid and assistance they need."

It looked for a moment as if Enys was contemplating refusing to help, but although he hesitated, he then seemed to remember what was likely to happen to his sister—might have been happening at that moment—and his jaw firmed.

"Madame, I have no sword, I left mine with my sister since she must wear it when she dines in Hall."

"I'm sure Captain Trevasker can find you one." Enys followed the boy down the deck where a motley crew of red-heads and wreckers were arming themselves with long knives, belaying pins. and a few with grenados hanging from their belts. Among them was Mr. Briscoe, looking considerably happier than he had earlier that evening.

Lady Hunsdon beckoned Dodd to lean in closer. "Mr. Janner Trevasker is Captain Trevasker's brother and he generally commands our cutting-out expeditions since these are his men. He is very experienced on the sea, less so on land. And so I would value your help." she said. "I have asked him to accept you as an advisor for I feel you may well have done something like this before."

Dodd rubbed his chin. "Ye'll no' be commanding us yersen, milady?" he asked, very straight-faced.

She beamed at him. "Of course, I should love to but alas I'm too old and stout for it and would slow you down to protect me. Like the Queen, I must ask brave young men to do my fighting for me, and very well they do it, too."

Dodd found himself bowing as if he were Carey. "It's an honour, my lady."

"Prettily said, Sergeant, my son must be teaching you his naughty ways."

"Ay." Dodd thought that must be the reason. "Ah, is this place a tower or a house?"

"As I understand it, this is a private house on the south bank quite a long way up river, well past Lambeth Palace. It will take you at least a couple of hours to reach it, even with the tide in your favour. However there may be a tower of some kind. The house is one of several owned by Mr. Heneage and let to Topcliffe for his disgusting pastimes and used by both of them when what they are doing is shadier than usual. I am quite sure Mr. Pickering knows its location as well."

"How many men does he have?"

Lady Hunsdon shook her head. "I have no idea, I'm afraid. It could be only a couple, it could a couple of dozen. You have the two gigs and ten men in each. You are not to use guns if you can avoid it, and you are to try not to kill."

Dodd snorted. A full assault on a defended house? No killing? Lady Hunsdon grimaced. "I'm skirting the borders of the law myself—my husband can probably smooth it over, but if it's a blood-bath…"

"My lady, why are you doing this for Mr. En…for Portia Morgan and Mrs. Briscoe? They're not your kin, are they?"

"Mrs. Briscoe isn't, but Mr. Briscoe looks a useful man in a fight and he'll be wanting to rescue his wife. Portia Morgan… well, I knew her family of course though not herself and her brother. She was in my service when she was taken, therefore she is my responsibility for good lordship. And also…" she leaned towards Dodd confidingly, "…I'm fair delighted at the chance to give Heneage a bloody nose for the way he treated my sons." She sat back again and rapped her cane on the deck. "Something I thought you might enjoy too."

Dodd smiled at her. "Ay, my lady. Whit about yer man Cecil?"

"What about him? I shall offer him my full hospitality, whether he likes it or not, until you come back with the women. We shall discuss many things. Off you go, Sergeant. Please conduct the raid as you see fit."

◇◇◇

It was pitch black night as the two gigs slid away from the ship and across the inky Thames. Even with the tide behind them again, they would have to row hard to get past the roaring leaping water at the bridge and into the relatively more peaceful upper part of the Thames. Going with Mr. Trevasker in the lead gig was the heavily bribed Thames waterman who had left his badge behind so as not to be blamed. Dodd took no part in it since he had no skill at boats at all, apart from the occasional fishing expedition in the Solway. They had no lanterns, relying on their nightsight and the fact that so long after sunset there would hardly be many boats ferrying across the river.

Even the lights in the city were gone out now, and their way only lit by starlight. The moon was at the quarter and not very bright. It was a harvest moon you needed for a good raid, silver-yellow light that turned the world to faery.

Dodd was sitting wishing very much for his comfy old clothes and jack and helmet. It seemed all wrong to be going into a fight wearing his fancy tight clothes, no smell of oiled leather and steel. At least he had his sword back. Perhaps he should have bought that poinard dagger after all. Briscoe was in the other boat. They had no guns since there was very little point in trying to keep the thing secret if they were going to be firing them—although their opponents might well have guns and would certainly shoot. The worst of guns was the notice they gave with the hissing and light of matches in the dark—and the *Judith* had no guns with snaphaunce or wheel locks because they hadn't penetrated to Cornwall yet. Their only real hope was surprise.

Enys was next to Dodd at the back of the boat and Dodd looked him over cautiously. He kept licking his lips but other than that, seemed steady enough. Still, you never knew with a man until you'd seen him fight and even then, you still never knew. Please God he was better at it than his extraordinary sister.

Enys claimed to know a small muddy beach where there was a path that led to Topcliffe's house—it couldn't be helped but they had to use the path as the house was on a small knoll in the middle of the Lambeth marshes.

They were at the Bridge, the slender pointed gigs pointing straight into what seemed a vast pile of foam where the tide and the river current came to blows. The White Tower gleamed a little in grey starlight. There were some incomprehensible shouts from boat to boat. They slowed, steadied, took aim and then the men started leaning into the stroke while Mr. Trevasker and one of the second mates, Ted Gunn, called the time.

With the creak of oars in the rollocks and the bellowing of the waters, Dodd found himself ducking down as low as he could to avoid the spray. The turbulence was appalling where incoming tide met the river flow, slow as it was from the summer. For a moment they held, trembling on the foam, the oars moving rhythmically. Even Dodd could tell that if the Cornish weakened or made a mistake in their rowing, the gigs would be turned sideways by the pounding waters and probably turn over and wreck. It was a ridiculous thing to do, as ridiculous as the salmon swimming upstream. Could they do it? Would they all die of drowning? Dodd knew he was holding his breath in fear of the boat sinking.

The vast wet starlings were moving, passing by as the oars speeded their rhythm. Gradually they seemed almost to climb up a mountain of water, battered one way and the other, under the arches with their echoing roar, under the bracing beams, and then out into the quiet of the broad reach of the Thames where the turbulence was less. Dodd heard the rasping of the men's breath as they eased their stroke. They had to keep rowing or the current would take them down under the bridge again but they were panting like men who had been in battle—which they had been. Without the tide behind them, the thing would have been impossible, and they still had three miles to go.

They settled into a steady rhythm after they had caught their breath and Dodd felt guilty for not helping—but this was no time for apprentices at rowing.

"How far do we go fra the river's edge to the house?" Dodd asked.

"Half a mile perhaps," said Enys. "The path is muddy but passable. It's narrow though. If they have anyone watching it, they might warn the house and they could lock the place up or even cut some throats."

"Ay," said Dodd, "We need to catch them unawares. Two men to go up the path on the quiet and cut any guards' throats…"

Enys coughed meaningfully.

"Oh ay, ehm…Capture them or something. About five more behind to get into the house and the rest to follow on if there's trouble. Are there stables?"

"Yes, at the back. But there was only me and everyone was asleep, so when I got in I just passed as one of them, taking the priest off for more interrogation."

"Why did ye kill him, really? It wasnae the coney-catching, was it?"

Enys said nothing.

"Hm," There was something Enys had said earlier that was niggling Dodd. He tried to track down what was worrying him. "Ye had the password, did ye?"

"Yes. And it worked. I must say, I was surprised."

"Cecil gave it ye?"

"Yes."

"And the men slept through?"

"Well neither Heneage nor Topcliffe was there, but yes…"

Dodd sniffed. "Ay well then, Cecil's got a man there and he drugged their beer."

Enys was silent and Dodd saw his teeth flash in a rueful grin. "And there was I congratulating myself on how cunning I had been."

No, it was still all wrong. It felt wrong. You took on a job to fetch a man out of imprisonment and then straight away you stabbed him in the back and heaved him in the river? It made no sense. Far better and far less effort to just stab him where he was in the prison and leave in a hurry. If that was your intent, of course. Perhaps Enys had intended to rescue him after all. But why had Cecil organised his escape in any case? Why couldn't

Cecil simply ask his father Lord Burghley to order Heneage to release him. From what Carey said, Burghley might have been old, but he was the chief man of the kingdom and the most trusted of all by the Queen…

Had Cecil ordered the killing then? But why didn't Enys say so? And if Cecil had ordered it, why did Enys feel he must run? And why use Enys at all instead of whoever it was he had working for him inside the house? Why make it so complicated?

Dodd stared into the darkness, sucked his teeth, and listened to the steady rhythm of the oars as the powerful Cornishmen shoved the boat upriver against the flow. What was he getting into? Was that where they would have taken the women? How did Lady Hunsdon know for sure? What about Pickering?

"Did ye know Jackson well?" Dodd asked, fishing for some kind of clue, somewhere.

"No, I didn't. Only by correspondance." Enys's answer was curt.

"Ah thocht ye came from a Papist family?"

"I do. I was in the Netherlands in the Eighties."

It was there, just out of reach, somewhere in the darkness. If he'd been paid to kill Jackson, why would he have broken him out of jail first? Had he been paid at all…?

Dodd stopped breathing for a moment. Enys had certainly been paid in advance—he'd had money to gamble with at Pickering's game who never allowed any kind of credit. Or…he had been given money at any rate, perhaps with the promise of more. Then he had been given careful instructions and he had followed them and successfully freed his man. And then, while in the boat on the Thames, no doubt heading for the Pool of London to take ship and escape, seemingly on a whim, Enys had put a knife in the back of the man he had just rescued at considerable risk and dumped him over the side with his feet still in chains to weight him down.

Dodd tried to imagine doing that kind of a job and what might make him put a knife in someone at the end of it. After all, you never really wanted to do it, did you? Killing someone in cold blood like that? No matter how many men you might have killed in battle or a fight or even on somebody else's instructions, you never wanted to do something like that at such close quarters, especially not in a boat. He might spot what you were doing and certainly would resist, you might fall in or be stabbed yourself. Unconsciously, Dodd shook his head. You wouldn't do it just because the man had coneycatched a lot of people, though you might disapprove of it. And you certainly wouldn't do it if the son of the most powerful man in the kingdom had just paid you to help the prisoner escape.

In Dodd's mind there was only one reason why he might put a knife in someone he had just rescued like that. He cleared his throat to ask Enys if that was the reason, then paused. All right. The only way the thing would work is if you realised that the man you had just rescued was going to try and kill you. Then it would make sense to put your knife in him first.

Why? Why would a priest who had just been rescued by Enys on behalf of…probably Cecil, possibly someone else…for what reason might he want to kill his rescuer? Well, they were alone in the boat apart from the boatman who had been well-bribed. One man goes upriver in a boat. A prisoner disappears from a safe-house. One man comes back, gets on a ship, and leaves England using the same name. And one man who knows too much about the scheme ends at the bottom of the Thames with a hole in him.

But you wouldn't expect a priest to behave like that, even a Jesuit. Also, how did Enys know for sure? His own voice came to him. "You were from a Papist family." Fr. Jackson was also a Papist—but what if Enys knew he wasn't what he claimed? Didn't all the Papists in a place tend to know each other?

Once again the backs of Dodd's legs went cold. Even the sounds of the oars faded to nothing as his mind slewed round to the new idea. Good God. Maybe? Perhaps little Mrs. Briscoe had been right and the corpse really had been her brother Harry Dowling, always in trouble, greedy for money. Perhaps the stern-looking Catholic lady who was not called Mrs. Sophia Merry was also right and the corpse was Fr. Jackson SJ. Perhaps they were the same man? In fact, thinking about what Ellie Briscoe had said of her brother and how he had refused to know her when she saw him in London, perhaps Harry Dowling was more of a coney-catcher than a priest. Perhaps he was working all the time for someone else…Such as Heneage? Or maybe Sir Robert Cecil? And both Harry Dowling and James Enys had been in the Netherlands where Englishmen tended to bunch together in places like Flushing or under the same captains. It was more than likely Enys and Dowling/Jackson had met.

So when he finally saw the man, Enys must have realised Jackson wasn't a priest at all. In fact, Cecil's involvement made it almost certain he was someone who had been spying for Cecil's steadily growing secret service. Cecil's involvement in helping him escape also suggested that he was someone who was valuable and knew too much to be left in Heneage's hands for too long. Enys had worked this out quickly because he knew the priest was lying, realised he himself knew too much to be allowed to live, and that the most likely way of getting rid of him was in the middle of a rescue.

But it had gone wrong for Cecil. Enys had fought in the Netherlands and he had struck first. The so-called Fr. Jackson went into the Thames still breathing and drowned—a nasty death, probably worse than the one Richard Tregian had suffered since Tregian had been hanged until he was dead. And Richard Tregian had died because Heneage assumed he was Cecil's man, so took him and put him to death publicly as a warning to Cecil. Enys had to lie low with what he had been given as a downpayment and being what he was had tried to gamble it into a nest egg and lost the lot. So he couldn't even pay his passage out of the country.

What had he done next? Gone to Cecil? Hardly, the man had tried to have him killed. Gone to…Well, obviously he had gone to Heneage who was the other side of the war he had stumbled into. He had gone to Heneage, spilled everything he knew. Probably he was trying to broker some kind of deal but of course Heneage had realised how that gave him a weapon. The taking of Briscoe's wife had been a side-game and a tidying up of loose ends in order to take Pickering's game. Heneage had arrested Portia Morgan to keep James Enys obedient and Portia Morgan would also be the bait that would draw the chivalrous and impulsive Carey into a trap, and alongside him that thorn in Heneage's side, Sergeant Henry Dodd. Enys was the stone that would kill two birds at once. You could hardly blame Heneage for not resisting the temptation. He had overegged the pudding when he ransacked Pickering's gaming chamber, but that was his habit as well.

However Carey had run to Court to speak to the Queen so he conveniently wasn't here to stick his neck in another noose.

What had Enys said ..."it was all a lie to coney catch great men at court."

Dodd's own voice came back to him. "Ye know nowt," he had said to Carey about another ambush. "Ye've been told."

Two boats? Sergeant Dodd as advisor, in command with Mr. Trevasker? Did Lady Hunsdon suspect something? He realised that he had sweat trickling down his back under his shirt, his stomach was crunched up, hiding under his ribs. This was far more frightening than a mere battle. He had been sixteen the last time he was this frightened. He looked across at the other boat which might as well have been on the other bank for all the talking he dared do. He couldn't even signal with a lantern for fear of being seen, and he certainly couldn't shout.

All right then. So they took Portia Morgan and had taken Briscoe's wife to make sure of Briscoe's help. It was provocative, an invitation to an attack. If there was to be an ambush there would be an alluring trail. And there was. Enys right there on the *Judith* where Carey would likely go to keep his father out of it, with the story of the house in the marshes, how he knew the path, how he had the key...

Dodd shook his head. This was all too complicated. It was simpler to think about it as if the Elliots had taken Janet and, say, Lady Widdrington.

No, perhaps not. Carey would be in the game then and make it complicated again. So. The Elliots have taken Janet.

You think they've gone to their chief tower, but it could be one of the others. What do you do?

You hit the one with the less obvious trail and hope they haven't double-bluffed you. In fact, you hit both towers, but you personally, Henry Dodd, you go to the less obvious one and make damned sure it's taken quickly before they can cut Janet's throat.

Which is less obvious? Lady Hunsdon and said "properties" so there were more than one. There was Heneage's large house in Chelsea and the one Enys had been talking about in the marshes on the south side of the river. Both houses accessible by boat, one on the north and one on the south of the river. One approachable through orchards and gardens, in the village of Chelsea where there are witnesses. The other out in the empty marshes along a single muddy path which you could mine, lay an ambush along, or simply wait until your attackers are in the house and then… say…blow it up. And which one has the more attractive trail?

Dodd showed his teeth to the night and relaxed. He leaned over and tapped Ted Gunn on the arm. "Can ye bring the boats together?" he asked. "I wantae talk to Mr. Trevasker?"

Gunn nodded and called in a foreign language across the water. It sounded a bit like the funny jargon you sometimes heard from Welshmen or Irish kerns. The other boat came cautiously closer.

"Mr. Trevasker," said Dodd, "I've a mind tae talk to Mr. Pickering."

Trevasker looked blank so Dodd repeated it as southern as he could and added "The King of London," Trevasker nodded hesitantly.

How and where could he find Pickering? Well, he was a headman who was also presumably about to go to war. He would have men placed on his borders to watch for him and tonight they would be awake.

"Take me to the nearest set of steps on the north bank," Dodd said, "Wait there for me," Mr. Trevasker was frowning slightly but eventually he nodded and the gig that Dodd was in began cutting north towards Blackfriars steps again. The other gig backed water well out from the bank.

Dodd was impatient to meet Pickering. He climbed out as noisily as he could, went up the steps a little way, then turned suddenly and laid hands on the two beggars quietly following him. They choked because he was holding both of them by the neck.

"I havetae talk to Mr. Pickering at once," he hissed. "You go tell him, you stay here wi' me."

Bare feet sprinted into the distance and Dodd settled down to wait. Pickering announced his presence by the unmistakeable pressure of a knife against Dodd's side and the smell of feet and sores. That was one of his henchman who had come up very silently next to Dodd despite the fact that he had his back firmly pressed to a wall from the old Whitefriar's monastery. In front of Dodd was the interesting sight of the King of London wearing rags and almost silent turnshoes.

Dodd grinned, knowing his teeth would show in the paltry moonlight.

"Well, Sergeant?" came Pickering's voice, steady in the greys and blues.

Dodd told him everything he knew, had worked out, and thought he knew. At the end of it, Pickering was silent for two beats of Dodd's heart, and then he chuckled. Dodd nearly chuckled back because there was nothing more satisfying when you were on a raid than to know there was an ambush and where it was.

"I got some news for you too, Sar'nt. The prisoners ain't in Chelsea, nor the marshes," Pickering said., "And they ain't at the Tower neither. They come off their boats at the Bridge. My bet is Southwark or the Bridewell."

"Ay," said Dodd, rubbing his chin. "But which?"

"We'll know in a minute or two, I've got young Gabriel watching the Southwark house for me. One of Topcliffe's places, but outside the City so 'e can play 'is games."

"Can Ah go and tell my lady Hunsdon's men whit's in the wind," said Dodd.

"Eh? Lady Hunsdon?"

"Ay, there's two boatloads of Cornish pirates that brought me here."

Dodd saw Pickering's eyes glint with mischief. "Well well, who'd ha' thought it. I know my Lord Hunsdon left Somerset House this evening heading up the Oxford road at the clappers."

Dodd almost smiled back. Careys on the move, eh? Ay well, the Dodd headman was on the move too. He nodded and went down the steps to where the gig was tied up with a large Cornishman standing on the boatlanding looking nervous. Dodd saw Enys still sitting in the boat, waiting patiently, his tense face giving back moonlight. Dodd beckoned Enys to him and the man climbed out of the boat and came over. Dodd clapped him on the shoulder.

"There's a change of plan, Mr. Enys," he said. "We're gaunae…" Then he punched the man as hard as he could in the gut, caught his shoulders, steadied him and put his knee into Enys's groin. It was very satisfying and the man went down with little more than a whine. Ted Gunn was staring at him. He listened while Dodd carefully explained what was going on as southern as he could, and then climbed out of the boat, tied Enys's arms behind him, and stuffed a bit of rope in his mouth. He and another Cornishman lifted him into the gig and laid him down along the length of it. Then Gunn raised his arm and whistled like a curlew across the water. Dodd could hear the rhythm of the oars as the gig came in to the boatlanding. He explained again to Mr. Trevasker who also grinned happily. Then he tensed and one of his men raised a crossbow.

Dodd spun on his heel to see Pickering with a couple of ugly mugs and a remarkably handsome young blond man beside him. "Gabriel 'ere says it's the Southwark house, but the Bridge is guarded," explained the King, "Not seriously, just someone watching. 'E also saw your boats climbing the Bridge rapids and the watermen says it was well-done but you was lucky not to die, and one of them lost ten shillings on it."

"Ay," agreed Dodd. "Will yer man lead us across the flow tae Southwark?"

"Course 'e will."

"Are there horses at the house?"

The blond man nodded. "Three of them for dispatch riders to Dover," he said in a deep voice.

"And where are the women?"

"Cellars of course," said Gabriel. "We 'eard 'em crying, couldn't see them."

"Crying?" asked Dodd, his blood chilling.

"Yer, screaming one of them was, like she was being tortured." The young man's face didn't change when he said it. "Or flogged," he added thoughtfully, "she was a bit breathless."

Dodd set his jaw. "Mr. Pickering, what would you suggest?"

Pickering sucked his teeth. "Gabriel tells me the house is locked up tight, no open winders, no outhouses to climb on. Front door's locked, o'course. There's a courtyard onto Upper Ground wiv men in it and dogs and one of the horses is there ready to take a message."

It was a pity Heneage wasn't sloppy nor completely stupid. No doubt the house in the marshes was mined and the house in Chelsea well-defended. Southwark would have the fewest men, but there'd be enough to defend against a sneak attack or a frontal assault just in case. Well then, what you needed was distraction.

Dodd squatted down with Pickering, Gabriel, Mr. Trevasker, and Ted Gunn and laid out what he thought would make a good plan. At the end of it there was a moment of shocked silence.

"Well, Sar'nt," said Pickering eventually, "You can go back to Newcastle…"

"Carlisle," Dodd corrected automatically.

"…the north, but I've got to live in London. This is my manor, you might say. And I've never done anyfink like that."

"Ay, and anither man has put a brave upon ye. If ye dinna hit him back wi' more and worse, ye'll no' be a headman for long," said Dodd with finality. "But if ye can think of another way intae a house that's defended and has hostages of yourn, I'll be glad to hear of it and take the news back tae the north country."

More silence. Finally Dodd recognised Gabriel's gruff voice. "'e's right, master," it said, "and that 'ouse is in a garden and right on the river."

There was the sound of teeth being sucked. "All right," said Pickering, "But we do it my way. We've got a bit of time to spare."

Ted Gunn was delighted with his part in the business and kept quietly snickering to himself.

Pickering, Gabriel, and a couple of his upright men climbed into the gigs and the waterman who had piloted them through the bridge went with Ted Gunn to direct the them going upstream against the difficult flow of the Thames without being sucked into any of the whirlpools or grounded on a sandbank. Both gigs were low in the water, but one crossed the current to the South Bank while the other with Ted Gunn and the still sleeping Enys in it continued upstream towards Chelsea.

saturday 16th september 1592, dark before dawn.

The boat kissed the boatlanding a little upstream of Heneage's house so Pickering, Dodd, Gabriel, Briscoe, and a couple of upright men that had fought in the Netherlands could get out. The boat carried on softly to the steps that led up to the garden of the house. There would be a wall and an iron grill, of course, but the Cornish had brought crowbars. It was at least an hour after midnight, maybe two, and Southwark was asleep, although the bakers would probably be stirring in an hour or so to light their ovens. There were lights from some of the bawdy houses to be sure, but Gabriel popped his head in one of them and spoke to the Madam who came out to curtsey to Pickering. The Bishop of Winchester may have been her landlord, if what Carey said was right, but Pickering was her real lord. She listened to what he had to say and then nodded, went indoors and started shouting at the girls. A little later all of them who weren't with clients came slinking out in their striped petticoats and elaborate hats and dangerously lowcut bodices. There was one striking redhead there with a cheeky grin and perfect white rounded tits that Dodd remembered from somewhere other. He had to swallow hard and pull his eyes away. He had always liked red-heads and the fact that the girl had a couple of freckles low down only made her more interesting…

Pickering elbowed him in the ribs. "If this lot works, Sar'nt, you only 'ave to say the word and she's yours."

Dodd coughed. "Ay, but Ah'm a married man."

"So what?"

"Ah, ma wife's got some…eh…powerful relatives."

"Oh. Well, never mind, they probably don't come to London."

That was true enough to be quite tempting. Dodd thought about it for a moment and then decided he'd better concentrate. The girls went with them as they quietly walked towards Heneage's house, led by Gabriel. It was indeed closed—the door locked, the windows shuttered tight. At the back was a walled courtyard but there was nobody visibly keeping a watch. From the house came a series of howls and screams which then bubbled away.

"Jesu," said Dodd, horrified. Nobody else took any notice. The girls fanned out and went and knocked on the doors of the nearby houses whilst Dodd and Pickering took a couple of the grenadoes that Trevasker had brought, lit them from a slow match that Trevasker had kept in a pot, and went round the back of the house.

Dodd hefted the heavy pottery ball filled with serpentine gunpowder and sawdust with the fuse coming out of the top. He hated grenadoes, always felt sick when he lit one because you never knew how long you had to throw it…Or whether someone brave might throw it back. But for setting fire to a roof, they couldn't be bettered.

Dodd threw the grenado overarm onto the thatch of Heneage's house where there was a dip between eaves. It landed, rolled, it was going to roll off the roof…And then it exploded—not as loudly nor as destructively as a petard which was the same thing made of iron rather than pottery—but well enough. A hole was blown in the thatch and the drier thatch inside caught alight immediately. Pickering's lob went neatly onto the roof, but then fell off and landed and exploded in the courtyard where arose an immediate squealing of pigs and a dog started barking manically.

Dodd went to the gate at the front of the house. Somebody fired at him with a pistol which missed, of course, and an arrow clattered against the shutter next to him. Another arrow followed it. He left a grenado there and took cover until that exploded too. Then he ran up to it and kicked it in as fast as he could while arrows and bullets clattered into the ground a yard behind him. They were shite, really. Quite clearly they knew nothing about defending a place, their angles of fire were all wrong.

Behind him he felt Briscoe, who was completely silent with a veney stick in one hand and a poinard in the other, behind Briscoe the other upright men, and then Pickering and Gabriel. He charged his shoulder into the remnants of the door, found himself facing a boy with his mouth open and an empty crossbow in his hands, and knocked him down with his stave. There was a mill in the part of the courtyard penned off for pigs and the two dogs on chains were barking themselves hoarse at it. An older man came at Dodd, who dodged and knocked him sideways. Briscoe took a man with a bow who was aiming at Dodd. Pickering and Gabriel were already across the yard and at the front door of the house itself. Gabriel knelt down at it as if he was praying while Pickering stood in front of him with a throwing dagger in each hand and an intent expression on his face.

Dodd's mouth turned down mournfully as he swapped blows with a swordsman, knocked the weapon aside, and sliced down through his shoulder. No jack. Was the man mad? On the other hand, Dodd had no jack on either and didn't think a fancy doublet could do much to protect him from a better-wielded sword. Somebody else came running at him and without thinking he kicked the men's legs from under him and knocked him out. Jesu, he'd never fought so gently in his life.

Gabriel was kneeling beside the lock with a hooked piece of wire in his fist and a grin on his face. Pickering opened the door, Dodd shouldered past him and spitted the man waiting with a raised sword.

Outside the harlots were helping to ring the firebell and shout fire. The next-door-neighbours were already forming a bucket chain from the Thames. Nobody had time to worry about the pitched battle around the house as the Cornish broke through the barred gate and into the garden.

Dodd knew he was in a dangerous state. The smell of the fire seemed to unroll the black rage in his belly and turn it into something like pleasure. He walked swiftly into the hall of the house which was already starting to fill with smoke, saw somebody start up from their sleep next to the fire, and hit him with his veney stick. It seemed a waste not to kill him, but Dodd was trying to do things the way Lady Hunsdon wanted them. There was somebody on the stairs so Dodd held his breath, burrowed through the smoke, grabbed him by the doublet front and threw him downstairs where Gabriel or Pickering coshed him.

There was a knot of them at the top of the stairs, two or three men, getting in each others' way as Briscoe fought his way up. Dodd pulled a painted cloth off the wall, threw it over their heads, and then beat everything round he could see with his cosh before throwing them down the stairs one after another. Gabriel laughed behind him as he stepped over one of the bodies.

Breathing as little as he could in the acrid smoke, Dodd slammed through several doors. Somebody shot a pistol at him again and by sheer luck the ball went into the wall not a foot from his face. Dodd's mouth drew down as he kicked through the door where the man with the pistol lodged, dodged the downswing of the ball of iron on the pistol's stock, knocked the arm aside, grabbed the front of the man's doublet, and headbutted him right on the nose. The man dropped his pistol and fell back clutching his flattened nose and mewing so Dodd kicked his legs out from under him and stamped on his hand. Behind him was Portia Morgan with her hands tied to a bedpost, her doublet off and her trunk hose half pulled down. What he could see of her arse was as marred with pockmarks as the rest of her, though nicely shaped.

Dodd looked at her face with the bloody nose and the black eye and the split lip and something told him what to say as he sawed through the rope around her hands.

"Ay, Mr. Enys, can ye fight?"

She paused, gulped, nodded. "Where's my sword?" She was making her voice deliberately deep. She was hitching her braces back over her shoulders, rebuckling her belt, coughing hard in the smoke. With shaking hands she caught up her doublet from the floor and slung it on, doing up the buttons quickly. Now he knew what to look for of course it was obvious; her hands may have been pock-marked but they were smaller than a man's and very deft.

"Take this," said Dodd, giving her his veney stick. "Where's Mrs. Briscoe?"

"She's in the cellar. Can't you hear her?"

Another earsplitting scream sliced through the building. Enys bent down to the man Dodd had flattened, who was trying to get up again. She pulled his eating knife from his belt and went to stab him in the chest with it.

"Better slit his throat," Dodd said, "It's easier."

Enys snarled, caught the man's hair in her fist and pulled his head back.

"Mind the blood," Dodd said to her, deliberately turning away. He felt she had the right. He still heard the soft sound of blade on flesh and the suck of air into a slit windpipe. Then he heard her being sick. The smell of the fire was gaining on him, the rage in him and the smell of blood: he wasn't angry exactly for there was none of the red mist of it, but he was far out the other side of the particular black rage that took him in situations like this and made him cold and ruthless and evil. He knew he was evil, but it couldn't be helped.

"Sar'nt," growled Briscoe from the door, "they're hooking the thatch off."

Outside the street was full of purposeful activity as men with long hooks pulled down the burning thatch and poured Thames water over it. In the courtyard at the front the pig was squalling so loudly and the dog was barking himself hoarse, you couldn't hear what was going on in the cellar—except there was something loud still happening there too.

"Mr. Pickering wants you downstairs, Sar'nt," said Gabriel.

Dodd was panting for air as not enough of it came through the holes in the roof, and he hadn't the breath to argue, so he turned, clattered down the stairs, followed by a still retching and swallowing Portia Morgan, through the hall and another door. Somebody erupted from a closet door behind him and found Enys in the way. She managed somehow to back-hand the man in the face with her stick. There was an audible crack as his jaw broke. He fell back as she kicked him hard in the knee and when he went down she grabbed his dagger from his belt and went to cut his throat as well. Dodd grabbed her arm and stopped her with regret.

"Mr. Enys," he shouted, "Milady wants us no' to kill tae many o' them."

She blinked, shook her head and—typical woman—said, "Why?"

Dodd didn't have breath nor time to tell her. He just shrugged, broke the man's knee properly with the hilt of his sword so he couldn't make trouble after, and carried on down into the cellars which stank badly of blood and shit. Pickering was standing in the middle of the place looking horrified, the heavy iron bound door had been smashed in and when Dodd braced himself to look through into the straw-scattered little cell, he understood why.

A sigh puffed out of him. There was young Mrs. Briscoe on her hands and knees in the straw squawking and howling. Portia Morgan blinked, took a long shaky breath, blinked again. Then she dropped her veney stick, went over, bent and stroked the girl's shoulder. "It's all right, it's coming."

Another horrendous shriek came from the girl as her belly moved. Enys saw Dodd standing staring, stood up, and came to him.

"Sergeant, can you get me two stools or blocks of wood this high, a big bowl of hot water or some aqua vitae, linen strips and a clean knife." The girl was howling again, calling for her mum.

"Now hush," said Portia Morgan. "You're not going to die, it's only a baby. Sergeant!"

She was lifting the girl's petticoats to look and Dodd turned quickly and ran up the stairs. Pickering came with him.

"God's truth," he said as Dodd stripped off one of the stunned men's doublet and hauled his shirt off over his head, then moved to the corner where there was a wood-basket and a promising looking small barrel. Dodd tapped some into a mug, tried it. The aqua vitae was cheap but drinkable, so he drank that to steady him, poured another one and gave it to Pickering to sustain him, and then put the barrel under one arm, picked up the woodbasket after slinging the man's eating knife into it along with his shirt, and carried the lot down the cellar steps to where Portia Morgan had her hand under the girl's petticoats and a look of concentration on her face.

"If you could find a real midwife, Sergeant," she said, "that would help, I'm having to try and remember what the woman did for...er...my sister."

"Ah've helped ewes at lambing and dogs wi' whelping," Dodd offered. "It's no' sae different."

At that point the girl squealed angrily again and started to cry. Portia Morgan turned again and looked under the blood-splattered petticoats. "It's coming, I can see it," she cried, and dug into the wood basket to pull out two large blocks of wood which she set on the floor. "Come on, Ellie, sit on these."

Dodd lent a hand to heave the girl off her hands and knees and sit her down with her legs spread, a buttock to each block, while Portia shoved the petticoats back and the girl grabbed her head and howled. Something black and bloody was showing between her legs. Suddenly he decided this was a lot more frightening than a lambing and ran up the stairs.

"It's coming," he said in explanation to Pickering who was sitting on the master's seat in the kitchen with his feet on the table, drinking from another barrel he seemed to have found. Dodd helped himself. "We canna move her until her wean's born now."

"I could see that, Sar'nt," said Pickering. There was a thundering about upstairs and the firebell had stopped ringing. "Fire's out, fank goodness. I've got Briscoe to check for any remaining cinders, keep his mind off things. I'll blame the fire on on you."

Dodd shrugged. What did he care what a lot of Londoners thought of him? His cold black rage had gone now, he felt as happy and relaxed as if he had…well, as if he had just had a pipe of Moroccan incense and tobacco.

At that moment there was a distant boom and all the shutters rattled. Dodd cocked an ear to it. The shriek from the cellars had almost drowned the noise.

"So it *was* mined," he said.

"Yer," said Pickering. "I wonder if that bloke Vent survived."

"Best not talk about it," Dodd said, "Whit do the neighbours say?"

"Oh they're all right. They know I'll pay 'em for their trouble. And the roof is off and the fire's out and Gabriel's tying up the men here in one of the bedrooms. There was only twenty of them and only a couple of dead."

"So the maist o' them will be at Chelsea or the marshes."

"Yer," said Pickering, "waiting for us with not the faintest idea." He laughed. "Until now, mind."

He laughed again and lifted his cup of wine in a toast to them.

Perhaps an hour later there was a clattering of a boat at the watersteps, a challenge from the Cornishmen. And then there were mutterings and Mr. Trevasker saying "milady" and "your honour." Pickering took his feet off the table and sat up warily.

Into the looted kitchen walked the small sprightly figure of Lady Hunsdon, pink-cheeked and happy. Beside her, dark and lean and bowed over sideways and forwards by the curve of his back, was a man in sober black damask and a white falling band, a fashionable black beaver hat shading a long face. And behind him trotted Shakespeare.

Dodd came to his feet and so did Pickering.

"Sergeant, my compliments on a very neat piece of work," said Lady Hunsdon, with her wonderful roguish smile that had caught Lord Hunsdon, the King's bastard, in a permanent web. "Sir Robert Cecil, Privy Councillor, asked to meet you at once."

Dodd bowed to her and inclined his head to the second son of the most powerful man in the Kingdom. From things Carey had told him, he thought that Burghley, Cecil's father, and Carey's lord, the Earl of Essex were at some kind of courtly feud. So why was Cecil so friendly with Carey's mam, eh?

"Ay," said Dodd, "Ehm…" How did you do it properly? "Ah, milady, may I present Mr. Pickering, the…eh…"

Pickering stepped forward quickly, bowed to Lady Hunsdon and Cecil and took his hat off. "Laurence Pickering, milady, your honour," he said. "Merchant of London."

From the half-closed eyelids and the faint smile, Dodd felt that Cecil knew perfectly well who this was. From the expression on Lady Hunsdon's face it seemed that she wasn't entirely sure.

"Ah…Mr. Pickering helped wi' the raid," Dodd finished slightly lamely, hoping he hadn't offended or insulted anyone. "He's…ah…a friend of Sir Robert's."

"An honour to be of service to you, milady, yer honour," said Pickering, staring hard at Cecil.

"Mr. Pickering," said the hunchback, inclining his body slightly, "I've heard a great deal about you from my mentor and friend, Sir Francis Walsingham, God rest his soul. I believe there was an…understanding between you?"

"Yes there was, yer honour," said Pickering, "I 'ad the…ah.. the honour of 'elping Sir Francis on several occasions. Though never as…ah.. dramatic as this time."

"Quite so." Sir Robert Cecil smiled and his dark face instantly transformed into a handsome and charming man. "I understand you run the only game that's worth visiting in London and that Heneage had the impudence to raid it?"

"Yerss, yer honour, that's right."

"Outrageous. I hope you will be continuing with it…"

"Of course, yer honour. When I get it set up again, shall I send your honour word of its whereabouts?"

"How kind, Mr. Pickering," said Cecil. "I would be delighted to learn to play properly."

Pickering bowed. Dodd could almost see the implied handshake between them. "Wiv yer honour's permission, I think I'll take my…friends…away now."

"Do so, with my thanks," said Cecil.

"And mine, of course, Mr. Pickering," said Lady Hunsdon. "How wonderful to meet another of my son's more interesting friends."

"Yersss, milady," said Pickering, rocking gently on the balls of his feet with his thumbs in his belt. "Your son has some very good friends." He turned to Dodd, winked, and left the kitchen, whistling through his teeth.

Cecil came forwards into the kitchen while Lady Hunsdon went and sat down in the chair with arms. She still had her silver and ebony cane which she leaned on. Cecil sat beside her on a bench, leaned his elbows on his bowed legs, and winced slightly. Shakespeare took up his unobtrusive position with his back to the wall near the door, his hands behind his back, the perfect servingman, listening for all he was worth.

"Well, Sergeant Dodd," Cecil said, "why not tell me the story."

Dodd told him. He told it as short as he could, not including the tangle over the Enys twins. There was no more shrieking from the cellar but nothing much seemed to be happening there. Dodd really hoped that nobody had died. Somewhere a cat was miaowing.

At the end of it Cecil smiled his shockingly charming smile again.

"I will elucidate a couple of points for you, Sergeant, since it seems you have worked out most of it."

Dodd tilted his head and prepared to be lied to.

"The Cornish lands that were hawked about London by Fr. Jackson, were of course, nearly worthless. Certainly there was no gold. Unfortunately…Very unfortunately many courtiers were taken in by his plausibility and bought them. Fr. Jackson was a Jesuit in that he had studied briefly at Rheims—long enough to counterfeit a Catholic priest—but his real name was Harry Dowling, as you surmised. He had offered to work for me against the Catholics but I naturally turned him down as he was not to be trusted."

Lady Hunsdon let out a small sniff of disbelief at this. Long practise allowed Dodd to keep his face completely straight. So did Cecil. By God, Burghley's second son would be very dangerous at primero.

"Among the spectators was Heneage. Being deeply implicated, he arrested Jackson to find out who he was working for. I engaged James Enys to free him and all did indeed fall out as you said. I heard no more from Enys. Heneage did not know what had happened to Jackson nor his rescuer. Heneage was also desperate to keep the secret of the lands he had bought being worth nothing much so that he could sell them to other innocent barnards. Hence he arrested Richard Tregian and after torture had revealed no information as to the whereabouts of Jackson nor to the source of the lay because of course the whole game was due to Jackson's greed, substituted him for the priest so that no one would ask questions about the priest."

Dodd inclined his head. That was more or less true. Except that he was even more sure that Cecil was the one who had set Jackson on to sell the lands. That coded letter had said most of the wheals were owned by Icarus—presumably Cecil's target. It still made sense that way. God, the man was twisty.

"And then you come into the mix and Heneage begins to panic. He knows he has no defence in law to your suits, and so he resorts to force against you." Cecil smiled and chuckled. "A very foolish man. He should have made you a respectable offer."

"Ay," said Dodd. Perhaps he would have taken it.

"And it ends here, does it not?" Cecil continued. "Unfortunately it seems that some ill-affected Papists have blown up another property owned by Heneage and that there has been a riot here between the rabble and scum Heneage chose to employ. You fortunately happened to be nearby with my Lady Hunsdon's men and you were able to quell the riot and out the fire—oh, and rescue a young lawyer and Mr. Briscoe's wife. You have not been able to kill Topcliffe?"

"He wisnae here," Dodd said. It had been a disappointment, that.

"How unfortunate," said Cecil with that charming smile again. "So both myself and my worshipful father owe you thanks for preventing worse bloodshed here. I shall be writing a report to him to that end and quite possibly, Her Majesty may choose to reward you as well."

From Carey's constant complaints on the subject, Dodd suspected that he would find a nest high in a tree that was full of suckling pigs before that happened, but still it was a nice thought. And it meant he was free to go?

"Ay, sir," he said, "Ah…I heard Mr. Heneage had a warrant for me on a charge of high treason."

Cecil tutted. "I am quite sure that is not the case, or if it was, in the heat of the moment, it will no longer be the case after I have spoken to the gentleman. Which I intend to do immediately at his home in Chelsea."

Dodd stood as Cecil levered himself to his feet and so did Lady Hunsdon. "Ay," said Dodd, feeling inadequate to the task of taking his leave properly from Carey's amazing mother. "Yer Cornishmen are fine fighters," he said lamely. "And…ah…it wis an honour to serve ye, my lady."

Lady Hunsdon beamed and held out her hand to him. Dodd knew what he was supposed to do, frantically thought back to what Carey normally did, dismissed it as impossibly complicated, and just took her hand and bowed over it.

He found her arms around him in a surprisingly fierce hug. "Sergeant," she said as she let him go, "like my husband, I'm honoured to have you with me. Give Robin my love when you see him." She paused and her dimples showed again. "If you can, my handsome."

Dodd coughed, "Ay. Thank ye yer honour. God speed, my lady."

◇◇◇

Dodd wandered out to the grey courtyard where he found a wounded and bleeding pig lying exhausted in its blood while the dog barked hoarsely on the end of his chain. Thoughtfully Dodd stepped up behind the pig and slit its throat quickly to put it out of its pain, then found a bone in the trough which he threw to the dog. In the way of dogs, the animal barked a couple more times and then starting gnawing on the bone.

There was something kicking and pounding at the stable door and neighing in panic, so Dodd went to the stable door and opened it, dodged the wild-eyed head that immediately tried to bite him, then looked hard at the animal. It was the nice one with the white sock he'd noticed at Chelsea, one of the regular dispatch horses no doubt which meant he'd be fast and probably quite strong.

Dodd unbolted the bottom door and slid into the stall quickly, then up close to the horse and speaking to him in his ear, stroking his neck and shoulder, gently fending off the teeth. "It's all done wi', ye stupid jade," he said since it didn't matter what he said, "And ye're coming with me,"

The saddle was hanging up and the bridle with it, so Dodd spent a little longer gentling the animal until it snorted and lowered its head for him, and then he brushed the coat down with a whisp of hay and put the bridle on and the saddle. Both were very nice, good leather and not too fierce a bit.

He had forty miles at least and wanted to be able to go quickly, so he checked the other stalls and found another perfectly good horse, not a gelding this time, but a chestnut mare also upset and relieved to see a man who patted her neck and called her a bastard in a soft and friendly voice. He put her bridle on as well and took the reins forward over her head, then led both horses out into the courtyard.

Gabriel was standing there, watching with interest. "Where are you going?"

"Och," said Dodd, "Mr. Pickering's a man o' parts here, but Ah'm not and I dinna wantae be in London when Heneage finds out whit happened."

"S'all right," said Gabriel looking offended. "There won't be any witnesses. Mr. Pickering and his honour said so."

"My lady Hunsdon said she didnae want killing."

"No, they just won't remember. Any of 'em."

"Ay, well. Ah'm tired o' London and now Ah've had ma satisfaction for the insult Heneage put on me, Ah've nae reason to stay."

"I'd stay for Molly, she likes you."

"Molly?"

"The mort wiv the big tits wot gave you the eye," said Gabriel, grinning. "She says her and Nick the Gent tried to tip you the marrying lay a few weeks back but it went wrong. She says you was fun, though."

Dodd could feel his face prickling with embarassment. So that's where he'd seen her before. "Ay, but that woman were blonde," was all he could say.

Gabriel sniggered. "Well, you never know what colour her 'air's going to be, so it's best to look at 'er tits, innit?"

"Tell her she can find me at Carlisle castle if she wants," Dodd told Gabriel with dignity. "Ah'm a married man."

Gabriel spread his hands in mock despair and turned away. "Gi' my respects to Mr. Pickering," Dodd shouted after him, "and ma thanks for coming out for me." He put his hand on the horse's withers and jumped up into the saddle and immediately felt happy and at home.

"It's been a pleasure," said Pickering's voice from the kitchen door, "'av a good journey norf now, Sar'nt."

Dodd nodded, took his hat off to Pickering, and was interested to see Pickering lifting his statute cap in return. Gabriel had already opened the courtyard gate.

Dodd came out of the gate with his remount trotting behind him, turned right to head west along Upper Ground to the horse-ferry for Westminster where he could pick up the Edgeware Road that led to Oxford. There was no point trying to cross London Bridge before the dawn broke when they would open the gates on the north side, and there was another hour to go at least.

Behind him he could now hear the outraged bawling of the new baby which was one of the happiest sounds in the world, he thought, even if it wasn't his. That ball of rage had been cleared from his stomach by arranging for the blowing up one of Heneage's houses, the burning and raiding of another, and reiving two good horses from him. Who knew what the court case might bring or what Sir Robert Cecil might do? So he laughed out loud, put his heels in, and cantered west along the south bank of the Thames, past the round wooden structure of the bear baiting and the scaffolding around another round building that was going up right next to it. Londoners were always building something new.

Behind him the sun rose.

GLOSSARY

A fortiori—stronger, moreover

Alchemy—the unacknowledged illegitimate grandfather of modern chemistry; an intellectually satisfying and logical theory of matter which featured four Elements and held that gold was the pinnacle of matter and could be made to order by using the Philosopher's Stone. Unfortunately, like many such theories, it was completely wrong. They found it was a little more complicated than that.

Apothecary—drugstore/druggist

Barnard—proposed victim of a coney-catching lay (scam)

Bartalmew's fair—London pronunciation of St Bartholomew's Fair. Please note that no "fair" is ever spelt "fayre".

Boozing ken—a small alehouse, often full of thieves etc (Thieves' Cant)

Border reiver—armed robbers on the Anglo-Scottish Border, organised in family groups called surnames who used the Border as a means of escape

Cloth of estate—a square tent of rich cloth traditionally set up over any seat occupied by a monarch

Coining—forging money

Colloped—cut into chops

Counsels—old-fashioned way of saying, trusted advice, hence Legal Counsel and Counsellor.

Cramoisie—dark purple red, a very popular colour in Elizabethan England.

Daybook—diary

Debateable Land—area to the north of Carlisle that was invaded and counterinvaded so often by England and Scotland that in the end it became semi-independent and a den of thieves, as often happens

Falling band—plain white turned down collar, Puritan style

Footpad—mugger

Henbane of Peru—an early name for tobacco

Insight—portable and saleable household goods

Jakes—outside toilet

Kinchin—child (Thieves' Cant)

Kine—old plural of cows

Lye—the all-purpose cleaning agent, made by passing water through woodash repeatedly, a powerful alkaline. Used to make soap as well.

Mort—woman (Thieves' Cant)

Nae blood tae his liver—it was believed that the blood in your liver gave you courage—hence lily-livered, said of those whose livers were pale. No doubt cirrhosis did make you cowardly.

Nipped that bung—stole that purse (Thieves' Cant)

Papist—Catholic

Playing a veney—exact equivalent of a kata in Karate or pattern/tul in Taekwondo, this was a set series of sword moves practised with a partner so as to build up strength and agility. To keep the deathrate down, pickaxe handls with hilts or veney sticks were used.

Poinard—long thin duelling dagger with an elaborate hilt, big brother to a stiletto

Polearm—any weapon involving a long stick with something sharp on the end

Praemunire—the short name of the statute of Henry VIII which forbade as treason any appeal to an authority higher than the king's—i.e. the Pope

Punk—whore

Pursuivant—literally—chaser, someone who acted for the State in tracking down spies, criminals and traitors. Often freelance.

Phlegm—mucus or snot, the cold and moist Humour, one of the four Humours of the body and a constant problem for the English who were renownedly Phlegmatic

Quod Erat Demonstrandum—as was demonstrated, QED

Red lattices—the shutters of any place selling alcohol would be painted red

Rickets—soft bones caused by Vitamin D deficiency in childhood, common among the Elizabethan upper classes if they allowed their childrens' diet to be supervised by physicians who advised against fresh vegetables (too Cold of Humour) and fish (too lower class).

Run wood—woodwild, mad

Serjeant-at-law—a senior lawyer with special privileges, appointed by the Crown, roughly equivalent to a QC today

Starlings—the piers of London Bridge

Statute cap—blue woollen cap that all common men had to wear so as to support the wool industry—a statute more honoured in the breach than the observance

Strilpit wee nyaff—untranslateable Northern insult meaning "weakling"

Surety—a Border system whereby the headman of a surname would hand over a lesser member of his family as a hostage for the good behaviour of another member of the surname

Swan Rampant—this was indeed apparently Hunsdon's badge and looked as described

Teuchter—incomprehensible Northern insult

To wap—to fornicate, as allegedly in "Wapping", a notorious haunt of whores

Upright man—gang leader

Utter barrister—outer barrister. At this time a lawyer who had been called to the Bar (of the court) and could stand outside it, thus having the right to be nearer to the judge than mere attorneys or solicitors (which then meant the equivalent of ambulance-chaser). Later they became the only people who could speak before a judge in court.

Venery—persistent naughty sexual behaviour. Now called sexual addiction, very common.

Wittol—idiot

To receive a free catalog of Poisoned Pen Press titles, please contact us in one of the following ways:

Phone: 1-800-421-3976
Facsimile: 1-480-949-1707
Email: info@poisonedpenpress.com
Website: www.poisonedpenpress.com

Poisoned Pen Press
6962 E. First Ave. Ste. 103
Scottsdale, AZ 85251